The
Last
Available
Man

Cindy Blake is an American writer living in West London with her two children. She is the author of *Girl Talk, Blood Sugar, Second Wives, Foreign Correspondents, I Saw You First* and the bestselling *It's My Party*.

The Last Available Man

CINDY BLAKE

POCKET
BOOKS

LONDON · SYDNEY · NEW YORK · TOKYO · SINGAPORE · TORONTO

First published in Great Britain by Pocket Books, 2002
An imprint of Simon & Schuster UK Ltd
A Viacom Company

1 3 5 7 9 10 8 6 4 2

Simon & Schuster UK Ltd
Africa House
64–78 Kingsway
London WC2B 6AH

www.simonsays.co.uk

Simon & Schuster Australia
Sydney

A CIP catalogue record for this book is available
from the British Library

ISBN 0–671–02265–2

Typeset by Palimpsest Book Production Limited,
Polmont, Stirlingshire
Printed and bound in Great Britain by
Clays Ltd, St Ives plc

To Sven-Goran Eriksson

Chapter One

The white wine was warm, the pub was grotty, the jukebox was playing an óld love song about Cupid. Georgina Harvey wanted to have a long chat with the lyricist of that one. Who thought it was a good idea for Cupid to draw back a bow and let an arrow fly straight into a heart? Hadn't anyone worked out that an arrow through the heart meant death, or at the very least severe disability? What was so romantic about an arrow? If Cupid had dispensed love by scattering rose petals on his targets' heads or making them drink a sweet potion, fine. But he worked his magic with a deadly weapon.

Of course, that might be the point. Love can be fatal. Because you can never be sure, when the arrow pierces your heart, that there's another one out there winging its way into the heart of the person you adore. You can be stuck there, pinned to the spot, while the object of your affection goes about his business entirely unscathed.

Taking a tiny sip of her wine, Georgie looked around her. She could sense some of the men in the pub staring at her. Well, let them. She knew what they were thinking: a thirty-something woman on her own in a pub must be trying to pull. Why else would she be there? They wouldn't believe she'd just had a business meeting, they'd think she was out to trap a poor unsuspecting bloke into marriage and a life of hell being chained to Her Indoors.

Why did men assume the purpose of women's lives was to ruin the fun of their own? Georgie wondered, aware that her thought pattern was heading into the groove of a rant, but unable to put a brake on it. Why did men think any woman over thirty was hell bent on getting a ring? What right did they have to feel so sought after? It's not as if men were precious jewels. Granted, there weren't very many of them, at least not very many decent unattached ones, but that didn't give them the right to stare at her as if she were some last-chance gold miner out to stake a claim.

Given her experience of the previous night, she was beginning to think it was useless even to try to understand the workings of the male psyche. Why bother when they behaved in such a lunatic fashion? Georgie replayed the scene again, as she had when she'd woken up in the morning. There she was, sitting on Adam's sofa, having a reasonable conversation about politics and wham! He gets up, this man whom she has dated three or four times, this seemingly sane, reasonably attractive thirty-eight-year-old gets up, turns on his video machine and sits back down beside her.

'Enough boring politics,' he says. 'This will relax us.'

'This', it turned out, was a porno movie. Georgie had been stunned to the point of speechlessness. Naked women, with what appeared to be Viking helmets on their heads, were rolling around in the snow together, grunting. Well, I'd be grunting too, was her first thought, if I were freezing my bum off. Her second thought, as a naked man with an even more elaborate horned contraption on his head joined them, was: would dogs do this? Would dogs pay money to watch each other have sex? She turned to Adam and asked him this question. He looked at her as if she had asked him whether the earth travelled round the sun or vice versa.

'Keep watching, it gets even sexier,' was all he replied.

'But I want to know. Would dogs pay to watch other dogs? Would cats? Why do humans do this?'

Adam didn't reply. Georgie wasn't deterred.

'I read somewhere that there are species of animals who eat in private and have sex in public. Which makes me wonder – do you think animals of those species would pay to watch other animals of those species eat? Would that be their way of getting kicks? Only fifty quid and you can see a full English breakfast being devoured bite by bite! Hang on, let's rewind and get back to the part where they're soaking up runny egg yolk with bread!'

'What *are* you on about, Georgie?'

'What are *they* on about?' She pointed at the television. Horses had suddenly appeared in the snow. Georgie hated to think what was coming next. 'I'm leaving, Adam. This isn't my idea of fun.'

'Whatever.' He shrugged, never taking his eyes off the screen. 'You're a really uptight woman, you know. You're frigid.'

Refraining from pointing out the obvious – that the truly frigid people were the ones cavorting naked in the winter wonderland – she picked up her coat and bag and left.

Don't go there, she cautioned herself as she stared at her glass of wine. Don't ask yourself what quirk in Adam's brain made him put on that movie, or what quirk in your brain made you think he was normal in the first place. Give up attempting to work it out rationally, give up men.

This was a solution she had thought of before, renouncing men, and one she believed she might be able to live with, but a personal demon kept stopping her, her Success Demon.

Georgina Harvey ran a financial services headhunting company in the City; she was good at her job; she was successful. Yet she had failed when it came to relationships. Yes, she had a good relationship with her stepsister, Jessica, but that wasn't the same as having a life partner. If you were single for long enough, if you were single for ever, people might start wondering what, exactly, was wrong with you. Soon enough, you'd start wondering what was wrong with you yourself. Georgie knew this was true because she'd already begun wondering.

Did she put men off because she was an independent, strong woman? Men were afraid of self-confident women, weren't they? Was that her problem? But men were also afraid of women who were weak. The few times she'd allowed herself to be carried away by passion, when she'd exposed a vulnerable side, men had backed off as quickly as they'd come on to her in the first place. Yet if she stayed strong, in control of herself, their male egos would rise up in revolt. There was no middle ground she could locate, no way to win.

Or was it her looks, not her personality, which made failure seemingly inevitable? Honestly, she couldn't believe that. Although she knew she wasn't, like Jessica, at the top of the Premier League looks-wise, she would have classed herself as somewhere near the top of the First Division, with the possibility, if she lost a little weight, of moving up. Her wavy brown hair, parted in the middle and set off from her forehead wasn't lank or greasy or a mass of split ends. Her eyes might be a little wide set, but she had a large, generous mouth and a decent enough nose. She was big-boned, yes, but not fat. People often assumed she had Slavic blood in her, an assumption she quite liked because it made her feel foreign and mysterious.

It couldn't be her looks, and it shouldn't matter anyway. Even if she found a 'perfect' man, Georgie had seen too much of love gone wrong to believe in the possibility of that perfection being sustained: her father and mother's divorce, for starters; her father and stepmother's marriage and divorce for the main

4

course; and her mother's remarriage to an alcoholic for dessert made for an unpalatable meal.

Couples she knew of her own age either fought all the time or looked as if they *wanted* to fight all the time. Who should cook? Who should do the dishes? Who should give the early morning feed to the new baby? John wants to stay at the party, Jane wants to leave the party – who gets his or her way? All sorts of little, and big, disagreements undermined what love there was or had been between once happy couples.

The way Georgie was beginning to see it, some supreme masochist, long ago, had figured out the hardest task for human beings – marriage – and imposed it on society. In marriage, two unrelated people are supposed to live together *for ever*, have sex only with each other *for ever*, deal with money, children, household work, work, socialize with friends one or the other might not like, live with all those potentially unattractive and irritating personal habits every person in the universe has, and – this was the hardest part of it all – be *happy* into the bargain. It was too much to ask of anyone.

So she knew men shouldn't matter, not as much as she let them. This inability to sustain a romance might be depressing but, if having a man meant pretending to enjoy the sight of Vikings getting it on in the Arctic Circle, she'd just have to learn to live without one. Correction, she told herself as she forced down another gulp of the terrible wine, learn to *keep* living without one. She'd have to forget that deep-seated instinct to find a soulmate, her need to share herself completely with someone who understood her, her desire for earth-shattering sex. Forget that amazing high of falling in love and concentrate on work.

Meanwhile she'd simply endure the stares of these pub crawlers and wait for Jessica to show up. As soon as Jessica walked in Georgie knew, those heads would swivel and stare elsewhere. They'd stare at Jessica. They always did.

*   *   *

Jessica Tanner pulled over to the side of Ladbroke Grove, turned off the engine and sat shaking. She'd almost killed that old woman. Somehow she hadn't seen the zebra crossing and before she knew it, there had been this figure in front of her, inches away. What if the brakes hadn't worked so quickly? How could she have lived with having killed someone? Her karma would have plummeted dangerously. What had she been thinking?

She hadn't been thinking, that was the point. She'd been daydreaming, imagining climbing Mount Everest, accompanied by a man with broad shoulders and a sensitive soul. She could see herself reaching the summit with this man by her side, stopping to digest the thrill of the conquest, congratulating each other on having climbed without sherpas, without oxygen.

It was the most ridiculous, far-fetched daydream she'd ever had. No wonder she'd almost run down the poor woman. Jessica had problems climbing stepladders. She was terrified of mountains. All those winters of her childhood, when her mother had taken her skiing, in Zermatt, in St Moritz, in Verbier, she'd had palpitations on the *beginners'* slopes. A simple snow plough was beyond her. She kept falling and then falling again. One of her skis would come off and she'd burst into tears with the effort of getting it back on again. Four year olds sped by her and laughed. Instructors invariably lost their patience. One in particular she remembered – a Frenchman – who had said, 'Look, see if you can manage not to fall off the lift and then we'll take it from there.'

Of course she promptly fell off the lift, the type of lift which had a bar you had to put between your legs. Her legs got tangled, her fear of falling took over, and she fell. The lift machinery had to be stopped; real skiers were temporarily stranded. The Frenchman skied over to her and shook his head in dismay, he swore, he looked at her with disgust and announced he was giving up on her. She wasn't worth the money he was being paid to teach her.

After that, the most dreadful of a million humiliating incidents, Jessica took to lying. In the mornings, she would go on a cable car to a café at the top of the mountain, sit with her skis, order coffee after coffee and wait. When her mother or anyone else in their group showed up at the café in the afternoon, she'd pretend she'd been skiing all day. By that point, she'd be so hyped up on caffeine that giving rhapsodic descriptions of her prowess was easy. Deceit had been the only way. She had to hide and lie or else be revealed as an uncoordinated coward.

Well, all right, I'm exaggerating a little, Jessica thought, as she re-started the car engine. I did manage to shine at the après-ski part of winter holidays. I came into my own in the evenings. The point is, I'm not about to go and climb Everest, I'm only daydreaming about it because it seems like such a dramatic romantic escape from my life at the moment.

I have to get out of the City, she said to herself as she swung back into the traffic, but how can I tell Georgie that? She gave me a job in her company, I should be grateful to her for rescuing me from the dire financial straits I was in. And the fact that I'm not a natural-born headhunter, that I know I'm not suited for this business doesn't help me much either. I need to make a living somehow. But what will I do if I do leave? I didn't go to university, I'm not qualified for any specific job, I don't have another career in mind.

A man would help. But there is no man in my life. Will there ever be or will I be as hopeless at finding one as I was at skiing? Am I scared of relationships? Is that my problem? If so, how do I get unscared? I don't have a clue.

I'm stuck she thought, as she located the pub and parked. Life, at this precise moment, sucks.

*   *   *

This used to be fun, Georgie thought. Meeting candidates in secret out of the way spots, having clandestine conversations, feeling a little like an MI5 agent was exciting. One of the pleasures of headhunting has always been the element of secrecy. But it's getting old. Or else I am.

Where's Jessica? And who's making these selections on the jukebox? Who is the sad excuse for a person who chose 'Moon River'? The lyrics make even less sense than the song about Cupid. Not only is the river a moon, but also a 'huckleberry friend', whatever a huckleberry friend is supposed to be. Which drug was the songwriter on when he wrote it? Give it to me and I'll make a fortune writing a song called 'Sun Ocean, My Raspberry Pen Pal'.

She felt it then; it couldn't have been tangible, but it was, this breeze created by men's heads turning at once, collective necks craning. That familiar thud of inferiority hit her stomach. She didn't have to look to know who had come in.

'I can't believe you had to meet the candidate *here*.' Jessica glanced around the pub and wrinkled her nose. 'This place is *squalid*.'

'He didn't want to be seen. The hush-hush factor. If anyone knew he was being headhunted, he'd be in trouble. You know, the usual paranoia of corporate executives.' Georgie shrugged and sipped her wine. 'And listen to this – he showed up in a motorcycle helmet. And . . . he didn't take it off.'

'He kept it on during the entire interview?'

'The interview didn't last long. Not once I knew he wasn't going to take the helmet off. What does he think – that he's so important he is tailed wherever he goes in case he might be meeting a headhunter? Please. Anyway, I suggested he should quit Goldman Sachs and start a new career in the stripogram business; you know, show up in leathers then take it all off but keep the helmet on. Many people would find that very sexy. For some reason, he didn't appreciate the advice. Anyway, thanks for coming to get me. I should have taken a cab, but for some reason I couldn't face it.'

'No problem. I wasn't doing anything. Actually, that *is* the problem, isn't it? It's Sunday night and I have absolutely nothing to do.'

'There's always TV. Is there anything good on?'

'E4 is doing the re-runs of *Ally McBeal* and *ER*. We've already seen the *Ally McBeal* and I don't think I can take the blood and guts of *ER*.'

'Our social lives are pretty pitiful when the high point is watching a re-run of a show we've already seen.'

'Don't remind me.' Jessica sighed. 'At least you had a date last night.'

'Don't remind *me*.' Georgie laughed. 'That wasn't just pitiful, it was tragic.'

'Do you think we'll be doing this in our sixties? Living together, watching re-runs of television shows? Is something wrong with us, Georgie?'

'That's what I've just been wondering. But no, I don't think so. I think something is horribly wrong with men. Which probably means we should be lesbians. But the problem with that is: A I don't fancy girls, B even if I did, can you imagine how awful breaking up with a girl would be? When romance with a man goes badly, you can always think: well, men are stupid anyway. Their emotional IQs are zero. You can't say that about women. No, lesbianism is out, which takes us back to square one. So, yes, I guess we *will* be watching re-runs of television shows in our sixties. I hope they're still playing *Frasier* then.'

'My mother rang.' Jessica picked up Georgie's wine glass, took a sip and grimaced. 'She has another Hooray Henry in mind for me. He's an estate agent – I've met him, actually.'

'And?'

'And remember Tim Park?'

'Yes.'

'He's even worse than Tim Park.'

'Impossible.'

'Possible.' Jessica nodded.

'Then tell your mother *she* should date him.'

'I wish I had.'

'Joanna doesn't stop, does she? Anyway, forget about her. She's always been a cow and she always will be. Come on –' Georgie stood up – 'let's go home. Unless you want to find yourself a little rough trade while we're here. That man over there with the tattoo and the shaved head? He's definitely hot for you – go for it. Honestly, I don't want to interfere with the course of true love. See, he's looking at you now.' Georgie waved at the man, pointed at Jessica and smiled.

'Georgie!' Jessica protested, but Georgie was five steps ahead of her and halfway out of the pub. She knew it would be useless to do anything except follow as quickly as possible.

I'm lucky to have her as a stepsister, she thought as she caught up to Georgie. Not many stepsisters are as close as we are. I don't think many real sisters are. But why is it that even though we're the same age, I feel like the younger one? Why is it that I'm her designated chauffeur? And why can she make comments about my mother being a cow when any time I say anything even remotely negative about her father, she goes berserk?

Sliding into the driver's seat, Jessica was struck by the impossibility of change. She and Georgie had established a pattern in childhood and it wasn't, as far as she could see, ever going to be different: Georgie would always be the one in charge, the one leading; while she would always be the kid sister, tagging along. If the person closest to you couldn't or wouldn't allow you to grow up, how could you ever think of yourself as grown up? As she started the engine, her brain began to trip up all over itself in an effort to work out this puzzle.

Georgie was tapping her fingers against the dashboard in time to some pop music Jessica hated. The car radio had always been a source of contention between them and Georgie always won the battle for control of it. Jessica always gave in because music had been the source of the worst row she could ever remember – one Sunday afternoon twenty years ago, when Georgie's father had put on a Country and Western LP and her own mother had accused him of being an uncultured yobbo.

It had been awful, that fight. Starting at lunchtime and continuing into the afternoon. I can't stand this, Jessica remembered thinking. Why do two people get married when they hate each other? She'd hidden under an old bed in the attic to get away from it. That had been her original purpose – escape. But as time went by, that had changed into wondering when her mother would notice that she had disappeared and come looking for her. The longer she stayed there, the more she felt she couldn't possibly come out. 'Here I am, here I am,' she'd wanted to shout. 'I know I'm thirteen and too old to be hiding, but come and get me.' How could she say that, though, when no one cared enough to notice she'd gone? It felt as if hours had passed before she finally heard footsteps.

'Here I am,' she said, inching out from beneath the bed.

'I thought you would be.' Georgie sat down on the wooden floor. 'This is a good place to hide.'

'Oh, it's you,' Jessica said blankly. She stopped moving. Her torso was out from under the bed, the rest of her was still beneath it.

'They finished the fight a while ago. Your mum has gone out somewhere; my father has gone out somewhere else. We're alone here. Want to watch TV? Or we could scream at each other like they do.'

'No thanks.'

'Listen, Jessica. They're wrapped up in themselves. They don't care about us – two thirteen-year-old girls don't matter to them right now. The best thing to do is to ignore them and get on with our own lives. We're in the same boat. I don't like this any more than you do. Let's get away.'

'Run away?'

'No – that's not practical. We'd end up begging or being murdered or something. Let's go to boarding school.'

'But you live with your mother in London during the week. That must be all right.'

'You don't know her new boyfriend.'

'Boarding school?'

Jessica finally extricated herself entirely from her hiding place and pulled herself up into a sitting position. Georgie was paying attention to her. That was so unusual in itself, she felt honoured. Before this, Georgie had made it painfully clear how uninterested she was in her stepsister. The first time they had been introduced, the year before, Georgie had shaken Jessica's hand, said 'Hello', turned away and asked her father what was for dinner. Their relationship hadn't progressed much since then. Jessica knew Georgie wasn't jealous of, or upset by, her, she simply didn't think she was worth consideration. And now, suddenly, Georgie was talking about going to boarding school – together. This unexpected reversal made Jessica forget entirely about her mother and slide sideways, closer to Georgie.

'Why not? They've got enough money to send us. You go to a posh public dayschool in this stupid country town anyway. My father would fork out the fees for me if only to prove to your mother that he's as classy now as she's always been. Boarding school has to be better than this. And we wouldn't be alone – we'd have each other there. We could be like real sisters. It could be fun.'

'You think so?' Jessica could feel her heart literally warming up. Until she had this sensation, she'd never known it had been cold.

'Do you want to listen to another screaming match?'

'No. I live with them all week, remember? I hear them all the time.'

'Then let's do it.' Georgie thumped the floor with her fist. 'I'll ask my father and you can ask your mother when things have calmed down a little. Meanwhile let's go and raid the kitchen and watch some TV.'

Georgie was heading down the stairs within seconds of saying this, with Jessica following her.

That was when it started, Jessica thought. From that point onwards I've been the one behind.

She reached over to the radio and turned down the music. Georgie reached out and turned it back up.

Chapter Two

Sadie had thought it couldn't get any worse. She'd been wrong. This time her hair was a blazing red, which was even more distressing than the green it had been the first time round. At least if you had green hair people might assume you were making a political statement. If anyone saw her now, they would think she was trying to colour-coordinate with a double-decker bus.

'Oh dear,' June, the eighteen-year-old trainee hairdresser said, stepping back a pace. 'It's not quite right this time either, is it?'

Sadie winced, thinking of the hours she'd already spent this Sunday sitting in this chair, being used as an experiment by a young girl who might need a job but who clearly should never get one as a colourist. June charged next to nothing for her work. Sadie now understood why.

I should have known better than to try to get cheap highlights, she said to herself. If I had wanted a facelift, would I have asked for the cut-price plan? A trainee plastic surgeon?

'Let me have another go at it,' June said. 'You know, third time lucky or whatever.'

All Sadie could do was nod.

14

Lisa, her friend and co-worker, had been the one who had suggested highlights to begin with. One of those women who would tell you if you had a piece of spinach caught in your teeth or a ladder in your tights, Lisa took pleasure in giving out advice on clothes, on romance, on anything that could remotely qualify as 'female'. That's what good girlfriends were for, Lisa believed, a twenty-four-hour helpline on the assault course of womanhood. Now, as she waited for June to mix up another batch of dye, Sadie wondered whether Lisa was consistently wise on these matters.

'I don't mean to be rude or anything,' Lisa had said on Friday after work as they shared a bottle of wine in the pub, 'but your hair, Sadie.'

'What about my hair?'

'Not to put too fine a point on it, it's – well, it's mousey.' Whisking a strand of her own blonde hair off her forehead, Lisa studied Sadie's hair so intently, Sadie began to wish she'd worn a hat. During slow times at work, Lisa was either sending friendly, chatty emails to her co-workers, reading glossy magazines or cutting out pictures of movie stars and poring over them. Lisa knew everything about nail extensions and hennaed tattoos and Tantric sex. If she ever left her job as receptionist at Harvey and Tanner, Lisa should, Sadie thought, become a door-to-door beauty and sex therapist.

But being the object of Lisa's attention at this particular moment was unnerving. Sadie hadn't spent a lot of time or effort on herself lately, in fact she'd let things slip. Her nails were uneven, she'd put on a few extra pounds, and now she was being told she had mousey hair. This past year hadn't been a good one for her: a broken heart had led to manic energy at work and sluggish behaviour at home. Sadie could have done without Lisa's appraisal, but she wasn't sure how to stop her without sounding defensive, so she poured another glass of wine and sat back to be judged.

Leaning forward, Lisa grabbed a clump of Sadie's hair, examined it, released it and smiled.

'I was thinking hair extensions, but they won't work on you. I can tell. And forget a perm with that hair. No – highlights. Highlights are the answer. I mean neither of us is ever going to be stunning, we're never going to be as glam as Jessica Tanner, but we can do all we can to help ourselves out, you know? I saw this place in Crouch End the other day, Hot Hair. There was an advert for cheap highlighting on Sundays. Why don't you go there? That could do the trick without costing you a fortune. Highlights will transform your life, Sade. Believe me.'

Reeling from the 'neither of us is ever going to be stunning' comment, Sadie had tried hard to grasp onto the lifeboat Lisa was throwing her: those magic words 'transform your life'. It was a struggle, though, partly because Sadie knew perfectly well that Lisa was at least *close* to stunning, that Lisa had put in that 'neither of us' line to ease the pain by supposedly sharing it. Still, she could get beyond that dangerous wave to safety if she concentrated on the possibility of almost instant transformation. Maybe highlights *would* do the trick. With lighter hair, she might have a lighter body, a lighter mind, a lighter heart. So she'd gone along with Lisa's suggestion, full of hope that she'd emerge from Hot Hair a different person. And now, as she sat looking in the mirror, all she wanted was to get back to where she'd been in the beginning. All she wanted was to be mousey again.

'Here we go.' June was behind her, brush in hand, slathering dye on Sadie's head for the third time with alarming non-chalance. 'This is fun, isn't it?' She waved the brush with a flourish. 'I always wanted to be a painter. I always wanted to be a ballerina too. But I bought those special ballet shoes once, and I kept falling over so I chucked that idea in. Now –' she stared at the collection of bowls on the cart beside her – 'which one was I using?'

Lisa was an impossible person to dislike. She was bubbly, she was funny, she genuinely cared. But Lisa wasn't, Sadie decided, someone she would ever take advice from again.

Three hours later Sadie Hawkes walked into her flat in Shepherd's Bush carrying bags of groceries. Her hair was no longer mousey, no longer flaming red, but an unnaturally dark brown with streaks of pumpkin-colour orange through it. June the trainee had managed to avoid any hint of normal highlights and had ended up foisting upon her a colour closely resembling shoe polish mixed with orange squash.

'Excellent!' she'd said as she examined her work. 'You know, you look like a really hip Catherine Zeta Jones. Cool.' Sadie knew June said that because June was tired and bored and couldn't be bothered to have another go at fixing the horror she had created. She knew she didn't look anything like Catherine Zeta Jones. She looked like a freak.

Andrew was at the computer in the corner of the living room. As soon as she came in, he swivelled in his chair, took one look at her and burst out laughing.

'That's not very nice.' She groaned.

'Your friend Lisa is not very nice if she convinced you to do that,' he replied, coming over to her, taking the bags from her hand and heading into the kitchen. He stopped at the doorway as she went past him to the fridge.

'It's not really Lisa's fault. I had a trainee hairdresser. Lisa was only trying to help.'

'Oh, yes. And Dr Shipman was trying to help all those old ladies feel better.'

'You're such a supportive brother. Such a big help in times of trouble.'

'Listen, what did you expect? Was I supposed to say, "Gosh, Sade, where'd you get that hot hair colour? Can I go there tomorrow and get mine done too?" I don't think so. Ready?'

'Ready.'

Andrew bent down, took a carton of yoghurt out of the bag and threw it to Sadie, who had already opened the fridge door. Catching it, she put it inside then turned for the next item, a package of ham slices.

'But look on the bright side. It will come in handy on Halloween. You'll bag loads of sweets if you show up at doors looking like that.' He pitched a carton of milk to her underhand, then lobbed a cauliflower high into the air. 'Watch it – tuna fish coming up.'

Sadie moved a step forward, caught the cauliflower, stashed it away, swivelled back for the tuna, put it on the shelf, pirouetting just in time to grab a flying jar of mayonnaise.

'Can't you do something to fix it?'

'By the time I finally got out of there, Boots was closed.' She bobbled a cucumber but managed to hold on and shove it in the salad compartment. 'And I don't have a secret stash of hair dye anywhere around. I'll have to wait to do something about it until I come back from work tomorrow.'

'Egg alert!' One by one, Andrew picked eggs out of their carton and threw them at Sadie, picking up the pace with each egg.

'Slow down!' she yelled, but he wouldn't, and she did what she always did every time they played this game: she missed an egg. Every time an egg crashed and splattered against a wall or the fridge or took a nosedive onto the floor, Sadie would start to giggle hysterically, Andrew would join in and they'd both laugh together as they cleaned up the mess. This time, though, Sadie didn't laugh or giggle. This time Sadie leaned against the fridge and burst into tears.

'I'll clean up later. I'll do it later,' Andrew was saying as he led her into the living room and sat her down on the sofa. 'Do you need something? Shall I get you some tea? A shot of whisky? A bottle of vodka? Some form of dangerous drug I don't have but am sure I can find on the street from a dealer, if the dealer doesn't mind taking a cheque?'

'No, nothing, thanks.'

She'd lost it, she knew. But why? Because she hadn't been transformed, at least not in any way that helped? Because she had let June, who was obviously as hopeless a hairdresser as she had been a ballerina, experiment on her? Because she knew she'd have to go in to work the next day and wait for the inevitable comments on her 'bad hair' day? No, she'd lost it because of one mobile-phone call.

'Yeah, babe,' Lisa had said, as soon as Sadie answered. 'How's it going? Are the highlights fabulous?'

'Not exactly.' On her way from Hot Hair to the bus stop, Sadie was trying not to notice people staring at her hair. She was grateful that Lisa had rung. Talking on a mobile phone at least made her look like a *busy* freak.

'I'm sure you look fantastic. I can't wait to see. Anyway, look, I probably shouldn't tell you this, and I've been having this big argument with myself about whether I *should* tell you this, but—'

'But what?' Sadie felt her stomach tighten. What was Lisa so nervous about telling her? Was she going to say highlights weren't enough, that Sadie actually needed an entire makeover, a cabbage soup diet, a new wardrobe, a personal reflexologist?

'Well, after you left the pub on Friday, Piers came in. He's back, Sadie. I spoke to him for a few minutes. He's been promoted and he's back working in the City.'

'Oh,' was all she could say. Her heart felt as if it had been slapped. Piers was back. He hadn't rung her. He wasn't going to ring her. Sadie kept walking, her eyes fixed on the bus stop ahead of her. If she could get there, she'd be all right. There would be a place to sit down. All she had to do was get there.

'I'm glad you're taking it so well.' Lisa sighed. 'He's a bastard, Sadie. He's not worth thinking about. You should have seen the slag he was with.'

'You're right,' she mumbled. She had to make Lisa stop talking somehow; this was too much terrible information. She wouldn't make it to the bus stop if Lisa told her anything more.

'I'm on my way home, but I have to stop at a Tescos and get some food,' she said. Talk mindlessly, she told herself. Fill up the airwaves with meaningless chatter and you won't have to hear another word about Piers. 'Did I ever tell you Andrew throws the groceries at me? It makes unpacking them more fun.'

'Your brother is definitely weird.'

She'd managed it. She'd stopped Lisa from saying anything else about Piers. And she'd made it to the bus stop. She was safe. Not only was she safe but she could see her bus approaching.

'Um, Lisa, this line is breaking up and my bus is here. Gotta go. See you tomorrow. Bye.' Sadie pushed the off button.

Bye, bye bye bye bye, she repeated to herself as she got on the bus and sat down at the back. Goodbye goodbye goodbye. Except Piers never said goodbye. He didn't tell me it was over. He came into my life unexpectedly and his departure from it was just as much of a surprise. 'The bank is moving me to Manchester.' That's what he had said. Not, and when I get there, I'm not going to ring you, I won't be inviting you there for weekends, and oh, by the way, I never want to see you again. Not, and if you are silly enough to ring me at the office, my secretary will screen my calls and you'll hear my voice in the background saying, 'Tell her I'm in a meeting.' Not, I won't give you my home phone number either which you'll find is ex-directory when you ring directory enquiries. Not, I won't respond to your increasingly desperate letters and emails.

'The bank is moving me to Manchester.' That's what he had said, followed by, 'I'm sure things will work out, though.'

Work out for whom? For you, Piers? For a convenient way for you to unload me after six months?

Don't think about it, she told herself. Think about the groceries, what I'm going to cook for dinner tonight. So what if Piers is back? What possible difference does that make now? I've moved in with Andrew. It's fun to be with my brother again. I'm fine.

You should have seen the slag he was with.

Get off the bus. Walk to Tescos. Buy the groceries. Catch the groceries. Pretend Lisa never said those words. Get on with it. Don't fall to pieces because you've dropped a stupid egg.

'Sade – what's the matter?' Andrew was staring at her with a frightened expression. She knew she should pull herself together. But she couldn't. The tears kept falling and she kept wiping them away and Andrew kept staring.

Piers had picked her up at a tube stop – Mansion House – as they were standing beside each other waiting for a train. The platform was jammed with people and this nice-looking man beside her kept looking around nervously, as if he expected policemen to rush in, find him in the crowd and haul him off to the station. She couldn't help but stare at him, wondering what he was so anxious about. He must have noticed because he smiled at her and said, 'I always think some nutter is going to push me onto the tracks when it's crowded like this. Stupid, isn't it?'

'No, not at all,' she'd replied. 'I mean, I don't think it's likely, but I can understand why you might worry about it.' They were so far away from the platform, the 'nutter' would have had to pick him up and carry him in order to throw him on the tracks, but Sadie wasn't about to point that out to him.

'Thanks for understanding.' His elbow was being pressed into her ribs by the crowd. She didn't try to move away from it. 'Are you a shrink by any chance?'

'No.' She laughed.

'Neither am I. Obviously.' He laughed too. Then groaned when an announcement was made over the speaker system saying the train was delayed. 'Do you think someone was pushed onto the tracks? Is that why it's delayed?'

'I don't think so. They just said there was a signal failure.'

'They lie!' He grabbed her arm. 'There's a dead body on the tracks, I know there is.'

'Maybe you should think about something else.'

'Maybe I should.' His eyes narrowed. 'Maybe I should think about you.'

Two weeks later she had moved out of the flat she was sharing with two friends and moved in with him. Six months after that he'd told her he was going to Manchester. For those six months she'd been sailing across a beautiful ocean in lovely weather, stopping at undiscovered tropical islands. Then the earth had turned flat and she'd been pushed off the edge. There'd been no warnings, no storms, no signs of trouble. I never saw it coming, she thought. How was I supposed to know he'd be the nutter who threw me in front of the train? Except I landed up sitting here on my brother's sofa, crying. Even a year later I'm still crying.

'What's wrong with me, Andrew?'

'Nothing. Nothing's wrong with you.' He said it with such force she knew he was relieved that she'd asked the question. As soon as she spoke, there was something tangible he could fix, a question he could answer in such a way as to make her feel better. They might squabble, tease each other mercilessly, push each others' buttons the way only siblings could, but when it came to any threat from the outside world, they protected each other fiercely. For a moment Andrew had been stumped by her sudden tears, but now she knew he'd do anything he could to help.

Only she couldn't tell him about Piers. If she did, he'd get angry. Andrew's hatred for Piers ran as deep as her own ambivalence towards him. She knew she was supposed to hate him too. She wasn't supposed to remember times they'd had together which had made her so remarkably happy. That was not only foolish nostalgia, but also bad for her sense of self-worth. He had humiliated her. She should hate him too. She did hate him. Most of the time.

'What a stupid question. Who told you something was wrong with you? Lisa? I bet she doesn't have a bloke. I only met her that one time, but I can tell you this – Lisa without a bloke is like a football hooligan without a can of lager.'

'Andrew,' Sadie couldn't stop herself from smiling, 'that's a ridiculous thing to say.'

'But it's true.'

'It's not Lisa's fault. It's—' she slumped back against the sofa.

'It's what?'

It's Piers. He's back. What if I see him on the street? Or the pub? How am I supposed to cope?

'It's work, actually.'

'I knew it!' Andrew thumped the sofa. 'Working in the City is soul-destroying, Sade. What's happened? Did someone in your company not get the Porsche they wanted? Did that drive them to commit public hari kari?'

'Nothing in particular has happened. I had a difficult week, that's all. It got on top of me, suddenly. I'm tired.'

'I can't help but wonder about your employers,' Andrew continued. He was, Sadie could tell, about to deliver one of his tirades about the City. Normally she'd object to his branding everyone in the business world as loathsome yuppies, but not now. Now she was happy to let him distract her. 'Georgina Harvey and Jessica Tanner, the scalp hunters of EC1. No – I'm wrong. They're not scalp hunters, that would be an insult to Native Americans, who shouldn't be insulted especially as they own and operate so many great casinos. No, Ms Harvey and Ms Tanner are Pod People. They came to this planet under false pretences. Tell me something – have you ever seen either of them bleed? Have they ever nicked themselves or cut themselves in your presence?'

'Andrew—'

'Exactly. They haven't, because they have no blood in their veins. In fact, they don't have veins. They have . . . they have *sap*!' Andrew stood up and began to walk around the room. 'Gooey sap. Sap that sloshes round their bodies. Sap that every waking second, and sleeping ones too, threatens to ooze out and infect every person in their vicinity, turning them into sap-filled business tycoons who walk and talk like normal human beings but who are fuelled by sloshing sap which will one day explode and swamp the planet, and the end of the earth as we know it will be nigh and—'

'Andrew, come on. They're perfectly normal people. You've never even met them.'

'We have to find the antidote to sap, Sade. This is really serious. It's worse than Armageddon. It's terrible.' He went over to the telephone on the desk in the corner and picked it up. 'Hello? Hello? Operator get me Bruce Willis. Now! It's an emergency! My little sister works for women who are masquerading as chief executives of a financial services headhunting agency in the City when all the time they're Pod People! Hollywood! We need the hot line to Hollywood!'

He'd done it. She was genuinely laughing now, despite herself. He was completely off the mark in his portrayal of Georgie and Jessica, but that didn't matter; he'd made her forget her terrible day. Life was all right again. She'd had a blip, that's all. Tomorrow morning would be a new start; everything would change for the better. She'd get lucky and find a seat on the Tube. When she walked into the office, she'd be told that Georgie had decided to promote her. A wonderful unknown man would then ring her up and ask her out to dinner.

On her lunch break, she'd go shopping and find a perfect dress with the new money she'd be getting from her promotion, a Liz Hurley, life-changing dress; after which someone from Vidal Sassoon would stop her in the street and tell her he'd make her hair beautiful.

Tomorrow her life would be transformed.

As long as she didn't run into Piers Tate.

'I guess Bruce is busy.' Hanging up the phone, Andrew came back and sat beside Sadie. 'Probably trying to patch things up with Demi. Do you think they should reconcile?'

'I hate to admit this, but I haven't given it a lot of thought.'

Andrew pushed his hand through his curly brown hair. He was dressed in a workshirt and jeans, both of which were too big for him. For the first time, Sadie noticed two deep wrinkles above his eyebrows. Yet he still looked like a teenager. She remembered when he had taught her to ride a bike, how amazingly patient he'd been with her. He should be a school teacher, she thought. He'd be able to get across all the necessary information and make it fun at the same time, the way he'd managed to make unpacking groceries into a game. What he shouldn't do was on-line editing for a boring dot com company. But then she shouldn't be in a job which she doubted would ever allow her to rise to a high position, either. Neither she nor her brother seemed to know the trick of how to progress in life.

Eight years before, when Sadie was twenty and Andrew twenty-two, they'd made a chart predicting what they'd be doing a decade later. Both of them would be married, both of them would have had one child. Andrew had put himself down as a director of television documentaries, Sadie had guessed she would be a management consultant. She didn't know why she'd written that exactly, she'd just liked the words. They'd be earning approximately the same money and would both be living in unmortgaged houses. A fight developed when Andrew insisted he'd be more famous, but then she'd countered him with her villa in the South of France so they'd more or less evened things out.

'We have to promise not to look at this chart until ten years from today, OK? But we have to remember we've done it and then check up on our progress. It's like a time capsule.'

'It's a deal,' she'd said.

Not one of their predictions had come true. Was that their fault, or was it life's? Sadie wasn't sure. All she did know was that she dreaded seeing that chart again and hoped Andrew had forgotten all about it.

'Well, *I* don't think they should reconcile. I think Demi can do better.'

'Really?' Sadie laughed.

'I think she'd do well with someone English, maybe someone younger. Someone with a lot of time on his hands which he can devote to her and those wonderful children with those fabulous names like Scout and Rumer, or is it Scout and Boy? I can't remember. Anyway, someone who really wouldn't mind being a kept man, who'd have no ego problems on that one. Someone who understands how hard it is to be a babe with a shit-hot body and—'

'Andrew.' Sadie shook her head. 'I think I should call Mum and Dad and tell them you need some help. You're in danger of becoming truly weird.'

'Sade –' he threw his hands in the air – 'has it occurred to you I've spent the last half hour talking to a person whose hair looks like a child's drawing of a tiger on LSD? If I were you I wouldn't mention the word weird until you've done something about it. And meanwhile—'

'And meanwhile?'

'You can get off your backside and help me clean up the egg.'

Chapter Three

The City of London was buzzing, and Princes Street, swarming with high-rise office buildings, banks, pedestrians, cars, was right in the centre of the hive. Technically, almost all financial transactions could be done by computer in the bathroom of a country house, the bar of a trendy hotel or a shack in Alaska, but there was still a visceral need for a place where the drones could congregate together, somewhere they could travel to during the week and get away from on the weekend. Adrenaline is hard to summon in private, staring at a computer screen. When everyone is in the same place pumping money, adrenaline is as natural as sweat.

Georgie loved this feel of the City; it suited her. She didn't like downtime, she needed action, purpose, deadlines. At school she'd always been the only one in class actually to want tests. Once, when a teacher had offered the choice of an essay – due in three weeks time – or an exam the next day, she'd voted for the exam. The other girls, she remembered, had looked at her with incredulity mixed with exasperation, and had moaned audibly.

They didn't understand that Georgie needed grades, so wanted as many exams as possible, as often as possible. She required them in the same way other girls required pop-star idols or the newest fashion. Grades gave her identity, they also scared her witless. With each test, she'd think she'd be found out; the teachers would realize she actually knew nothing and had faked her way through all her previous endeavours. The only way to calm her fears was, paradoxically, to take another test and get another A. For a moment, the sight of that A would comfort her, until the prospect of the next grade loomed and anxiety would return with a vengeance. Constantly seeking to prove herself, she went through school on a knife edge of insecurity, never sure how long she could pull it off, always desperate to confirm that she could.

Other successful people, she'd since learned, had the same 'I'm going to be found out' syndrome, but none of those people, she thought, had it as profoundly as she did.

In a well-planned and well-executed progression, she had garnered grade A in her maths, economics and French A Levels, spent her gap year working for a Japanese stock-broking firm based in London, gone to university, received a degree in economics, joined an investment bank as a trader dealing in Japanese bonds, taken a year off to do a post-graduate training course in management skills, and then found work as a consultant for capital markets in a large headhunting firm. That particular firm was broad-based, dealing not only with financial services but also property, law, the media, technology and pharmaceuticals. After five years there, Georgie reckoned she could run her own headhunting company, specializing in financial services only.

Finding the backing to do it was relatively easy, but that didn't mean Georgie could relax. Each day when she went into her office, she had to take a few minutes at her desk warding off the 'today they're going to realize I'm a fake' attack. Only manic work could help dispel it; if she let down her guard for a second, the nameless amorphous 'they' would pounce, she knew, and she'd be left without a company, without a job, without anything. If she didn't feel stressed she was uncomfortable, wondering what she had overlooked or missed. Time spent away from work was time 'they' could use to find her out.

It was exhausting, this lifestyle of hers. At moments she wished she could give it up and try to lead a relatively normal life, but she had no practice in the normal; she'd been an overachiever for so long, she was afraid if she stopped, she'd go straight to an old persons' home and spend the rest of her life in a rocking chair.

At nine fifteen on this Monday morning she was especially relieved to get back into the office. Weekends were always difficult for her – all that free time, which was supposed to be spent relaxing, the activity which least suited her – and this past weekend had been particularly hard. Adam and his Vikings had been a disaster on Saturday. Yes, she'd managed to schedule that meeting at the pub for Sunday night, but then the man had shown up in his motorcycle helmet and that interview had also turned into a disaster.

After she and Jessica had returned home from the pub they'd fixed themselves their usual Sunday night scrambled eggs and bacon supper and turned on the television, finally settling on a made-for-television film. An Olympic-hopeful skier had a terrible car accident and had to have both of her legs amputated. No longer able to pursue her dreams of glory, she became a model of courage, trained herself to walk on her prosthetic legs, and pursued a new career as an aeroplane pilot – not just an ordinary aeroplane pilot, but one who did stunts and aerial acrobatics. Meanwhile, of course, one of the male aerial acrobatic pilots fell passionately in love with her and they lived happily ever after.

Jessica wept. She started weeping after the car accident and continued weeping throughout.

'Jess? What's wrong? That was supposed to be a happy ending.'

'She was so brave.'

'Exactly. She was brave and she triumphed. A story like that is supposed to uplift you, not leave you blubbing.'

'She really loved that pilot.'

Jessica broke down again. Georgie couldn't begin to understand what the problem was, but then she'd never understood the reasons for Jess's tears when they came. During their first few weeks at St Anne's boarding school, Jessica had cried constantly. How could she be homesick? Georgie couldn't fathom it. They'd both *wanted* to leave home. Their respective parents had made almost no effort to hide their relief when the boarding-school plan hatched in the attic had been broached to them. Jessica's mother Joanna was not the type who baked cakes or had a lot invested in the concept of 'nurturing', and Jessica's actual father, from what Georgie had picked up, was a distant, unemotional, upper-class club bore. Georgie's father showed no interest in his stepdaughter; in fact, the only trait Georgie's father and Jessica's mother seemed to share was a disregard for the stepdaughters their marriage had foisted upon them.

It wasn't as if they'd left a loving, functioning home, so why was Jessica crying? Jessica, unable or unwilling to answer the question, allowed herself to be comforted by Georgie, and, within a few months, she was getting along fine at school. It was Georgie who was struggling. She didn't understand the social structure which dominated the atmosphere of the school, the snobberies which lurked in every conversation. You would be looked at with disdain if you said the word 'toilet' instead of 'loo', with disbelief if you mentioned you'd never travelled outside England. There were right clothes and wrong clothes, even right make-up and wrong make-up. God forgive the girl such as Georgie who didn't wear any make-up at all.

At the beginning, with her competitive instincts on full throttle, she'd tried to fit in with the other girls, but somewhere along the line she'd been branded as an outsider – probably, she reflected, on her first day. She worked out that if she put all her energy into it, she might be able to change the tag and become one of them, but that would mean not giving as much as she could to her studies, to those all important grades.

She could bear the 'swot' reputation, she got used to not being invited to parties, mostly because Jess, despite her own resounding popularity, never even came close to dropping her. Jess had been loyal, which Georgie knew must have been, at times, hard for her. Georgie could live with having few friends as long as Jess was there. What she could never do, though – and this sometimes made her wonder about herself – was to cry.

'Hey, Jess, come on. Chill. It was only a story.'

'It's wrong.' Jessica shook her head. 'It's all wrong.'

'What's all wrong?'

'Everything. I'm so alone.'

Moving closer to Jessica on the sofa, Georgie stifled her immediate response. She wanted to say 'pull yourself together' but she knew Jessica in moods like this. There was a lost quality to her, the same sad vulnerability she'd showed that afternoon in the attic.

Georgie hadn't believed it at the time – posh, disgustingly pretty Jessica hiding under a bed in the attic. Until then, she'd kept her distance from her new stepsister when she spent weekends at her father's house. Everything about Jessica and her mother Joanna was foreign to her: their expensive clothes, the way they talked, how they behaved themselves. It was clear to Georgie that, having made a sudden windfall in his fibre-optic business, her father had decided to trade up by leaving her mother to find a glamorous upper-class woman, buy some boring house in the boring country and attempt to be some kind of nouveau riche squire. She wanted as little to do with it as possible. Yes, she'd visit at weekends, but she'd keep herself to herself. Which was also what she did in London during the week as soon as her mother linked up with the drunk boyfriend.

Her mother and father weren't lower class, they were squarely in the middle of the social scale, but they hadn't sent her to public school, they wouldn't have dreamt of buying her designer clothes. Jessica and her mother discussed leg waxing, clothes shopping and ski trips together. It was all, to Georgie's thirteen year old mind, extremely unpractical and fairly stupid. What was the point of paying someone to rip hair off your legs when there were razors? Who wanted to wear someone else's name on their clothes? Yes, she would have liked to go skiing, but she knew there was no chance Jessica's mother would ever ask her along.

They might be the same age, but otherwise she and Jessica Tanner had nothing whatever in common. Until that afternoon.

The row had been uglier than any of the others. The shouting had risen like heat through the house, reaching her in her bedroom, stifling her in its thick smoke of nastiness. Finally doors had slammed; she had looked out of her bedroom window and seen Joanna drive off in her Mercedes, her father drive off in his.

'The wankers,' she remembered saying to herself before setting off for some quality TV-time downstairs. After half an hour or so of watching pure drivel, she'd turned it off and sat on the huge sofa feeling sorry for herself. After another half hour, she got bored with that as well and went to find Jessica. Little Miss Prissy was probably putting on make-up in her room or trying on all her cupboardsful of clothes, but watching that would be marginally better than watching the *Waltons*.

Jessica wasn't in her room. She didn't seem to be anywhere.

For the first time, in the year since she'd been coming to this house at weekends, Georgie wondered about Jessica. Maybe her life wasn't so fantastic, either. Maybe Jessica had hated hearing that fight as much as she had. Maybe they had more in common than she thought. She couldn't quite bring herself to believe that. Jessica was Jessica. She was probably out taking a walk and trying not to get her shoes dirty.

Still . . . Georgie kept wondering. Jessica didn't take walks. So where was she?

If *I* were hiding, where would I go?

I'd go up to the attic.

As soon as she heard Jessica's feeble, 'Here I am,' Georgie knew everything had changed. Jessica Tanner needed her. Jessica Tanner was her friend. Jessica Tanner was her sister. Jessica was the only real family she had and she was going to look after her. No matter what.

And I've done just that, she thought as she looked over at Jessica. Even though she drives me mad sometimes, even though she is still wrapped up in her social world and her appearance and her clothes. I've looked after her. I've rescued her whenever she's needed help. I've been as good a sister as there could possibly be. And now she's sitting here crying and I need to help her again.

Jessica wouldn't respond well to 'pull yourself together', Georgie knew. Luckily, she also knew exactly what Jessica *would* respond to.

'There's a bottle of champagne in the fridge, Jess. Let's shake it up and then drink it.'

'There is?' Jessica smiled. She sat up straight.

'It's right there in the fridge. Do you want to?'

'Absolutely.'

Georgie went to the kitchen to get it, thankful that this trick always worked, trying to remember when she'd latched on to it in the first place. It must have been during those first days at St Anne's, when Jess was always crying. At some point, she must have said, 'Why don't we try to find some champagne and shake it up again,' and Jess must have laughed. For some reason, that memory of shaking champagne bottles was precious to her stepsister. To Georgie, it was only a silly stunt they'd pulled, but for Jessica it meant instant happiness. Why? Georgie couldn't work it out.

They'd been hanging around the house one summer weekend, the summer before they'd gone to St Anne's, not doing much of anything. There was going to be a dinner party that night, Jessica's mother and Georgie's father were already arguing about who should sit beside whom, and Georgie had pulled Jess aside. 'Let's have some fun,' she'd said. 'Let's sneak into the kitchen before the party starts and shake up the champagne.'

'What for?' Jess had asked.

'Because then, when they open it, it will explode all over the place.'

'Really?'

Jessica's dove-grey eyes widened, a gleam of pure pleasure in them. Like co-conspirators, Georgie and she went on to plan the execution of this subversive act down to the last detail. When the moment came, they hid at the top of the stairs, peering through the banisters down into the sitting room. They couldn't hear what was being said by the party guests, but they could see Georgie's father taking hold of a bottle, preparing to uncork it. Jessica grabbed Georgie's hand a second before the blast. Champagne sprayed everywhere, a gusher of gold liquid splattering across the room. It went over dresses, furniture, paintings. After cleaning up the mess, Georgie's father made the fatal mistake of going to get another bottle. This time, Jessica didn't stay to see the explosion. She fled from the landing and ran into her bedroom, Georgie in hot pursuit.

'Jess, what's the matter?' She thought Jessica was crying, that's what it looked like. Jessica was curled up on her bed, a pillow over her head. But when Georgie removed the pillow, she saw that her stepsister was stifling wild laughter, not tears. She'd try to stop but then she'd begin again, laughing so hard Georgie thought she might be about to rupture her appendix. Jess was so out of control it was actually a little frightening.

The mystery of the shaken champagne bottles was never solved by their parents. Georgie had been impressed by Jessica's poker face under questioning. And still slightly baffled by Jess's unrestrained hilarity whenever they were alone together and the subject came up. Now, she knew, it was a sure-fire short cut to cheering Jessica up, the easy way to make her happy. She used that knowledge whenever it was necessary, though she always wondered when the power of it would fade and Jessica would say, 'Enough.'

This strange magic worked again, though, after the movie. Jessica took the bottle from Georgie's hand, shook it furiously and laughed and laughed. Waiting for a while until the fizz subsided, they then opened it and polished it off. Jess's tears seemed to have been forgotten by the time she went to bed. Georgie, going up a few minutes later, was surprised to find on the side table, under the lamp she was about to turn off, a copy of *The Wasteland*. Had Jess been reading it? If so, why? What the hell could she be doing reading T. S. Eliot? It made no sense. Jess was a Danielle Steel type of reader. Still, reading *The Wasteland* would depress anyone.

Perhaps this was why she had been weeping, why she had come out with that 'I'm so alone' line. Jessica Tanner had taken up poetry. God help her, Georgie thought, as she turned off the lamp. If there were such a thing as the Gianni Versace Book of Light Verse, maybe Jess could get to grips with it. But *The Wasteland*? Now, that was truly bizarre. What Jess needed was a career, not poetry. If she had work to think about, she might forget how 'alone' she was. But would she ever manage to get a grip on the headhunting business? So far, it didn't look likely.

Although she had social connections which could be occasionally helpful, Jessica Tanner was not and probably never would be a player in the financial world. After failing to get into university, she'd wasted years doing, effectively, nothing. Once in a while she'd motivate herself to take a course, but they were courses like 'Seventeenth-century Musical Instruments' or 'Cultivating the Zen You', and all the while she was living off her parents' money. That money, despite her mother having had a huge settlement from Georgie's father when they finally did the sensible thing and divorced, had run out. For whatever reasons, the upper-class club bore father refused to support his daughter, so Jessica was suddenly left floundering. Georgie had suggested they move in together, and then, in an act of supreme generosity, brought her into the business.

She wasn't any good at it. Jessica's attention span was short at the best of times. Although she understood the general concept of finding jobs for people, she was hopeless at the details of the business. If she heard the words 'debt origination', her eyes would glaze and she'd start searching through her bag for lipstick. Trying to find things for Jess to do was a job in itself and Georgie was running out of patience.

She has to apply herself, Georgie thought as she climbed the stairs to bed. I can't carry her any more. I have to help her learn how to concentrate.

'You know, Jess . . .' They were in the car travelling to work the next morning, stuck in a traffic jam on the Embankment. Jessica was driving. Georgie, unhooking her seatbelt, shifted her body so that her back was against her window. 'I think it's time I taught you more about the business.'

'What do you mean, exactly?'

'I mean I could tutor you in the evenings.'

'Tutor me?'

'Yes.'

The car ahead of them moved forward ten feet or so. Jessica stayed stationary.

'Would this involve homework?'

The car behind honked. Jessica kept her foot on the brake.

'Homework would be part of it, yes.'

'Homework?'

'Jess – people are honking. You can move up.'

'Oh.'

The engine revved, the car lurched forward, Georgie shouted, 'Watch out!' two seconds before Jess slammed on the brakes. They missed a fender bender by inches. Georgie put her seatbelt back on.

'Jess!'

'Sorry.' Jessica shook her head.'I wasn't concentrating.'

'Anyway, I was thinking you could start by reading the *Financial Times* every day.'

'Mmmhmmm.'

'I'll get you a subscription to some good business magazines, too.'

'I'm not feeling very well. Can we talk about this later?'

'What's wrong?'

'I have a headache.'

'All right. We'll talk about it tonight, then.'

They didn't speak for the rest of the journey. When the traffic cleared, Jess drove like a lunatic, putting her foot on the accelerator, then braking for no reason, then speeding up and then braking again. The constant stopping and starting made Georgie feel so nauseous she wondered how Jess could stand it with her headache.

As soon as she reached the sanctuary of her office and turned on her computer, Georgie's stomach settled. There were seventy emails waiting to be read. The weekend was over. Life was back on track.

Chapter Four

Jessica had her head in her hands. *Homework?* There wasn't a worse word in the English vocabulary. Except for 'exam'.

It was definitely time to get out of Harvey and Tanner.

Why had Georgie put the Tanner into Harvey and Tanner to begin with? She'd explained at the time, when she started the company, that she'd been racking her brain for a name to go with 'Harvey' – because it sounded, on its own, like some American man you'd meet in a bar – and had decided that Tanner was perfect. Did Jess mind? No, she didn't mind, not then. But now, when she was in the office every day and people looked at her as if she should know everything about the financial services sector because her name was on the name plate, it was definitely a disadvantage.

The only way out of H&T, though, was to get another job, some way to support herself. Every time she had this thought, and she'd had it thousands of times over the last few months, she ran up against the wall of the obvious: what job? Who, besides Georgie, would employ her?

Jessica picked up the phone on her desk. She dialled a number but hung up before it rang. It wouldn't work, she knew. Ringing her mother would only make things worse. What would she say? I need a job? Her mother would say,

'Darling, you need a husband. Any prospects on the horizon? Remember that nice man I was telling you about yesterday? I know an estate agent may not be . . .' And she'd have to say, 'I don't want to meet the estate agent again. It has nothing to do with his job, Mum, it's his personality that darkens a room,' and then listen to her mother sighing.

That was supposed to be the education she'd had – courses in how to find a man. You go to the right ski resort or the right restaurants and parties, you wear the right clothes and you smile the right smile and you meet the right, acceptable, high-earning man and you marry him. Yes, you might then divorce him, as Jessica's mother had done twice now, but you were well paid for your time. It was an old-fashioned, anti-feminist outlook, but Jessica's mother was certain it was the only outlook to have.

'Listen to me carefully, sweetheart,' Joanna had said on the day Jessica turned eighteen. 'I'm going to give you a little lecture which will help you in life. Nowadays male–female relationships are all about the market economy. Women have a limited window of opportunity to exploit their potential in the marketplace. Between the ages of eighteen and twenty-eight, they're in a good selling position, but they hit a brick wall at ninety miles an hour when they reach twenty-nine, thirty. That's because they start to think of their future and panic – as they should, of course. They get that desperate look in their eyes and men can see it. They can smell the fear. Women think, "all right, I'm going out with him now, but if we break up, it will take a year to recover and a year to find someone else and how much time do I have left before my time runs out?" So they start to push hard, and the men, feeling pushed, run away. Do you see what I'm saying?'

'No,' Jessica mumbled.

'Well, you will, if you ever have the misfortune to be in that position. You'll be thirty or older and there will be the men wanting twenty-five year olds who don't have the baggage, who are fresh, who are relatively innocent. Then you'll have to start looking for divorced men who have children, or bottom-feeding men who can't get the twenty-five year olds and your power in the marketplace will disappear. Now do you understand?'

'No.'

'Sit up straight, Jessica. I'm sure you won't have to deal with any of these problems. I'm just trying to give you advice so you won't have to. You wouldn't believe the number of female wrecks littered on the shoreline of the age-depreciation process. What I'm pointing out to you is that that process starts earlier than you may think. It doesn't begin at thirty-five, it begins in the late twenties. It's not about the biological time clock – whether you can have children or not. These days, you can have children on your own, for God's sake, get some sperm from some clinic or somewhere and you'll get the baby. It's getting a *man* I'm talking about – that's a much, much harder proposition. Men are spoilt for choice. Women are ever-decreasing assets. Sell at your highest value, darling. Twenty-four, twenty-five. I'm sure this sounds ruthless, but I promise you, I'm only being practical.'

Jessica was now thirty-three. Her mother was pushing estate agents and their ilk at her like medicine for a consumptive.

Was that really what she was destined for? A career in marriage with love being an unnecessary bonus? Are you supposed to settle for someone who bores you or who irritates you or who you're not attracted to, simply in order to settle? Jessica had dated plenty of respectable men, but they'd all made her feel uncomfortable in one way or another. There had been many times in many restaurants when she'd wanted to run screaming from the table after the first course, not even sure why she was so put off. What makes a dream man? She didn't have a clue. All she knew was she hadn't found one – a state of affairs which was driving her mother mental.

And now Georgie was offering to tutor her in the art of headhunting, an occupation Jessica knew she would never understand, even if she worked day and night trying to. The City had a language of its own, a financial language with buzz words and phrases and peculiar grammar. Jessica had never been good at languages; she'd copied Georgie's Latin homework her entire time at St Anne's.

The image of Mount Everest reappeared. This time she was standing on top, her arms wrapped around a gorgeous vision of the male species, while a storm raged around them.

What she wanted was to get lost in passion, to be swept away. She wished she could laugh the way she had that night when the champagne bottle exploded.

That was the favourite moment of her life. It was the most daring thing she'd ever done. As she had watched Georgie's father uncork the bottle, she'd felt as if she were taking a step off a high diving board not sure if there was water in the pool. It was heady, it was funny, it was against all the rules she had lived by. Not only had it been a waste of champagne, it had been the waste of bottles of Cristal champagne, the most expensive of the lot. Money was being splattered over the living room for no good reason. It felt as if an anger she'd never been aware she had was suddenly being released. Nothing had come close to that feeling of liberation since, not even sex. She'd never been able to let herself go like that in bed. She was far too ill at ease, she knew, between the sheets, and as for more exotic love-making locations – on the kitchen table, on the floor, in a park – she couldn't do anything except wait for it to be over and hope the man in question hadn't noticed how self-conscious she was. No man had ever managed to make her forget her inhibitions. She didn't know where those inhibitions had come from, but they looked like staying for eternity.

Jessica remembered being seven years old, playing Snow White in a school production. She'd had to sit alone on stage at the beginning, singing a song. Her voice wasn't particularly good, she knew she'd got the part because of her looks, and she'd been embarrassed to sing. She'd been terrified, actually, at the thought of having to perform for people. 'You'll be fine as soon as it starts,' her parents had said. 'The minute you begin the song, you'll forget about being afraid.'

They were in the audience – she could see them in the second row as she opened her mouth, sang the first line and then choked. No sound would come out, nothing. She sat, blinking, as disappointment took the place of pride on their faces. The words kept refusing to come out, but the tears had no problem whatsoever. As they rolled down her cheeks, she rushed off the stage. The teacher in charge of the play dragged her back on and sat her down. The music started up again. Everyone in the audience, she could sense, was willing her to get it right.

'Somewhere waiting for me,' she sang, 'there is—'

That was it. That was as far as she could get. The tears weren't just falling, they were cascading with the force of a burst pipe. The music wouldn't stop playing, the audience wouldn't stop staring at her, all she could do to get away from the horror of it was to flee yet again. This time the teacher didn't drag her back. Some other child was pushed on as a replacement Snow White while the teacher went out and found her parents and told them it might be wise to take her home.

'I'm disappointed in you, Jessica,' her father had said in the car.

'You're disappointed in everyone, Sam,' her mother had said in a cold, hard voice. 'And I don't care what time of day it is, *I* need a Martini.'

Jessica couldn't remember what had happened when they got home. She was, though, relieved that four and a half years passed since the play before they got a divorce. Otherwise, she knew, she would have blamed herself for their splitting up.

Turning on her computer to read emails she either didn't understand or didn't care about, she began to sing to herself.

'Somewhere, waiting for me . . .

At that point, her tears, which had been waiting in the wings since Georgie had said the word 'tutor', took their cue, walked to centre stage and started to fall.

Chapter Five

There was a long queue at the newsagents' – of course there was, Sadie thought. She'd snuck out of the office to get herself a chocolate fix and now she was stuck waiting, wasting precious time. If she stayed away too long, Georgie would notice and be irritated.

Being a PA to Georgina Harvey could be difficult. Georgie was a work-obsessed perfectionist who expected everyone in the company to be as committed to Harvey and Tanner as she was. Yet she was, generally, fair. On the whole, if you did what she wanted and did it quickly and efficiently, you were treated well.

Sadie realized she had put herself in an impossible position regarding her career, but she didn't know how to extricate herself from it. She had been happy enough to get the PA job eighteen months ago, as it paid reasonably well and she had been excited about the prospect of getting in on the beginning of a new company. Georgie had promised in the interview that Sadie's work would be reviewed every six months and that she believed wholeheartedly in promoting from within. Now Sadie wanted to move from being a PA to become a researcher, but she also knew she had been such a good PA that Georgie was loath to lose her. Yet if she didn't do her job well, she'd most likely be fired. It was a *Catch 22* scenario. She knew she had to sit down and have a talk with Georgie, but she wasn't sure what was the best time to do it. Today certainly wasn't, that much she knew for certain. Not only was Georgie in her Monday morning, preoccupied mood, but something was very wrong with Jessica.

Technically, Sadie was Jessica's PA as well, but Jessica, as far as Sadie could make out, didn't do anything. Occasionally Jessica would call Sadie in to her office and ask her to set up a lunch or a dinner date. That was pretty much the sum total of Jessica's requirements of a PA. At first Sadie wondered what exactly Jessica was actually doing there, but she had so much work to do for Georgie, she stopped wondering and was grateful. Two Georgies would have been too much. This morning, though, because Georgie was busy answering emails, Sadie had knocked on Jessica's door to see if she could help her in any way. When she got no response to the knock, she opened the door and took a tentative step inside Jessica's office. Jessica was sitting at her desk crying.

'Jessica.' Sadie took another step toward her. 'Are you all right? Is there anything I can do?'

Jessica waved her away and buried her head in her arms on top of the desk.

That was when Sadie had decided it was time for a chocolate fix.

When she finally reached the front of the queue at the newsagents', she heard her mobile ringing.

'Sorry, just a second. God I hate these things,' she said apologetically to the man behind the counter who was looking at her as if she were holding up air traffic at Heathrow.

'Sade, where are you? I didn't see you come in. And now I can't find you. I have to see the hair.'

'Lisa, I'm in the newsagents', I'll be right back. Do you want some chocolate or anything?'

'No, no, no. Not hungry. I forgot to ask. Did they cut it too? I should have told you to get it cut too.'

'No, they didn't cut it,' Sadie answered, thinking: thank God.

The man behind the counter put his hands on his hips. He was one of those men whose every available inch of skin was covered in a mat of thick black hair. It sprang through his shirt, it had colonized his arms, it was everywhere except the top of his head. Sadie grabbed a Dime bar from the rack of chocolates in front of her and put it on the counter.

'Did you see that ridiculous email Jessica sent – must have been last thing Friday night? About how we should all dress. The woman is bonkers. She has nothing better to do. I mean, as if I don't know how to dress already, as if she's the style police. All right, she has those designer frocks, but pay me enough and I'll buy them too. I'll spend my lunch hours at Harrods, I'll . . .'

Pinning the mobile to her ear with her shoulder in a contorted Quasimodo position, Sadie opened her bag, fished out her wallet and saw she only had a fifty-pound note. How had that happened? She couldn't remember ever having a fifty-pound note, but there it was. She handed it over to Mr Hairy.

'You can not be serious.' He stared at her. There was not one iota of pity in his eyes. 'If you want change for a fifty, you'll have to buy something for more than thirty p.'

'Oh, and fine, when I'm at Harrods,' Lisa was saying, 'I'll grab a little Moschino number. And why not, while I'm at it, scoop up some Manolo Blahnik shoes? What a name. Blahnik. Blah, blah, blahnik . . .'

Sadie took a quick inventory of the shop – what could she buy?

She saw him then, at the back of the shop, by the stand of greeting cards. A man with sandy hair. A man approximately six feet tall. His back was to her, but she knew. She knew it was Piers.

'And Manolo – sounds like a football player. Or some health cereal. Crunchy manolo, good for the heart . . .'

Covering the mouthpiece, Sadie leant forward and whispered, 'Please give me change. I have to get out of here. Now.'

'I said, buy something for more than thirty p and I will.' The hairy man was sweating. So was Sadie.

'Not that it's not important to eat healthy stuff. Excellent for the skin. Do you take those fish pills I told you about? I know they take a while to kick in and I know they're expensive, but I promise you, Sade, your skin will . . .'

'Lisa, I've got to go.' Sadie cut off the call, threw the mobile back in her bag. She had to get out of there before Piers saw her. 'Here.' She grabbed a plastic football from a bin at her side. 'I'll have this. Please be quick.'

If Piers was still looking at the cards, she might be able to sneak past him. What she couldn't do was have a civil conversation with him, a 'Hello, how are you, oh you're back, are you?' conversation. Not now. Not ever, if she was honest with herself. She didn't want to see his eyes or his smile, she especially didn't want to hear his voice. All it would remind her of were those words, 'Tell her I'm in a meeting.'

Her phone rang again, just as Mr Hairy handed her the change. Finding it seemed to take forever – it was hidden in the bottom of her bag. When she finally took it out and answered it, she heard Lisa saying, 'You can't totally rely on them though. The fish pills. They work, yes, but you need to drink at least three litres of water a day and . . .'

She could feel Piers moving, sense that he was making his

way to the front of the shop. She cut off the call again. Grabbing the football, putting it under her arm, she kept her head down and started for the door. A few more feet, she thought. Only a few more feet and I'll be safe.

The impact jolted the ball out of her hand. Her bag crashed to the floor as well. She'd done it. She'd walked straight into Piers.

'I'm so sorry,' he said, leaning down to retrieve the bag. 'Hang on,' he smiled up at her as he handed it to her, 'I'll get the football too.'

'*I'm* sorry. It was my fault.' She wanted to hug this man for not being Piers. She wanted to kill him because he had the same hair colour and was the same height. Instead she took the football from him and said, 'Thank you very much.' The relief she felt was so monumental she actually skipped to the door. On her last jump for joy, she crashed against a male body coming through the entrance.

'Nice to see you again, Sade.'

He was holding her by the shoulders, Piers Tate was holding her by the shoulders, while she hugged the football to her chest as if it were a baby.

'Aren't you going to say hello?'

'Of course.' She raised her eyes, looked at him, looked away. 'Hello, Piers. Long time no see.' *Long time no see?* How could I have said that?

'Come with me while I get some fags.' He took her elbow and guided her back to the front of the store. The queue had disappeared. 'I'd like twenty Bensons please.' Piers handed Mr Hairy a five-pound note. 'You see I still smoke.' He turned to Sadie. 'Still haven't managed to quit.'

'Oh.' Sadie couldn't move. Say something, don't just stand here like a buffoon. Say something like Lisa says she said to some man who'd dumped her – what was it? – 'The only big thing you have is your ego.' No, that wasn't it, but it went along those lines.

'Listen . . .' Piers collected his cigarettes and change, stuffed them into his pocket in exactly the same way he always stuffed change and cigarettes and pieces of paper into his pocket. The familiarity of the movements he made seized and squeezed her heart. 'I'm sorry about the way things ended, I should have handled it better. But – you know . . .' He shrugged. 'Men behaving sadly.'

'Don't—' Sadie began and stopped. Don't what? Apologize? Or don't say the word 'ended', because maybe it was preferable not hearing anything at all from you to hearing you speak that word, especially in a bloody newsagents' shop in front of this ape-like man who was listening to every word.

'No, honestly, I was a bastard, I know. I've felt really horrible about it, really guilty. I don't know why I was such a coward. I should have told you face-to-face, before I left, I should have told you it was over—'

'No.' Shaking her head quickly, Sadie backed away. 'Don't—' She thought she was going to be sick. Get a grip, she lectured herself. Don't give him the pleasure of seeing you so shaken.

'You know Piers,' Sadie tried to align her features into some semblance of normality, 'the only thing about—' No, wait, how did it begin? 'The only big thing about—' What? What came next? It didn't matter – she couldn't say it whatever it was.

'What? What's the only big thing?' Piers moved toward her, a solicitous look on his face. She'd managed not to look at his face very closely before this moment. Now she had no choice; it was right in front of her. His eyes hadn't changed colour, he hadn't developed scores of wrinkles, his nose hadn't been broken. This was the same face she'd woken up to for six months.

'Smoking is bad for you. That's a very big thing.'

'Well, what a newsflash, Sade. I think I knew that. Are you OK?'

'Fine, fine.' She forced a smile, took another step back. 'I thought you should know, that's all.'

'Do you think we should tell other people that smoking may be bad or keep it our little secret?'

Don't blush, she told herself as she felt a furnace start up in her face.

'So, Sade, have you been playing a lot of football lately?'

'What?'

'That football you're clutching. I figured it must be yours or you wouldn't be holding it so tightly.'

'It's for a friend.'

'A friend? What kind of friend?'

She was tempted, she really was, to make up a boyfriend. Tell Piers she was engaged to a wonderful Brazilian striker who'd just been bought by Manchester United.

'A friend friend.'

'Ah. Anyway, would you like to meet up for coffee some time?' Pulling a Palm out of his inside jacket pocket, Piers studied it. 'I have some free time next week – no . . . week after next – how about that? We could catch up on each other's lives.'

What? Like a reunion? Sadie thought. And I'd be the one with same job, sharing a flat with my brother in crack-infested Shepherd's Bush, boyfriendless, while you'd be the one with a new promotion and a new girlfriend and your Palm full of appointments and things to do? I don't think so.

'Sounds great,' she said.

'I'll ring you. Are you still at H and T?'

'Yes.'

'Excellent.'

'Excellent.'

Awful. Terrible. Bad, bad, bad.

'I'm off. Ciao, then.'

'Ciao.'

Fuck off. Leave me alone. Go and smoke five thousand cigarettes. I hate you. Coffee week after next. How lame is that?

She watched him as he headed out of the shop and turned right. When he walked, he swung his arms up and down as if he were propelling himself with them rather than his legs.

Finally forcing herself to move, to leave the newsagents', Sadie tried to console herself. She hadn't fainted, she hadn't prostrated herself at his feet, she hadn't thrown a fit of any kind. She may not have handled herself perfectly, but given the situation, she'd made a decent job of it. That was something to be pleased about. It could have been worse.

Why did he have to come back? she asked herself as she slowed down to a walk. *Why didn't he stay in Manchester?*

I'm not going to think about him any more. It doesn't matter that he's back. I'm over it. So what am I doing with this football under my arm?

Going over to the side of the pavement, Sadie placed the football in front of a bookshop, hoping someone who needed it would pick it up and make use of it. *This might make someone's day*, she thought. *Maybe a father will give it to a little two-year-old and he will become the next David Beckham. Yes, and maybe I really do look like Catherine Zeta Jones*, Sadie muttered to herself, wishing she still had the football so she could kick it.

As she was walking into the lift in the Harvey and Tanner office building, Francesca, from accounts, was walking out.

'Quick!' Francesca grabbed her and pulled her into the lobby. 'Evacuate! Flee! Let's get out of here until the dust settles.'

'What dust? What's going on?'

'You mean you missed it, Sadie? Lucky you. Although I have to say it was almost worth watching. You know that email from Jessica about dress code? Her tips on fashion? You got that one too, didn't you?'

'Yes. Jessica copied it to everyone.'

'Exactly.' Sadie and Francesca walked a few feet to the side of the lobby and huddled. 'Well, Lisa got it too, of course. And Lisa, being Lisa, decided to have a little fun. She sent an email to Lucy in research saying: "Suitable clothes? The sisters should be thinking about fuck-me clothes. How long has it been since either of them got shagged, do you think? Two more uptight, sex-starved females I have not seen since my days in the convent school. Actually, my guess is that they are virgins, but I'm willing to open a book on it." And –' Francesca grabbed Sadie's arm – 'she pressed the wrong bloody key. It went out to the whole office.'

'You mean . . . ?'

'Absolutely. Around five minutes ago, Georgie and Jessica had the pleasure of reading about their own sex lives, or lack of them.'

'I don't believe it.'

'Lisa didn't believe it either. She's in Georgie's office now.'

'Is Jessica there as well?'

'Yes, my spies tell me Georgie hasn't drawn breath and Jessica is sitting there filing her nails. "Uptight, sex-starved females". Don't you love it?' Francesca's laugh was infectious.

'I hope Lisa doesn't get sacked.'

'Me too.'

Sadie saw a look of amusement suddenly pass over Francesca's face.

'Um, that's interesting,' Francesca said coyly.

'What is?'

'That . . . you know . . . new hair thing you've done.'

Sadie put her hand to her head. Her hair. She'd forgotten about her hair.

Chapter Six

'Virgins? She thinks we're virgins? I should have sacked her.'

Georgie bent down, took off one of her shoes and pounded it on the desktop in front of her. The week before Jessica had seen an old newsclip of some Russian doing just that when he was having a temper tantrum at the UN. She couldn't work out why he was so angry, but she doubted it was because he'd been called a virgin.

'Lisa didn't really mean it,' Jessica said, thinking, the only reason I sent that email about a dress code was because I was so bored I couldn't think of anything else to do. I don't want Lisa to lose her job because I was pretending I have a job.

'It shows disrespect. Unbelievable disrespect.'

'But . . .' Jessica frowned.

'But what?'

When she was angry, Georgie's right eye wandered. Actually, to be precise, it strayed a little to the left of its usual position, giving her face an off-kilter aspect which for some reason Jessica always associated with Napoleon.

The comparison wasn't entirely surprising, though. Georgie was an emperor in her own way at Harvey and Tanner: an efficient, tenacious, tyrant. If not Napoleon exactly, Jessica could imagine her stepsister as a Moscow Mafia Queen, reigning over a horde of well-heeled hoodlums.

'But Lisa has a point. I mean, we may not be virgins, but—'

'But what?'

'But we're . . .'

Georgie reached into her desk and pulled out a packet of cigarettes. Watching her light up, Jessica winced. Georgie rarely smoked. When she did, it signalled she was either in the middle of a fit of rage or a fit of nerves.

'We're what, Jess? What are we exactly?'

'We're alone.'

'Alone. Alone, alone, alone.' Georgie flung her hands in the air. Jessica was worried that the cigarette was going to take flight as well. 'What is this? National Alone Week?'

'More like National Alone Decade,' Jessica said under her breath.

'I heard that Jess. And you might as well make it century. But we're not the only ones. Everyone is alone, really. I mean, think about it. How many happy couples do you know?'

'Mr and Mrs Post Office Pover – they were married fifty-five years, weren't they?'

'But we don't know if they were happy. All we know is they worked in the post office and were married all that time.'

'Well, if they hated every minute of it, they would have burnt down the post office so they wouldn't have to see each other, wouldn't they?'

'I'm not sure that's entirely logical thinking.' Georgie drummed her fingertips on the desk. 'But, OK – I'll give you the Povers. Who else?'

'I don't know.' Jessica made a mental search of the couples she knew. 'I can't think right now.'

'See – only the Povers.'

'No, no. I'm sure there are others, I just can't think of them.'

'There might be a very good reason you can't think of any.'

'God, Georgie, sometimes you're incredibly depressing to be around. You might not believe in love, but I do.'

'You and Mrs Pover.'

'Please, could we stop talking about the Povers. They always frightened me. Every time I went into the post office they asked me when I was going to go to church.'

Laughing as she put out her cigarette, Georgie said, 'They never asked me. I think they gave up on me when I washed their car for charity that time – remember? I used some chemical or ammonia by mistake to wash it and all the paint came off. It took all their Christianity to forgive me. Seeing me in church would have been too much for them to bear. But you've put me off the track. I was talking about Lisa's email. "Uptight, sex-starved." Please. Well, all right, sex-starved maybe.' Georgie grunted. 'But uptight? Never.'

'I don't know. She might be right about me. Perhaps I *am* uptight. Sometimes, anyway.' Jessica looked away from Georgie, out the window. 'I wonder sometimes if I'm uptight because I've never really loved a man. I know I've had crushes. But true love? I don't think I've fallen in true love – except maybe once.'

'Once? Who was this once?'

'Daniel.'

'Daniel?'

'Daniel Canter – remember him?'

'Jessica?' Georgie tilted her chair back, folded her arms across her chest.

She was wearing a blue suit with brown shoes. Jessica had never understood why her stepsister had such a disastrous clothes sense. Maybe I was unconsciously thinking of Georgie when I sent that email, she thought. I can't bring myself to tell her she should dress better, so I lectured the whole office.

'You're not talking about the Daniel Canter who lived next door to us in the country ages ago? Tell me you're not.'

'I am. He gave me flowers once. I think he stole them from a graveyard. But, still, it was a sweet gesture, wasn't it? Incredibly romantic.'

'Was that before or after he'd done his stretch for car theft?'

'Daniel wasn't a criminal, not really.'

'No?' Georgie rolled her eyes. 'Did the car's rightful owner have temporary amnesia and forget he'd given it to Daniel?'

'People make mistakes, Georgie. It was a . . . a youthful indiscretion. But I *was* in love with him. I used to write to him in gaol.'

'The Povers probably censored your letters.'

'And you fancied Daniel's brother, didn't you? What was his name?'

They hadn't reminisced like this for a long time, though Jessica often tried unsuccessfully to pull Georgie back into the past. Jessica loved talking like this, it gave her a feeling of family and belonging. Besides, discussing Daniel Canter was hugely preferable to discussing Georgie's tutoring project.

'Mark. Daniel's brother was named Mark.'

'That's right. He had a club foot, didn't he?'

'Jess! A club foot? His little finger had to be amputated when he was three years old. There was absolutely nothing wrong with his foot.'

'Why did Mark's finger have to be amputated?'

'Daniel thought it would be fun to try sawing it off. Apparently he didn't do a very professional job.'

'No. That's impossible.' Jessica shook her head. 'Daniel would never have hurt anyone. He was an angel.'

'Angel? Jess – what's happened to your memory? Daniel was a thug.'

'He was not!' She tried to visualize Daniel Canter. Dark-haired, tall, thuggish? His jerseys always smelled of autumn leaves, and he had a motorcycle. That much she remembered perfectly. That and the fact he kissed like an eighteen-year-old angel.

'You are really worrying me. Are you seriously saying you didn't know Daniel sawed off Mark's finger?'

'Well, no. How was I supposed to know?'

'That's fairly crucial information. You might have asked. You could have said, "Daniel, darling, what happened to your younger brother's finger? Did a car door slam on it? Did he pound it to smithereens with a hammer? Or, did you, by any chance, try to saw it off?"'

'I was too busy fancying him to ask him questions.'

'Oh, God.' Tipping her chair back down, Georgie put her elbows on the desk and her head in her hands. 'That's the problem with women, isn't it? We don't ever think straight when it comes to men. Some cute man walks into our lives and – kaboom – we're at his mercy. We don't ask questions, we believe everything he tells us, all rational thought goes out of the window. We should make them give us a CV before the first date.' She looked up. 'Honestly, think about it. Then we'd have a history, we'd know what we were dealing with. If, for example, you'd known Daniel had sawn his brother's finger off, you wouldn't have been so shocked when he stole that car – and you were totally shocked Jess, I remember. In fact, you had one of your fainting fits when we heard.'

'Make men give us a CV? That would be like applying for a job. It's not exactly romantic.'

'Being a good lover *is* like a job. It's serious work.'

'Would they have to have an interview too?' Jessica laughed.

'Wear their best suit and tell us how they plan to get ahead in the relationship?'

'Why not? It's not that crazy an idea.'

'Yes it is. You know, you're as bad as my mother.'

Am I? Georgie asked herself. And is this really a crazy idea? Joanna wants Jess to get married because that's the 'done' thing; I want Jess to find someone because I want her to be happy.

Looking at her stepsister across the desk, Georgie took in what she normally took for granted because she saw her every day: the high cheekbones, the long legs, the long eyelashes, the high forehead – everything about Jess was either high or long. She's like a cathedral, Georgie found herself thinking. All light and air and space and clean lines.

Joanna can't find a man for her but that doesn't mean I can't. Why *shouldn't* romance be like a business deal? Why couldn't it work to approach it from a different, more practical angle? The traditional ways certainly haven't worked so far. But how exactly am I going to get men to give over CVs and do interviews and . . .

'Jess?' Georgie stood up, went over to the corner of the room, grabbed a leather chair and pulled it up beside Jessica. She crossed her legs, her shoeless foot bobbing up and down.

'Yes?'

'Tell me something. What are we doing here?'

'God, I don't know, Georgie. I think about it all the time. That's why I've been reading poetry, I've been trying to find some meaning. The problem is, I can't really understand a lot of it. I mean, *The Wasteland* – it's so complicated and dry and I'm not quite sure what he's trying to say.'

'No, Jess. Forget poetry. Poetry's crap. A lot of words and images everyone tries to make sense out of and no one really understands. I meant what are we here in this building for? What's our job here?'

'We're headhunters.'

'Exactly! We're headhunters. We find people. Someone wants a position to be filled, we find the person to fill it. Which means we put people together. Who else does that?'

'Other headhunting companies.'

'Yes. And?'

'And dating agencies. Oh, no – I don't think I like where this is going, Georgie.'

'But you're going there, aren't you? You see – it's a natural connection. Harvey and Tanner is like another form of a dating agency. We're matchmakers.'

'Don't –' Jessica shook her head. 'Stop now before it's too late.'

'Come on, it makes total sense. We matchmake for other people, why can't we do it for ourselves?'

'Because there's a difference between jobs and love. You really are turning into my mother.'

'I am not. You want to find a man, I want to find a man. People like us, at a certain point, after lots of bad experiences, *do* sometimes end up going to dating agencies. There's nothing wrong with that. But we don't have to go to a dating agency because, effectively, we have one of our very own. We have thousands of people on file here. All we have to do is go through those files and select suitable male candidates – for ourselves.'

'You can do it. Forget about me.'

'Why? Why dismiss it like that? Think about it. At this point in our life we meet the same people at the same parties. I hire mostly women and the few men who work here are off-limits, not that they're talent romantically speaking anyway. How are we ever going to find anyone? I, for one, don't have a clue.' Georgie stood up. 'I *will* do it for myself. But you might want to take advantage of it too. And it would help me a lot if you did this with me, if we took on this project together.'

'Um, let me think about this.' Jessica rubbed her forehead, flicked her hair back from her head, then bit her lip. 'You're basically saying we should employ ourselves to find ourselves a man?'

'Yes.' Georgie smiled. 'That's exactly what I'm saying.' She stood up, clicked her fingers, did a little dance. 'Sisters are doing it for themselves! Why not?'

'You're nuts,' Jessica said. But she smiled when she said it.

'Remember up in the attic that afternoon? Remember what I said about going to boarding school?'

'You said it could be fun.'

'And it was, wasn't it?' Georgie asked, thinking: it was for *you* anyway.

'After the beginning bit, it was, yes. I had fun at St Anne's.'

'And we could have fun doing this too.'

'But how do we do it? Where would we start?'

Georgie picked up her telephone and punched a button.

'Sadie? Could you please cancel that lunch I have with the man from Coutts? Say I have the flu or something. Jessica and I are going out – we have an important project to discuss. Great. Thank you.'

Deal closed. Deal signed, sealed, delivered, Georgie said to herself. I'll find her a man. She'll think she's helping me find one and all the time I'll be doing it for her. Jess will be walking down the aisle by spring. She and the man I find for her will be the Mr and Mrs Pover of this generation.

And who knows? While I'm at it, I might just find the love of my life myself.

Chapter Seven

Sadie was busy putting together a file for Georgie on a candidate for a job with a major trading firm. This man had been touted as an up and comer, a star in the making whom Harvey and Tanner wanted to approach. At the moment he was in a perfectly good job in another trading firm – Georgie's brief was to convince him he should make a move. He'd be offered a better salary, more perks, a bigger title.

How wonderful that would be for him. Or would it? Occasionally, Sadie found herself wondering if headhunting was equivalent to breaking up a marriage. This man hadn't come to Harvey and Tanner, they were going after him, like an attractive woman at a party offering a spoken-for man a glimpse of a different, more exciting life. 'Your wife may have been fine for a while, but she doesn't really understand you the way I do, I can give you everything you've always wanted.'

Would he be better off staying where he was, with the company who had seen his value from the beginning, or did Harvey and Tanner have every right to tempt him?

The ringing phone on her desk stopped her from pondering any more on the moral aspects of her job.

'Is the coast clear?' Lisa asked

'They've gone out to lunch. Yes.'

'Are you positive?'

'Yes.'

'Do you think they're going to buy guns so they can come back and shoot me?'

'It might take them a while to get a licence.'

'All right. Be there in a minute.'

Lisa hung up and Sadie smiled. She was pleased Lisa hadn't been fired; Harvey and Tanner would be a sadder place without her. The heading of Lisa's email 'Horny and Talentless' should have been enough, she thought, to have landed Lisa in deep trouble, much more the content, but Georgie and Jessica had left for lunch with smiles on their faces. How could that be? Georgie had been, by Francesca's account, furious about the email, and only an hour or so ago, Jessica had been sobbing at her desk. Now they were going off to lunch to discuss an important project. When Jessica had never been involved with any important project? And after they'd read that email? It didn't make sense.

But if they were happy campers, who was she to question why? The day had already been horrible enough. At this moment, all Sadie wanted was for it to be over, so she could go home and finally wash the colour out of her hair. The thought that Piers had seen her like this was one she kept pushing out of her mind. Each time it re-entered, it brought pain and embarrassment. If she'd had a sense of humour about her relationship with him, she could, she supposed, have laughed off the run-in with him, the aptness of the fact that he'd palmed her off with his Palm. She would have giggled about her hideous hair.

His apology for ditching her had been unheartfelt – that was the word she finally lit upon to describe it to herself. He hadn't been filled with remorse, only a brief discomfort at the sight of her. Well, one thing she knew was that she'd never humiliate herself again. Not like that. By the end, she had harassed Piers with emails, letters, phone calls to tell him she *wasn't* harassing him – that was the supreme irony. Aware that he must think she was obsessed, she obsessively tried to contact him to tell him she wasn't. As he never responded, she had had no chance to let him know she wasn't crazy. And now, unless she stalked him, she'd have no chance to tell him how her hair had been mangled by a well-meaning trainee.

Lisa opened Sadie's door, took one look and put her hand over her mouth.

'Don't say it.' Sadie warned her.

'No.' Lisa flopped onto the chair. 'I . . . oh shit.'

'You just said it.'

'I'm sorry, Sade. Oh, my God – how did it happen? I mean how could it have gone so wrong?'

'You're so tactful, Lisa.'

'Well, I mean, really . . .' She nodded her head from side to side, narrowed her eyes. 'There's no point in pretending, is there?'

'No, I suppose not. Not a lot. And guess who I ran into at the newsagents'?'

'Not Piers?'

'Yes, Piers.'

'Shit. Fuck.'

'My thoughts exactly.'

'What did he say?' Lisa crossed her long legs and twirled a strand of her hair with her forefinger.

'That he's sorry he behaved so appallingly and that we should meet up for coffee in a few weeks' time. It was truly awful.'

'Bloody hell! We've both had fantastic days, haven't we? Can you believe I sent that email? Can you believe they read it? I feel awful, I really do. It was supposed to be funny. I mean, it's not as if they'd ever be my best friends, but I got carried away with myself while I was typing.'

'They seemed to have recovered well. When they went out to lunch together they were smiling.'

'You're joking?'

'I'm serious.' Sadie smiled herself. 'I don't know how long the mood will last, though.'

'Well, I know I'm going to keep my head down for a while, hide from them both. Georgie was fuming. I'm totally surprised she didn't sack me.'

'And Jessica?'

'She didn't say a word. Georgie kicked off and I apologized and said I hadn't meant it, you know, it was a joke, and Georgie said she didn't appreciate my sense of humour and gave me an official warning and I got out as quickly as I could. Before she could change her mind and sack me.'

'Good strategy.'

'I was terrified, I'll tell you. When Georgie gets angry, something spooky happens to her eye. She should have it looked at. I mean, it's unnatural. It goes wonky and sort of travels around her eye socket like it has a life of its own. If she does ever find a man, he'll run a mile when he sees that.' Lisa stood up. 'I have to run now, I've got lunch with Leslie. I need a few drinks after that close call. But, Sade? The way I figure it, things can only get better, so keep your pecker up.'

'You too.'

'You know, sometimes I wish I had one – a pecker I mean.' Lisa had paused by the door. 'But then again, be careful what you wish for, right? You might get it.'

With that, she left and Sadie was alone, feeling a mixture of amusement and bemusement. This was a normal enough reaction to have after being with Lisa, she knew, but this time she felt it particularly keenly. What did that mean, exactly, 'be careful what you wish for, you might get it'? Should she take it as advice not to wish for anything at all in life or only certain things? How could you go through life without wishing? To monitor all your wishes, making sure none of them could be dangerous if they happened to come true, was an exhausting prospect. Sadie knew what she wished for: promotion, a boyfriend who was kind and funny and reliable, a perfect body – she couldn't put them in order, but there they were. Did any of them harbour seeds of doom or disaster? Maybe they did, but how would she ever know unless they did come true? It was as frustrating as that old maxim 'you can't have your cake and eat it too'. What was the point of having a cake unless you did eat it?

Sadie, tired of riddles, had picked up her telephone and dialled Andrew. 'Hey, have you got hold of Bruce yet?'

'No, but I've text-messaged Demi. She'll get back to me soon.'

'What makes you think that?'

'I told her I worship her. I told her I had a lot of time on my hands at the moment to devote to her. I said I had experience babysitting and that children naturally flock to me. I said I have a wide variety of musical interests though, unfortunately, am unable to play an instrument myself. I said—'

'This was a long text message.'

'Listen – I had a lot to say. Anyway, I told her I am an honest, caring, humble man. And . . .'

'And?'

'I signed it Russell Crowe.'

'Excellent move.'

'Aren't you proud to be my sister, Sade?'

'Dream on, you dumb slob.'

Chapter Eight

Georgie's mind was racing and she loved the feeling of it, the click after satisfying click which came when a plan was falling into place. She'd brought her laptop along to the restaurant; this was, after all, a business proposition. They needed to be methodical, they needed to have a strategy. Organization was always the key to success.

'Where do we start?' Jessica asked, after she'd ordered a salad and a mineral water. 'How do we begin?'

'Well, we already have a database, we have all these men and women on file, so we comb through our files, we select the appropriate men and we interview them.' Georgie tried to keep a businesslike voice despite the fact that Jessica's choice of food and drink had irritated her, reminding her of all those cloned girls at St Anne's, every one of them watching her weight, every one of them appalled by Georgie's tendency to devour mounds of stodgy food. She knew the sight of Jessica's salad would somehow force her to finish every bite of the pasta she'd ordered for herself.

'But we have thousands of men on file.'

'Well, we go through the thousands systematically and weed the good ones out. But first we need to focus. We need to decide exactly what it is we're looking for in a man. What

I'm thinking is, if we make a list of our basic requirements now, you can go through our files and find men who meet them. Then we interview them – pretending we're doing it for work reasons.'

Georgie was forced to pause as their lunches were delivered. Could Jessica handle this task? she wondered. Did she even know how to access their database? Would she end up having to take over from Jess and do it all herself? She had a business to run. Perhaps this wasn't such a good idea after all.

Picking up her fork, Jessica speared a piece of lettuce and ate it without making a sound. What was she being roped in to here? Once again, she was going along with one of Georgie's ideas, playing follow the leader. And this idea was truly bizarre. How could anyone look for romance in such an emotionless way? Treating it like a business deal robbed it of all its magic. But then again, Georgie was a highly effective businesswoman – was it so impossible to transfer those skills to the dating arena? Wasn't it worth a try?

Plus, this project would give her something to do, which was a big bonus. The only problem was how to actually do it. She had no idea how to set about accessing files – conquering the email part of computer technology had been a personal triumph. She hated the word 'web', she was afraid, each time she turned the computer on, that she'd unwittingly activate some virus and wipe out all Harvey and Tanner's records.

I'm a throwback, Jessica thought. I should have been born in the eighteenth century. But I have to try. For Georgie's sake, I have to try. She needs a man, she can pretend she doesn't but I know her. Beneath that aggressive, compulsive desire to succeed, she has a soft heart, I've seen it – up in the attic, at St Anne's countless times. She shouldn't show it only to me, she should fall in love. If she doesn't, she'll end up lonely and jaded and cynical. This project might just save her. She's saved me in financial terms; by working with her on this, maybe I can pay her back in emotional ones.

'Georgie?'

'Yes?'

Georgie had just taken a swig of Coca Cola.

'Do you absolutely have to drink all that sugar?'

'Yes, I absolutely have to, Jess.'

'Wouldn't Diet Coke—'

'No, it wouldn't. Now what were you about to say?'

'I was just thinking – I can help, but with some of the more technical parts, the database and all that, maybe Sadie could help too.'

'That's a brilliant idea, Jess. Brilliant.'

'You don't think she'd think it was . . . well . . . strange?'

'I might have thought that before, but –' Georgie shovelled penne into her mouth – 'did you see her hair today?'

'That's true.'

'Anyway, it doesn't matter what she thinks. The point is, she's being paid.'

'I suppose you're right.'

As long as Sadie knows this isn't *my* idea, Jessica thought. I don't want anyone thinking I'm this desperate.

'So . . .' Georgie put the laptop, on the table and started it up. 'Let's make a list of our requirements. I'll open a file now. Why don't we begin with age. What do you think? Between thirty-five and forty-five?'

'How about thirty-five and fifty? Older men can be very attractive.'

'Fine.' Georgie typed, Age: between thirty-five and fifty. 'Done. I suppose height's next.'

'Six feet and over.'

'That's a little tall, don't you think?'

'No midgets, Georgie. No dwarves.'

'OK. How about five ten and over?'

71

'Fine. And he has to have a driver's licence.'

'A licence? Why a licence?'

'Don't you just hate those men who don't drive? It shows a serious inability to cope with reality.'

'Current driving licence.' Georgie said as she typed. 'I suppose that makes sense. Sort of. OK, it's my turn. Ability to swim.'

'What?'

'Think about it – you're on your honeymoon in Barbados, you've had a few drinks, you go for a swim, you start to drown and he's standing on the beach like some useless prat, watching you as you die.'

'What made you dream up that particularly gruesome scenario?'

'It could happen.' Georgie pursed her lips. 'I don't see what's so strange about planning for all eventualities.'

'Would that be down in the files? Is everyone who is interviewed at Harvey and Tanner forced to sign a document which proves they can swim?'

'Look, you seem to want a driving-school instructor and I want a lifeguard. At least we're getting somewhere now.'

'This is unbelievable.' Jessica began to laugh. 'What is going on? Shouldn't we be talking about sense of humour or charm or, I don't know – intelligence, maybe? Shouldn't we start with the basics?'

Basics, Georgie said to herself. What is my *basic* requirement in a man? That he not have any ex-girlfriends. How about that? Jessica would laugh if she said it, she knew, but then Jessica hadn't gone out with Martin. Martin, the man Georgie had dated two years ago. Martin who had seemed wonderful in every respect, until he'd introduced her to his group of friends, a whole gang of people he'd hung out with at university and still, at the age of thirty-four, saw constantly. At first they'd seemed like pleasant people.

Funny, bright, lively, they'd all welcomed Georgie into their close-knit circle.

What Georgie hadn't known to begin with was exactly how close-knit that circle was. Martin had, it transpired, slept with every single woman in it. This fact was supposed to be amusing. In the course of conversation, it would come up often and Martin and his ex-partners would all laugh and the men in the group would all laugh too and it was all so jolly it was unbelievable. Completely unbelievable. Georgie didn't buy it for a second.

As far as she was concerned, when a woman had sex with a man, she was like a South American tribesperson who had had her photograph taken by an anthropologist; she had, as it were, given away a little part of her soul. Women never forget sex, they just don't. Nor do they think it's particularly funny. In the interests of the group dynamic, these women had obviously come to think of their stints in the sack with Martin as casual sex, but Georgie could feel the underlying possessiveness. Their friendly overtures to her were laden with a subtext: we knew him before you, we slept with him before you, we could get him back if we wanted to. The only reason you're here is because we have allowed you to be.

Any woman involved with Martin had to endure these females staking their claim, making those telling comments. Isn't he cute when he shaves naked? Don't you love the way he hogs the bed? Georgie resented the choice she had to make in these situations – either she went along with them and laughed at all of Martin's silly little bedside traits, colluding with them in making Martin a figure of fun, implicitly joining in with their supposed relief that they were no longer sleeping with him, or she could refuse to play this game and thereby alienate the group, which meant, of course, alienating Martin. That was what had happened in the end. She'd tried to wean Martin away from them. She'd failed.

No ex-girlfriends. That's what she wanted to put down on this list of theirs. But she might as well put down 'priests only'.

'You're right, Jess. Back to basics. OK. Intelligence. Should we have university graduates only?'

Jessica turned her head away. But Georgie had caught the look in her eyes.

'I didn't mean to say intelligence is dependent on having gone to a university. Honestly, I didn't mean that.'

'What did you mean?' Jessica kept her face averted.

'I don't know.' What a tactless mistake. Jess had always been touchy and defensive about not getting into university. It was a sore spot Georgie had learned not to touch. 'Anyway, education is meaningless, Jess. All that matters is what you can do with what you know. For example, you know much more about art and culture than I do.'

'That's true.'

'So, let's just say, our perfect man should have *knowledge*.'

'Knowledge of what?'

'Knowledge of how to make women have multiple orgasms, how about that?'

Jessica laughed. Georgie laughed along with her. Thank God, she thought, for sex. Sometimes it's the answer to everything.

Aware that her laugh might sound false, Jessica tried to pitch it so that it matched Georgie's. Georgie, obviously, had experienced multiple orgasms. Jessica hadn't had even one. At this point in her life, she doubted that she ever would. Something held her back from the brink, but she wasn't going to admit that, not to anyone, not again. The one time she hadn't faked it and had actually told a man her problem, he'd spent the next week working so hard trying to sort her out, she'd ended up feeling as if she'd been in a boxing ring with no referee to stop the fight. 'Please, it's not that important,' she'd kept saying, but Hugh wouldn't listen. He was so determined to be the one who gave her her first orgasm, he'd exhausted himself and her in the process.

Hugh was a champion cyclist. He was extraordinarily fit. Jessica hated to remember the nights of so-called passion they'd spent together, all the hours he'd toiled away, all the tricks he'd attempted to use, her own desperate struggle, which, by the end, was more for his benefit than for hers. She wanted him to accomplish this Herculean task, if only so he'd finally stop and leave her body alone. When she tried to put an end to it by faking as usual, he knew that's exactly what she was doing. The moment when he did eventually admit defeat, the look of bewilderment and pain on his face was horrible to see.

'If you'd come cycling with me, we might crack this,' he'd said. She couldn't fathom what cycling might have to do with sex, all she could think of was the French ski instructor telling her not to fall off the lift.

'I don't think I can do anything I'm *supposed* to do,' she'd replied. 'I mean, I'm not good at being taught. I was hopeless at school.'

'You have to learn how to let yourself go.' By this point, Hugh was panting, he was sweaty, he was glassy-eyed with fatigue.

'I'm sure you're right,' she said. What she wanted to add was, 'But wouldn't the right person make it easy for me to let myself go?' By that time, he was getting dressed, in a purposeful way; the purpose being to get out and stay out. She thought if she said that, it would only be another challenge to him and he'd start all over again. That was a prospect she couldn't face, any more than she could face the thought of going on fifty-mile cycling trips with him coaching her the whole way. She'd fall off the bike. He'd go mental.

No, she would laugh along with Georgie and pretend

she knew what she was laughing about. Some secrets were necessary to keep.

'The problem is,' Georgie said, 'you can never tell whether a man is good in bed until you get into bed with him, can you?'

Jessica shook her head.

'So we can't really put sexual knowledge down on this list, much as we'd like to. We're not doing very well here.'

'How about no pot bellies?'

'No pot bellies? That eliminates ninety-nine per cent of men on this planet. Sense of humour – now, that's basic.'

'Definitely. And he should be sympathetic, creative, spiritual . . .' Jessica was counting these qualities off on her fingers.

'Hang on.' Georgie sighed. 'We've moved from the driving instructor to the Dalai Lama in about ten seconds. But, all right, I'll type those in. Articulate, polite, successful in whatever field he works in – how does that sound? Oh, and no criminal record.'

'You'll never let me forget Daniel, will you?'

'Never.'

'Can we find someone who looks like George Clooney?'

'Why not? George Clooney lookalike – it's in. Anything else?'

'I can't think of anything more.'

'OK.' Georgie sat back. 'Here he is, the perfect man: he's between thirty-five and fifty, over five foot ten, he has a sense of humour, no pot belly, is sympathetic, spiritual and creative, articulate, polite, successful, with no criminal record to date; he has knowledge – of what we're not sure yet, but hopefully of how to give great sex. He looks like George Clooney and, if we get really lucky, he can drive and he can swim. Sorry, can I just add no y-fronts to that? Boxer shorts men only?'

'Absolutely.'

'And no porno freaks.'

'Agreed. And no man who spits in public.'

'Good thinking – no spitters. And no one who thinks lavatory humour is hysterical. No man who'd put whoopee cushions on chairs and think it was a fabulous joke. We won't be able to tell all that much from our files, but the interviews will sort out the men from the boys, so to speak.'

'Georgie, hang on, aren't we forgetting something crucial?'

'What? No men with false teeth?'

'The most basic requirement of all.'

'Which is?'

'He has to be available.'

'Oh, God yes. Available – I'm putting that in capital letters and italicizing it. We don't want to muck around with married men. Even if they can drive and swim and wear boxer shorts over their toned bums.'

I won't, Georgie said to herself, ever be a mistress. Those, 'Sorry I can't make it tonight' last-minute phone calls, the, 'Oh my God, I think I know that person at that table in the corner, we have to get out of here even though we've just sat down' scenes in restaurants. I won't do it and neither should Jess.

'It would help if he was heterosexual too.'

'That would be a big help. Well –' Georgie finished typing and looked up from her laptop – 'this should definitely be fun.'

'You really think so?'

'I know so. Trust me, Jess. You'll – I mean we'll – have the time of our lives.'

Chapter Nine

Michael Henny
50 years old. 6'4"
Morgan Stanley, Mergers and Acquisitions
Divorced, one child
American expatriate

Beard. No one should leave off 'bearded' in any description of a male, Georgie thought as she shook Michael Henny's hand in the Café Med. Particularly if it is a beard so bushy it looked as if it could be hiding a nest of black widow spiders.

'Nice to meet you,' Michael said, sitting down and unsuccessfully trying to fit his legs under the table. 'Sorry to be late, but I was at a parents' meeting at my daughter's school and I couldn't get away.' Crossing his legs to the side of the table, he flicked what looked like bits of congealed pasta off his trousers.

Don't be put off, she said to herself. Beards can be shaved. Trousers can be dry-cleaned. He's obviously a committed father. Jessica would appreciate that.

'That was nice of you, Michael, to go to the meeting. I don't think my father ever came to one of mine.'

'Oh, Jasmine is so intelligent I wouldn't have missed it for the world. An A starred on every single one of her GCSEs.'

'How clever she must be. I should hire her when she's finished university.'

'You should hire her now.' Michael's chest literally expanded with pride. 'She's a chess wizard too, she can beat me most of the time.'

'Gosh.'

This was the first 'date', the first man they'd chosen to inspect. If she'd had her way, Georgie wouldn't have been here, Jessica would. But Jess had insisted that, as this whole project had been Georgie's idea to begin with, she should start it off. In one sense, vetting Michael on Jessica's behalf would be easy; Georgie had a better idea of what Jessica needed than Jess did herself. And setting up the meeting had been simple; she'd rung Michael and suggested they get together. While Michael would think this was a business meeting of some sort, that he was being headhunted, Georgie could check him out. What would happen if he was a candidate worthy of Jessica, how she would then manage an introduction between them, she hadn't worked out yet. Still, she knew she'd be able to, if he fitted the bill.

There had been times during interviews when Georgie had found herself studying the man on the other side of her desk and wondering more about his expertise in bed than in business. She'd managed, on those occasions, to haul herself back into professional mode, knowing it was never a good idea to become personally involved, especially if you were a female headhunter. Rumours were always circulating around the City about women executives who slept around. Until now, Georgie had been paranoid about being talked about in that fashion. She couldn't believe, though, that she'd ever been attracted to Michael, and struggled to remember her interview with him. She had recalled an American she'd thought was fanciable, and mentioned that to Jess. Was that American Michael? Could she ever have succumbed to his charms? What charms?

Michael's boasting about his daughter was off-putting, definitely. It was, however, what most parents seemed to do. The couples Georgie knew who had kids never failed to inform her that their children were the best, the brightest, the stars of the universe. Little Johnny could read when he was six months, little Sally could ride a horse before she could walk, blah blah, blah. As far as Georgie could make out, not one child born in the last twenty years had been normal; they were all geniuses, megastars, future world leaders.

'I know this sounds like boasting, but –' Michael paused, a pause full of significance, as if he were about to announce the Second Coming – 'Jasmine would be number one on the tennis team if it weren't for the tits.'

'Sorry?'

'The tits, you know. You wouldn't believe how fast we're developing in that area. It seems like yesterday we were in the M and S training bra and now we're up to 38C, heading for 40, 42 – God knows where it will end up. What size *was* Marilyn Monroe?'

'I'm afraid I have no idea.'

'We went through real hormone hell during puberty, but I think we're beginning to come out the other side, so to speak. Once the painters came in, life eased up a lot.'

'Excuse me?'

'Her period.' Michael smiled. 'That's how we say it in our house.'

'I know what it means, Michael. I just can't believe you—'

'I believe in talking about things openly and honestly – all the details are important, you know. Sex, periods, masturbation – the whole nine yards.'

'Don't you think ... I mean, don't you believe in the concept of privacy?'

'I can see –' he leaned back in his chair, folded his arms across his chest – 'you're one of those repressed women who suffered a lonely, desperate adolescence. As you said, your father never came to school meetings, you were afraid of discussing the workings of your body. You know what you need, Georgina?'

'I'm afraid to ask.'

'A hug.'

'Maybe not right now, Michael, if you don't mind.'

'It would be so good for you.'

'I'm sure, I'm sure. But later, OK?'

'Oh, come on. Don't be shy. Stand up.' Michael rose. Georgie pressed herself as far back into her chair as she could.

'Come on.' He took her hand, pulled her up and crushed her to him. She held her breath, kept her eyes tightly shut. 'There –' as he released her, he grabbed her bum and squeezed it – 'isn't that a whole lot better?'

'It made all the difference in the world. I'm a new person.'

'So . . .' They both sat down again. 'What's this meeting all about then? I'm a big fan of yours. As you must remember, you got me my present job. Do you have something special to offer me now?'

'Actually,' Georgie was thinking fast, 'this meeting has nothing to do with Harvey and Tanner. I'm a Jehovah's Witness, Michael. I thought you'd be interested in hearing about our beliefs. It would only take a few hours of your time.'

'Um.' Michael's eyes darted away from hers. 'That's very interesting, Georgina. Of course I have great respect for people who believe in God, but I personally don't—'

'I have lots of literature I know you'd love to read. And there's a meeting tonight we could go to.'

'Gosh.' Michael looked at his watch. 'I couldn't find a babysitter and poor Jasmine is all alone. I have to go now. Sorry to leave so suddenly – all my fault. Another time, maybe.'

'Absolutely. Whenever. Just ring me. I can help you on the path to truth, Michael.'

'Yes, yes, of course.'
Michael didn't walk out of the restaurant, he ran.

Greg Trainer
36 years old
5′9″
Single
Account Exec Barclays

'Wonderful to meet you, Jessica.' Greg Trainer shook her hand. It was a weak handshake, the kind of handshake Jessica immediately distrusted. 'I always wondered what the Tanner in Harvey and Tanner looked like. And now –' he clicked his fingers – 'I know.'

Would Georgie like this man? Jessica asked herself. He was attractive, no doubt about it. Smooth and sleek and well put together. His handshake might not bother Georgie, his looks would definitely please her. Perhaps this project was worthwhile after all. Sadie had pulled Greg Trainer out of the files and Jessica had nodded her approval. As it was turning out, Sadie was doing most of the work, researching the potential candidates, narrowing down the field, and Jessica was grateful, not only for her help but also for the fact that Sadie hadn't made any snide comments about this scheme of theirs, she'd apparently taken it in her stride.

Jessica and Greg had arranged to meet in the ground-floor bar of Mortons in Berkeley Square. Greg, ten minutes late, had no difficulty in spotting her, she was the only woman there. They made their way to a booth; Jessica sat and Greg slid in beside her.

'I'm sorry,' she said. 'Could you sit opposite me? I find it difficult to talk this way.'

'Whatever.' He slid out again. 'So what's this all about? Are you going to make me an offer I can't refuse?'

There was something wrong with Greg Trainer, but Jessica couldn't identify exactly what it was. Was he a little too smooth? A little too sure of himself? Or was it his hideous, bright-purple tie?

'Let's talk business later.' She'd practised this line. It seemed to work. Greg smiled and shrugged. 'Tell me how things are going with you in general. How's life, Greg?'

'Mmm hmmm hmmm hmmm hmmm.' Greg seemed to be humming something, or did he have a stammer? 'Life's a beach and I have the bucket and spade to prove it.'

'Oh. That's nice.' Having no idea how to respond to the bucket and spade comment, Jessica glanced around the dark bar and tried to get over her growing distaste for this man. Greg was good-looking. She should concentrate on that salient fact. He wasn't the man for her, but he might be the man for Georgie.

'I'm hot, I'm cool. Life is sorted. Mmm hmmm hmmm hmmm hmmm.'

'That's wonderful.' She hadn't imagined it before, he was definitely humming. But what was he humming? 'New York, New York'? Or was it a very poor rendition of 'La donna è mobile'? Jessica rubbed her forehead, trying to get her thoughts back on track.

Find out his hobbies, Georgie had instructed her, that's a good way to get a handle on his personality.

'I'm sure you lead a very pressured life, though, Greg. Tell me – what do you do to relax?'

'Relax – don't do it.'

'But you *should* relax, Greg. We all have to sometime.'

'Frankie Goes To Hollywood.'

'Sorry?'

'Whatever happened to them?'

'To who?'

'Frankie.'

'Who's Frankie?'

'Frankie Goes To Hollywood.'

'You just said that. Does he go there often?'

Jessica felt as if she were in the middle of one of those dreams that made no sense and never would, the kind of dream you're very happy to wake up from. Where was the waiter? She needed a drink.

'The band. Frankie Goes To Hollywood. You know, Jessica. "Relax".'

'Oh. Of course.' She was beginning to understand – he was talking about a pop group. She could just remember the name now. But she didn't appreciate being told to relax. 'I'm actually a very stress-free person, Greg.'

'And what about Dexy's Midnight Runners? They disappeared without a trace too. They were great. "Come on, Eileen".'

'My name is Jessica.' She sat up straight.

He laughed. He laughed and laughed. 'It's a song, Jessica. "Come on Eileen". Dexy's Midnight Runners.'

'Oh.'

'Don't tell me you've never danced to that one at the end of a long night. God, where have you been? In a cave?'

Who was interviewing whom? What right did he have to make her feel stupid because she hadn't danced to some pop song? Why was this dreadful man still laughing?

'I don't see what's so funny.'

'You don't?' He wouldn't stop laughing. 'I love it. I mention "Come On Eileen" and you say: "My name is Jessica." What a laugh!'

She was already sitting very straight, but she managed to raise her chin and sit up even straighter. The thought of having this man for a stepbrother-in-law was appalling.

'There was a very, very important position I was going to talk to you about tonight, Greg. An incredibly luclative job on offer. Now I think you're the wrong person to fill it. I don't find this amusing at all.'

'Luclative?' His laugh was booming out. 'A luclative job? Would that mean I'd be paid in filthy lucla?'

'I didn't say luclative, I said lu*crat*ive.'

'You said luclative. It doesn't matter, Jessica. Don't look so offended. You're too beautiful to worry about words. I bet you wow them all down in the City. I bet all those boring bankers go apeshit when they see you. I'm sure you give them a whole new spin on *head* hunting.'

Jessica's breathing was speeding up, it was getting shallow, too. She grabbed the edge of the table with both hands.

'Oh, come on, don't go all PC on me here. Take a compliment – who cares if it's a sexist one? And don't stress, I was going to turn down whatever job you were offering anyway. A luclative or a non-luclative one.' He had stopped laughing but he had a disgustingly pleased with himself smirk on his face. 'I'm getting out of this whole banking rat race anyway. I'm going to do something *interesting*.'

'Well, bully for you.'

'Whoa – you should loosen up a little, sweetheart. Mmm hmm hmmm hmm hmm.' He switched then into words, something about Barbie girls.

Jessica put her head in her hands to steady herself. I can be humiliated for Georgie's sake, she told herself. This is all for Georgie's sake, after all. I have to remember that. There have been times, going through the files, when I've thought of these men as possibilities for *me*; even today, on the way here, I wondered whether *I* might like Greg Trainer. But this isn't about me. Poor Georgie had her own awful time with that Michael person last night. My coming here tonight has spared her another night of horror. I've done a good deed, so it's been good for my karma. That's the way I have to look at it. And it's the way I will look at it from now on.

Lifting her head, she looked Greg straight in the eyes.

'I think I'll leave now, Greg. We don't have anything more to talk about.'

'Uh oh, I've offended you, haven't I? What can I say . . . oops, I did it again!' He began to laugh so much his shoulders were shaking. People around them were staring. Jessica stood up and walked with as much dignity as she could out of Mortons. Greg's laughter followed her all the way out to Berkeley Square.

They can't, Jessica said to herself as she hailed a taxi, they can't all be as horrendous as Greg. Can they?

'So, Cameron, does it bother you – the Cameron Diaz thing?'

'I don't know what you mean.'

He had floppy dark hair and mud-coloured eyes. He worked for Price Waterhouse. He was forty-four and five foot eleven. Divorced, no children. His hobbies were canoeing and . . . canoeing. Georgie had placed him in his job a year before and had decided, when reviewing her files, he was a decent candidate, especially because of his canoeing – Jessica had been dating men who were into sport recently. Canoeing might not be the most exciting sport in the world, but it was a start. They were sitting in All Bar One, and Georgie was trying to convince herself those muddy eyes of his were mysterious and sexy, not dull and duller.

'You know, Cameron Diaz, the movie star.'

'Why would that bother me?'

'Because she's a woman. And she has a man's name – your name.'

'I'm afraid I'm not following you. She doesn't have my name. I'm Cameron *Holt*, not Diaz.'

'Right.' Drop that conversational gambit, Georgie, she said to herself. 'So . . . have you been canoeing anywhere wonderful recently?'

'Unfortunately, I haven't had the time.' He didn't drink. He didn't smoke. He didn't seem to talk much either.

'Price Waterhouse is keeping you chained to the desk, then?'

'They're hardly going to *chain* us. That would be absurd.'

Now she remembered. Why hadn't she written it down at the time, this man's breathtaking literal mindedness? How could she have forgotten? All she had in her notes were the words: competent, driven, divorced, childless, canoe freak. She must have been so bored she couldn't be bothered, and now she was paying the price.

'Which company is interested in me? Can you tell me that now?' Cameron leaned forward. His shirt had a pattern of goldfish on it, the top button hung by a thread. Jessica would delete him for those two things alone, Georgie thought. 'Because I'm not interested in leaving Price Waterhouse, you know, but I'd be interested to know who wants me.'

'I'm afraid I'm not at liberty to tell you that at this precise time, Cameron.'

'Then why are we here?'

'Good question. This is a getting-to-know-you process. It's helpful when we're putting people together. It's a short cut of sorts.'

'I don't understand. I don't need a new job, I'm not looking, but if someone is interested in me I think I should be told. Does this have anything to do with "Potholing For Pleasure"?'

'Potholing for pleasure?'

'The newsletter I started up a few months ago.'

'I thought you were a canoeist or whatever it's called.'

'I pothole as well.'

'Crikey!' Georgie shook her head. 'How amazing! A potholer! I never would have guessed!'

'So this has nothing to do with my newsletter?'

He looked crestfallen, as if he hadn't managed to squeeze

into one of those dank tiny tunnels that led to another dank tiny tunnel. Or as if he'd been stuck somewhere in the middle and that silly headlamp lunatic potholers wear had run out of batteries. Which was preferable: a man talking about his daughter's tits or a man talking about potholing? Neither, was the answer. She'd give him five minutes more, max. Just in case she'd missed something crucial. She'd learned in her business dealings that you shouldn't judge too quickly, and she'd already made Michael run for the nearest exit. She'd stay and finish her drink, at least.

'Um, Cameron, excuse me, but what could a potholing newsletter possibly have to do with the financial services sector?'

'I didn't say it did. I asked a question.' He pouted. Georgie wished she could tell him to go up to his room and stay there until he had a major attitude adjustment.

'Have you ever had an emergency? I mean, have you ever had to be rescued and winched out? Is that what happens? Do you get hauled out of the pothole by your toes, or what?'

'No.' Now he looked affronted. 'I've always been successful in whatever I do.'

'I'm sure.' She finished off her wine in one long gulp. The only way Jessica would spend more than two minutes with Cameron was if she were on drugs. Jessica didn't take drugs.

'Well, Cameron, I think we've wrapped things up here.' She signalled a waiter for the bill. 'Thanks for your time.'

'Hang on a minute –' he reached out and grabbed her wrist – 'you rang me. You said you needed to see me. And now, after –' he looked at his watch – 'five and a half minutes, you leave, without telling me what this was all about?'

'Five and a *half* was it?' Georgie shook off his hand and stood up. She'd pay at the bar so she wouldn't have to wait for the bill. This man was not just chronically unprepossessing, he was a pain in the neck. 'Well, five and a half is all it's going to be.'

'You know –' he stood up – 'you remind me of my ex-wife.'

'What a wonderful thing to say,' she replied. 'Some day you'll have to tell me the difference between potholes and assholes.'

Two disasters, she thought as she hailed a taxi. But it's too early to get discouraged. They couldn't all be this bad. Could they?

If three men travel across a river at the speed of two knots per hour with a four-kilo bag of peanuts and it takes them twenty minutes to arrive and the current is going against them, how many kilos of peanuts will they have when they reach China? Was that what William was asking her? Jessica struggled to remember, she had tuned out after the bit about 'two knots'.

'Sorry, William, I don't have a clue. I was never any good at those sorts of questions.' They were in the bar of the Groucho Club. Had anyone in the history of the Groucho Club asked someone a question like this? Where did he think he was, at a Mensa meeting?

William Peters, aged thirty-eight, was an accountant at Coopers and Lybrand, and a widower. On paper, he'd seemed more than reasonable, in the flesh he was jowly and pudgy and had these little wisps of blond hair that made him look like an overweight, ageing, cherub – a cherub who had gone to seed. Jessica could tell he'd probably been an extremely attractive child. But, as her mother would say, he'd lost his looks, and he wasn't ever going to find them again. Within two minutes of sitting down, he'd set her this absurd question about peanuts. But then, Georgie was good at maths. Jessica knew she shouldn't dismiss him immediately.

'It's simple, really.' William pulled the bowl of peanuts on the table toward him and started arranging them in little piles.

'You see, here are the peanuts and –' he grabbed the salt shaker – 'here is the boat and—'

'Honestly, however you try to explain it, I won't understand. My stepsister might, though, she—'

'I promise you I can make it simple for you.' He wasn't going to give up. He was determined to go on with this.

'I promise you you can't.' Jessica grabbed some peanuts from one of the piles and put them in her mouth.

'It's only a question of the current. Once you understand that—'

'William. Please. I don't think you understand that I don't want to understand. I have no interest in peanuts.'

'The peanuts are irrelevant, as I said.'

'Then why put them on the table?' She clenched her fists.

'Because they are a part of the equation, but they are not the relevant part. Look.' He raised the salt shaker. 'This is the boat, yes? Are you with me so far? I know women have a problem with these sorts of problems, women's brains don't comprehend the complexities—'

'Excuse me?'

'Well, women aren't called the "weaker sex" only because they're physically weaker than men, although of course they are physically weaker, but they're also intellectually weaker. Why? Because they don't exercise their brains. Brains need mental aerobics to keep fit. Problems like this are a form of mental aerobics. In a business like yours, you should be doing these problems every day. You should, during any slow times at your office, work on brain teasers. I'm not saying you'd ever surpass the male intellect, but you might get up to speed. I can recommend various books—'

'Thank you, William, but that won't be necessary.'

Georgie would loathe this man. On a bad day, Georgie might actually murder this man.

'Fine, but concentrate now, why don't you? Let's start at the beginning again. Here –' he plonked the salt shaker in front of her – 'is the boat.'

Jessica slumped in her chair.

Chapter Ten

'So –' Andrew yawned and stretched his legs out. 'How is the "Find a Mate For the Pod People" project going? By the way, do you want a drink?'

'No thanks.'

'I think I'll have one.' Standing up, he went over to the built-in bar by the bookshelf. 'This item of furniture never fails to amuse me,' he said as he reached for a bottle of vodka. 'Five years in this place and I'm still trying to work out why our landlord is so keen on the Spanish look. What was that soap that failed? *Eldorado* – that was the name. Do you think Christophe had a bit part in that?'

Andrew was right, Sadie thought. The flat was a miniature version of a Costa Brava poolside casa, minus the pool, of course, but complete with downmarket Spanish tiles, a built-in bar with a mirrored back, and a heavy reliance on the colour orange. She'd grown so used to it she didn't notice any more, but it didn't make much sense, given that Christophe was Polish and, as far as she knew, had never been to Spain in his life.

'At least he didn't decorate it along the lines of the Queen Vic.'

'Anyway,' Andrew plopped some ice into his drink and went

back to his original position on the sofa, 'you've been working on this available-man project for months now. Have they hit paydirt yet? Are the trendy people across the country rushing to buy designer hats for the impending nuptials of Georgie and/or Jessica?'

'No. It's awful, actually. Each man I find seems to be worse than the last one, and the files are running low. In fact, I've almost reached rock bottom. I don't know how to tell them this project is over.'

'What if *they* got married? To each other, I mean. Wouldn't that be fun?'

'Hilarious. Anyway, they're both out interviewing potential romantic candidates tonight. Maybe something wonderful will happen. If it doesn't, I hate to think what moods they'll be in tomorrow.'

'Correct me if I'm wrong, but weren't you hired to work for a headhunting business? Since when did you join a dating agency?'

'Since they handed me Project X.'

She'd been baffled and unbelieving when Georgie and Jessica had explained this new project to her. They wanted her to help them headhunt themselves a man? Georgina Harvey and Jessica Tanner were that desperate? Part of her was relieved that these two attractive, successful women were in as dire circumstances as she was as far as men were concerned, while another part of her was deeply disappointed. If Georgie and Jessica couldn't manage to get a love life in a conventional way, what hope did she have? If they were successful in their search, should she hire them for herself? God, could she even afford to hire them? That was the strange route her thoughts had taken when what they had dubbed Project X had been explained to her. From then on, she'd decided to view it as just another part of her job. But as the months went by and candidate after candidate failed the interviews, Sadie not only worried that there wasn't a halfway decent available man left in the world for anyone, including herself, but that she'd get the sack for not being able to find the impossible. The only comfort she took was from the fact that Georgie and Jessica would have a hard time explaining why they'd fired her. What would they say? 'She couldn't find us a good date?'

'Tell me something, Sade. Are they planning to tell the poor blokes, assuming, that is, that some miracle happens and they both find them tonight, how they went about finding them? In the middle of some romantic evening, are they going to say, "Oh, by the way, Tom/Dick/Harry, did you know my personal assistant headhunted you for the job of boyfriend?" Is that the plan?'

'I don't know. I don't think they've sorted out any type of plan. At first I thought I was searching for men for both of them, then Jessica pulled me into a corner and told me this was all for Georgie and, approximately two hours later, Georgie called me into her office and explained to me that this was all for Jessica. All I know is that we started this off in September and it's now December and it's been one disaster after another.'

'Life in the romantic lane is tough for us all, Sade. I mean, Demi hasn't rung back, she hasn't even text-messaged and you haven't been out on a date since The World's Most Obnoxious Man left town.' Tugging on his earlobe, Andrew narrowed his eyes and stared at Sadie. 'Please, please tell me you haven't heard from The World's Most Obnoxious Man. Pretty please with molasses on top? I'm holding my breath here.'

'I haven't heard from him.'

'Thank God –' Andrew exhaled, took a gulp of his drink – 'for big, huge favours.'

Sadie stifled a fleeting urge to defend Piers to Andrew. Why should she? He hadn't rung. She hadn't even had to make an excuse not to have coffee with him. All that palaver checking out dates on his Palm had been a charade of politeness. Piers *was* The World's Most Obnoxious Man. Andrew was right.

'I have to say, Sade, your choice of men makes me seriously question your taste.'

'Well, your choice of women hasn't been exactly brilliant either.'

'Excuse me?'

'Andrew, think back. Scroll through your memories and tell me one of your girlfriends who would make me think you have a brain cell in that fat head of yours.'

His forehead furrowed, his finger tapped his glass.

'There was – no, all right. But then there was – no, forget her. How about . . . ?'

'Yes? How about who? Which one?'

'How about . . . how about Theresa?'

'Theresa?'

'That girl I dated a couple of years back. You remember, the waitress at Pizza Express.'

'Oh, her.' Sadie nodded. 'She *was* nice. But you only went out a few times, didn't you?'

'Five times. Then her old boyfriend came back. You know, maybe I should give her a ring tomorrow.'

'What about the boyfriend?'

'Maybe the boyfriend is dead by now.'

'Andrew!'

'Well, he might be. Who knows? It's worth a try.'

'You're sick.'

'No, I'm just extremely practical.' Andrew smiled. 'Listen, Sade . . .' His smile faded. 'I hate to mention The World's Most Obnoxious Man again, but I have to ask. You're over him now, aren't you? You haven't had any relapses?'

Sadie felt Piers' hand grab hers. He always grabbed it and squeezed hard when they were in a tube station. But he never did anywhere else. Why hadn't she taken that on board at the time? He'd never been physically demonstrative when they were with his friends. In the presence of other people he treated her more like a friend than a lover. He'd met her underground, he'd kept her underground.

'No, no relapses, Andrew. I'm over him.'

Sadie was amazed. Something very odd and magical had just happened. This time, when she said she was over Piers, it felt like something at least approaching the truth.

'Good.' He got up and went over to the bar to refill his drink. 'Because otherwise I would have had to find a hitman to take him out and I don't know whether hitmen will take credit cards these days.'

'You're so naive.'

'I know.' He spread his hands. 'But devilishly attractive nonetheless.'

Chapter Eleven

It had happened so quickly that Georgie could barely remember how they'd ended up in his flat. Drinks had naturally turned into dinner at Momos, then they'd naturally shared a taxi and she had naturally agreed to stop at his flat in Chelsea for a coffee. Well, why not? He was all the adjectives she'd noted down after her original job interview with him, and more. She hadn't put 'sexy', which he most definitely was, nor had she described the incredible blue colour of his eyes. Oliver Ransome, a single, forty-three-year-old human resource manager, was gorgeous. What a relief.

She and Jess had been on date from hell after date from hell for the past three months. At this point, Adam the Porno Watcher was looking like a catch. She'd suffered through evenings with Lawrence, the coke-head; Charles, the accident-prone one who kept knocking glasses and bottles over and apologizing so profusely Georgie had finally suggested that he go to a confidence-raising course; Larry who sweated so much she thought he'd drown himself; Harry, the Gilbert and Sullivan freak; not to mention Michael and Cameron, or all of Jess's equally hopeless encounters. They had a depressingly long list of men they'd pay any amount of money not to have to see again.

And now, finally, she'd found heaven in the form of Oliver Ransome. Jess would love him. No doubt about it. There was only one small problem. Georgie hadn't managed yet to turn the conversation to the subject of her stepsister and how fabulous she was and how Oliver should meet her. Somehow she'd forgotten about Jess.

As soon as we relax in his flat, she told herself, as soon as we get comfortable, I'll start talking about Jessica.

'So, Georgie –' Oliver had taken off her coat, hung it up in the hall closet and led her to his sofa. His flat was decorated in a masculine, minimalist style. 'We were supposed to be talking business, weren't we? But somehow we haven't got around to it.' He grinned. 'Which is fine by me. Why not put pleasure before business for a change, right? It's a lot more fun.'

'That's true. By the way, did you know my stepsister works with me?'

'How nice, keeps it in the family.'

His arm slid behind her.

'Her name's Jessica.'

'Nice name.'

His fingers were tickling the back of her neck.

'She's very beautiful.'

'Runs in the family, does it? Even in the stepfamily?'

His mouth was on her mouth. His tongue was playing with her tongue.

Georgie pulled back. But not instantly.

'Um, Oliver, do you have any coffee around?'

'Absolutely.' He grinned again, shed his jacket, stood up. 'Whatever the lady wants, she shall have.'

Trouble, trouble, trouble. Stop, stop, stop. Get a grip. Fine, you know he's a good kisser. But that's as much research as you can do on Jess's behalf. What would I say? You'll love him, Jess – he kisses like an artist and he's fantastic in bed, too. I thought you should know everything about him before

I passed him on. No. I'll have the coffee and then I'll figure out a way to set him up with Jessica.

But ... I can see him doing jack-knives and swan dives, cutting a swathe through the water like a sleek shark. Jess doesn't care about swimming. Does she deserve him?

Oliver clearly liked fresh air; all the windows of the flat were open and the December cold was beginning to get to Georgie who was shivering in her sleeveless blue dress. She reached over and took his jacket. I'll see how this plays out, she told herself. I'll see whether he loves classical music, whether he cares about poetry, if, by any wonderful chance, he doesn't have a drivers' licence. I'll find out if he and Jess would really be suited. I'll give him a Jess Compatibility Test and I'll be scrupulous about it – if he passes it, then I'll step aside. If he doesn't ...

As she put Oliver's jacket on, she felt a strange buzzing. For a split second she thought she was having a minor heart attack, then realized it was only a mobile phone vibrating in his inside pocket. Delving into the pocket to retrieve it, intending to go into the kitchen and hand it to him, she pulled two items out. One was the phone. The other was a wedding ring, which slipped out of her fingers and plopped into her lap.

'I'll be there in a second. Just have to make a quick pit stop,' Oliver called out.

It's going to be a permanant pit stop, she thought after she read the text message on his phone: 'Missing my husband. Love, love, love.'

Georgina Harvey took off Oliver's jacket, laid the phone and the ring on top of it, tiptoed to the closet, retrieved her coat, let herself out of the flat, took the lift down to the ground floor, stepped outside, hailed a taxi, got in, and only then allowed herself to feel the full force of her outrage.

'You know, I'm fascinated by the way clouds move,' Jessica

was saying, 'sometimes they waltz, sometimes they foxtrot, sometimes they—'

'Tango.' Stephen finished the sentence for her. 'I know. I've often thought that myself.'

'You have?'

'Yes.' He nodded. 'Often.'

He's so sensitive, Jessica thought, staring at this vision of beauty across the table from her. Was it possible to fall in love this quickly? Well, why not? He fitted all the qualifications: he was thirty-eight; divorced with twin ten-year-old sons; a lawyer at J. P. Morgan (how Georgie would laugh at that, she thought, given all her recent jokes about Daniel Canter's criminal past); just under six feet tall; not even a smidgeon of a pot belly; and had beautiful, silky blond hair. *And* he loved poetry. That revelation, coming early on in the evening, had saved her from hours of angst and suffering, of wondering whether he'd be the perfect man for Georgie. Georgie had called poetry 'crap'. That was a basic, undeniable fact. Even if Georgie met Stephen and fell for him, she'd have to realize they were fundamentally incompatible. Nothing was more fundamental than poetry.

'I've never understood why Byron described clouds as "lonely".' She ran her hand back through her hair. This gesture, she knew, would accomplish two things at once: he'd notice what lustrous hair she had, and he'd understand she really did have a poetic soul. Poets always raked their hair when they were thinking deep thoughts. 'Clouds aren't lonely. Clouds socialize. They bump into each other all the time.'

'Byron?' He laughed.

She didn't see what was funny, but it was a warm, deep laugh, nothing like that maniac Barbie-girl man's taunting laugh, so she forgave him.

'Don't you love Byron, Stephen?'

'I do. Absolutely. As it happens, I love Wordsworth, too.

You know, Jessica, you're a very beautiful woman. More beautiful, even, than a lonely cloud.'

'Thank you.'

'Is that a Gucci jacket you have on?'

'Yes.' She smiled. Taste. He had taste. And his eyes were almost exactly the same shade of blue she'd had her bedroom painted – Sanderson Historic Range, Number 21.

'Have you ever thought of cutting your hair? Short would suit you.'

'You think so?'

'Definitely. Audrey Hepburn in *Roman Holiday*, that's who you remind me of. You look just like her. She was stunning with long hair but even more breathtaking with short.'

Done, Jessica thought, I'll make a hair appointment tomorrow. Screw work.

'Shall we have some coffee?'

'I'd love some.'

A seamless progression this evening had been. From drinks, to dinner, to coffee, to – she could only hope. He hadn't asked her why she'd rung and arranged this meeting; he didn't seem to care whether Harvey and Tanner were headhunting him for some amazing new job; as soon as they'd sat down, they'd started chatting about life, each passing sentence only proving how made for each other they were. Poor Georgie, she thought, she's probably with another in the long line of the creeps we've had to suffer. I hope she's found someone too tonight. If she hasn't, I'll feel awful. I was supposed to be helping her and now I seem to have helped myself. Still, the poetry. Don't forget the poetry problem. Maybe Stephen has a friend. Maybe Stephen has a brother.

Stephen waved at the waiter, who came over immediately, another good sign. He commanded attention effortlessly.

Stephen Conway. Jessica Conway. Mr and Mrs Stephen Conway. And their son, Harry and their daughter, Sophie.

The twins would presumably live with the ex. If they didn't, that would be fine, too.

I'll make a terrific stepmother, she thought. I'll remember every rebuff I had from Georgie's father; all the times he ignored me. All I have to do to be a good stepparent is to be the exact opposite of James Harvey.

Maybe I'll be able to let myself go with Stephen tonight. And then I'll be able to talk about multiple orgasms.

I'll be a different person, a fearless person.

And my mother will get off my back. My mother will finally get off my back.

'Can I get you two beautiful people something else?' the waiter asked. He was grinning, obviously happy to be in their proximity, enveloped in their cloud – yes cloud, of blossoming love. All evening he'd been friendly and sweet and attentive, this nice young Australian boy who was quite gorgeous himself. She should take down his name and number when they left. He deserved a better job and she could get Georgie to find one for him. In years to come, when Stephen and she discussed their first meeting, or told other people about their first date, this waiter would be part of the story. She could hear herself say: 'And now that waiter is head of a multinational corporation; and all because he was in on the first enchanted moments. Oh, and he's godfather to Harry!'

'Some coffee please.' Stephen grinned back up at him. 'If it's not too much trouble.'

'No worries.' He winked at Stephen.

'Someday my prince will come,' Jessica sang underneath her breath.

But why was Stephen turning around in his chair? And why did he seem to have his eyes fixed on the waiter's retreating backside?

Even if she'd packed a parachute, it wouldn't have had time to open and cushion the impact on her heart. No, no, it can't be, she tried to tell herself, he has *twins*. But when he turned back she caught a fading gleam of pure lust mixed in with Historic Range Number 21.

'Nice waiter, isn't he?' She hoped he hadn't noticed the fear in her voice.

'"Nice" doesn't do him justice.' After raising his eyebrows and tilting his head, Stephen licked his lips and grinned. 'I'd say indescribably delicious.'

Oh, shit, Jessica said to herself. I can't bloody believe it.

This one topped them all. He beat the forty-one-year-old chartered accountant who picked his nose, the forty-six-year-old insurance company director who had whichever phobia it was called when you had to wash your hands every five seconds, the forty-nine-year-old, thrice divorced futures trader who must have had a truly deranged plastic surgeon – the plethora of undesirable, strange males she'd had to meet during the course of this project.

Stephen had outdone them all, because for almost two hours she'd believed love was not only possible, it was sitting right there in front of her. Well, she'd been half right, anyway. Stephen and the waiter might have a glorious future in front of them. She could walk out now and leave them to it. In which case she'd have to go back home and tell Georgie about yet another fiasco.

It was a well-deserved fiasco, though. The company of a good-looking, flattering man had thrown all her good intentions to the wind. She was supposed to be rescuing Georgie, not thinking about herself. Her feeble excuse for putting her own emotions first by seizing on Stephen's liking for poetry had been just that – feeble. What if he'd hated poetry? Would she have then handed him over to Georgie or kept him to herself? She didn't want to answer that question. She hadn't, thank God, *had* to answer that question.

This whole project was silly and it hadn't done either of

them any good. You couldn't hire yourself romance, nor should you. She never wanted to hear about Project X again. As far as she was concerned, it was over. This ridiculous dating agency was shutting up shop.

'So, Stephen –' she pushed her hair back again, mentally cancelled the hair appointment – 'tell me. When did you first realize you were gay?'

He smiled. He shrugged. And then he began a very long story. If the coffee hadn't been as strong as it was, she would have fallen asleep at about the time his wife walked in on him and her best friend's husband.

Georgie couldn't believe it. There were only two files left. Sadie must have made a mistake. There had to be a whole other file of suitable candidates somewhere, but she had already searched Jess's office and found nothing else which was relevant to Project X. Absolutely fuck-all, except these two left on Sadie's desk who didn't fit the bill anyway. One was sixty and clearly terminally unemployable; his CV contained so many jobs in such a short period of time, he must have been an arsonist or embezzler, the other was thirty-three but five foot one. Not a midget, but close enough. And that was it, the end of the line.

She'd come to the office straight from the Oliver debacle, hoping for a chink of light, a small drop of hope that their search was ongoing, that they'd simply been unlucky up till now. And here she was at eleven p.m., sitting at her assistant's desk, almost weeping with frustration and fatigue. There weren't any decent men, it was as simple and as sad as that. Could it be that she and Jessica had set their standards too high? Georgie put her head down on the desk. Too high? All they'd asked for was someone of a reasonable height and a reasonable intelligence and a liveable-with personality who was available. Driving licences and swimming expertise had gone out of the window months ago. So had the adjective 'handsome'. George Clooney? Mr Bean was more like it. And honestly, could either of them really be expected to date a man who potholed for pleasure?

Raising her head and fishing the mobile out of her bag, she punched in Jessica's number.

'How's it going?' she asked when Jess answered. 'Do you have a live one there with you?'

'I wouldn't say that, no.'

'Another dead duck?'

'Yes.'

'How bad is it?'

'Very.'

'You'd – we'd – kick him out of bed?'

'Neither of us would have the slightest possibility of ever getting him there in the first place.'

'Then why are you still there with him?'

'I have no idea.'

'Great. That does it then. I'm in the office, at Sadie's desk. We're down to the last two and they're no-hopers as well.'

'We have to stop this now.'

'You're right. And I thought it was going to be fun. It's been hell. Complete and total hell. See you later.'

'Ciao,' Jessica said in an artificially upbeat voice.

Georgie sat back in Sadie's chair. They were back to square one. Project X was patently ridiculous. This was a headhunting company, not a dating agency. She'd been searching for an easy solution to Jess's 'I'm so alone' problem and come up with a disastrous one instead. All she'd managed to prove was how difficult it was to find any man worth more than a second's thought. Perhaps Jess was destined to be single. Perhaps she was as well. Was that so terrible? Not for her, not exactly. She had her work, she didn't have to be a wife and a mother to be fulfilled. Jess needed all that, she didn't. Not really. But there were times. Times when having a man around would have been nice; someone to look after her, someone to protect her, someone . . . Georgie shut off that mental tap. There is no such person, she told herself. I've been effectively alone for a long time now. I've had to take care of myself and I've done a good job of it. Anyone coming into the picture now would make demands I couldn't meet, he'd never understand who I am and how I've made myself successful against the odds. He'd want to change me. It's too late for me to be someone who would compromise in a relationship. I'm too set in my ways.

Face it, Georgie, you're a spinster, she said to herself and tried to laugh. Forget these months of misery, forget those few moments with Oliver, when you had the sad illusion this project might work for you as well as for Jess. Men are all the same. They're all disappointments in the end. Get back to real business and let Jess find herself a man in some normal way. She will, eventually. Don't be like Joanna and push her into it.

As Georgie pushed back the chair and bent down to retrieve her bag from the floor, she caught sight of a piece of paper under the desk. It wasn't like Sadie to leave anything important lying around on the floor, she knew. Therefore it had to be junk or one of the Project X discards, probably the Gilbert and Sullivan freak. She picked it up, went to toss it in the bin, but her curiosity stopped her. One little look. Just to make certain this was another non-starter. Just to make her feel even more resolved about calling the whole thing off. If it wasn't the 'I'm called little buttercup' fanatic, it would probably be a ten-year-old City wunderkind stamp collector with braces.

There, typed on the A4 sheet were the words:

MORGAN BLAINE
BORN: July 17, 1965

HEIGHT: 6'0"
OCCUPATION: Writer (see *Voodoo Women,* published
   1999)
Go For It

And that was it: that was all there was. Georgie sat back
down, put the piece of paper in front of her, read and re-read
it. What was it doing here? What the hell was Morgan
Blaine doing in a Harvey and Tanner file? *Voodoo Women?*
She'd not only read *Voodoo Women,* she'd read it in one
go, completely enthralled. Morgan Blaine, she remembered,
was American. He couldn't have been looking for a job in
England, could he? Why? Why would a writer, especially
a successful writer, go to a financial services headhunting
agency in a foreign country? It didn't make sense. And
why that 'Go For It' line at the end? Who could poss-
ibly have typed that? And why? Georgie reached for the
phone.
   'Sadie?'
   'Yes?'
   'Sorry to ring so late and on a Saturday night, but I'm at
the office. Underneath your desk was a file on a man named
Morgan Blaine. What was it doing there?'
   'Underneath my desk?'
   'Yes.'
   'I'm afraid I have no idea.'
   'It's only one page, only age, height and occcupation. That's
not a normal CV. Then there's a line at the end that says: "Go
For It". Did you write that?'
   'No, never. I've never seen that piece of paper.'
   'Well, it's here. It can't have flown here on its own.'
   'What was the name again?'
   'Morgan Blaine. The writer. *Voodoo Women.*'
   'Who do what?'

'*Voodoo Women.*' Georgie smiled. 'It's a novel. By this man Morgan Blaine. What's he doing in our files?'

'I'm really sorry, I don't know. I don't recall the name.'

'Have you told anyone about this project, Sadie? You promised us you wouldn't.'

'I haven't. Honestly, I haven't.'

'So who wrote: "Go For It"?'

'I don't have a clue.'

'Well, let me know if you remember anything that might clear this up, will you? It's a mystery.'

'I will.'

'Thanks.'

Hanging up, Georgie swivelled in the chair, left to right, right to left, until she felt dizzy and stopped.

Someone in the office might be playing a practical joke. But who? Sadie had always been discreet, she wouldn't, Georgie believed, lie. Someone might have found out, somehow, but still . . . Morgan Blaine was the right age. The right height. Had she kept her copy of *Voodoo Women*? Yes, definitely. It was at home, in the bookshelf by her bed. Was there a photograph of Morgan Blaine? Any background material on him? She couldn't remember now, but there was an easy way to find out.

Georgina Harvey leapt out of her chair.

The hunt was back on.

Chapter Twelve

'Look, look, look – he's not bad, is he? Look at his shoulders. Fantastic shoulders.' A copy of *Voodoo Women* was on the coffee table, Georgie and Jessica were hunched over it.

'But that's all we can see of him.' Georgie was examining the photograph on the back flap with a magnifying glass she'd been given for a birthday present when she was ten and was now thankful she'd been foresighted enough never to throw away. All right, she hadn't used it to start a fire in the woods, but it had come in handy after all. 'Why did they take the picture from the back? Is he so ugly it would put people off reading him if they saw his face?'

'Georgie, you don't understand. This is a sensitive, sensual picture. Moody.' Jessica sighed. 'Poetic. Just like his writing.'

'I read it before you did.'

'One day before I did.' Jessica pulled the book towards her, Georgie grabbed it and pulled it back.

'The violent bits aren't poetic, Jess. They're strong, macho, tough. He's not a wuss.'

'I never said he was a wuss, for God's sake. Being sensitive does not mean you're a wuss. You're so black and white. You never see the shadings.'

'Yes, and you never see the fact that your boyfriend is a

thug or the man you fall deeply in love with over dinner is a poofter.'

'That's not fair.' Jessica drew back and stiffened.

'OK, OK, I'm sorry. Let's not fight – this is too exciting.' Georgie bent over until she was within an inch of the photograph, her magnifying glass right on top of it. 'Do you think he's blond or dark? Why couldn't they have taken a colour picture?'

'I wish it said more about him,' Jessica swiped the book out from under Georgie's gaze. 'All it says is, "Morgan Blaine teaches creative writing at Columbia University. He is currently working on his next novel, *Lightning at Dawn*." That's not much information to go on.'

'Jess, that's a huge amount of information. It's everything we need. First and foremost,' she put the magnifying glass down, got up and began to pace around the room, 'if he was married, odds are it would have said so. You know, "Morgan Blaine lives with his wife and three children, blah, blah, blah". Authors always put down if they're married or their spouses get offended. Secondly, we know where he works. Thirdly, he's clever. He doesn't feel he has to name his next book *Warlock Men*, he isn't into that pathetic sequel business, he's self-confident—'

'And creative.'

'And creative.'

'Do you remember that scene in the bayou, the one where the heroine – what was her name? Eva – that was it. The one where Eva heard the music playing and followed the noise and found Rick in the clearing and they didn't have to say one word to each other, the one when she had an orgasm just looking at him?'

'Do you think that's physically possible?' Georgie stopped pacing. 'I mean, has that ever happened to you?'

'Um . . .' Jessica took a deep breath. 'I'm sure it's possible. It must be.'

'I don't know if it is, but wouldn't it be amazing if it were?' Georgie stared into space for a minute, in silent contemplation. 'Anyway,' she shook her head to clear her thoughts, 'I loved the bit when Rick killed the rapist with the machete. I know it was very graphic, but somehow it didn't make me squeamish at all. I was really into it. I mean, what was Eva doing trying to stop him? How crazy was she?'

'She didn't understand him, not at that point. She didn't know what was going on, why he had the machete. She was terrified of him, remember?'

'That's right, the stupid cow. Anyway,' George put her hands up in the air, 'the point is, we have to meet him.'

'But how *can* we meet Rick?'

'Rick? Jess, Rick's a fictional character.'

'Of course,' Jessica raised her chin. 'I *know* that. I was trying to be funny. Do you really think I'm that thick?'

'No, I just thought you'd mixed up fiction and reality.'

'Why don't I believe you? Do you want a glass of wine? I'm going to get one for myself.'

'Yes, please.'

Jessica was sulking; Georgie could tell from the way she walked to the kitchen, her shoulders tense and high. They happened sometimes, these little misunderstandings between them – normal for anyone who lived together, Georgie thought, especially stepsisters. For the most part they disappeared as quickly as they occurred, but occasionally they lingered and the atmosphere in the house reminded her, on a small scale, of the laden, heavy air in their old house, when their respective parents were arguing. Jessica, in those days, had tiptoed through the minefields, either shutting herself in the bathroom for hours, or sitting with a dazed, anxious expression in front of the television, while Georgie had buried herself in her studies.

Whoever wrote that book *You Can't Go Home Again*, was

right, she thought, but the title makes it sound as if you'd want to. I don't want to remember any of it.

As she watched her stepsister return, carrying two glasses of wine, Georgie noticed what Jess was wearing – a pink silk blouse and black silk trousers. How much had that outfit cost? Joanna had spent more money on clothes than was humanly possible, a fact which had caused at least 80 per cent of the arguments in the house. Georgie's father would open the bills and go ballistic. 'What is this, your religion?' he'd shout. 'Do you pray at the temple of Gucci?' Like mother, like daughter, Georgie thought. It's genetic.

'Thank you,' she said as she took the glass Jess offered her. 'That was nice of you, to get the wine.' She knew there was an edge to her voice, she also knew Jess hadn't noticed it. Jess wouldn't remember what had put that edge there, she'd never think an incident which had happened thirteen years before could suddenly spring to Georgie's mind now, nor would she understand why it should. That day all those years ago hadn't meant anything to her. But it had to Georgie.

It had been the one time she had been excited about going to a party, and it had also been the one time Jess's mother had ever offered to help her.

The party was for the eighteenth birthday of one of the few girls at St Anne's Georgie got on with – Martha. Martha was studious too, and had a cousin she'd told Georgie about. 'He's dishy, he's intelligent and he'll be at my party,' she'd said. 'You have to meet him. You two will fall in love at first sight.' Georgie found herself wanting very much to meet this cousin and looking forward to the party. Someone wonderful might fall in love with her at first sight. She might get to do all those things normal teenage girls did. She might be able to swoon and walk around in a daze and possibly even forget about work, for a little while, at least. It was a heady, thrilling prospect.

'You'll need a nice dress, Georgina,' Joanna had said, 'for this party tonight. And there's not much time to find one. Don't you have to be in London by eight? Why don't you come shopping with Jessica and me now and we'll find something?'

'I can't. I have to study,' Georgie had replied, not quite willing to accept the offer straight away. She wanted to, she was desperate to, but she had such a strained relationship with Joanna, she thought it would be a kind of surrender, one that Joanna would never let her forget. The idea of owing Joanna anything, even a trip to the shops and advice on clothes, was making Georgie hesitate.

'Suit yourself,' Joanna said. And then Jessica had piped up.

'I can find something for you, Georgie. If you have to study, let me look for you. If I find anything good, I'll bring it back and if you don't like it we can return it and get credit.'

This was the perfect solution, Georgie had thought. This was a weekend away from school, but one in her A Level year. The time she could spend studying on this Saturday morning was important and shouldn't be missed. She could study while Jess shopped. Perfect. And she wouldn't have to suffer watching Joanna playing Lady Bountiful Stepmother.

Jessica would be going to the party as well, but Jessica, of course, already had plenty of dresses she could wear.

'I can find you something beautiful,' Jess had said.

'All right,' Georgie said. 'Nothing *too* frilly, though. I don't like frills.'

'Don't worry. You know I know about clothes. Trust me.'

Georgie had trusted her. She'd trusted her when Jessica came back from the shopping expedition with armfuls of bags. She'd trusted her as they ran upstairs together, into Georgie's room, where Jess giddily opened all the bags and took out four dresses.

'Here.' Jess laid them out on Georgie's bed. 'Now all you

have to do is choose. I couldn't resist getting all of them –
they're so stunning. I couldn't choose just one.'

The dresses *were* stunning. They were perfect. And not one
of them fitted.

Joanna was standing at the threshold when Georgie tried
to wriggle into the last of the four.

'Oh, dear,' she said, smiling at Jessica, 'we got the wrong
size, didn't we?'

'You know my size, Jess.' Georgie gave up wriggling, pulled
the dress back over her head and threw it on the bed. 'You
know my size.'

'I know, I know.' Jessica grimaced. 'But I thought maybe one
of them . . . anyway, they didn't have these in your size.'

'So why did you get them?'

'Sizes do vary,' Joanna said calmly. 'We were hoping that
would be the case with one of these.'

Georgie was in her underwear, standing at the foot of the
bed. She looked at Joanna. She looked at Jessica.

'Did you try them on, Jess?'

'Yes.'

'And they fitted you?'

'Yes.'

'Right.' Picking up the dresses in a heap, Georgie threw them
at Jessica. 'They're yours.' She walked out of her bedroom,
down the hall, into the bathroom and slammed the door.

Jessica spent the whole train trip to London that afternoon
explaining why she thought one of the dresses might have
fitted. Georgie didn't listen. She was wearing a pair of black
jeans, a white cotton shirt and trainers. Defiantly unhappy,
she sat in silence while Jessica droned on. Georgie didn't want
to forgive Jess, what she wanted was to stop being jealous. She
was tired of hearing people say, 'Oh, you're Jessica's sister?
Isn't she beautiful!' Georgie knew Jess was beautiful; why did
everyone have to rub it in? She'd try to set the physical apart,

allow herself to hate Jess's looks at the same time as loving her as a person, but envy made the distinction hard to hold on to. If Jess had been good at school, Georgie didn't know what she would have done. All her love might, she knew, have vanished in a frenzy of competition.

Georgie knew her jealousy was shameful. Only at times like this, after an incident like the one with the dresses, did she really allow herself to feel the full force of her envy. But feeling it only made her angrier at Jess for causing such an unseemly emotion in the first place. When would it stop? She didn't know. She knew only that she couldn't wait for this train trip to be over so she could get away from Jessica Tanner.

As soon as she walked into the party, she was informed by Martha that the dishy cousin wasn't coming after all. Georgie proceeded to spend the evening on the sidelines, feeling contemptuous of the world, watching the boys buzz around Jessica. Jessica, who was wearing one of the four dresses.

Jessica, who kept the other three dresses as well. And wore them often.

Georgie never made a comment, not once. After all, clothes didn't matter, boys didn't matter, and besides, Jess couldn't help herself, Georgie knew. Any more than she could help having Joanna for a mother.

This was the worst possible time to have this particular memory assault her, Georgie thought. There was Jess, sitting on the sofa, with her wine – still the possessor of that face and that body. And there was the copy of *Voodoo Women* lying on the coffee table like the pot of gold at the end of the rainbow.

Morgan Blaine was an amazing writer. He could well be an amazing man. Yes, she'd set up this whole project for Jessica, but did she have to sit on the sidelines and watch Jessica waltz off with all the dresses and the amazing man as well?

'You know,' Jessica took a sip of her wine, 'you say you found

115

that piece of paper on the floor by accident, but it wasn't an accident, not really. It's fate. It's karma.'

Karma? Georgie stared at her stepsister, trying to work out what was going through her brain. Karma? Poetry and now Buddhism?

Whose karma? she wanted to ask. Yours or mine? What size karma? Ten or twelve?

'So do you think we should try to find Morgan Blaine?' She asked this question carefully, in an even, unemotional tone. 'Do you think we should go to New York?'

'I don't know.' Jessica tilted her head. 'It's an exciting idea, but can you take the time off? I could go, find out if he really is single, do some advance investigating on my own. It's not as if I'd be missed much at work.'

Ah ha! She wants to go alone. She wants him for herself. I thought so.

'I can take the time off. No problem.'

'Really?'

'Really.'

'You're sure?'

'Absolutely.'

'Then we should go, yes. Morgan Blaine might be the perfect man for you.'

'Or for you, Jess.'

'Oh, no, I'd just be going to keep you company.'

As if, Georgie thought as she watched Jess take another sip of wine. You don't fool me. I know when you're faking, there's that little squeak in your voice. The same squeak I heard that whole bloody train trip when you kept trying to make excuses for yourself.

'Fine, then.' Downing her wine in one long mouthful, Georgie put the glass back on the table with a bang. 'We'll go together. And, now that I think about it, we should take Sadie with us. She can keep a handle on work, while we find

Morgan Blaine. Is Monday all right with you? Because, as far as I'm concerned, the sooner, the better.'

'Monday's fine by me.'

'It's Monday then.' Georgie forced a smile. 'I can spend tomorrow making calls to cover for my absence at Harvey and Tanner.'

'It will be fun, won't it? I really hope he's the man for you, Georgie.'

'And *I* really hope he's the man for you.'

'You know, your eye, sometimes your eye . . .' Jessica paused, stopped entirely.

'My eye what?'

'Nothing.' Jessica turned her head away, then stared at the floor. 'It's lucky we're so totally uncompetitive, isn't it?' She looked up then, straight into Georgie's gaze. 'I'd hate it if we were. Competitive, I mean. It's such a relief that we're not.'

It was Georgie's turn to find the floor suddenly fascinating.

'It's a huge relief,' she said.

Chapter Thirteen

Sadie knew she would have loved the skyscrapers if she could have seen them. On the way in from JFK she caught a couple of glimpses of the skyline, but she was at the far side of the taxi and it was hard to crane her head past Georgie and Jessica who were sitting beside each other like statues, their bodies stiff, their faces rigid.

Something was seriously wrong. The atmosphere in the cab was all strained politeness and brewing rancour. But no one said a word and Sadie was left feeling that she'd embarked on a surreal journey. Here Georgie and Jessica were, in America, hunting down some man they'd never met, a famous writer who had somehow ended up as a name on a piece of paper on the floor of an office. It was as if Andrew had decided to stop joking about text messages and gone to find Demi Moore because he'd passed a rubbish bin which had her picture in it.

While Project X had been fairly mad, it had at least had a touch of sanity in it. Why not trawl throught the files and see whether there were any suitable men in them? It wasn't that far off from using a dating agency, Sadie could see some logic in it. But this? Flying across the ocean, tracking down a writer, and then – then what?

Making dates with men on their files gave Georgie and Jessica a spurious excuse: they could claim they were meeting these men for business purposes, make up stories to cover their true intentions. How could they do the same with Morgan Blaine? What could they possibly say to him?

Was the tension between these two a product of this mad pursuit, or was it due to something else? Sadie couldn't work it out, nor could she answer the question Andrew had posed as soon as she had woken him up with the news that she was going to New York; she'd run into his bedroom after Georgie had rung her on Sunday morning, bounced up and down on his bed and yelled, 'I'm going to New York, I'm going to America. Georgie and Jessica have found their available man, a writer named Morgan Blaine, and that's where he is. And they're taking me with them tomorrow!'

'Hey, Sade,' he'd grunted, hoisting himself up and leaning against his pillow, 'fantastic. Be sure to let me know.'

'Know what?'

'How they do it.'

'Do what?'

'Divide this poor bastard into two. Haven't you noticed the fatal flaw here? Think about it. There's only one available man, and there are two available women. Will they use a chainsaw? Or a simple kitchen knife? Maybe cut him in half with a pair of nail scissors? There's going to be a lot of blood whichever method they choose. Better take some cleaning fluids.'

Sadie *had* thought about it on the flight as she read *Voodoo Women*. Were Georgie and Jessica discussing the fatal flaw up in business class? Had they worked out what to do if he *was* still available and both of them fancied him? Perhaps they assumed that because they had such different personalities, they'd always have different taste in men; yet both of them were here in this taxi, both of them were on this chase. And both of them were acting as if the other were a stranger. When had this tension started? She hadn't noticed it at Heathrow, but then she'd been busy checking in and buying a few things in duty free. Had it begun while they were sipping champagne in business class? If so, Sadie was pleased to have been relegated to economy.

'Would you mind very much opening the window, Georgie?' Jessica asked, in what struck Sadie as an exaggeratedly posh accent.

'It's the middle of December, Jess, but of course, if you want me to, I will.'

'I find it very stuffy in here.'

'Fine.' Georgie hit the button which made the window descend. She kept it down until the entire window was open.

'That's *too* far. We'll freeze.'

'Whatever.' Georgie pressed the button again. The window zoomed back up. Now there was only a tiny sliver of it open. 'Is this all right with you?'

'Yes,' Jessica answered. 'Thank you very much.'

'You're welcome.'

'And if it's not too much of a bother, I'd appreciate it if the taxi could drop me on the way to the hotel. I can catch up with you later.'

'Drop you where?' Georgie didn't turn to look at her stepsister as she asked this, she stayed staring ahead.

'There's a beauty salon on 66th and Madison, I want to have my legs waxed.'

'Really? As you said, it's the middle of December. Are you planning on wearing shorts?'

'No, I'm not. But I don't like the feeling of having hairy legs.'

'Of course you don't. One doesn't, does one?' Georgie's arms were crossed over her waist, her hands were fists. 'One must get rid of all extraneous hair whatever the circumstances. Even if that means getting legs waxed after a transatlantic flight. I know *I've* always found that to be the case, haven't you Sadie?'

Sadie didn't know how to respond, nor did she want to. Georgie was trying to recruit her on to her team to exploit the fact that there were three people on this trip and one of them was a free agent. If she were forced into taking sides, Sadie knew she should choose Georgie's. It would be the correct political decision given that Georgie was the person who signed her pay cheques, not Jessica. But she resented being put under this pressure, and so early on in the trip as well. She wished this ill-will between them would finally explode into an argument and then dissipate.

She and Andrew had never had moments like this. When disagreements threatened to escalate out of control, one or the other of them would turn whatever the source of the problem was into a joke. Was that because they were different sexes? If Andrew had been a girl, would they have engaged in this kind of frosty, cutting conversation? What if Andrew had been a girl *and* a stepsister? How would the dynamic have worked then? Sadie stopped wondering and concentrated on how to keep herself from being the pig in the middle.

'Mostly I shave my legs,' she finally replied. 'Sometimes I wax them, though.' This was about as neutral a comment as could be made; there was nowhere to go with it, she knew, and Georgie would understand it was a signal that Sadie wasn't going to play the game and choose between them – not until she absolutely had to, anyway.

'That's practical of you, Sadie.' Georgie nodded. 'Well –' she put her hands up in front of her, examining them – 'if you're going to have your wegs waxed, Jess, I think I'll have a manicure.'

'That's a very good idea.' Jessica lifted her chin. 'As long as we're going to be there, I might as well have my eyelashes tinted too.'

'Excellent. That will give me time to have my eyebrows shaped.'

'Well, then, I might as well have a pedicure.'

'Perfect. Then I can go on the sunbed.'

'You'll look like a lobster.'

'Thank you so much for caring, Jess. Do you think they might have something there that will help with those little lines that are beginning to show around your eyes? That would be nice, wouldn't it? Or, do you like them just the way they are?'

It can't get any worse, Sadie thought. She leant back against the torn upholstery and closed her eyes.

An hour later, she was lying on the bed in her hotel room, trying to get some sleep. Georgie and Jessica had suggested she take the luggage and check in while they had their beauty treatments. Despite the bagfuls of clothes they'd brought with them, they had also decided to go on a shopping expedition after they'd finished at the salon. Sadie was relieved to have this time alone. This trip had been such a surprise and her excitement about coming to America for the first time had been so intense, now she'd arrived all she wanted to do was collapse for a few hours in a bed and compose herself. She needed rest. If this high voltage step-sibling rivalry continued, she'd have to be on full-scale alert to negotiate a path between her employers.

She still couldn't get over the fact that they were on this hunt in the first place, that they had had to go through all this to find a man. Looking at Jessica, anyone would think she'd spent most of her life turning men down. And while Georgie wasn't as technically attractive as Jessica, she had a sexy robustness to her. If she weren't in the City, Sadie could see her on a farm, hoisting pails of milk, the wench with an eye on the taciturn local teacher. She knew it was an absurd thought as soon as it crossed her mind, but it made sense on a visceral level.

Looks must count for something, she said to herself. Maybe their not being in a relationship had to do with timing. Either they'd met the right man at the wrong time or the wrong man at the right time. Who could say? All Sadie knew was that she hoped, for her sake as well as theirs, that something good came out of this trip. The best possible result would be if Morgan Blaine were married, or if he had no interest whatsoever in either of them. The competition would die down, they'd be back to their usual selves. But even that might not make a happy ending for her. Every time Georgie or Jessica looked at her, they'd probably remember this ridiculous, failed project. They'd be embarrassed by it, therefore they'd be embarrassed by her presence. One way or another they'd figure out a way to get rid of her. And then what would she do? She wished she'd never been involved in all this, she wished she were back at the office doing her usual job. A trip to America was wonderful, theoretically, but in these circumstances? It was a lose-lose situation. Unless Morgan Blaine *was* the perfect man, with superhuman powers, one of which was the ability to clone himself.

Taking her seat at the table Georgie had found for them in the bar of the Carlyle, Jessica put her shopping bags on the floor beside her and smiled. She was secretly thrilled. The hours spent at the salon had been worthwhile. And afterwards, on the shopping trip, Georgie had bought a loud tartan suit which made her look like a Scottish dental hygienist, while she had found a perfect pair of Armani trousers, a jacket and an elegant, soft, white blouse to go underneath. Morgan Blaine would like the subtlety of her outfit, the casual understated look. Yet there was a twinge of fear in her heart. What if he talked about pop groups she'd never heard of? What if he immediately dismissed her and fell for Georgie?

But how had this all come to pass? How could she be sitting here, waiting for Georgie to return from the loo, plotting how to capture the heart of a man she'd never met, for no other reason than to *beat* Georgie? When had this project turned so ugly and so competitive? Jessica couldn't put an exact time to it, the moment when something changed between her and Georgie. That moment may have started as soon as they were in a tug of war over *Voodoo Women*, snatching it back and forth from each other, but that had been almost playful, almost funny. And then? And then she'd brought Georgie a glass of wine and nothing had been the same since, as if a potion had been dropped into the glass, a deadly poison. Georgie wanted Morgan Blaine to herself, that much Jessica thought she knew for certain. What she didn't understand was why she wouldn't give him to her. 'Go to New York on your own,' she should have said. 'Tell me all about it as soon as you meet him.' What had stopped her? Georgie's angry eye? Her tone of voice?

A terrible envy had invaded her psyche. All Sunday, from the moment she woke up, scenes from her past had pushed into her mind and wouldn't leave. There was Georgie, reeling off her amazing grades to her father, while she stood watching, anxious not to have to tell her own bad ones to her mother. There was Georgie, in the English class they took together, putting her hands over her eyes when Jessica said something obvious about a book. And there was Georgie, humiliating her in their final year at school. They were discussing what university everyone wanted to go to, what chance they all had of getting in. Jessica had kept quiet during this talk in a local coffee bar. She'd kept her legs tightly crossed and a

smile on her face. Names of universities swirled around in
the haze of smoke from teenage cigarettes. There were boys
from the neighbouring boarding school there as well; in all
there were seven boys and eight girls sipping coffee, smoking
and discussing the future. Jessica had counted them and was
mentally pairing off couples as a way to avoid having to think
about what they were all saying; a conversation she had no
part in.

'Well, at least Jess doesn't have to worry about any of this
university business,' Georgie had stated. Loudly. 'All she has
to do is figure out which man she'll marry whose credit card
she can shop happily ever after with.' The entire group had
laughed. Every single one of them. And then the discussion
about universities had continued. Jessica had wanted to say
something. She had been desperate to say anything to erase
the mark that laughter had left in her heart, but there wasn't
anything to say. She knew perfectly well she'd do badly in her
A Levels. There was almost no point in taking them. Georgie
was right. All she had to worry about was the day when her
prince would come. But did Georgie have to announce it
like that in front of everyone? Pick her out when she'd been
sitting so quietly and show her up to be nothing more than
a wife-in-waiting?

Jessica could feel it even now, the sense that she'd been
lifted up and slammed against a wall, the instinctive reaction
she'd had to flee and go to the ladies'. 'I'm sorry I don't
do well at school,' she'd said to herself, as she had locked
herself into a cubicle. 'I'm sorry I can't get to the top on
a ski lift. I'm sorry for everything. I want someone to say
"I love you" right now. I feel thirsty and hungry and empty
and homesick and I don't even know what home I'm sick for
because it isn't any home I've ever lived in. Georgie should
know that. And she should talk about something I can join
in on, instead of sitting there rabbiting on about university

and pretending I don't exist. Pretending she doesn't know how miserable I am.'

You can't have him, Jessica thought as she watched Georgie making her way back to the table. I went to the loo that day and cried. You must have seen afterwards that I had been crying and you didn't care. You must know how embarrassing it is for me to be in that office every day doing nothing and you don't care. All you care about is having me as a sidekick who makes you look better, brighter, more successful in comparison. You can't have him. Morgan Blaine is mine.

'So –' Georgie plopped herself into the chair, sat back, crossed her arms – 'I think the best way to go about this is to go to Columbia tomorrow morning to find him. He teaches there so he must have an office there. We can sit outside it and wait.'

'All right.'

'And then we'll introduce ourselves and take it from there.'

'Fine.' Jessica shrugged.

'You don't seem very excited, Jess. After all, this may be the beginning of a new life for you.'

'A man whose credit card I can shop happily ever after with?'

'What? I didn't hear that.'

'Never mind. It wasn't important.'

'So, if we get going around nine or so? Does that make sense?'

'Perfect sense.'

The waiter came with the wine Georgie had ordered, and Jessica was grateful for his interruption. A flashback had appeared before her eyes, a picture of Georgie riding on the back of Daniel Canter's motorcycle, her arms locked around his waist. It was a true picture. It had happened,

Jessica knew. At some point in time, Georgie had taken a ride with Daniel. But why? If Georgie had thought Daniel was such a thug, why had she gone on his motorcycle with him? And why hold on quite so tightly?

'Georgie?' Jessica took a sip of wine. 'You never secretly fancied Daniel Canter, did you? In your heart of hearts?'

'No, Jess, I've never fancied any of your boyfriends. And my heart of hearts doesn't go out to criminals.'

'But you went with him on his motorbike once, I remember.'

'He took me on a ride once. It doesn't mean I fancied him.'

You're lying. You did fancy Daniel. Where did you go on that motorcycle? Why were you on it to begin with? He was my boyfriend. What actually happened that I don't know about?

'Excuse me.' A man was suddenly standing beside their table, his eyes fixed on Jessica. 'Don't I know you from somewhere?'

'No.' Jessica shook her head. 'You don't.' He was in a business suit, his hair was swept back off his face, he had a large nose and small eyes.

'Are you sure?'

'Positive,' Jessica said dismissively.

'Could I know you from now, then? From this very moment? Could this be the beginning of our knowledge of each other?'

'No.'

'You're sure?'

'Positive.'

'So nice not to have known you,' Georgie remarked as she watched him walk away. 'What a creep.' She turned back to Jessica. 'Why did you ask me whether I fancied Daniel? That came from nowhere, Jess. What made you ask me that?'

'I was just wondering,' Jessica brushed her hair back, 'that's all.'

'Did you ever fancy any of my boyfriends?'

'No.'

'Well, that's fine, then. As you said before, it's lucky we're not competitive.'

'Isn't it?' Jessica's eyes slid away from Georgie's and found the floor.

The panic didn't hit Georgie until they'd left the bar, she'd seen Jessica to her room, and gone on to her own. But when it came, as she was unpacking her suitcase, it arrived with such force she had to sit down on the bed and try to calm herself. That businessman hadn't approached her with his feeble come-on, he had gone straight for Jessica, the man-magnet. The fact that Jess hadn't had a successful relationship with a man didn't mean she hadn't been besieged by offers. Jess was like one of those candidates every business wanted to hire. She may not have found the right match yet, but that wasn't for want of men trying.

How could she have been so stupid? Why hadn't she kept her mouth shut about Morgan Blaine and come to New York on her own? Why give him the chance to look at Jessica? This was like taking on Abba in the European Song Contest. She couldn't win. She didn't have a prayer. Unless . . . unless she got to Morgan Blaine first. But how? She didn't have a clue.

What she did have, though, was a Manhattan phone directory. It was on the top shelf of her closet, she'd seen it when she was searching for an extra pillow. Morgan Blaine might be in it. And if he was, she'd know where he lived. She could get to him before he went off to teach, waylay him, possibly even dissuade him from teaching at all that day, thus keeping him out of sight of Jessica for hours.

Was that unfair, was it cheating?

No. Jess had all the physical advantages, the odds were stacked in her favour. Georgie had entered this race with a handicap; the only way to even those odds was to get to Morgan first. That wasn't cheating. That was applying simple mathematical principles.

Why do I suddenly want him so much? Because I'm afraid I can't have him? Is this like getting the dreaded F on an exam? Because I want to win something that wasn't supposed to be a competition but has somehow turned into one?

Georgina Harvey walked slowly to the wardrobe and took the telephone directory down from the shelf. Sitting on her bed, she thumbed through it to Blaine. Blaine, A., Blaine, B., Blaine, Connie, Blaine, George, Blaine, H. Blaine, L. Blaine, Louis, Blaine, Morgan.

Blaine, Morgan: 308 East 81st Street. Telephone number 288-3109.

Should she ring him? Now? No, how could she explain herself over the telephone? Also, he might be hideously ugly. Jessica could have been wrong about the 'soulful' photograph and she might have been right – he didn't want people to see him from the front for a very good reason. No, better to stake out 308 East 81st Street early in the morning. Check out if it was an apartment building or a house, do some dawn undercover detective work and then decide whether to ring his bell and present herself or . . . or . . . she didn't know. She'd decide when she got there.

Meanwhile she'd try on her new suit once more, set the alarm for six o'clock and banish all guilty feelings from her brain. Jessica would forgive her. Jessica would be fine. Jessica wouldn't fancy him anyway. After all, the love of Jess's life so far had been Daniel Canter. She'd been thinking about him

129

only minutes ago. Perhaps Jess liked the element of danger, the men who were always either in trouble or on the verge of it. In that case, she wasn't keeping Jessica away from the man of her dreams. Whatever else Morgan Blaine might have accomplished in his life, it was close to a dead certainty he hadn't done a stretch in Wormwood Scrubs.

Chapter Fourteen

It was nine in the morning and Sadie, who had been up since six, was busy dealing with Georgie's emails on the laptop. Although Georgie had delegated a lot of her work by phoning her two top consultants on Sunday, saying she and Jessica had to take an unscheduled trip to New York, there was still a fair amount for Sadie to do. She'd almost finished and was about to give herself the luxury of ordering breakfast from room service when the telephone rang. Startled by its unfamiliarity, the way it rang once and paused before it rang again, unlike the two quick, successive English trills, she waited three rings before she answered.

'Sade, it's Lisa. I just found out you're in New York too. What's going on? Why the sudden trip? Come on, tell me. I need to know.'

'I don't have to tell you not to disclose the real reason why we're here to anyone in the office,' Georgie had said when she'd phoned Sadie's room the night before. 'Jessica and I will be out tomorrow morning. No one from H and T needs to know more than they've been told. Understood?'

'Yes,' Sadie had replied.

Now faced with a direct question from Lisa, Sadie side-stepped it with, 'I don't even know all the details of the trip, and I'm here with them.'

'Lucky you.' Lisa sighed. 'In New York City. I wish they had taken me.'

No, you don't, Sadie thought. Or rather you wouldn't if you knew what it was like travelling with them.

'If there are any problems there, something that needs Georgie's attention immediately, ring me. I can try to sort them out from here.'

'No worries.' Sadie could hear Lisa turn a page in a magazine. 'I don't like this season's shades of pink. Do you?'

'Not much.'

'Listen, before you go, did you see my *Voodoo Women* man?'

'What?'

'The piece of paper I left on your desk on Friday. I know all about this whole sisters-doing-it-for-themselves-find-a-man scheme, you know. So I thought I'd—'

'Lisa! How do you know about it?'

'You know Connie?'

'No.'

'Well, Connie is a friend of mine who works for Lloyds and she was at the restaurant with the Twisted Sisters when they were talking about it and she heard everything because she was at the next table and she loves listening in on people and she would have told me ages ago only she got ME – which, by the way, I totally believe in, I mean I absolutely think it's a disease – anyway, she told me when she got back to work last week and then I did some listening-in-behind-doors detective work myself and found out you were helping them and I thought: "Blimey! This is beyond belief, you know." It's hysterical when you think about it, these two sex-starved businesswomen chasing down men. Anyway, I'd just finished reading this book *Voodoo Women* and I thought,' another page turned, 'I – God it's *all* bloody pink now, pink everywhere – anyway, I thought, if they want some magic man, why not throw in this bloke who wrote the book on it, you know? Voodoo Women? How perfect is that? Go for it girls!'

'Oh my God.' Sadie felt her grip on the receiver tighten. 'You put that piece of paper on my desk?'

'Yeah, like a CV. With the writer's name – I can't remember it now. I made up his age, too.'

'Why? Why did you do it?'

'I was bored. My horoscope for that day said I should have fun and do something creative. It was a fun thing to do. I'm really pissed off at you for not telling me about this whole find-a-man thing, by the way.'

'Lisa.'

'What?'

'Nothing.' Sadie shook her head. 'Please don't tell anyone else about the whole find-a-man thing, OK? You were in enough trouble with the email. They don't want anyone to know.'

'No shit! I wouldn't want anyone to know if I were them. But don't worry, I won't broadcast the juicy info. I haven't told anyone. I need this job.'

'Lisa, I've got to go.' Sadie was desperate to hang up and work out the implications of this new information.

'Cool. When are you coming back?'

'I'm not sure. Soon. Probably very soon.'

'Let's go out to the pub as soon as you do. I need to hear *everything*. Have they found a bloke yet?'

'No.' Sadie closed her eyes. 'They've more or less stopped looking.'

'Well, hey – tell them to look up Voodoo Man while they're there, why don't you? It said on the jacket he lives in New York. They could . . . hang on. *Hang on!* They haven't . . . don't tell me . . . you didn't give them that piece of paper, did you? They're not in New York now to find him, are they?

Tell me that isn't why you're there. It was only a joke. Some fun. Oh, God.'

Sadie didn't respond.

'Oh, no. They're after him, aren't they? That's why this sudden trip. I *made up* his age, Sade. There was a photograph, but it was taken from the back. He could be eighty. You'll cover for me, won't you? You won't tell them I'm the one who wrote it?'

'I won't. I promise.'

'I can't believe it. I mean, how mad are they? How absolutely, totally mad are they to chase across an ocean for a bloke they don't know? And besides, even if he is thirty-eight and gorgeous and all that, there's only one of him.'

'Exactly.' Sadie rubbed her forehead so hard she could feel it start to turn red. 'Exactly.'

After she'd hung up, she called room service. She needed some food, badly. Lisa had put that piece of paper on the desk and it must have fallen on the floor. Why did Georgie have to see it? What a complete, unbelievable mess. She'd cover for Lisa not only because she didn't want to get Lisa sacked but also because she didn't want to go back to London on the next flight with Georgie and Jessica in even worse frames of mind than they were already. Not telling them the truth might be selfish but that was her choice. She'd spent months working on Project X, which was, technically, not her job at all. They'd bent the rules roping her in on it, now she was bending the rules by not telling them. And in the end, what difference did it make if they found out from her that Morgan Blaine might not be the man they thought, or if they found out for themselves? In the first case, a friend of hers might lose a job she liked – that was the only real difference.

I don't know if I can leave this room or what I'm supposed to do now, she thought. I'd like do do some sightseeing but should I be on standby in case they need me? What would they need me for? They're going to find Morgan Blaine, whoever Morgan Blaine turns out to be. I suppose if they find out he's gone to Hawaii they'll need me to organize the next leg of this treasure hunt. In which case I have to wait here, at base camp.

Georgina Harvey and Jessica Tanner: women explorers off to find the Yeti, Big Foot, the Loch Ness Monster. That's what they were. Two women on Mission Impossible. Sent by a receptionist whose horoscope had told her to have some fun.

When the waiter arrived with her food, Sadie, noticing he was good-looking, thought for a moment of bribing him to impersonate Morgan Blaine, dragging him to Georgie and Jessica, where he would then announce that he was married. Or gay. He might as well have been Morgan Blaine. Any man could be Morgan Blaine as far as those two were concerned. Because, Sadie was beginning to understand, this trip had nothing to do with Morgan Blaine. And everything to do with Georgie and Jessica's relationship with each other.

The two stepsisters had been forced together because of their respective parents' divorce, then the marriage which had thrown them together had broken up as well. It was not a terrific basis for a loving relationship. On the other hand, they might have bonded just because of these difficult circumstances. They could, because of what they'd been through together, be closer than real siblings. It didn't seem entirely plausible, but then Sadie wasn't at all sure where plausibility entered into relationships and love, especially male–female love. What was love about, anyway? Companionship? Sex? Or a projection? This man loves me therefore I must be lovable. I am loved therefore I love.

That was partly what had attracted her to Piers, she knew. He had homed in on her and she'd felt flattered. She'd then proceeded to invest him with rare and sparkling qualities – whether he actually possessed those qualities wasn't an issue. People tended to love people who loved them. That was a simple human response. When Piers stopped loving her, she had never asked herself whether or not he was the right man for her, she had blamed herself for being inadequate. That was a simple human response as well. But that didn't mean it was necessarily the correct one.

The telephone rang again. Sadie hoped it wasn't Lisa with even more unwanted news.

'Sadie –' it was Jessica who sounded breathless – 'come to my room. Four-o-three. I need you here. Now.' Click. Jessica had hung up.

What could have happened? Sadie wondered as she threw on a pair of trousers and a top, to make Jessica so jumpy? Whatever it was, at least she had something to do, somewhere to go. The second after Sadie knocked on the door of Room 403, Jessica swung it open and started to talk.

'Georgie's gone. She's fucking *gone!*'

Never having heard Jessica swear before, Sadie found herself instantly shaking.

'She's gone? Has something terrible happened to her?'

'Terrible? Something terrible is going to happen to her when I see her. She's *cheated*. She went to find him first, I know she did. She *cheated*.'

'Are you sure? Couldn't she be having breakfast downstairs?'

'I checked downstairs. No, I know her. I know she bloody well *did* fancy Daniel, after all. The liar.'

'Daniel?' Sadie was still standing on the threshold of Jessica's room.

'Daniel Canter.'

'I thought . . .' She grimaced, trying to understand. 'I thought his name was Morgan Blaine.'

'It is.'

'Then why—'

'She was all over him on that motorcycle. She probably went behind my back and wrote to him *all the time* in gaol.'

'Georgie was in gaol?'

'She should be in gaol. The thief.'

'I'm sorry.' Putting her hand up to her forehead, Sadie tried to force her brain into making some sense of all this. 'Did Georgie steal a motorcycle from some man named Daniel or was Morgan Blaine in prison, or—'

'Never mind. Come in.' Jessica motioned her into the room, then went to the table and picked up her bag. 'I'll explain it all in the taxi on the way to Columbia. We have to get there. Right away. Ready?' She was dressed in an Armani trouser suit and she grabbed a fake leopardskin coat, Sadie hadn't seen before, off the bed. 'She might not have caught him yet. We might still be in time. What time do classes start there?'

'I'm afraid I don't know,' Sadie replied, following Jessica out, thinking she should ask why she needed to go along as well, but knowing she preferred to be along on this chase than to be sitting alone in her room. At least this way she'd get to see some of Manhattan. 'I'll just run to my room and grab a coat. I'll be back in a second.'

'Hurry, Sadie. Please hurry.'

During the entire taxi ride to the Upper West Side, while Sadie took in Central Park, Broadway, the throngs of people crowding the streets, the buildings, the *hustle* of New York, Jessica ranted. Daniel had been *her* boyfriend but Georgie had gone on his motorcycle with him and Georgie had probably gone off with all her boyfriends behind her back and Georgie would stop at nothing to win and yes, she'd been generous, she'd given Jessica a job and a place to live, but now she was talking about handing out *homework* and Jessica wouldn't be able to learn anyway because she hated the City, but that wasn't the point, the point was Georgie had *cheated*.

Struggling to take in all this information, Sadie felt simultaneously curious and anxious. Jessica confiding in her like this was riveting, the idea that Georgie *could* steal a boyfriend of Jessica's was riveting, as was Jessica's hatred of the City, but she knew having too much personal information was dangerous. Jessica would, at some point, regret having spilled her guts like this. No one liked confessing their fears to an employee. This taxi ride could be the equivalent of a one-night stand, with Jessica waking up the next morning regretting what she'd done. Sadie knew that in the mood Jessica was in she would have told all this to the cab driver if Sadie hadn't been there. That would have been a safer option, though. The taxi driver would get his money and disappear. Sadie wasn't able to disappear from Jessica's life. Or Georgie's. Even more distressing, by dint of being in this cab to begin with, Sadie knew she'd ended up in Jessica's corner in what was now clearly a heavyweight title bout.

When the taxi pulled up in front of huge iron gates on West 116th Street, Jessica paid and got out. It had started to snow. She looked so frantic and so out of place as she stood on the pavement while students passed by, staring at her fake fur coat, that Sadie felt sorry for her.

'Where do you think we go now?' Jessica asked miserably.

'Excuse me.' Sadie stopped a young man as he walked by them. 'How do we get to the English department here? That's where they teach creative writing, isn't it?'

'Yes.' He smiled. 'You go through the gates, walk across the campus and it's the building on your right at the end.'

'Thank you.'

'No problem. I love your accent.'

'Thank you.' Sadie blushed, but she didn't have time to be embarrassed by her red face because Jessica was already striding off. Her usual slow walking pace had been abandoned, she was almost cantering.

Sadie caught up with her at the exact moment it happened. A man walking a few steps in front of them as they crossed the campus yelled, 'Morgan!' Another man, walking in the opposite direction, heading straight for them, stopped. The two stood talking, only a few yards away. Jessica had pulled up short as soon as she heard the name yelled, and grabbed Sadie's arm.

'It's him,' she whispered. 'It's Morgan Blaine. Look. It's him!' She started tiptoeing towards the men, pulling Sadie along with her.

As soon as they were level with them, Jessica began to search through her handbag as if she'd just discovered she'd lost her keys. Sadie couldn't help but smile, it was a clever ploy which allowed them to stand still and overhear the conversation.

'Do you have a class now?' the first man was asking Morgan.

'No, I'm not teaching today.' Morgan answered. Sadie could feel Jessica's excitement. If fake leopardskin could melt, it would have then.

'So how's the book going?'

'Slowly.'

He was tall, a little over six feet, he was wearing glasses and had, Sadie thought, a shy, open, kind face. He might have been in his late thirties or early forties, she couldn't tell, but close anyway to Lisa's invented thirty-eight. Not drop-dead handsome, not someone she would normally associate with Jessica, Morgan Blaine looked like a benevolent, unassuming man who wouldn't get the promotion but would be sincerely happy when a friend of his did. Someone who would never forget his godchildren's birthdays. Someone who would have tons of godchildren.

Thank God I didn't tell her about Lisa, Sadie thought. I almost did in the taxi. But now Lisa's little joke may not be so misleading. Morgan Blaine might not be a Greek God, but he is presentable, definitely.

'No wedding ring,' Jessica whispered, continuing to rummage around in her bag.

'Would you like to grab a cup of coffee?' The first man stamped his feet in the cold. Sadie felt a sense of excitement mounting. This must be what it feels like when hunters find a fox, she thought, only there's no terrible killing at the end. I hope.

'Coffee would be great.'

Morgan and the man headed off through the campus with Jessica and Sadie following closely behind.

'Look at his shoulders. Wonderful, stunning shoulders, same as his photo. I would recognize them anywhere.'

'He looks nice.'

'I think I fell in love at first sight. Has that ever happened to you?'

Dazzled by the first personal question Jessica had ever asked her, Sadie was speechless for a few seconds, before saying, 'Once.'

'It's *never* happened to me before. This is the real thing. I just know it.'

'What are you going to do when we get to the coffee place?'

'I don't know. I don't know.' Jessica pounded her fist against her lips. 'I have to make him notice me.'

'That shouldn't be difficult. I mean, I doubt that there will be any other woman as beautiful as you there.'

'You think I'm beautiful?' Jessica reached out, put her arm around Sadie's shoulder and hugged her as they scurried after their prey. 'You are *so* sweet, Sadie. You know that? I'm so glad we brought you with us. I couldn't have done this without you. I can't believe we found him this quickly. It's fate. I know it's fate. I can't tell you how much I believe in fate. Georgie's probably in that English building now, waiting. I hope so. I hope she sits there for hours.'

They left the campus and stopped as Morgan and the other man waited to cross the street. The tempo of the falling snow was picking up and Sadie wondered when, if ever, it would stop.

'I feel as if I'm in a television show,' Sadie said. Don't think about Georgie, she told herself. Don't even think about how livid she's going to be. Your job is probably gone, anyway. It was probably gone the moment you agreed to help them in this crazed project. Enjoy this moment. Jessica has found the Yeti, Jessica is now going to try to *talk to* the Yeti. This is a scientific discovery of monumental proportions. It's a cross between being hysterically funny, hysterically weird and thrilling.

'Look. Look!' Jessica elbowed Sadie in the ribs. 'They're going down those steps. It's a coffee place. A basement coffee place.' They crossed the street, then Jessica halted abruptly, pulled out a brush from her bag, ran it through her hair, put it back, pulled out a compact and opened it. 'How do I look?' she asked, staring into it with a little frown. 'Aeroplanes – they're terrible for the skin.'

'You look fine.'

'Really?'

'Really.'

'Good.' Snapping the compact shut, Jessica threw it into the bag and took Sadie's arm again. 'Here we go. Oh, my God, I'm nervous. You have to help me, Sadie. We have to get his attention in some way. Should I spill a cup of coffee over you? That might work.'

'There might be a better way,' Sadie mumbled, following Jessica down the stairs.

Morgan Blaine and the man were sitting in the middle of the room. Both looked up and stared at Jessica as she steered Sadie to a table beside theirs. No one else was in the coffee shop and Sadie found herself thinking it would have been a little more subtle if Jessica had sat at more of a distance, but who was she to give anyone, especially Jessica, romantic advice?

'Brrrr.' Jessica rubbed her hands together as they sat down across from each other. '*La neige. La neige tombeau.*'

La neige tombeau? Sadie was speechless. Morgan and the other man continued to stare. An ancient waitress wearing an apron approached, put two coffees in front of the two men, turned to Jessica and Sadie.

'What'll you two ladies have?'

'We'll have two *caffé au leche* – no, no,' Jessica's hands fluttered in distress, 'two *caffé con lait* or is it . . . ?'

'Two coffees with milk, right?' The waitress sighed dramatically and moved away. There was silence. Sadie could sense that Morgan, who was sitting on her side, only a foot or so away, had his eyes locked on Jessica. His friend, who had red hair and the beginnings of a beard, was also clearly captivated, but managed to take his eyes off Jessica and turn back to Morgan.

'You know, Morgan, I'm finishing *my* book soon,' he said. 'I have to say, I think it's damn good.'

'New York is so charming, don't you think, Sadie? All these . . . all these little cafés and so many . . . so many interesting people. But,' Jessica raised her already loud voice a notch, 'I always think when I come to this country that what I really would like to do is to to visit the bayou. The mystery, the *heat*, the atmosphere. The bayou is my spiritual home.'

'I always thought that about you.' Sadie was getting into this now. She reckoned, if she helped out enough, she might avert the prospect of having hot coffee dumped on her. 'You've often said how much the bayou appeals to you.' She knew they were the setting for *Voodoo Women*, but what was the bayou exactly? she wondered. Some sort of swamp?

'I'm sure your book is fantastic, John.' Morgan leaned forward, his hands around his mug of coffee. 'Did I ever tell you about my trip to Louisiana? The research work I did there for my last book? In the—'

'Bayou?' Red-haired John interrupted. 'Yes. Of course. But did I tell you about *my* trip there? You know I play the blues. People used to say I could have done it for a living – played the guitar. God knows why I chose academia. It's not really me.'

The waitress delivered their coffee. Jessica swept her hand back through her long black hair, stood up, took off her coat and walked slowly to hang it on a peg at the side of the room. Both men's eyes followed her. Neither of them spoke.

'It's such a shame we don't know anyone here, Sadie,' she said when she had returned and sat back down again. 'I mean, obviously we have many friends here, but we never really get a chance to speak to anyone who . . . anyone who . . .'

'Would treat us like tourists,' Sadie jumped in to the rescue. It was so easy doing this on someone else's behalf, helping Jessica on her quest. If she'd had to do it for herself, she wouldn't have known where to begin. 'Everyone we know assumes we know New York backwards. They don't take us to the Statue of Liberty or the Empire State Building so we've never actually been. At least I haven't. Have you, Jessica?'

'No, you're so right. I haven't either. Of course I've been to the museums, but now that you've made me think about it, I realize I've always gone on my own. I'd love to go with a native New Yorker some time.'

'Speaking of my past hobbies, Morgan,' John's voice was even louder than Jessica's, he could have been heard over a Concorde taking off, 'Did I ever tell you I used to be a tour guide? Right here in Manhattan?'

'No, you never did, John.' Morgan sounded desperate not to be eclipsed in this conversation. At least he wasn't shouting, Sadie thought. He was scoring points for being a little bit less transparent. 'Did I tell you about my summers working in the Natural History Museum?'

'Christ, how boring!' John chuckled. 'You worry me some-times, you know?' The chuckle faded and turned into a solicitous tone. 'You don't ever get out. You stay cooped up all the time, writing. You never go to clubs or bars or anywhere fun. If you don't watch out you'll be a real nerd.'

Whoa, Sadie said to herself. Brutal. This is like watching a David Attenborough programme on the mating dance of the rare and vicious species called human beings.

'Really, Morgan,' John continued, his voice full of pity. 'I should take you out and show you the town some night. I've got plenty of time on my hands, you know. Single, footloose, fancy-free, that's me!'

'Excuse me,' Jessica directed these words across the table to Morgan. Sadie knew she was about to move in for the kill. 'I'm sorry to interrupt and I know it's rude to listen in on someone's conversation, but I couldn't help overhearing – you did say you once worked at the Natural History Museum, didn't you?'

'Yes.' Morgan blushed, put his hand up to his glasses, removed them, then replaced them immediately. 'I did.'

'How fascinating. I've always wanted to go there. I was saying to my friend Sadie here only yesterday how much I'd like to see the Natural History Museum, wasn't I Sadie?'

'You were.' I feel like a straight man in a comic routine, Sadie thought. Except this isn't about comedy, it's about romance. Though at this particular point in time the two have a lot in common.

'I'm Jessica, by the way.' Stretching her hand toward Morgan, Jessica's face was suffused by a luminous smile. 'So sorry to interrupt.'

'Don't apologize, please.' Morgan shook her hand. 'And I'm Morgan.'

'And I'm John,' the footloose, fancy-free bachelor put in quickly, offering his hand. 'You two are English, aren't you?'

'Yes, yes we are.' Jessica gave John's hand a cursory shake. 'And this, as I said, is Sadie.'

Morgan shook hands with her, John didn't bother. He was too busy talking to Jessica.

'Morgan and I are both professors at Columbia. Right across the street. We would consider it our civic duty to help you get to know our city better. I'm from Boston originally and I've always regretted that silly tea party we threw.' John chuckled again. 'I love the queen. I'm an Anglophile extraordinaire, as it happens. Can't get enough of Buckingham Palace, Wimbledon, all those strawberries and cream – I lap it up. Unfortunately, Morgan here is busy working on his book, but I'd be pleased to take you to the Natural History Museum any time you'd like. In fact, if you'd like to go now, it would be no problem whatsoever.'

Jessica's eyes narrowed.

'How very kind of you to offer, John, but I couldn't possibly go now. However,' Jessica smiled, 'Sadie would love to go with you, wouldn't you Sadie?'

'Absolutely,' Sadie said, trying not to mind the sight of John's face falling. 'That would be wonderful.'

'Now?' John asked, his voice trying to backpedal out of the fix he'd put himself in.

'You did say you were free, and now's as good a time as any, isn't it Sadie?'

'Now would be excellent.' Sadie nodded.

'But you want to go too, Jessica,' John protested. 'You don't want to miss out, do you? We could go later on in the day. Or tomorrow, or any time you'd like.'

'Oh, I'd love to John, but I wouldn't want to stop Sadie from her chance now. She's had such a bad time lately with the accident and everything, she deserves a lovely trip to a museum with a lovely, gallant man such as yourself. Poor Sadie has been stuck with me for ages. She needs a break – don't you Sadie?'

Sadie could only nod, marvelling at how professionally

manipulative Jessica was, how she'd managed to slip in a reference to this unspecified 'accident' which would make John, effectively, an unfeeling monster if he declined to take her.

'Sadie, I hope you won't mind if I say you're looking a little pale.' John looked over at her with an overabundance of anxious concern before turning back to Jessica. 'I wouldn't want to get in the way of her recovery.'

'Nonsense, her leg needs the exercise! The surgeon said so. Off you go, you two.' Jessica waved them away as if they were bothersome insects. 'I'll see you back at the Carlyle, Sadie. Have fun! Enjoy! But don't overdo it!' She shooed them off.

'Goodbye, John, goodbye, Sadie.' Morgan looked a mixture of confused, pleased and very, very nervous. 'Nice meeting you. I'm sure you'll like the museum.'

'They'll *love* the museum,' Jessica smiled, 'they'll *adore* the museum.'

As Sadie left with the recalcitrant John, she could hear Jessica saying, 'Shall we get another cup of coffee, Morgan? I'd love to hear about your writing.' She couldn't hear his response, though, because John was holding the door open for her and muttering something, the only word of which she could make out was 'sandbagged'. As quickly as she could, Sadie limped up the stairs to Amsterdam Avenue.

Georgie had no idea where she was. She had the blue BMW in sight, though, and that was the important thing. She'd pulled it off; the stake-out had worked, more or less. The point was she'd found Morgan Blaine, she was following Morgan Blaine and wherever he went she'd go too. Poor Jessica, left behind in Manhattan, chasing after a man who wasn't there. He was here, on some American motorway, driving the car in front, and at some point he would have to stop. She'd beaten Jessica, she'd found him first, she had a chance now. And she was going to take it.

How clever she'd been to find him. It had been cold at six thirty in the morning. Standing in the street, rubbing her hands together, afraid to go and get a cup of coffee in case she missed him, she'd been freezing, bored and uncomfortable. At times she'd almost given up. But it had come good. She'd worked out that it was a house, not an apartment: there was only one bell, only one door knocker. All the blinds were pulled down when she'd arrived so she had assumed that he was asleep; all she had to do was wait. Waking him up might be disastrous, for all she knew he could be one of those men who were grumpy in the morning.

She'd positioned herself across the street from his house so she could get a better view, thinking that as soon as she saw the blinds go up on one of the top floors, she could move straight to his front door and wait for his departure. As she was rehearsing various ways of introducing herself – bumping into him accidentally on purpose saying, 'Oh, my God, you're Morgan Blaine, aren't you? My favourite writer!' and tripping up in front of him and pretending she'd sprained an ankle were the two top runners – she saw, too late, his front door open and a tall man who looked to be in his early forties with crew-cut dark-blond hair emerge, carrying a small suitcase and a bag of groceries. He hadn't opened the blinds, he'd given no hint of departure and he had, before she knew it, put the groceries in the boot of a car parked outside his door and was climbing into the front seat. At the same time as she saw a woman coming out of the house next door to Morgan's wave and heard her shout, 'Have a good time, Morgan', she realized that he had already started the car engine.

Watching Morgan manoeuvre out of his parking place, Georgie was, for an instant, rooted to her spot across the street. Only for an instant, though. Looking around wildly for a taxi, she saw one two cars away from Morgan's and flagged it down. God was on her side. An unoccupied taxi at eight in the morning in Manhattan, not just an unoccupied one, but one with a driver who simply said, 'Sure thing,' when she came out with the most ridiculous phrase she had ever used in her life, 'Follow that car.' Well, to be precise, she had said, 'Follow that blue BMW,' but it felt as silly as 'follow that car'.

At first, as they went along the Upper East Side Drive and then over the Triborough Bridge, she assumed he was going to the airport, either LaGuardia or JFK. It might, she knew, be a little tricky to follow him across the globe without any clothes or even a toothbrush, but she had plenty of cash and a variety of credit cards, so it was possible. Anything was possible, as long as she kept her wits about her and didn't lose his trail. Within a short time, however, it became clear that the airport was not his destination and Georgie stopped worrying so much. He wasn't driving too quickly, it was easy enough for the taxi to keep up with him, she could, for the first time since she'd woken up this morning, sit back and relax a little.

Poor Jessica, she kept repeating to herself. She's probably at Columbia now, asking anyone she can find where Morgan Blaine is. Would people there know where he was going? Was he on his way to a country house he went to regularly? Would Jessica find out and come after him herself? If she did, she'd be hours behind. There really wasn't any need to worry, not yet anyway, not until Jessica finally caught up with her.

'You sure you want to keep going, lady?' the cab driver, a man with a ponytail, probably in his mid thirties, turned back to look at her.

'I'm sure,' she answered. 'I don't care how much it costs. And don't worry, I have cash. Wherever that car goes, we go too.'

'Right.' He nodded and turned back to the road. 'Good to get out of the city,' he added. 'Looks like a lot of snow. The city is a bitch in snow.'

'I'm sure.' For the first time, Georgie took in her surroundings and noticed that the cab was decorated throughout with ET memorabilia: signs saying, 'phone home', photographs of ET in varying poses, a little ET doll hanging from the rear-view mirror. 'So . . .' she said, thinking she might as well be friendly as he had unwittingly saved her in a tight spot, 'you like ET, I see.'

'Love him.'

'How sweet. Steven Spielberg would be pleased.'

'Who's he?'

'You know, the director, the one who created ET. Steven Spielberg.'

'I don't know what you're talking about.'

'The film. You saw the film, didn't you?'

'What're you talking about? Someone creating ET? You trying to say someone made him up?'

'Um . . . yes.' Georgie looked at this man's eyes in the rear-view mirror. Was it her imagination or did they bear a scary resemblance to photographs of Charles Manson's eyes? 'Sort of,' she amended. 'In a way.'

'In what way?'

'I'm not sure exactly.'

'Because,' he reached behind his head, undid his ponytail, shook out a mane of greasy blond hair, 'if you're trying to say he's not real or anything, you're outta here.'

As in rubbed out? As in dead? Oh, my God!

'I think there's been a misunderstanding,' she said, very slowly. 'You see, I'm English.'

'So?' He'd stuck a cigarette in his mouth and was puffing away. The fact that it was unlit wasn't very reassuring.

'So, I'm . . . I'm not as familiar with ET as you are. But I'd like to be, obviously. I mean, I love him too. From a distance.'

'So what was all that crap about that Steven guy creating him?'

'A mistake. I'm jetlagged. I wasn't thinking straight.'

''Cause I can pull over right now.' He demonstrated his ability to do just that by swerving to the side of the highway.

'No, no, don't, please.' Georgie felt panic, pure panic. 'Listen, please. I've been in a mental institution. I don't know what I say sometimes. I say crazy things. But I don't mean them. Really. Please. Can we just forget what I said?'

'Well, sure.' He laughed, straightened the wheel. 'People think I'm crazy too sometimes. As if.'

'As if,' she repeated, joining in on the laughter with the manic abandon of relief.

'Hey, look. The BMW is taking this exit. Follow that car, huh?'

'You said it.' She gulped.

'Wow! This is fun!' After taking the unlit cigarette out of his mouth and stubbing it out in the ashtray, he turned around and looked at her. 'You gotta love this country, don't you?'

Georgie nodded her head so vigorously she thought she'd break her neck.

Chapter Fifteen

'Damn.' Red-haired John made a show of looking at his watch and then slapping his hand against his forehead. 'I can't believe it – I forgot. I have a meeting with one of my students. I have to get back to the campus. I'm sorry, Sadie. I'm afraid the Museum of Natural History is a no-can-do right now.'

'That's all right.' Sadie was, in fact, relieved by this pathetic lie. The idea of having to limp round a museum with someone who had no interest in being there with her wasn't enticing. 'I should be getting back to the hotel, anyway.'

'I'll get you a cab.'

'No, thank you. Could you tell me where I could get a bus, though?'

'You could get the subway on 116th street. There's an IRT stop.'

No, Sadie thought, I'm tired of the underground.

'I'd prefer a bus.'

After he'd told her how to get to the right bus stop, he shook her hand.

'I hope I'll be seeing you soon. You and Jessica,' he said the last word hopefully. 'What are you guys doing in the city?'

'It's a little complicated to explain.' Sadie smiled.

'Well, hey, pip pip and cheerio, then!' He forced a fake laugh. 'Later.'

John was obviously disappointed by how his day was turning out, but Sadie wasn't. She was in Manhattan, on her own, free to do whatever she wanted, at least for a while. Jessica would be charming Morgan, Georgie would still be hunting him down. She could walk the streets, ride the buses, be footloose and fancy-free herself.

Surprised by how easily she found the bus stop, Sadie stood waiting, gazing up and down Riverside Drive. New York City in the snow was magical, no doubt about it.

I could be someone different here, she thought. This is the kind of place that transforms people. Maybe . . . she stopped herself. She was here only as long as it took for Jessica and Georgie to work out whatever they had to work out with Morgan Blaine. When they were finished, she'd fly back to England, back to Shepherd's Bush.

It might be time to move out, she thought. I should let Andrew get on with life on his own, not depend on him as I've been doing. I can cope on my own now, or at least I think I can. It's time to try it out and see.

She was the only one to get on when the Number Four bus pulled into the stop. It was half full and Sadie found a seat towards the front, across from three beautiful young black girls who couldn't have been more than six years old, all of whom shared the same features. Were they triplets or siblings of close but different ages? She couldn't be sure, though the woman Sadie took to be their mother because she kept trying to restrain their fidgeting, looked tired enough to make triplets a strong possibility.

'Chill,' the little girl in the middle said to the one on her right before leaning over and tickling her mercilessly.

'Would you stop that . . .' the mother began, but her voice

was drowned out by the man sitting beside Sadie who had a mobile phone to his ear.

'Fucking hell. It can't be that fucking difficult to get fucking snow tyres on. You're lazy, you know that? You're fucking lazy.' He was in his twenties, wearing a dark heavy wool coat and a red baseball cap with the name Fred embroidered across the top. Sadie glanced across at the children and saw they were staring at him. She wanted to tell him to watch his mouth in front of them, but didn't dare.

'Suck it up, sweetheart,' Fred was shouting. 'I mean, get a fucking grip. I work, you don't. Get the goddamn tyres on and keep your mouth shut.' Everyone in the bus had turned to stare at him.

'Excuse me,' the man on his other side tapped Fred on the shoulder, 'language?'

'You got a problem with English?' Fred snapped, then returned his attention to the phone call. 'By six, right? You get the tyres on by six, or you're in fucking trouble.'

The man who had interrupted Fred stood up. He was tall and blond, attractively on the edge of handsome, but without crossing that good-looks line which led to self-conscious vanity. Dressed in casual trousers and a dark-blue sweater, he looked at Fred with a 'you've made a mistake' expression, reached out, grabbed the phone away from him and, as Sadie sat transfixed, walked the few steps to the front of the bus, which was at that moment pulling into the next stop. At the precise instant the doors opened, he threw Fred's mobile phone through them and out into the street.

'What the fuck?' Fred was shouting as he reached the other man at the front. 'What the fuck have you done?'

Taking a wallet out of his trouser pocket, the blond man flipped it open, pulled out a card and handed it to Fred.

'Sue me,' he said, in what Sadie recognized was a slight

southern accent. And then he smiled straight at Fred. Everyone was watching this drama, including the bus driver, who hadn't moved off from the stop.

'Fucking right I'll sue you!' Fred pushed the blond man aside. 'You.' He pointed at the driver. 'Wait here.' He stepped off the bus, and as he did, the bus driver closed the door and stepped on the accelerator, leaving Fred shouting and shaking his fist on the pavement.

'Nice move,' the blond man said to the driver.

'You too, bud,' the driver replied.

Sadie looked across at the tired mother and saw that her face had lost a decade. 'How very fine,' she said in a jubilant voice. Someone towards the back started to clap and the applause spread throughout the bus.

'My pleasure, folks.' The blond man bowed, then returned to his seat. As he passed her, he looked at Sadie and raised his eyebrows. She could feel her own eyebrows rising in return.

'Mommy, mommy, did you see what that man did?'

'You bet I saw.' The mother laughed, glancing at the blond man. 'We've just seen an endangered species, girls, a gentleman.'

'What's a gentleman?' one of the other girls asked.

'A man who isn't a dog.' She grinned and winked at Sadie. 'Come on now, little ladies, get ready, we're getting off at the next stop.'

Laughing quietly, Sadie stole a quick look at the blond man. His eyes were closed, his face at rest; he looked like he was having a perfect dream. Life must have worked out well for him, she thought. He'd have a nice flat and a good job and a beautiful wife. Maybe a few children. His wife wouldn't worry about any predictions she'd made with her brother years ago which hadn't come true. No, the Gentleman would have a wife who was a Superwoman and what's worse, most probably a likable Superwoman.

But *I'm* the one who was on this bus and saw that wonderful moment, Sadie said to herself. And *I'm* in a new place, seeing different people and being winked at by strangers with triplets. I wouldn't have missed this for the world.

So why am I being a prat and checking out the fourth finger of his left hand? The fact that he doesn't have a ring on doesn't necessarily mean anything. For God's sake, he's not trying to chat me up, he looks like he's *asleep*. It's hardly as if he's fascinated by me. I'm behaving like a fool staring at him. Georgie and Jessica's man-mania must be contagious.

I'll get off when the bus gets to Madison Avenue. If he opens his eyes and speaks to me before then, well . . . well, what? Am I going to spend my life getting pulled on public transport? I don't think so.

Still . . . he has those incredible green eyes. Traffic-light green. I've never seen anything like them before. Close up, they must be even more amazing. And he *did* raise his eyebrows at me. So he noticed me. Sort of.

Ten minutes later, as the bus swerved to the side, Sadie stood up and moved to the door. This was her stop. She didn't want to get out. She would have liked to stay in this warm bus, driving in the snow, spectating on New York City from her safe seat for the next three weeks. When Christmas day dawned they could stop at a restaurant and celebrate, sing carols together. She would know the life story of everyone on board by then. She and the Gentleman would have told each other secrets. For the rest of their lives, they'd be bound by this magical-mystery tour. Just before she stepped out, she looked back at him and saw his eyes were still closed. 'Well, that's that,' she thought. 'But it was fun for a while. And it was the first time I've thought of a man besides Piers in eighteen months.'

She didn't want to go straight to the hotel, she wanted to keep exploring on her own. 'I'll just get another cup of coffee,' she said to herself, 'and then I'll work out where to go next and how to get there.' Across the street she noticed a coffee shop, right beside a nail salon. Maybe I'll get my nails done too, she thought, and then shop for some clothes I can't afford. Then I'll stop in at the hotel, see if Georgie or Jessica have left any messages for me, and if they haven't, I'll do some sightseeing. This is like being a truant from school. I'm sure there's work I could do, but I'm not going to hurry back to do it. What's the point? Jessica has found Morgan Blaine, I helped her find him, I made sure she was alone with him. All of which will doubtless cause Georgie to go mental. I might as well enjoy myself while I can.

Feeling enormously proud of herself for not being intimidated by a foreign city and for having had the foresight to buy a guide to New York at Heathrow, thrilled by an increasing sense of reckless freedom, she crossed the street, went into the coffee shop and sat down at one of the stools at the counter. After she ordered coffee, she got out the guide from her bag and began to look through it.

'Is this, like, a date, or what?'

The question was being asked by a teenage girl sitting on Sadie's left. She had a nasal accent, a mess of curly black hair, a nose stud and was wearing a tight short black skirt and a long-sleeved fake-velvet red top.

'I dunno. Maybe. I guess.' The adolescent male to the left of the girl who answered, sounded painfully nervous. Sadie, who had raised her eyes from her guide when the girl spoke, was surprised to see the boy dressed in a suit and tie which looked as if they could be his father's. His dark hair had an inordinate amount of gel on it and he kept twirling the stool back and forth. Why weren't they at school? she wondered. Who had a date at a coffee shop at ten thirty in the morning? Jessica and Morgan, she answered herself, smiling. Perhaps this was the best time and the best method of dating yet to be invented.

''Cuz it's not like this *has* to be a date if you don't want it to be or anything.' The girl bit her lip. Sadie forced her eyes back to her guide.

'I don't mind.' He sighed audibly. 'I, like, like you and whatever.'

Biting her own lip to keep from laughing, Sadie couldn't help herself: she had to look, to see their facial expressions. She tried to be discreet by observing them in the mirror which ran along the wall behind the counter.

'But I'm not talking love or anything,' the boy added, frowning.

'I'm not either, babe.'

The girl said this so quickly and Sadie heard such defensiveness in her voice, she winced. At the same time a blast of cold air hit her. Someone had come in. Someone was taking a seat at the stool beside the boy's, three away from her own. And this someone was the Gentleman. But it couldn't be! He'd been asleep on the bus minutes before. Was she imagining things again? Like thinking she'd seen Piers the first time in that newsagents' shop? Sadie carefully, slyly, looked in the mirror behind the counter. Same hair, same face, same man.

'I feel sick,' the teenage boy said, continuing his twirling.

The Gentleman ordered a cup of coffee from the woman behind the counter. Sadie tried to breathe normally.

'Oh great.' The girl snorted. 'You going to throw up?'

'No, I mean sick like nervous sick.' Grabbing his tie and loosening the knot, the boy sighed again. 'It's, like, I'm not sure what to say to you. So my stomach's kind of twisted or something.'

He was smiling, the Gentleman, as the cup of coffee was placed in front of him. 'Thank you,' he said, glancing up at the woman who had served him. Sadie caught his eye in the mirror, she saw his expression of surprise, followed by amusement. He raised his eyebrows. She raised hers.

'Yeah, well, I'm nervous, too. It's not like we know each other so good. It's kind of nerve-making. Like going to school for the first time in a new class or something. Oh, fuck, that sounds so lame.' The girl shook her head. 'I wish I had a cigarette.'

'Me too.'

Sadie could see the Gentleman shake his head almost imperceptibly in a gesture of disapproval at the mention of smoking. They were watching each other watch the teenagers, strangers observing a romance in progress, commenting silently from the sidelines. She found herself unnaturally interested in the outcome of this conversation and the two people having it. 'Don't mess this up,' she wanted to say. 'You two might be made for each other. Look, he's worn a *suit* – isn't that cute? And she's put on lipstick and mascara. You both care. Don't be afraid of each other, go for it!'

'You know, I got this friend who says I shouldn't be seeing you,' the boy blurted out.

The Gentleman put his elbows on the counter and his head in his hands.

'What friend?' the girl's voice could have cut concrete.

'Nobody you know.'

'If I don't know him, why's he dissing me?'

'He's just like *heard* of you, is all.'

'Heard *what*?'

'That you're a heartbreaker.'

'A heartbreaker?' The girl paused, took a breath, then giggled. 'Yeah, right.'

The Gentleman's head was out of his hands, his smile had reappeared.

'I mean it, 'cuz, you're so pretty and everything.'

Sadie could see it all, the girl's flushed face, the boy's

anxious, devouring stare, the Gentleman's thumb pointed up by the side of his coffee cup.

'You wanna take a walk or something?'

'Sure.' The boy practically leapt from his stool. 'You're really cool, you know?'

She kissed him. A quick, passionate kiss. Then stood up, smoothed down her skirt and let him put his arm around her and walk her out of the door.

The Gentleman swung his stool around to face Sadie.

'Whoa,' he said. 'They had me worried there for a second. That comment about the friend saying he shouldn't go out with her, that was a close call.'

'I know. I could feel her bristling beside me.'

'But he pulled it out of the bag with "heartbreaker". Nice move.'

Like you on the bus, she thought.

'Very nice move.' She nodded.

'Young love.' He shrugged. 'It's a killer.'

You're the killer, Sadie Hawkes said to herself, and I'm dead in the water.

Jessica was confused. After she'd asked Morgan about his research work in the bayou, he'd spent twenty minutes detailing its flora and fauna. At least that's what she *thought* he was doing; it was difficult for her to follow the technical terms. She wanted him to talk about the spirit, the soul of the bayou, not the bugs. But then again, as she knew, God was in the details. Morgan wrote so beautifully about the South because he knew every plant and organism. He must have worked from the inside out, studying the minutiae in order to get across the bigger picture. That was admirable, definitely. He was a serious person, not just a popular writer. She should be pleased, she should try and concentrate. She really should.

'So, Morgan –' she interrupted a treatise on the properties of moss. Concentrating so hard had made her eyes tired and her brain limp. Any more of it and she'd be a piece of moss herself. 'You don't have a Southern accent. Where do you come from originally?'

'Boston. Like John. But we hadn't met before we met here, if you see what I mean.' The face he made showed his displeasure with himself. 'I'm sorry. I'm not a scintillating conversationalist, I'm afraid. You ask me about the bayou and I go on and on about boring things and you ask me a straightforward question and I flub it.'

'Oh, don't apologize, please.' Jessica could hear her own voice stuttering slightly. What did 'flub' mean? What did anything mean? Her brain wasn't functioning at all. It felt as if the mosquitoes he'd been describing before he'd launched into the moss had invaded her head and were swarming there like airborne maggots. Was this love or was it a caffeine overdose? While her foot was tapping under the table, her nails were tapping on top of it. Where were they in the conversation? She could tell he expected her to say something, but what? Boston. That was it. He came from Boston. She should ask him about Boston.

'Boston.' She grimaced. What about Boston? 'Are there lots of mosquitoes in Boston?'

'Some.' He laughed.

I came across an ocean to find you. I fell in love with you at first sight. But I can't tell you that, can I? You'd think I'm mad. You already do. Maybe I am.

'I haven't spent a lot of time in Boston, though.'

'Really?' Jessica grabbed the edge of the table. Get a grip she told herself. This is not the place or time to have an identity crisis. Focus. Stop breathing so quickly. 'Why's that?'

'My parents sent me away to school in New Hampshire when I was twelve.'

Reform school? Was he another Daniel Canter? Well, that wasn't so bad. In fact, it was a good sign. Unless . . . didn't mass murderers spend their youths pulling wings off flies? Was that why he was so interested in nature? Could that be why he could write such violent scenes? Because he'd killed someone when he was twelve? Car theft was one thing, murder . . .

'Do you mind me asking what you did?'

'Excuse me?'

'What did you do to be sent away?'

'Oh —' he laughed again. 'I didn't do anything. Except be born, I guess. My father went to this school, so did my grandfather, it was a family thing, St Paul's. That whole WASP, boarding-school business. It's a joke, really.'

Boarding school. It couldn't have been better. They had so much in common. But her breathing wouldn't slow down. And the mosquitoes were still buzzing. They wouldn't leave her brain. She could see them — little dots swirling and buzzing.

'Jessica? Are you all right?'

'I want to sail to Tahiti.' She was staring at her coffee cup. Now the mosquitoes were inside the coffee cup and they were drawing her into it with them. 'I hate my life.'

'Jessica . . .'

Her name was a faraway, faint sound. The sound her head made when it hit the table was a lot louder.

ET's biggest fan turned down the dirt road, following the BMW at a discreet distance.

'Stop here,' Georgie commanded, before remembering the dangerously loony person she was talking to and adding, 'Please.' She wanted to hang back a bit, give Morgan time to get out of his car and into the house before she approached him. There weren't any other cars around. The house, at the end of the mile and a half private road, looked deserted.

'Is that guy your ex?' the driver asked as he put on the brakes.

'No. He's someone I want to surprise.'

'This place looks spooky. All these . . . all these trees and shit.' He waved yet another unlit cigarette in the air. 'I'd be scared if I were you. Looks like a witch's house. Those gables. And out in the middle of nowhere. Woo. Blair Witch Two.'

So he does watch movies. Then why . . . ? Georgie shook her head. Now was not the time to figure out the deranged psyche of this cab driver. She could see Morgan in the distance getting out of his car and heading for the porch. He was a big man. She hadn't noticed in Manhattan how big he was. Nothing wrong with that, she thought. He doesn't have a paunch, just a large frame.

'I'm calling it two hundred, even. How's that?'

'Fine.' Pulling out a wad of notes, Georgie counted off two hundred. Did he need a tip? Who knew what he'd do if he didn't get one? She peeled off another twenty, hesitated, then added another twenty as well.

'You sure you'll be all right here?'

'I'll be fine, really.'

''Cause I could hang out here for awhile.'

'No, no thank you.' Go and talk to your alien friends, she thought. Go and phone home. The screen door closed. Morgan was in the house. No other cars were visible, no lights were on in the house, he was there alone. She was in luck. 'There's a place for you to turn around here. You don't need to go up the driveway any further. I'll walk.'

'Cool.' Putting his hair back in a ponytail, the cab driver said: 'Groovy,' and then, 'Peace,' as Georgie got out of the back seat. Hippy or alien? Or both? she asked herself. As if it matters. That's one person I'll never have to see again, thank God.

*　　*　　*

162

The large clapboard house did, indeed, look spooky, mostly because it was set so far back from the main road, had no neighbouring houses around and was topped by the gables the driver had mentioned. It seemed in decent enough shape, though. No signs of obvious decay. In the summer it would be lovely. The perfect place to get away from the city and relax. Georgie started walking towards it, slowly, practising how she would introduce herself to Morgan. The sprained-ankle ruse was clearly out, unless he'd believe she'd happened to take a random walk in the snow down a mile and a half of road before falling over two inches away from his porch. An edited version of the truth, she decided, was the best option. The, 'I love your book so much I came to see you' line. There was the risk he might think she was Kathy Bates in *Misery* but it wouldn't take her long to disabuse him of that. He'd be pleased; authors were always thrilled to know they had readers. They could discuss *Voodoo Women* over a cup of coffee, then move on naturally to other subjects.

It would have been helpful, she was aware, as she crunched over the snow, if she'd worn boots instead of heels, and maybe this suit wasn't exactly right for a country setting, but then again tartan had an air of healthy Scottish walks on the moors to it, so she could have done a lot worse.

And I can tell him about the mad cab driver as well, she thought. That should be good for a few laughs. Poor Jessica. Where is she now? Sitting outside an empty office in Columbia, fuming? Well, she'd get over it. Sometime.

Just as she reached the steps that led up to the porch, she saw Morgan Blaine open the door and step out.

'Who the hell are you?' he asked. His voice was as rugged as his looks. Unprepared for the aggressive tone, Georgie found herself speechless – speechless and frightened. It struck her in that second that she didn't actually know anything about

Morgan Blaine. Yes, he might be a great writer, but the taxi driver had been perfectly competent at his job as well. She was stuck in the middle of nowhere with a stranger who could rape and strangle her, hide her in the woods, and no one would even know she'd been here.

What was she doing? Why had she taken an hour and a half taxi ride with a lunatic to follow a man she'd never met? Somehow, it was all Jess's fault, this predicament she was in. She would have never followed Morgan Blaine into the woods if she hadn't been so intent on finding him before Jess did. What crazy game were they playing? And why? Why exactly were they playing it?

'I'm Georgie,' she finally forced herself to speak, 'Georgina Harvey. I'm a big –' don't say 'fan' she cautioned herself, remember Kathy Bates – 'admirer of your work. I've come a long way to find you.'

'Which work is that?' His squinting eyes stared at her, up and down, then up again, landing on her face.

'*Voodoo Women*,' she responded quickly. 'I loved *Voodoo Women*.'

'Is that right?' He didn't move. She didn't either.

'Yes, absolutely. I've come a long way to find you. I don't mean to disturb you, I just—'

'If you don't mean to disturb me, what do you call this? Showing up out of the blue? And how did you get here?' The voice was unrelentingly harsh. The hands were on the hips. Morgan Blaine was not pleased.

'I took a taxi. Look,' Georgie moved a step forward, then, seeing his expression, retreated, 'I know this is going to sound a bit mad, but, well, people do mad things sometimes and . . .' she faltered under his oppressive stare. This was *so* mad, she realized, there was no rational explanation. The whole thing was a disaster from start to finish. What was she supposed to do now?

'If you want me to leave, maybe you could call a cab for me.'

'Of course I want you to leave. But while you're here –' he pulled a set of keys out of his pocket – 'bring in the grocery bag out of the trunk.' After tossing her the keys, which she managed not to catch, he turned his back on her and went into the house.

This was so humiliating, Georgie was flabbergasted. The man was a rude son of a bitch, ordering her to unpack his car like that. But what choice did she have? If she wanted him to call her a taxi, she'd have to play by his rules. *What am I doing here? I should be in the office where I belong. What's happening while I'm not? Is it going to pieces without me? Have I given up everything I've worked so hard for because I happened to remember that scene with Jess, Joanna and the dresses? Why did it have to come back at me like that and throw me off balance, toss me into this finding-Morgan-Blaine-first frenzy?*

Georgie bent over and fished for the keys in the two inches of snow. It was bloody freezing and she hadn't put on a proper winter coat, she hadn't eaten properly, she was in the middle of the woods with a surly, up his own ass author and she'd have to shell out another two hundred dollars to get back. *Fantastic*, she muttered to herself as she opened the boot of the BMW. *Bloody fantastic. This is the trip from hell.*

Jessica could remember flashes of what had happened: the waitress and Morgan beside her; someone lifting her; someone – was it the waitress? – saying, 'She needs to lie down.' Then Morgan saying 'Should we go . . . ?' The cold air of the street. But before that, the clarity of knowing she didn't want the leopardskin coat they were draping over her, trying to throw it off, desperate to get it off her. Then a taxi. A building. A lift. Morgan carrying her across a threshold. A bed. Clean sheets. A washcloth on her forehead. The comfort and bliss of sleep descending.

And now, waking up to Morgan Blaine. Who was sitting beside her bed, reading a book.

'You rescued me,' she said, with a lazy, weak smile.

'Hey.' He shut his book. 'How are you feeling?'

This was a dream world, a world where she was tucked in and looked after and happy.

'I fainted, didn't I? And you rescued me.'

'Well, I wasn't going to leave you in that coffee place, was I?'

'You carried me, I remember.' He must have taken off her coat and shoes; otherwise she was dressed as she had been.

'Um . . .' He had a sideways smile. It was possibly the sweetest smile she'd ever seen. 'Was that a good thing or a bad thing to do?'

'Good.' She never, ever wanted to leave this bed. 'I came from England to find you. I'm so glad I did.'

'You . . . ? Jessica, listen, you must be exhausted and really confused. I was going to take you to the hospital, but the waitress said you'd fainted and people do faint and it would take hours to be seen in the emergency room with horrible stab victims everywhere and what you needed was some rest.'

'She was right.' The peace. The unbelievable peace and relief of knowing that some day had arrived and her prince had come. She felt as if she were in a cocoon, protected from every single thing that might go wrong in life.

'Do you faint a lot?'

'Occasionally. I have incredibly low blood pressure. Any time a nurse takes it, she does it again because she can't believe she has the right reading. But I haven't fainted for a long time and I've never fainted quite so dramatically. I was tired – I didn't sleep at all last night because I was thinking about meeting you. And then I met you and there were those awful mosquitoes in my coffee.' There was no point in trying to stop smiling. She couldn't begin to stop smiling. 'I want to be honest with you straight away, Morgan. I don't want to hide anything. You don't mind, do you? Being tracked down? Georgie – my stepsister – and I came on the spur of the moment. There was Project X, which didn't work out at all. And then . . . oh, God, it's such a long story.'

'Are you sure you're feeling all right? Can I get you something? Some tea?' Morgan took off his glasses, then immediately replaced them.

'No.' She reached out for his hand. 'Don't go. Don't leave, Morgan. Promise?' Jessica was weak with happiness. Love, she decided, didn't give you energy, it paralysed you. Was this what it felt like to take drugs, as if you were on another planet and everything had slowed down and the world was floating, all time suspended?

'I promise.' He squeezed her hand. He was wearing dark-blue corduroy trousers and a blue workshirt. Everything about him was clean and fresh.

'There were so many awful people we interviewed and then there was Stephen. He was different. At first, I thought . . . but then there was this waiter . . .' Jessica tensed. 'That boarding school of yours, what was it like there? I mean, was it all male?'

'It used to be, but not by the time I went. Thank God.'

Thank God.

'You believe in fate, don't you, Morgan?'

'I'm beginning to.'

That sideways smile. No one else should get to see that smile. It should be reserved for her alone.

'Um, Jessica, I think maybe you hurt yourself more than you know when you banged your head. I think you need to get your strength back. I'll fix you something to eat.

Lie back and relax, I'll be back with some food in a few minutes.'

'Voodoo.' Jessica watched Morgan exit the room then closed her eyes. 'It's magic.'

Chapter Sixteen

It wasn't impossible to lug the heavy bag of groceries into the house, but it wasn't easy either. Georgie, struggling with it, slipping, almost falling over into the snow as she made her way up the stairs to the porch, couldn't believe it. Wasn't Morgan Blaine at least going to open the door for her? Apparently not. There was no sign of him, so she put the bag down, opened the door, held it open with her foot and picked the bag up yet again.

'Put it in the kitchen – in the back on the right,' she heard him yell.

'Screw you,' she muttered as she followed his instructions, walking down a hallway past a living room which she could see was full of maritime objects – a carved swordfish above the fireplace, paintings of old sailboats, two antique life preservers, and oars on the walls. When she reached the kitchen, she dropped the bags on the kitchen table and stared. It was painted sea blue. A mural of swimming tropical fish ran through it. Morgan Blaine was as mad as the taxi driver. Why, if he had such a deep attachment to the ocean, was he in a house in the middle of the woods?

'You can unpack it now.' He was standing behind her, at the threshold. His voice, close up, was even more scornful than it had been at a distance. It stopped her instinctive 'fuck you' response and had her immediately obeying his command without turning to look at him. Taking a tin of canned corn out of the top of the bag, she stood uncertainly, wondering where the hell she was supposed to put it.

'The cupboard,' he said, 'is generally a good place for tinned food. Oh, and shout when lunch is ready.' She turned and stared at him. He turned and walked out.

He must have been six foot two. He had a military haircut. His face was tanned, not artificially, but with a colour that came from constant exposure to the wind, and, Georgie thought, the sea. Ahab. She was standing in the kitchen of Captain Ahab's house. Did that make her Moby Dick?

Alone, with a can of corn in her hand, she sank onto a pine kitchen chair and weighed up her options. Stay and be humiliated some more. Leave. The latter was definitely the better one.

Georgie, for a reason she couldn't begin to explain to herself, put the can of corn away into a cupboard, before leaving the kitchen.

'Mr Blaine?' she called out from the living room. 'I think I should leave now. Can you ring a cab company?'

'So what's the deal?' He was coming down the stairs, his feet clomping heavily on the wood. 'Can't find the can opener?' He was at the door to the living room. 'Problems with lunch?' He stepped towards her.

'I want to leave, that's what the deal is.' You've stood up to bullies before, she told herself. Most of the men in the City are bullies. This man is no different. Stand up to them and they'll back down, otherwise they'll walk all over you.

'You want to leave?' He crossed his arms. 'You've come all this way – and judging by your accent, it's a very long way indeed, to see me – to sit at the feet of the great author. And now that you're here, at the end of this epic journey, you want to leave? That doesn't seem right. Don't you want to feed me? Give me sustenance for my hungry creative soul?'

Why was he so obsessed with food? More importantly, how was she going to force him to ring a taxi?

'Sit down,' he barked, then went over to the fireplace, took a box of matches from the mantelpiece and proceeded to light the papers underneath the kindling and logs, before turning to face her. Georgie had disobeyed him and remained standing.

'Let me guess. Reasonably attractive young woman tracks down famous author in his country hideaway. Famous author thinks: oh lucky me! Oh, goody, goody, goody,' Morgan Blaine clenched both fists and pumped them, 'I am so fortunate to have her here. We can talk about my work. She will understand my every heartbeat, each thought that comes into my sensitive brain. We will make tender, caring love. No, scratch that. We'll have jungle sex. Orgasms by the thousands. Guinness world record breaking orgasms. After which we'll share a cup of hot chocolate and our innermost secrets in bed and presto!' He snapped his fingers. 'My God, we're engaged! Was that the plan?'

Reasonably attractive?

'No.' Her own voice was unfamiliar to her. She'd never whined before, never. But then she'd never been in such an embarrassing situation before.

'Why don't you tell me what the plan was, then?' Dressed in a lumberjack shirt and jeans, he looked like he could enter a bodybuilding contest. His eyes were dark blue and full of contempt. If he weren't so nasty, she thought, he'd be good-looking, but this superior attitude made his face so harsh it was impossible to imagine him in any moment of intimacy.

'There was no plan per se. I was more or less—' she couldn't think of an appropriate word.

'Winging it?' he suggested.

Georgie nodded.

'Hey, Idiot, I'm here!' The voice came from the hallway and belonged, Georgie could see as she swivelled to see its owner, to a blonde woman. She was dressed almost identically to Morgan, but with a bright-blue ski jacket on, and her hiking boots clomped as she made her way into the living room. A wife wouldn't yell out, 'Hey, Idiot!' would she? So who was she? His girlfriend? She looked to be in her late twenties, her hair was straight and shoulder-length, she was smiling as she brushed snow off her jacket. As soon as she saw Georgie, her smile broadened.

'Company. You didn't tell me.' She threw a sidelong glance at Morgan, who was still standing in front of the fire. 'I would have dressed for the occasion.' Her eyes travelled back to Georgie, and rested on her suit.

'This is . . .' Morgan smiled for the first time. 'This is someone whose name I have forgotten but who is a huge fan of my work.'

'Really?' The blonde turned to Morgan. They were both grinning now. 'Which work exactly?'

'*Voodoo Women.*'

'Ah . . . *Voodoo Women*. I keep forgetting how popular that is.'

'She came a long way to find me. She's foreign.'

'Does she speak English?'

'I *am* English.' Georgie said, flustered. Knowledge of the absurdity of her position escalated. Were they laughing at her? Yes. Not openly, but with those complicit grins of theirs, and their way of talking as if she were a stray dog who had wandered into the room. Which, she knew, she was. In a way. If they'd known the whole truth, the story of Project X, they'd be rolling in the aisles.

'Excellent!' The blonde walked over to Morgan and slipped her arm around his waist. 'God, you're amazing, Morgan.

A world-wide reputatation. I'm so proud to be related to you.'

Sister? Sister-in-law? What? And why, Georgie asked herself, do I feel a sliver of jealousy? This makes no sense at all. Two minutes ago I couldn't wait to leave. Now all I want to know is what this woman is doing here.

'I'm this great writer's cousin,' the woman said, gripping and pinching his waist. 'Eliza. And you are?'

'Georgie. Georgina Harvey.'

'That's it!' Morgan snapped his fingers. 'That's her name. I should have remembered. We're practically engaged. All we need is sex and hot chocolate to clinch the deal.'

'Look –' Georgie felt her body tense. Enough was enough. She hated being made fun of like this, even if she was well aware she had offered herself up for heaps of ridicule. It was time to get her pride back. Somehow. It was time for her to go on the offensive. 'I realize I've intruded on you here, and I apologize. If this is the way you treat your readers, however, Mr Blaine, I think you're a very patronizing person.'

'Jesus, Morgan. What have you been doing to her?' Eliza asked.

'All I did was ask her to make some lunch.' Morgan shrugged. 'Is that so patronizing?'

'It's not very friendly.'

'She showed up on my doorstep, for God's sake. Am I supposed to cook for her?'

'I'm here.' Georgie was aware that she shouted this. 'I'm in the room. You don't have to keep saying "she".' She looked at Eliza. 'I'll call a taxi if you'll just give me the number. That's all I want now – to leave.'

'I'm afraid that's impossible,' Eliza said.

Oh, no. Is she in some conspiracy with him? Are they a pair of sadists, do they want to keep me in this house and torture me?

'The snow is officially a blizzard now. I heard it before I trekked over here. The roads are closing. You'll have to wait for a snow plough. Of course you can borrow some boots and heavy clothes and trek back with me to my place, but that's three miles away and you won't be able to get a taxi there, either. I think you should stay, Georgina.' Letting go of Morgan, Eliza moved over to the sofa and seated herself. 'You know, Morgan will never discuss his work with me. I've always wanted him to talk about *Voodoo Women*. Maybe we can gang up on him and force him to speak. That would be excellent. Hell, *I'll* cook the lunch if it's such a big issue between you guys.'

'Kind of hard to get a taxi back to England anyway, isn't it?' Morgan cocked his head to the side.

'Manhattan. I'm staying in a hotel in Manhattan.'

'You don't say.' Morgan rolled his eyes at Eliza. 'And I honestly thought she had cabbed it here from London.'

Georgie wanted to disappear. She'd walked straight into that one and it hurt badly.

'Truce?' Eliza put her hands in the air. 'Time out? Behave, Idiot.' She glared at her cousin. 'We're going to have a serious discussion about literature. What were the first lines of *Voodoo Women*? Wait a second, I've got it. 'Women in the bayou know their business. And that business is magic.' Whoa. We could take a lifetime on that one. Okay, I'll go get lunch. You two try to be civilized while I'm in the kitchen.'

Eliza left the room. Georgie stared at Morgan. Morgan stared at Georgie.

'Why do you have all these nautical things and fish in a house in the middle of the woods?' she finally asked.

'Why do you wear such weird clothes?'

Georgie closed her eyes, shook her head, and clenched her teeth. She pictured Morgan Blaine with a fishing hook in his eye. That made her feel a little better.

*　　*　　*

174

Morgan brought Jessica's food in on a tray. He'd made chicken sandwiches and a mixed salad, accompanied by a glass of sparkling water and slices of apple. There was a clean white linen napkin, and a small blue vase with a pink tulip in it. Jessica sat up, as he arranged the pillows behind her, and said, 'Yum.'

'You need some sustenance.' He patted the pillows. 'You've had a shock, fainting like that and ending up in a stranger's apartment.'

'I couldn't be better,' she replied. 'Honestly. I feel wonderful. And you're not a stranger, not really. I told you. I came from London to find you.'

'Uh huh. We can talk about that later.' He sat down at the foot of the bed. 'You know, you said something before you fainted. You said, "I hate my life." Is that true?'

'Sort of.' Jessica picked up one of the sandwiches, took a bite. It was delicious. Everything was delicious. She had never been happier in her life. She was so happy it was impossible to remember why she'd been unhappy before. Is this what it feels like to be born again? she wondered. Have I had a religious experience?

'Why did you sort of hate it?'

'I don't know.' Don't chew and talk at the same time, she told herself. It's unattractive.

'Jessica,' he leaned forward, 'I'm worried about you. Some of the things you've said, they don't make sense.'

'I'm fine, Morgan, really I am. Would you like some chicken?' He shook his head. 'A piece of apple?'

'OK.'

Jessica passed a slice of apple across the bed. I'd like to put it in his mouth, she thought, but not yet. Not quite yet. She lay back and watched as he ate it. He didn't seem to chew at all – was *he* nervous about eating in front of her as well?

She watched as he swallowed and swallowed again. He

175

coughed. His face went pink. He coughed again. His face turned red.

'Morgan? Morgan?'

Morgan's hand was at his throat. His eyes were bulging.

'Oh, my God! Oh my God! Morgan!' What was she supposed to do? What was it called – the Hemlock Manoeuvre? Or what? Whatever it was, she didn't know how to do it. 'Morgan!' Jumping out of bed, she rushed round behind him, put her arms around his chest – she'd seen people do something like this on TV – and pulled in as hard as she could. Nothing happened. 'Oh my God, oh no!' Jessica began to thump his back. She pummelled it with her fists. 'Breathe! You have to breathe! Swallow some more! Please don't die!' The telephone. Where was the telephone? Not in this room. Where? And what was the emergency number in this country? She was out of the door and in the hall when Morgan called out. 'Jessica – Jessica –' he appeared on the threshold – 'I'm all right now. I've swallowed it. It's OK.'

'Oh my God.' Jessica ran into his arms. 'You scared me.'

'I scared myself.' He said, hugging her. 'Now *you've* rescued *me*. You saved my life.'

'No, no, no. I didn't know what to do. That Himmler Manoeuvre or whatever it's called. I never took first aid. God.' She leant her head against his chest. 'That was awful.'

'Come back to bed.' Steering her back into the bedroom, Morgan insisted she get under the covers. 'We seem to be prone to medical mishaps.' He smiled. 'What a pair we make.'

We're a pair already. Excellent.

'Well,' he took off his glasses, sat back down on the end of the bed. 'There you are, lying in my bed and I don't even know why you're here – in New York, I mean. Are you here on business? Do you work or do I have a fabulously rich and famous heiress between my sheets?'

'Um. I work,' she said, panicking. He was a famous author.

She was a non-functioning headhunter. He probably hated people who worked in the City or Wall Street. He'd prefer someone who had a creative job, a painter, a sculptress. How could she explain why she had such a non-job?

'My stepsister, Georgina. She and I—' Georgie – she'd forgotten all about Georgie. Any minute now and Georgie might be ringing his bell. Clever, totally successful Georgie. Jessica sat up straight, her mind in a whirl of dismay. 'Oh, God, Georgie might ring your bell at any second. Did I tell you? I should have told you. Project X was her idea. But we were supposed to be in it together. She's already cheated. She went to find you without telling me. She'll be furious with me for finding you first. Don't answer if your bell rings – promise you won't answer.'

'Jessica, Jessica.' He moved to the chair beside the bed and took her hand. 'Poor Jessica.' Morgan brushed her hair away from her forehead with his other hand. 'Should I call Sadie at the hotel? You said you were staying at the Carlyle didn't you? Would you like her to come over and help out?'

'No, please. Don't. I like it like this – just us.'

'I really don't want to take advantage of you in this condition. You should talk to someone you trust.'

'I trust you, Morgan.'

'What's Sadie's last name?'

'Hawkes. But don't ring her. Believe me, I'm fine. Just a little tired. It's jetlag, that's all.'

'Then sleep. Sleep as long as you like. I'll be here when you wake up.'

'Promise?'

'I promise. Look, I'll leave the tray on the side table there and you can have some more sandwiches if you wake up and are hungry. But no apples, OK? Just in case.'

'You won't let Georgie in if she rings your bell?' she asked as she watched him remove the tray and place it on the table.

'Jessica, please.' Morgan bent over her. 'Get some sleep. We'll talk later, when you're better.'

As she turned over on her side, Jessica looked around the bedroom. It was painted white and had beautiful framed pictures of flowers hanging on the walls. Why hadn't she listened properly when he was talking about nature before? He could talk about moss for ever. As long as he talked to *her* about it, not Georgie.

'You wouldn't like her suit,' she said, yawning. 'I know you wouldn't.'

'I'm sure I wouldn't.' He patted her on the shoulder. 'Sweet dreams.'

She was standing in a clearing, barefoot, moss underneath her feet. Music was playing, someone was singing, but she couldn't make out the words. Walking slowly, feeling the spongy moss between her toes, she went into the woods on the edge of the clearing, listening, trying to hear the words. The murmur became more distinct the further she went forward. Yet the music had stopped and there were only the words now, in hushed tones.

'I called the hotel. Her friend Sadie wasn't in her room. I'm not sure what to do now. She's so confused.'

'Did she hit her head when she fainted?'

This was a female voice. The woods began to recede. When they disappeared altogether, Jessica opened her eyes.

'Yeah, she banged it on the table. I'm sorry to call you like this. But I didn't know what else to do, whether I should take her to a hospital or not. I figured you'd know what to do.'

'She might have concussion. You should have taken her to the hospital, Morgan.'

'I know, I know. Shit. She's so messed up. She was saying she'd come all the way from England to find me and that she was up all last night thinking about me.'

'God, she must have *really* banged her head.' The female voice laughed.

'And there was something about some Project X. Plus she hates her life. And there's a stepsister she's terrified of who she thinks is going to turn up here at any second and something to do with a suit.'

'A law suit?'

'A clothes kind of suit, I think. She said I'd hate the suit.'

'We might have to get her a psychiatric evaluation at Saint Luke's. I know one of the psychiatrists there, he's good on delusional patients.'

Jessica, who had been on her side facing the far wall, sat up abruptly.

'I'm fine. I'm absolutely fine.'

'Jessica,' Morgan and the female were standing by the doorway of the bedroom, 'I'm sorry if we woke you up. This is a friend of mine, Louisa Stafford. I called her up and asked her to come over because she's a doctor.'

'I'm absolutely fine.' Jessica scrutinized Louisa Stafford. Mid thirties. Reasonably pretty in a sloppy, dishevelled sort of way. Baggy trousers, baggy sweatshirt, oval face, short, dark hair. 'I fainted. That's all. I don't need a doctor.'

A psychiatric evaluation? Who's the crazy one? This Louisa woman who wants to lock me up.

'Let me look at you, anyway. It won't hurt.' Louisa started toward the bed. Jessica shrank back into the pillows.

'You can't put me in some loony bin.'

Or could she? Was it against the law to lock someone up in America without her consent? Or did they do it all the time because they had so many crazy people wandering around?

'I'm from England,' she said forcefully. 'I have friends who know members of the royal family.'

'Jessica, please.' Morgan came to the other side of the bed, opposite Louisa. 'She only wants to look at you. Of course no one is going to put you in a loony bin.'

'Which members of the royal family?' Louisa smiled at Jessica. 'I'm only asking because I have a little crush on Prince William. And hey, don't tell me I'm too old for him, OK? I know already.' She took Jessica's wrist in her hand and felt for her pulse. 'So you know the queen? That's very nice, Jessica.'

'I don't *know* her. I never said I knew her.'

This was not going well. This was going very badly.

'Morgan tells me you were talking to him about some Project X. Do you want to tell me a little about that? Is there a conspiracy going on you'd like to talk about?'

'No there is not. I – there's nothing to tell.' Jessica felt her lips form a pout. No way would she tell her about Project X. This doctor with her professional voice and her baggy clothes could take a long walk off a short pier. Even though she'd slept in hers, even though she'd been through as much as she'd been through this morning, Jessica's clothes weren't as creased or as sloppy. She had that much over Louisa, at least.

'And your stepsister who might show up any second – why are you so frightened of her?'

'I'm not. We're very close, actually.' She shook Louisa's hand off her wrist and sat up straighter. Pride, she said to herself. Get your pride back. 'I appreciate your concern, but it's unnecessary, really. We came here because we're great admirers of *Voodoo Women*. Is there something wrong with that?'

Louisa narrowed her eyes. Then turned to look at Morgan again. Jessica couldn't make out what the expression on her face conveyed.

'No, of course there's nothing wrong with admiring voodoo women, Jessica.' She stood up. 'I've never met a voodoo woman myself, but I'm sure if I did, I'd admire her. Very, very much. Anyway, you seem fine, physically. I think you might need a few tests, though. Just to make sure that bump didn't affect you in any way. I'm going to make a quick call to St Luke's—'

'No!' Jessica sprang out of bed. 'I told you. I'm fine. All right,' she ignored Louisa and concentrated on Morgan, 'it was a crazy project. I admit that. But if you knew what hell we went through, if you knew how I had to sit and watch some bonkers accountant tell me a salt shaker was a boat and all that peanuts and knots and current business, if you only knew, you'd understand. I know other fans must want to meet you. We came further than most people to find you, that's all. I don't need any bloody psychiatric tests. I shouldn't have told you about it all but I wanted to be honest with you. I didn't want to play games. I thought—'

'Morgan,' Louisa interrupted in a preternaturally calm voice, 'you and I should have a talk in the living room. Jessica, I'm going to get you a Valium from my bag, all right? It will calm you down.'

'I don't need any bloody Valium. Morgan, please—'

'I think Louisa knows what she's doing, Jessica. A Valium won't hurt.'

Louisa left the room, Jessica stared at Morgan. What she saw in his eyes made her drop her own eyes to the floor.

Her shoes were beside the bed. She put them on, grabbed her bag and coat off the bedpost, stood with her feet planted like a boxer's.

'I'm leaving now, Morgan. You know where I'm staying—'

'Jessica, please, don't. Louisa's not going to—'

'I'm leaving. I don't know why you have treated me like this. Rick would have never called a doctor in to try and tranquillize Eva, would he?' She waited for his response. He didn't make one. 'Would he?'

'Um. I guess not. Jessica, I don't know what you're—'

Jessica pushed past him, out into the hallway, where Louisa was heading straight for her.

'Jessica—'

'Fuck you and your drugs and your loony bin.' Jessica shoved her to the side with her elbow and ran, her head held high, out of the door.

Chapter Seventeen

And where was Sadie?

Walking along Fifth Avenue.

Surrounded by crowds of people.

On her own.

Not minding in the slightest that people were jostling her or that the snow was seeping through her shoes.

The Gentleman had asked her to meet him in the same coffee shop for breakfast the next day. That was after he'd said he had to run, he was late, oh hell, he was always late but this time he was even later than always and he'd like to talk to her some more but he had to go and could she meet him there tomorrow morning at eight thirty?

Which was, he added, before rushing out, a safe time to rendezvous with a stranger, wasn't it? Those traffic-light eyes of his signalling 'go', 'say yes', while she nodded, knowing she was blushing as red as any stop signal.

She hadn't had time to ask him what he was doing there in the first place, how he had happened to appear when the last time she'd seen him he'd been sitting on the bus, apparently asleep. They hadn't even exchanged names.

She'd have to wait until eight thirty tomorrow to find out another way of thinking of him aside from 'the Gentleman' as a name to pin on him. Well, any name would do. Unless it was Piers.

The whole episode had been so dreamlike, unexpected and unlikely that she'd actually asked the waitress behind the counter, after the Gentleman had left, whether she knew him.

'Yeah, he comes in every morning,' she had responded. 'He seems nice enough. Always leaves a decent tip. I wouldn't worry about getting picked up by him, sweetheart. I wouldn't worry one fingernail's worth.'

Sadie wasn't worried about being picked up by a stranger. She was worried she'd imagined him. People didn't throw rude men's mobile phones off a bus and say 'sue me', not any people she knew. They didn't get spontaneous rounds of applause. They didn't have eyes as green as his and they didn't talk about young love being a killer and they didn't speak in Southern accents. If people like that did exist, they wouldn't ask her out to breakfast. Therefore she must have made him up. But the waitress was real and the waitress backed up the fact of his existence.

Loath to go straight back to her hotel, back to reality, Sadie had started walking and kept at it. She'd cut across to Fifth Avenue and headed downtown, past the Plaza Hotel, past St Patrick's Cathedral, past the Rockefeller Center, all the way to where she was now, the Empire State Building. There was no point in going up it, not in this weather, so she turned around to retrace her steps. She couldn't classify this trip as window-shopping because she hadn't looked in a single window. All she had done was to replay every moment with the Gentleman, starting from her first glimpse of him on the bus, ending with her last sight of him exiting the coffee shop. Each time she came to the end of the tape, she rewound it in her mind and pressed replay, aware the entire time that she was getting far too carried away by it. Not that the knowledge stopped the tape from playing.

I'm allowed to indulge myself, she thought. Even if tomorrow is a disaster, if he doesn't show up, or if he tells me he's married with three children, I will at least have had an afternoon of anticipation and happiness. I'm allowed that. This isn't the same as my situation with Piers, all those months when I kept thinking he'd call, kept hoping he had a valid excuse for shutting me out of his life so abruptly, that was self-delusion. This is pure fantasy. There's a difference.

At 79th Street, she crossed back onto Madison. Until she caught sight of the Carlyle, she hadn't stopped to think properly. But as soon as she saw the hotel, she did. What if Georgie and/or Jessica needed her at eight thirty tomorrow? The odds weren't high at that time in the morning, it was more likely they'd be asleep, yet nothing about this trip had been likely from the beginning of it. Could she dare tell them the truth? Wouldn't they understand given their Morgan Blaine fantasies? Or would Georgie be in such a temper because Jessica had nabbed him first that she'd want to pack her bags and force Sadie to accompany her home? She had no way of contacting the Gentleman if something like this happened. And no way whatsoever of telling Georgie 'no'. Her trip had been paid for, she was their employee. How could she quit and strand herself in New York without a job, without money?

'Hey, honey, are you all right?'

A well-dressed older woman was standing in front of her, addressing her with a concerned look.

Startled, Sadie tried to smile, but a vicious headache brought on by the moisture-laden air had lodged behind her left eye and it wouldn't let her mouth move.

'You look lost.'

'I'm fine,' she mumbled. 'Thank you.'

She managed to make it to the hotel and up to her room before kicking off her wet shoes and collapsing into bed. After ten minutes, she rolled over and searched for the extra strength

Nurofen she always kept in her bag. Like a hungover raver, she stumbled to the bathroom and forced herself to take two, almost being sick in the process of swallowing. The best way to survive this sort of headache, she knew, was to lie still in a lukewarm bath.

The pounding behind her eye wouldn't go away, even when she was lying as still as she could, stretched out in the bath. Louder and louder and louder, until she thought her head would explode.

'Sadie! Sadie! Are you there?'

Damn, Sadie swore, getting out of the bath and reaching for a towel. Which is worse – a headache smashing my brain to smithereens or Jessica banging my door down?

It was too close a race to call.

Eliza had managed to create a pasta salad with tuna fish, cherry tomatoes and canned corn niblets, which was, Georgie reflected, surprisingly tasty. She was absurdly hungry and had to stop herself from devouring the whole bowl. Showing any weakness or rude table manners in front of Morgan Blaine would not be a good idea. He would make fun of her, tease her, send sly glances to Eliza, do anything whatsoever to embarrass her. That seemed to be his purpose on earth, to make her feel ridiculous. The enjoyment he took in this was disproportionate to the situation, she kept thinking. So a fan of his work had showed up at his door, was that so horrible?

'You know, Morgan, you write about the bayou as if you've been there. Which I know for a fact you haven't. How do you manage that leap of imagination, you blockhead?'

Georgie tried not to look as disappointed as she felt seeing Eliza help herself to the last spoonful of salad as she asked Morgan this question.

'Talent.' Morgan shrugged. 'A feel for words.'

'Uh huh.' Eliza nodded. 'Does that go for the sex scenes

too? I mean, were they based on real life experiences or a feel for words?'

Eliza resembled Morgan in the outdoorsy air she had, the sense she gave off of healthy hikes, of hockey games. Yet when she asked about this aspect of Morgan's work, she did so in a husky, amused, naughty voice which was so far away from innocent it could have been used on a demonstration tape for phone-sex operators.

'*Voodoo Women* is not about sex, Eliza. *Voodoo Women* is about life. How we live, how we die, how we survive, how we struggle, how we conquer the forces which rule our passions, how we live under the stars which guide our souls.' Morgan, as he made this statement, spread his arms in an all-embracing gesture suitable for the chorus of 'He's Got the Whole World in His Hands'.

'God.' Sitting back in her chair, Eliza put her hand over her heart and sighed. 'God, Morgan. You're *so* deep.'

'Excuse me?' Georgie couldn't help herself. She'd never heard such crap in her life. 'You're not being serious, are you?' Her eyes honed in on Morgan.

'Why wouldn't I be serious?' Morgan popped a cherry tomato from his plate into his mouth and talked as he chewed. 'You said you loved the book. I assume you recognize talent and depth when you read it.'

'Yes, I loved *Voodoo Women*. But it's not exactly *War and Peace*.'

'She doesn't understand.' Morgan said to Eliza.

'No, she doesn't understand,' Eliza replied.

'She's English.' Morgan said sadly.

'She's English,' Eliza echoed.

'So was Shakespeare,' Georgie shot back.

'No?' Morgan cocked his head. 'Really? You don't say.'

'I've had it.' Georgie stood up. She could feel her entire body quivering. 'I've had enough of this. I want to leave now.'

'It's a long walk back to Manhattan,' Eliza said, smiling.

'I don't care. I *do not* care.'

'Oh, sit down.' Morgan waved his hand. 'We don't have to talk about great literature if it upsets you so much.'

Georgie sat down. It was, indeed, a long walk to the end of the driveway, much less all the way back to the city. In a blizzard. No one spoke for a few seconds, until Eliza suddenly said, 'Hey, we could go sledding.'

'Excellent idea, Eliza. We can go sledding. Come on.' Standing up, Morgan clapped his hands together. 'The sleds are out front on the porch. It's snow time, folks!' He stomped off, out of the kitchen and into the hall.

'Do you want to come sledding, Georgina?'

'No, thank you, Eliza.'

I want to sit here and stew and hate both of you, she thought. You and your cheer-leading heartiness, him and his self-proclaimed genius.

'Look, I'm sorry if we teased you a little on the English thing. Morgan and I always tease each other. We have since we were kids. I guess we're so used to it we figure other people can take it too. It's harmless really.'

What irritating children you must have been. What brats you still are.

'Of course. I understand. But I'm fine sitting here. Really.'

'Georgina, listen –' Eliza paused, then shook her blonde head. 'No, never mind. Okeydokey. There's some instant coffee in the cupboard, there's the kettle on the counter. Help yourself if you want any.'

'Thank you very much.' She could hear herself using Jessica's voice as she said this. The upper-class accent designed to put miles of culture and history between herself and these American fools. The exaggerated politeness which, she knew from being on the receiving end, never managed to mask disdain. 'Do you think the blizzard will last long?'

'It'll probably be over by tomorrow morning and the snow ploughs come pretty early. You'll be able to call a taxi after they've been.'

'Fine. Thank you very much.'

Shit, she said to herself as she watched Eliza go to find Morgan. Shit, shit, shit. I'm stuck here all night? With these miserable sods? That's all I fucking need. The sooner I leave this country the better. I'll tell Jessica what a nightmare Morgan Blaine is, how I saved her from meeting the biggest creep in the world by my stupid cheating and we'll fly back home tomorrow night. I'll call Jess now to put her out of her misery. I'll apologize five million times and tell her I've already been punished for my sins.

Remembering that there was a phone on a side table in the living room, Georgie got up to go and use it.

'Hey.' Morgan, towering over her and blocking her path, was standing a step inside the kitchen. 'Have you changed your mind? Do you want to come sledding? I'm sure I can find you some reassuringly weird sledding clothes.'

'No, I haven't changed my mind. Actually, I was going to make a phone call if you don't object.'

'I don't object. Unless you have many close friends in Japan.'

His eyes locked onto hers. They didn't move, they didn't blink, they cut through her, reached into her, grabbed and held her – hard.

'But I think you should come sledding after you've finished,' he said.

'Why?'

'Because I think you need to have some fun, Georgina.'

He turned and left the kitchen. Georgie sank back down onto her chair. She wasn't sure what had just happened with that look of his, but something had happened, definitely. Something slightly scary and very exciting.

*   *   *

189

Jessica was incoherent. Sadie, sitting at the end of her bed, a towel wrapped around her, her head still pounding, tried to make sense of the woman sitting in a chair opposite her, talking so quickly and so agitatedly it was hard to make out her words, much less their meanings.

'So this woman was going to *drug* me – Valium – I don't know, some Saint somebody's psychiatric ward and then he looked at me as if he thought I was mad as well. Which was crazy.' Jessica paused, stared up at the ceiling. 'Yes, I said I hated my life, but that was before my head hit the table and it doesn't mean I should be institutionalized or drugged. There are loads of people who hate their lives, maybe you even hate your life but I wouldn't force Valium down your throat, or—'

'Jessica.' Sadie put her hands to her temples and rubbed in circles. 'Slow down, please. Can we start from the beginning? The last time I saw you, you were sitting with Morgan Blaine at that coffee place. How did doctors and Valium get into the picture? I honestly don't know what you're talking about. I can't help unless I understand what's gone on. Maybe you should take a few deep breaths and start again.'

'Right. Right.' Sadie could see Jessica visibly trying to pull herself together. 'You're right. I have to calm down. I have to breathe.'

For the next few minutes, Sadie sat in blessed silence as Jessica inhaled, exhaled, inhaled, exhaled. And then slowly retold the events of her morning and early afternoon, ending with the plaintive question, 'What do I do now?'

What should Jessica do now? Sadie had no clue, but at least her headache was beginning to loosen its grip. The Nurofen were kicking in.

'What do you *want* to do?' she asked.

'I want to convince him I'm not mad. I want to marry him.

Oh God—' Jessica suddenly fluttered her hands. 'Did I just say that? Oh God. Maybe I *am* mad. The thing is, something happened to me when I was in his flat. It's hard to explain, and maybe it had something to do with banging my head, but I felt as if I could tell him everything. I was floating, Sadie. It was the strangest experience, I've never felt anything like it. I was in the bed and I wanted to stay there and hold his hand and just *talk* – well, maybe do something else besides talk, but I felt . . . I felt as if he'd opened me up. And that suddenly, I wasn't alone any more. Not that I'm alone when I'm at work or with Georgie, but, well, you know what I mean, don't you?'

'I think so, yes.'

'And now he thinks I'm a madwoman.'

Her legs were curled up beneath her, her face was pale and worried. When Jessica had said, standing in the middle of the Columbia campus, that she'd fallen in love at first sight, Sadie had been dubious. Now, though, she was beginning to think it might be the case. Jessica's vulnerability was palpable, Sadie could feel it, that female uncertainty which could affect even the prettiest of women. Lisa had once been in a state of panic because she was afraid the man in her life might catch her unawares some late night or early morning and see her without her false eyelashes on. No matter how much Sadie told her that couldn't possibly make a difference in their relationship, Lisa had refused to calm down. That particular man had, indeed, buggered off, but not because he'd seen Lisa eyelashless – Lisa had never once shed them in his presence. He'd left because, as he told her, he preferred more 'natural' women.

'The bastard before him said I wasn't sophisticated enough. You can't fucking win.' Lisa had sighed. Sadie had sighed along with her. Now she was sighing along with Jessica. This wasn't Girl Power, this was Female Fragility. Not a good slogan for the millennium, but, possibly, a historical truth.

'You told him everything? All about Project X?' Sadie hoped Jessica wasn't going to answer 'yes'.

'I mentioned it. I didn't tell him all about it, no. I don't think so, anyway. I wanted to be truthful. I wanted—' Jessica stopped, stared at Sadie with desperate eyes. 'How stupid have I been? Oh, no.' She knocked her fist against her forehead. 'I told him I'd come all the way from England to find him. He must think I'm a desperate stalker. I can't believe I talked like that. I *never* talk like that. Men hate it when women talk too much and come on too strong. What got into me? How could I have? Oh no.' She put her head in her hands. 'Oh no.' She lifted it again. 'He thinks I'm a stalker, doesn't he?'

'Well—'

'Don't answer, don't answer. I know he does. A bunny-boiler, a psychotic floozy. What can I do?'

They sat in silence, Jessica looking at Sadie with beseeching eyes.

'I could take it back!' Jessica exclaimed suddenly. 'I could say I said it because of hitting my head. That doctor said I might have concussion. I'll tell him that was exactly what happened. Concussion. I had no idea what I was talking about.' Standing up, Jessica regained some of her natural colouring. 'Project? Did I say project? No, I'm here on business. I'm a sane woman of independent means who came to New York on business and had the misfortune to hit her head. I ran into a professor in a coffee shop, I had no idea who he was, I fainted, I hit my head, I've come back to my senses now. That works, doesn't it? Tell me it works.'

'It sounds reasonable. But—' Sadie couldn't bring herself to finish the sentence.

'But what? Tell me.' Jessica sat down beside her and grabbed her by the wrist. 'Tell me, Sadie. But what?'

'But only if Georgie doesn't get to him in the meantime.'

'Oh my God! Oh, no. Georgie. Where is she? Have you seen her? Has she rung?'

'No. Neither. I don't know where she is.'

'She might be in his apartment right now. Eating the chicken sandwiches I didn't get the chance to finish. I'm dead.' Jessica hung her head. 'I'm finished. At least he'll think we're both mad, that it's not just me.'

He'll think madness runs in the family, Sadie thought. And he'll be right.

The telephone rang then, making them both jump. Sadie clasped the towel firmly around her and went to answer it.

'Hello?' a male voice said. 'Is this Sadie? Sadie Hawkes?'

'Yes.'

'This is Morgan – the man you met in the coffee shop with Jessica. I was calling because she ran out of here in a hurry and she'd fainted before and I was worried about her.'

Putting her hand over the receiver, Sadie mouthed, 'It's Morgan,' to Jessica who leapt up so fast she looked as if she were in a new 'get to the telephone quickest' Olympic event.

'Actually, she's here, Morgan, would you like to speak to her?'

Jessica grabbed the phone out of her hand before Sadie could hear his answer.

'Morgan, Morgan, hello. I'm so glad you rang.' Her other hand was clutching Sadie's arm for support. It was clutching so hard Sadie could feel the blood begin to drain out.

'Yes, yes, I'm fine, thank you. You must have thought I was bonkers, running off like that. And talking the way I did. It was the concussion. I wasn't thinking straight. I was making no sense, I know. But I'm fine now. How are you?

'Yes, yes, I'd love to see you again. I can come over any time. Um, that lovely doctor friend of yours isn't still there, is she? No? Well, why don't I come over now, then.' She picked up the pen from the bedside table. 'What's your address again? Right.' She scribbled on the hotel note pad. 'Excellent. I want to thank you again in person for rescuing me . . . You did too . . . we won't fight about it, but you did. All right. Wonderful. See you in a while. Goodbye.' She put the phone down. 'Yes!' She pumped her hand in the air. 'Yes!' She hugged Sadie. 'Yes, yes, yes!'

'I'm happy for you,' Sadie said. Meaning it.

'I can't wait. Do you believe this, Sadie? I've met Morgan Blaine, I've fallen in love with Morgan Blaine and he wants to see me. He said we make a pair, so he must – no, I have to be cool, I have to be in control. I can't get ahead of myself here. Still . . .' Jessica beamed, but the beam was soon followed by a frown. 'If Georgie rings, please, please don't tell her what's happening. Please, Sadie? If she gets involved, she'll take over. I don't know what's happening between us, why it's all gone so badly, but I know she won't be happy about me and Morgan. I need some time alone with him before she comes into the picture. You don't have to tell her, do you?'

If Sadie had had any doubts before about keeping her job after this trip, they were gone now. She knew she'd lose it. Lying to Georgina Harvey was tantamount to tying herself to a railway track and waiting for the Harvey and Tanner express train to run over her. But she couldn't let Jessica down. Not now. They were in the same position, they were both in love with men they'd only just met and were dying to see again.

'I won't tell her.'

Jessica hugged her again and headed for the door. Just as she reached it, the phone rang.

'If it's her, I'm not here. Right?' Jessica stayed where she was, her hand on the doorknob.

'Right.' Sadie nodded, thinking: please don't be Georgie. Please don't make me lie. She picked it up reluctantly and said hello.

'Sadie, it's Georgie. Is Jessica with you by any chance?'

'No, Georgie, she's not here.' This was the fatal flaw, she reflected as she lied, not the fact that there were two women chasing the same man, but that they'd brought a third who was taking sides.

'Good, good. Listen, I'm in the country and I'm staying here overnight'.

'You're in the country and you're staying overnight?'

Punching the air after hearing these words, Jessica waved at Sadie, mouthed, 'Bye,' and left the room.

'Yes, Sadie. That was what I said. You don't have to repeat it back word for word. There's a blizzard, so I can't get back to the city.'

'Oh. Why—'

'Anyway, the thing is, I've met Morgan Blaine.'

'What?' Sadie sat down on the bed.

'But I don't want you to tell Jessica.'

'You've met Morgan Blaine?'

'Sadie, has something toxic invaded your brain? Yes, I've met him and, well, this is hard to explain, but I think I might like to get to know him a little better. There's so much snow I couldn't move even if I wanted to, but certain things have happened. I can't quite explain it, but the point is I need some time with him before Jessica comes into the picture. Can you tell me if she has any idea where he is yet? Is she on the trail?'

'Sorry to sound stupid, but are you saying you're with Morgan Blaine right now?'

'That's what I'm saying. Look, I know I cheated—'

'But Jessica is—'

'I know. She must be furious. I know it's a lot to ask, but if you could just throw her off the scent for a while, distract her somehow—'

'You're absolutely sure you're with Morgan Blaine?'

'Yes, I'm absolutely sure. And now I'm going sledding

195

with him. Are you trying to say you won't help me out here?'

'Georgie, Jessica is distracted already. *She's*—'

'Great, terrific. I'll see you tomorrow and explain everything. Jess will forgive me. You won't believe the stories I have to tell . . . ciao, babe.'

Ciao babe? Since when had Georgie called her 'babe'? What was going on? How could she be in the country with Morgan Blaine when Jessica was in the city with him?

For a moment, Sadie considered chasing after Jessica to tell her about this. That moment ended as soon as she realized a salient fact: if Jessica was going to visit her Morgan Blaine and Georgie was ensconced with *her* Morgan Blaine, the chances of either of them somehow ruining her date the next morning with the Gentleman receded into thin air. Besides, they were both happy. There was no point in bringing to light the fact that one of them had found the wrong man. The war would begin again and she'd be back in the frontlines of it.

Sadie picked up the receiver she'd just put down. She couldn't wait to ring Andrew. Not even he, in his wildest imaginings, could come up with a scenario this bizarre.

Chapter Eighteen

Georgie had never been sledding. She wasn't an outdoorsy type of person. At school she'd been good at sports as well as a swot, though she'd never been captain of any of the teams she played on. That, she knew, was down to the fact that once, in her first year at St Anne's, during a netball match she'd elbowed another girl so hard in the ribs that the girl had fallen to the ground and howled in protest. The headmistress had promptly called her into her office and delivered a lecture on sportsmanship and the dangers of being 'too competitive'. Making all the right replies, vowing she'd never do it again and saying she had been momentarily carried away in the heat of the match, Georgie had been stunned the next morning to find herself ordered to visit the school counsellor.

'Why do you think winning is so important to you?' the improbably young and pretty counsellor had asked as soon as Georgie had sat down.

'Isn't winning important to everyone?' she'd asked back.

'I'm not asking anyone else, I'm asking you. Why don't you tell me a little bit about your parents.'

Grudgingly, Georgie gave a quick and unemotional account of her parents – their divorce, their remarriages, her father's success in his business. When she'd finished, she was surprised to see a sad look on the counsellor's face.

'While all of this was happening, what was their relationship with you?'

'The same as always.' She shrugged, beginning to feel nervous, but not wanting to show any anxiety to this stranger.

'What was "always" like?'

'I don't know. They did all the usual parent things, I guess. They were pleased when I did well at school. I don't really remember much. They were around – sort of. They had other things to think about.'

'What *things* exactly?'

'Their marriage breaking up, my dad's work, all that. I think they thought—' she stopped, wishing she could get up and leave but knowing she couldn't without creating more problems for herself.

'What do you think they thought?'

'I think they thought I was sort of in the way.'

'And do they still think that?'

'Sort of. I mean . . .' she felt a pressing need to defend her parents. 'They *do* have other things to think about. My father and his second wife aren't getting on very well, they argue a lot, my mother's new husband is – well, he drinks a lot, so she has to deal with that. I'm fine, really, so they don't have to worry about me. Why should they worry about me if I'm fine? I'm sorry I did that in the netball match, but she overreacted, honestly. I didn't push her as hard as she said I did.'

'However hard you did or didn't push her, you got attention, didn't you?'

'I wasn't trying to get attention.' Georgie felt hot and claustrophobic even though the room they were sitting in was large and airy. 'I wanted my team to win, that's all.'

'Your academic record is excellent, you're a high achiever, but you don't have many friends here, do you?'

'I have Jessica,' Georgie blurted out. 'She's my friend, she's my sister. And Martha. And . . . and anyway I'm concentating on my work. I thought that was what I was *supposed* to be doing in school.'

'Because your parents only pay attention, are *pleased* as you said, when you do well at school? Are you concentrating so hard on work, on winning, on doing well, because your parents aren't concentrating on you?'

'I don't see why they should have to concentrate on me. I can take care of myself. I don't cause them any more problems than they already have. Why should I? Am I supposed to make their lives more difficult? Is that what you want me to do?'

'I don't want you to do anything, Georgina. I'd *like* it if you came and talked with me some more. Would you like that?'

'No,' Georgie caught herself shouting, and immediately lowered her voice. 'No, thank you. I won't push anyone again, I told Mrs Franklin I wouldn't and I won't. I'm fine. You can't make me come, can you?'

'No.' She shook her head. 'I can't.' That sad look on her face came back. Georgie turned away from it and stood up.

'I'm fine,' she said. 'Really. I'm fine. You don't have to worry about me.'

'*Someone* should, Georgina. Someone should worry about you.'

Georgie left, a terrible mixture of anger and fear in her heart. She wasn't going to go back, she didn't want to talk about her parents; all she wanted to do was get her A levels and go to university and succeed in life without anyone finding out she shouldn't have been able to do any of those things. The counsellor was one of those terrible 'they' people who could expose her failings and show her up as the fraud she was. By asking a few simple questions, she had pushed buttons in Georgie's psyche that, for reasons she didn't understand, left her feeling ashamed and humiliated.

Now she'd spent the morning feeling those same emotions, but this time it was Morgan Blaine who had brought them on. In a moment not unlike that time she had elbowed the girl to the ground, she'd lost control of herself in the heat of a passionate competition, thrown all her rational thought processes into a skip, and chased a strange man into the woods. She wasn't surprised, on reflection, that he had, in effect, called her into the headmistress's office and lectured her for her sins. Yet she wanted to go out and play in the snow with him, she wanted to see that look again, the one that had cut through to her heart and lodged there. He hadn't said she had to talk about her past or analysed her in any scary way; he'd only told her she needed to have fun.

Would sledding actually *be* fun? What if he and Eliza were champion sledders and she couldn't keep up? What if she made a fool of herself?

As if I haven't made as big a fool of myself as it is possible to make already, she said to herself. I've got nothing left to lose.

After ending her conversation with Sadie, Georgie left the comfort of the warm living room and headed for the great outdoors.

She could hear Morgan and Eliza, out behind the house, whooping like demented children. Venturing off the porch, following the screams, she sloshed her way, in her already soaked heels, around the side of the house. The hill they were sledding down wasn't very steep, but it was high enough to make a decent incline for their sledges, old-fashioned sledges which looked like replicas of the original Rosebud in *Citizen Kane*. Morgan was in mid-sled, halfway down the hill, lying on his stomach. Eliza was right behind him, on her stomach as well. Morgan reached the bottom, Eliza's sledge rammed into his and they both fell off in a jumble. They looked like oversized Smarties. He was wearing a neon-yellow all-weather jacket, hers was neon blue.

The scene was idyllic, in a picture-postcard sort of way, Georgie thought. Pine trees everywhere, snow swirling, grown-ups at play as if they didn't have a care in the world. If this had been a movie, this was the point where she would have expected to see a rifle trained on Morgan's forehead. And if there hadn't been the rifle or something equally foreboding to cut the cute factor, she would have walked out.

'Hi there,' Georgie called out. 'Mind if I join you?'

'Hey! Sure!' Leaping up, Eliza brushed the snow off herself and walked toward Georgie. 'Come on, I'll get you some clothes to wear.'

I want Morgan to get me the clothes. I want to be in a room alone with him again. I want that look, whatever it was. That voodoo.

'What made you change your mind?' Eliza asked when she reached Georgie's side.

'I don't know. The snow is so beautiful. The trees. And I could hear you having fun.'

'Well, kiddo, you made the right choice.' Eliza clapped her on the shoulder. Georgie winced.

'So . . .' They were in the house and Eliza was taking jackets off pegs in the front hallway. 'Here, this should work.' She handed her an oversize denim one. 'And I'll run upstairs and steal some of my aunt's jeans and a sweater and boots.'

'Morgan's mother? Where is she?'

'In the Far East. She's a travel writer. Morgan's father, Uncle Ted, died when Morgan was five and his mother had to bring him up on her own. At first she did local travel stories; when he grew up, she branched out.'

She watched Eliza bound upstairs and bound down again minutes later with a load of clothes and after she'd changed into them in the bathroom off the living room, Georgie felt as if she were dressed for a weather women's convention in Lapland. Not only did she have the jeans, the jacket, gloves, a jersey and boots, she was also equipped with thermal underwear and socks so thick she couldn't feel where her toes were.

Eliza was waiting for her in the hall. 'Excellent. Let's do it!' she said, grabbing Georgie by the elbow. 'Watch out for snowballs, though. Morgan throws a mean one.'

Morgan, as she was soon to learn, threw *vicious* snowballs. The first one caught Eliza on the shoulder as they were approaching him, the second slammed into Georgie's thigh.

'Sleazeball!' Eliza shouted, proceeding to roll her own and fling them in his direction, while Georgie stood, rubbing her thigh.

I can't believe I'm with these lunatics, she thought, before the logical bit of her brain took over and she ran for cover behind a tree. All thoughts of Morgan Blaine the author, vanished. This was Morgan Blaine the snowball hurler and she wanted revenge, pure and simple. She wanted to get the bastard. So she pondered her strategic position and decided on the element of surprise attack. She'd circle him from behind while he was ensconced in his snowball fight with Eliza and ambush him.

Scooping up a mound of snow and crafting a hard, cricket-ball-size missile, she set off on her charted course, keeping out of sight in the treeline until she came to the point where she could cut in behind him. Then, slowly, noiselessly, she approached. His massive back was to her, his hands were busy warding off the attacks from Eliza and making his own in return. She had to get close to make it hurt, throwing from too great a distance would be ineffective. When she was five yards away, she began to tiptoe. The snowball she held was almost pure ice. If she caught him on the top of the head, he'd be in agony. The prospect was a satisfying one to contemplate.

Two yards away, she stopped. She drew her arm back. She

aimed. Just as she was about to let fly, she saw him turn. The moment of release, when her snowball flew out of her hand, was also the moment she was tackled. He was on top of her. He had her hands pinned, spreadeagled in the snow.

'Say "Uncle",' he commanded, his mouth breathing hot air in her ear.

She lay there. Panting. Mute. A crumpled, defenceless snowwoman.

'Say "uncle" and we'll get Eliza together.'

'I don't understand. What do uncles have to do with anything?'

'"Uncle" means surrender in American. So say it.'

'Uncle,' she whispered.

As soon as he let go of her arms and took his weight off her body, she grabbed as much snow as she could with both hands, hurled it straight at his face and set off as fast as she could go, heading back to the trees.

'I did it, I did it!' she crowed, realizing at the same time this feeling of triumph was even greater than any she'd had in her business dealings. 'I got him!' When she stopped to catch her breath, she turned back to the scene of her crime and saw Eliza pelting Morgan with snowball after snowball as he sat in a heap, rubbing his face.

Primitive childhood playground politics took over. Georgie instinctively switched loyalties and went for the obvious target, the current winner in this fight, Eliza. She charged her, running headlong at her, grabbing her around the waist and toppling her over into the snow, pinning Eliza's arms to the ground just as Morgan had pinned hers.

'Traitor!' Eliza yelped. 'You're supposed to be on *my* team.'

'Surrender? Uncle?' Georgie, sitting astride Eliza's stomach, put a touch more pressure on her arms as she asked this.

'Yeah, Lize.' Morgan was standing above them, laughing.

'I think you better surrender. She's got you there. Go on – say uncle.'

'All right – uncle. Can we call a truce now?'

'I don't know.' Morgan crouched down beside them. 'What do you think, Georgina? Truce? Or should we make her suffer a little more? You could keep holding her down while I tickle her – or, I could pull out her fingernails, maybe. One by one.'

It was as if she'd been here before, a déjà vu of a childhood she'd had, which made no sense whatsoever because she hadn't had it. She'd never felt such uncomplicated a sense of fun, she had never frolicked in this way, but it was a familiar sensation nonetheless, and the word 'truce' came naturally to her when she said it. This wasn't school, where she felt compelled to get better grades than anyone else, or work, where she had to prove herself time and time again, this was a snowball fight and she could do whatever she wanted to do, including calling a halt to it.

'So,' Georgie released Eliza's arms and got off her stomach, 'Can we go sledding now?'

'Georgina,' Morgan made a little bow, 'Queen of the Snow. We'll do whatever you want.'

Chapter Nineteen

Jessica was enchanted by Morgan's apartment. There was a calmness about it which soothed and relaxed her; a feeling of safety. The walls were all muted colours and, as in the bedroom, the paintings and photographs he'd put up were all of flowers. The floors were wooden, polished, but not overly gleaming. Even the armchair she was sitting in was snug. Like the bedroom, the living room was a place she'd be happy to fall asleep and wake up in.

Furniture could cost the earth. There could be vast sofas upholstered in perfectly matching materials, antique dining-room tables, four-poster beds, but that wasn't a guarantee of comfort. Jessica knew this to be the case because she'd lived in houses full of the 'right' pieces all her life. Until this moment of complete ease, though, she had never understood how much tension there was in furniture which was made for the eye, not the body.

As she sat, her legs curled up beneath her, her hands wrapped tightly around a mug of tea, she studied Morgan's face carefully. He had a high forehead and high colouring, a nose apparently fashioned for glasses to perch on with open, trusting, innocent blue eyes behind the lenses. She could picture him at that boarding school of his, a scarf loose about his neck, hurrying to a class. Other boys might have teased him. But other boys wouldn't have seen what she was seeing now – his huge heart. The sweet boy in him would always be visible, she decided. Whether he was ten years old or ninety.

Yet there had to be a hidden side to him. Otherwise he wouldn't have been able to write those violent scenes in *Voodoo Women*. From the minute she had arrived, he'd treated her like a recovering invalid, settling her in the armchair, bringing her tea, attending to her like a male nurse. Wherever the macho machete part of his psyche lay, he wasn't putting it on display with her. And though there were bookshelves near his desk in the corner, she'd noticed there weren't any copies of *his* book in them. Morgan Blaine was hiding his fame as well. His modesty was appealing. He wasn't one of those Americans who bragged noisily, he was English in his restraint.

Of course she was hiding herself too. Sooner or later, Georgie would reappear. Having managed to convince him she wasn't a mad stalker, Jessica would have to admit that was exactly what she was. Her only hope lay in the thought that by that time he would have begun to know her and would understand and forgive. If not, she was doomed.

'Are you sure you're feeling better now?'

'Yes, definitely. I'm fine.'

'You had me worried, you know. I couldn't figure out what the hell you were talking about. You mentioned some waiter and there was that project and your stepsister and boy –' he shook his head – 'I was lost.'

'Mmm, it was the concussion. It made me say ridiculous things.' Change the subject. Now. 'Your friend the doctor – Louisa? Have you known her long?'

'A few years. Her fiancé is an old friend of mine.'

'I'm sorry she had to see me in such a state.'

'Oh, don't worry. She sees people in a lot worse states.'

He smiled. 'It was funny, though. After you left, she said she thought that for some inexplicable reason you might have been telling the truth – about coming all this way to find me, I mean –' he rolled his eyes – 'as if. I said, "Absolutely, Lou, she's so desperate she decided to fly across an ocean to track me down in a coffee shop. That's how she goes about life, picking random strangers across the world to accost on snowy mornings."' He laughed.

'Ha.' This was a feeble effort, Jessica knew. 'Ha, ha, ha.' Actors could make themselves cry, why couldn't she make herself laugh properly?

'We weren't laughing at your expense, I promise, but the part about admiring voodoo women was pretty wacky, you have to admit.'

He was laughing again.

'Morgan –' Jessica rose and went over to the armchair he was sitting in. She knelt down in front of him. 'I love the fact that you're so modest, it's—' before she could finish her sentence he'd leaned over and kissed her. A kiss to build a million dreams on, she thought as she let herself get lost in it. It was the only conscious thought she had.

'Sorry,' he mumbled as he pulled back. 'I'm really sorry, I couldn't resist. There's something about you, Jessica. I don't know how to explain it—'

'You don't have to.' She was the one who leaned forward this time. She was the one who kissed him.

The kiss is the moment of truth. The kiss is like the gypsy fortune teller predicting the future. If the kiss is good, all else falls before it, if it's not good, if it's sloppy, bumbling, awkward, it presages disaster. The kiss is the key to the heart. If men only knew that, Jessica thought, if they only knew that one thing, they wouldn't worry so much about size or technique or staying power. They wouldn't need to study pictures of the Kama Sutra or work out more and more impossible sexual positions to prove their manhood. They'd concentrate on their mouths and tongues and hands. They'd take courses in kissing. They'd get degrees in kissing. They'd . . .

'Jessica? Hello?'

She was in his bed. He'd carried her in his arms again, undressed her, undressed himself and continued where they'd left off in the living room. Soon they'd make love. They'd been on the verge of it before, but Jessica had pulled back and said, 'I just want to hug for a while, Morgan.' He'd immediately drawn her to him, not pressing for more. She'd stopped because she was frightened of not having an orgasm. She didn't want to feel the disappointment of not having one. Sometimes she wondered if the whole orgasm thing was a myth, whether women had made it all up and were in league with each other to pretend it was real. Every magazine article about orgasms might be total fiction. They might not exist. In which case she wouldn't have to worry about not having one. On the other hand, if they were real, she might have one with Morgan Blaine. Tonight. But what if she didn't? Jessica's brain was so enmeshed in this mental dilemma, she'd forgotten that she was lying in his arms.

'Morgan . . .' She lifted her head from his chest. 'Sorry, I was lost in thought.'

'Are you OK?'

'I'm fine.'

'All of this has taken me by surprise.' He hugged her. 'I didn't plan this, you know.'

'I know.'

'It wasn't my intention. I mean, I didn't lure you over here to get you into bed.'

'I know. It was like Rick and Eva, wasn't it?'

'Sorry?'

'The way they got together, except for that bit in the clearing, when they only had to look at each other to –

you know – although actually, it wasn't so different, not really. I mean, fine, there wasn't any clearing the first time I saw you—'

'Clearing?' Disentangling himself from Jessica, Morgan sat up and switched on the bedside light. 'I'm afraid you've lost me again.'

Sitting up as well, drawing the bedsheets around her, Jessica smiled at the dishevelled Morgan. No, he wasn't wildly handsome, he wasn't exactly what she had expected, but in certain lights, at certain times, like this one now, his creativity shone through his face. For a while there, in bed, she'd almost forgotten who he was: Morgan Blaine, the writer. Now that was all she could think about. This was the man who'd written *Voodoo Women*, the talented, successful author. And she had him to herself in this bed.

'Would you read to me, Morgan? The book you're working on now? Would you read the beginning to me, here in bed? It would be so romantic. I'd love it.' And it might put me in exactly the right mood, she thought, *Lightning at Dawn*. It might be Lightning at Midnight tonight.

'Well, sure.' Morgan wrinkled his nose and scratched his forehead. 'If you want me to, sure. Let me go get my glasses.'

Jessica sat waiting for him in a haze of expectation, unbelieving that she had such fortune. He was going to read to her, to share his creation with her. She might be the only person who had heard these words. A private reading of *Lightning at Dawn*. Just for her. Georgie would drop dead from envy. If Hollywood made the book into a film, she could go to the Oscars with him. Mr and Mrs Morgan Blaine and their two children, Morgan Jr and Catherine. Of course they'd refuse to do a photo shoot for *Hello!*, that would be tacky, but . . .

'OK. Ready?' He was carrying a manuscript and had his glasses back on.

A naked author on the foot of the bed, Jessica thought. How

fabulous is this? Relaxing back against the pillows, she closed her eyes and waited. Morgan cleared his throat.

'*Microbiotic Organisms in Flux*, Chapter One. To paraphrase Tolstoy, all microbiotic organisms are alike, but each microbiotic organism when in flux is different. A clear picture of this dissimilarity is gained by the study of the environment, the causes which activate the flux, the meaning, as it were, of the term "flux", which, though defined by Frederick Derring in his ground-breaking essay on the subject (see footnote 1), has subsequently been questioned in such a way as to necessitate the need for further study. Although not wishing to disassociate myself from Professor Derring's brilliant work, I feel it will be useful for those in the field to—'

'Morgan?' Jessica's eyes had opened. There was a certain amount of fear in them. 'What are you doing?'

'I thought you might be bored.' He shrugged shyly. 'But you did seem interested when I talked about moss before. And you did ask for it.'

'Oh.' Jessica struggled to make sense of this. Why would he write such a boring beginning to a novel? Was it some sort of take-off? A satire about . . . about what? Was it possible to write a satire about organisms in flux?

'I guess I'm not literary enough to understand. Is this some sort of avant garde approach? To start off a novel like that? I don't mean to criticize, really I don't, but don't you think you might put off the reader in the first paragraph? I'm not pretending to be a literary critic, but, you know, the beginning of *Voodoo Women* was so different. I guess—' Jessica found herself waving her hands in the air helplessly. She'd made a slip and mentioned *Voodoo Women*. He'd know she knew who he was. But it was too late now, she'd done it. Perhaps he hadn't noticed. 'I guess it just sounds such hard work to start off with, you know, microbiotic organisms? What are they when they're at home?'

Morgan scratched his forehead again. 'You *keep* losing me, Jessica. I don't understand what you're talking about. This isn't a novel, it's a scientific book. Am I being really dense or something?'

'No.' Jessica frowned. 'I picture you writing novels, poetic, romantic, thrilling novels, that's all. Not scientific books.'

'That's the nicest compliment I've had in a long time.'

He got up. She knew he was going to come and kiss her, but she motioned him back down. They could kiss later, they could kiss all night. She wanted to know what had happened to his work.

'Novels like . . . novels like *Voodoo Women*.'

'Um . . .' Instead of scratching his forehead, Morgan drew his hands slowly down his face. 'Is your head feeling all right? Maybe that concussion has come back. Maybe I should call Louisa again.'

'Oh, please.' Frustration with him made Jessica want to get out of bed and shake him by the shoulders, but she was suddenly self-conscious of her nakedness, so she stayed put. 'What do I need a doctor for? All I'm doing is telling you that you should stick with what you're good at. Fine, you suddenly seem to care about science, but can't you do that in your spare time?'

'Jessica, I *am* sticking to what I'm good at.'

Any more of this and she'd start beating her head against the wall. It was time to stop this charade of his. His modesty, which had been sweet at first, was becoming aggravating.

'Morgan, listen, I know who you are. That doesn't mean I'm stalking you, I promise. But I do know who you are.' Jessica got out of bed and went to sit down beside him. 'And do you honestly think the public who love Morgan Blaine, who love *Voodoo Women*, want a scientific book about microbiotic thingammmies? You're so talented, Morgan. I don't want you to waste your talent, that's all. I . . . I . . . I'm only saying this because . . . because I've fallen in love with you. Don't you see that?'

'Ah.' Morgan rose. He looked up at the ceiling, down at the floor, rubbed his chin. 'I think I do see. Now. I think maybe I do.'

He walked over to the chair in the corner of the room where his clothes were and began to put them on. Jessica stayed still, stiff with disbelief. She'd told him she loved him and he'd gone to get dressed? What was that all about? Was he another one of those non-commitment freaks? A phoney, pretending to care until he'd got her into bed and tricked her – well, almost tricked her – into having sex, at which second he would turn away and abandon her? Or was he hurt by the criticism she'd levelled at his scientific book? Authors were famous for having fragile egos. Had she wounded him or was he a typical 'now that I've got her I don't want her' creep?

When he had finished dressing, Morgan walked back to the foot of the bed and sat down again, taking her hand in his.

'We have a slight problem here, Jessica. Let me ask you a few questions to determine exactly the extent of this problem, all right?'

'I tell you I love you and you want to cross examine me?' Jessica raised her chin. If he was going to back away from her, she was going to make it extremely hard on him.

'Bear with me, all right?'

As soon as she saw that sideways smile, she abandoned her high horse and simply nodded.

'I'm Morgan Blaine, yes?'

'Yes.' She nodded again.

'And I wrote *Voodoo Women*, a hugely successful novel, right?'

'Right.'

'And –' he let go of her hand, steepled his fingers – 'let's see . . . do I do something else? Like maybe teach creative writing at Columbia? Something like that?'

'You're being very silly, Morgan.'

'So I do?'

'Yes, of course you do. If you go on like this, *I'll* have to ring Louisa.' Jessica laughed. Morgan didn't.

'And, in reality, in actual fact, you *did* come to New York to find me.'

'Well . . .' Jessica wanted to dive back under the covers. The moment of truth was coming more quickly than she would have liked. But what choice did she have? He already knew she knew who he was. He'd find out from Georgie eventually that they'd chased him down. At least they'd had their passionate kisses. If she phrased it well, if she explained very carefully, he might not mind so much.

'In a manner of speaking, yes. I did come to New York to find you. But I wasn't stalking you, Morgan. I only wanted to meet you, to tell you how fabulous your work is, to see what you were like in person. People do like to meet their heroes. It's a natural impulse, don't you think?'

His eyes weren't sympathetic. They were boring into hers as if he were a policeman and she was a criminal. She had a brief pang of empathy for Daniel Canter.

'And this stepsister you were talking about before, she's here too? What is she doing in New York?'

'Trying to find you too,' Jessica answered meekly.

'So where is she?'

'Um, in the country somewhere. She went to find you first and she must have got lost, I don't know. It's not as mad as it sounds, Morgan. I know it's hard for you to understand and you might feel a teeny bit threatened having two women chasing you, but we weren't really *chasing* you, we just wanted to meet you. Actually,' Jessica gained some courage, 'you should be flattered. I'd be flattered if I were you.'

213

'I doubt that.' He grunted. The silence that followed was so oppressive Jessica thought it might last forever, that she and he would be locked in these same positions, not speaking, for the rest of their lives, until one or the other or both of them keeled over and died.

'Actually, it's pretty funny,' Morgan finally said. Relief travelled through every part of Jessica's body in one rush.

'It is, isn't it?' She beamed a high-voltage smile at him.

'Yeah, it is. My guess, Jessica, is that your stepsister *did* find Morgan Blaine.'

'Ha!' The chill she felt didn't infuse her whole body, it went straight to her heart and lodged there. She grabbed the sheet from the bed and wrapped it tightly around her. 'That *is* funny, Morgan. Are you saying you've cloned yourself?'

'No, I'm not saying that. I'm saying I'm not Morgan Blaine. My name is Morgan Hancock. Which means, and this is pretty hysterical you have to admit, you got the wrong man.'

'I—' Jessica stopped. Her mind went racing back to the basement coffee shop. Had he said his last name when they were introduced? No. But Morgan is not a common first name. How could there be two Morgans teaching at Columbia? Evidently, easily enough. The man staring at her, scrutinizing her, was not Morgan Blaine. He didn't write *Voodoo Women*, he wrote books about microbiotic organisms. How could she? How could she have made such a huge, such an unbelievably huge mistake?

'Hmmm.' Morgan finally turned his eyes away from hers and focused on the ceiling. 'To tell you the truth, I don't know what bothers me more. The fact that you and your stepsister have been hunting down some unsuspecting author, or the fact that you're so incapable of hiding your disappointment when you find out I'm not that unsuspecting author. I mean, really!' He stood up, went over to the bedroom window and stared out. 'Why not pick on Ben Affleck or someone *really* famous, if that's what you're after. Why settle for a writer, why not go the whole hog, hitch that pretty wagon to a star? Go faint on his latest movie set, see if he can be bothered to pick you up. That was a really slick move, that fainting business. When did you dream that one up?'

'I didn't—'

'Right. Of course. Absolutely. Someone who is prepared to fly halfway across the world to find a famous writer would never stoop so low as to pretend to faint, would she? Jesus, what a sucker I was. This beauty falls into my lap and I actually believe she might like me. If you knew how happy I was when you asked me to read my book to you – I thought . . . I thought . . . oh, forget it.' He turned around and faced her. 'I think you should go now.'

She could hear the pain in his voice, she could see the hurt in his eyes, but she couldn't respond to it. All she could do was look at him and think, 'He's not Morgan Blaine. Georgie must have found Morgan Blaine. I not only found the wrong Morgan, I almost had sex with the wrong Morgan. How foolish have I been?'

A small connection in her brain cells was made, a connection leading to the thought: so what? Who cares if he's the wrong Morgan? He's *my* Morgan. The connection was made, it sparked and then it fizzled like a dud firecracker. The whole point of this trip was to find Morgan Blaine. The real Morgan Blaine who was a successful novelist, not a shy scientist.

She could see it all playing out in front of her: Georgie, sitting arm-in-arm with the real Morgan Blaine on the sofa at home, basking in her triumph, the successful career woman with the successful author, facing Morgan Hancock and herself on the opposite sofa. Georgie had just asked Morgan Hancock what he did for a living and was pretending to be fascinated by his stories of moss and organisms in flux. Morgan Blaine was trying to hide a yawn.

'He's perfect for you, Jess,' she could hear Georgie say. He's perfect for you because he's not Morgan Blaine and he isn't a huge success. That would be the unspoken subtext. She, Jessica, would be the little sister who would get invited to all the literary parties and the Oscar nights, only because she was related. The little sister. Always, always, the little sister.

It didn't take long to get dressed, though it seemed to take ages because she had swept up her clothes, fled to the bathroom and was putting them on in silence, while her mind searched for and found ways to justify what she was doing. She hadn't meant to hurt him. Her intentions weren't bad. A mistake had been made. Mistakes happen. There was no point pretending she didn't want to meet the real Morgan Blaine when she did want to. If she stayed now, it would be out of pity. Morgan Hancock wouldn't want to be pitied. He wasn't her type, not really, And she wasn't his. Those feelings of peace and comfort and rightness she'd felt in this apartment were due to her fainting fit, something had gone wrong in her head and she'd mistaken it for happiness. She wasn't leaving because he wasn't Morgan Blaine, she was leaving because they didn't have anything in common. That was the crucial bit in all this. Yes, she'd pictured that scene with Georgie and Morgan Blaine, but that wasn't what was really at the heart of her leaving; if it were, that would be shameful. It was strictly a matter of compatibility. She had nothing to feel guilty about. Absolutely nothing whatsoever.

When she came out, she found Morgan in the living room, dressed and sitting at an old oak desk in the corner.

'I'm sorry, Morgan, I'm very sorry about all this,' was all she could think of to say.

He spun around in his chair, the sideways smile on his face.

'Hey,' he said. 'Don't worry about it. John was right, I don't get out enough. This has been an adventure. More or less. But

Jessica,' he took off his glasses, 'when and if you find Morgan Blaine, don't get into bed with him on the first date, OK? He might get in over his head and do something stupid like fall in love. I mean, I know that's probably the point of this whole exercise of yours, but give the guy a break, huh? Give him a while before you bring the heavy artillery out.'

'Morgan, I—'

'Forget it. Go find the voodoo man.'

Jessica hung her head and walked to the front door.

'Wait a second. Jessica?'

'Yes?' Turning around, she found him standing a few steps away.

'How did you find me? I mean how did you know I was in that coffee shop?'

'I heard John calling your name on the campus. I assumed there couldn't be another Morgan who taught there.'

'And you're what? In some kind of race with your stepsister to get to Morgan Blaine?'

'That's not why—'

'Please, shut up, Jessica. You've said enough already. But if your stepsister hasn't found him already, let me give you a tip. Instead of hanging around Columbia, why don't you just look in the phone book? He's in there – I checked while you were getting dressed.'

'Really?'

'Boy, that gleam of anticipation in your eyes is frightening. How could I have ever thought— Forget it. Go back to your hotel, look him up and give him a call. But do me one favour, OK? Don't tell me what happens. Because whatever happens, I don't want to hear about it.'

Morgan walked away.

Jessica walked out.

Chapter Twenty

Sitting in front of the fire, her legs stretched out, her back resting against the sofa, Georgie basked in the afterglow of her afternoon in the snow. Night had arrived, they'd all taken hot baths and changed, Eliza having found more of her aunt's clothes for Georgie to wear, and all was right with the world, especially as Morgan had opened a bottle of red wine.

'So admit it, Georgina, you had fun with the damn Yankees, didn't you? You like our rough and tumble antics, our uncultured idea of a good time.'

Morgan was bending over, picking up logs and putting them onto the fire as he asked this.

'I did have fun.' She smiled. 'Yes. I admit it. Uncle.' She held up her hands in a gesture of surrender.

They'd polished off a frozen pizza Morgan had heated up and come into the living room to be more comfortable. Eliza was sitting a few feet away from her, cross-legged on the floor. The difficult atmosphere of the morning had evaporated and Georgie found she was beginning to like Eliza, whose wholesome appearance didn't entirely hide a wild side. Not only that, she was starting to believe this nautical themed living room was actually very cool.

'You should emigrate,' Eliza said. 'Come join the rebel

colonials over on this side of the world. Did you know the War of Independence started with a snowball fight on Boston Common?'

'I didn't know, but I believe it, especially now. My thigh still hurts from that snowball Morgan threw – which he threw before I knew we were even having a snowball fight. I call that cheating, Morgan. It's not on, as we say in my country.'

'Shit!' Morgan dropped a log, shook his right hand in the air. 'Shit! A splinter. Ouch.'

'Poor baby.'

'Don't mock me, Eliza. It hurts.' He held his finger up, examined it. 'I think it's in deep. Uh oh. Time for an operation.'

'Oh, good!' Jumping up, Eliza headed for the kitchen. 'I get to operate! Let me sterilize a needle. I love hunting for splinters.'

'What she means,' Morgan grimaced, 'is that she loves inflicting pain.'

He was a different man to the Morgan of the morning. Georgie couldn't get over what one afternoon in the snow had accomplished. His rough tone had gone, his patronizing, cynical manner had vanished, he seemed to have forgotten how angry her appearance on his doorstep had made him. In this mood, she could imagine him writing the romantic scenes in *Voodoo Women*, creating the relationship between Eva and Rick. What she'd been exposed to before had obviously been his violent, machete-slicing side. But then what side of her had he seen at the beginning? The demented author-chasing female, that's what. Over dinner, she'd told them about her work and he'd talked about his mother working and raising him on her own. He'd expressed admiration for women who managed to hold their own in tough circumstances; and she'd actually seen what she thought might be a touch of respect for her in his face when she explained how she'd raised the funding to start up Harvey and Tanner.

'Here we go.' Eliza was back, waving a needle which looked like it came from a sewing kit. 'I put it in the fire of the stove to sterilize it. Hold out your hand, Morgan.'

Putting out his right index finger, Morgan closed his eyes.

'Squeamish, are we?' Eliza bent over and peered at the finger. 'Let me see. Hmmm. There it is. Splinter located. Now –' she jabbed the needle into his finger. He yelled. Georgie flinched as she watched Eliza dig around in the finger.

'Jesus, Eliza, you're butchering me. Stop—'

'Hold on, I've almost –' she pushed the needle in further – 'I can't quite . . .'

'Eliza!' Morgan grabbed her hand and yanked it away from his finger. 'Enough. What are you, a card-carrying sadist? Leave it. The splinter will work its way out.'

'Can I try? I'm very good at it,' Georgie suggested, having never taken a splinter out in her life.

'What is this?' He looked from Eliza to Georgie and back again. 'Is this your way of ganging up on me? Are you going to take turns torturing me?'

'Let her try.' Eliza walked over and handed the needle to Georgie. 'It's deep in there. Don't be afraid if you draw blood. Just keep going until you get it. Dig deep.'

'Oh, thanks. Thanks a lot,' Morgan moaned.

Georgie approached the fireplace. She took Morgan's finger in her hand and fought off her immediate desire to put it in her mouth and suck the splinter out.

'Right.' She held the needle up so it was hovering above his finger. Her own hand was shaking as she searched the skin to find the splinter. 'I see it. Here we go. Right.'

'You have no idea what you're doing, do you?'

'I know exactly what I'm doing.'

Before she started, she glanced up at his face, he wasn't

closing his eyes, he was staring at her, with that same look he'd given her before. This time, though, his eyes had affectionate amusement in them as well, not just that intense, searching quality.

Georgie focused. Finding this splinter and removing it was suddenly as important as anything she'd done in her life. But the dark line in his finger, barely visible beneath the skin, was so sliverlike she couldn't see how she could get enough purchase on it to take it out. Act authorized, she told herself. This was the mantra she'd repeated at the most difficult moments in her career.

'Ready? I'm starting now. Don't move your finger.' In order to keep him still, she grabbed the underside of it with her other hand. 'Now. Count to three.'

'What?'

'Count to three.'

'One . . . two.'

Georgie pushed the needle in, broke the skin, came at the splinter from the side, and yanked it out with one quick movement.

'Three.'

'Done.'

'Done?'

'Done.'

Morgan looked down at his finger, then up at Georgie. A beautiful, gorgeous grin slid across his face. 'You're a superstar, Georgina,' he pulled her to him and kissed her quickly. On the lips. 'A true genius. See Eliza – see what talent is all about?'

'Yuck. If I'd done it I would have had to get a kiss? Yuck.'

Pick up another log, get another splinter, just let me do that again. Please.

They went back to their original positions, although this time, Morgan came and sat beside Georgie on the floor, his legs and arms almost, but not quite, touching hers. The proximity was beyond sexy, it was in a realm of excitement that was making her feel so light-headed she couldn't think of anything to say, all she could do was wish Eliza would leave them alone, yet be terrified at the thought of Eliza leaving them alone.

Oh my God, he's George Clooney, she said to herself. I didn't notice the resemblance before. He really is George Clooney. How could I not have seen it?

'Yo, Georgina!' Eliza was clicking her fingers. 'Hello? Where are you? In never-never land? I asked you what you thought about Tony Blair.'

'Sorry. I was—' Georgie shook her head. 'Somewhere else. Tony Blair? What do I think about Tony Blair? I don't know.' Georgie used to know what she thought about Tony Blair. This morning she could have talked about Tony Blair for half an hour without stopping. But now? She couldn't be coherent. Until she got her act together and recovered from that kiss, conversation wasn't an option for her, listening to Morgan and Eliza having one was all she could manage.

'Actually, I'm tired of politics. You know, I've been wondering. Do you do a lot of your writing here, Morgan? Is this a good place to create in?'

He turned away from her gaze, looked up at the ceiling, then down at his hands, then all over the room, his eyes covering every inch except the space where she was stretched out; he seemed to skip over her deliberately before returning his concentration back on his hands. This one act of omission caused her pain, a physical pain she could feel in her stomach and chest.

'I find it is, yes. Authors need space, a sense of infinity, a feeling of being at one with the world.'

Something had gone horribly wrong. His voice had reverted to the contemptuous tone it had possessed in the morning. Although they were still sitting side by side, in exactly the same position they'd been in before, Georgie felt as if he'd picked himself up and gone to the far corner of the room.

'Morgan . . .' Eliza shook her head. She was in a chair, her legs tucked up beneath her. 'You're such a dufus.'

'Who is the one who *wanted* me to discuss my work, Eliza? Who said this morning she was dying to hear me talk about it? Wasn't that you?'

'That was before.' Eliza frowned.

'Before what?' he shot back at her.

'Come off it.'

'*You* come off it. You know I get this all the time. You know how much it bugs me.'

'I'm sorry.' Georgie was so flustered, so unaware of what could have caused this change in him, she felt panicky. 'It's my fault for bringing it up again. Let's talk about something else.'

'No.' Morgan stood up abruptly, started to pace around the room. 'I want to talk about it now. I am, after all, Morgan Blaine. The famous author, Morgan Blaine. People want to know about Morgan Blaine. They want to know how his mind works, how he comes up with his ideas, what he has for breakfast, you name it. It's so much fun being a celebrity. I pity the poor people who are normal, who work at a normal job, who live normal lives, who don't create masterpieces. No one wants to know about them, do they? You wouldn't be here now –' he stopped pacing and pointed a finger at Georgie – 'would you, if I weren't Morgan Blaine?'

'I suppose not,' she answered. 'But—'

'There – you see, Eliza?' His hands were in the air, palms up. 'You see? Georgina is sitting with us now because, and only because, I wrote *Voodoo Women*. She wants to sit at the feet of a writer and ask him how he does it. I'm giving her what she wants. So . . . let's see.' He began to pace again, his hand on his forehead. 'Where was I? Oh, this place. How it helps me to create. The being at one with nature bit. Does John Grisham have a place in the woods? Probably. The last time I saw him, at that award ceremony, he told me: "Morgan, life is all about nature and nature is all about life." And how wise John is. If anyone understands the creative process, my old buddy John does . . . he called me the other day and—'

'Morgan.' Standing up as well, Eliza went over to Morgan, stood facing him, her hands on her hips. 'I think I'll go to bed. Enough is enough.'

'OK. You can sleep in Mom's room. Georgina can have the guest bedroom. All right?'

'Fine.' Eliza started to move away from him, turned back. She whispered something to him, turned away again, said, 'Goodnight Georgina, see you tomorrow,' and left the room.

Georgie, alone with him, wanted to ask what was going on, why this sudden change of mood, what Eliza had whispered.

'I hope you don't mind putting me up for the night,' she said instead.

'No problem.' He moved to the mantlepiece, picked up a remote control, switched on the television in the corner of the room. 'I think it's time for some entertainment.' He didn't look at her, simply settled himself on the sofa facing the TV.

What? Why? How? Georgie was at a loss. When she'd been eight years old, her godmother had given her a glass horse for a birthday present. Despite the fact that Georgie didn't ride and had never been particularly interested in horses, she loved this object with a passion. She couldn't remember exactly how it had broken, all she could recall was looking at the pieces of glass splayed across the floor – an ear there, a leg there, a tail over there – a shattered horse. Years later, at school, when she'd read the play *The Glass Menagerie*, she'd been so affected by it and her teacher couldn't understand why. Georgina Harvey always got As in English, but English was not a subject she loved or was excited about – maths was what she was most involved in. Why this sudden overwhelming interest in a play? the teacher wanted to know, but Georgie couldn't explain. What she'd felt reading it was what she'd felt looking at the broken horse, and what she felt now sitting with Morgan Blaine watching television. An empty, sad, lonely, hopeless mix which, when put together, became the certainty of unfulfilled dreams.

The snow was still swirling outside, the fire was crackling, Eliza had gone to bed, and Morgan Blaine was channel-surfing. Georgie sat down on the sofa at a distance from him.

Click – a rerun of *Seinfeld*. Click – CNN. Click – *Friends*. Click – basketball. Click – ice hockey. Click – Audrey Hepburn and George Peppard in the rain. *Breakfast at Tiffanys*. Morgan didn't click again. He sat and watched as the film ended and the credits rolled. 'Cue Henry Mancini,' he said. 'Cue "Moon River".'

'You know I've always wondered—' Georgie began, tentatively.

'About huckleberry friend?' Morgan cut in.

'You . . . ?' Georgie couldn't finish the sentence. She stared at Morgan Blaine. He stared at the television.

'Huckleberry friend ranks up there with the cake-melting lyrics to "McArthur Park" as the most stupid lines ever penned.' His head had swivelled, he was looking at her now.

We're getting it back, she thought. Whatever that magic was we had before, we're getting it back. I didn't imagine it, the way we work so well together. Who else would have the exact same response to that line? Who else in the world?

'So . . . time for bed.' He turned the TV off, stretched. 'Your room is the first on the left upstairs. I put some pyjamas out for you and a towel. The snow plough comes early, it will probably wake you up. I get up early anyway, so if you want to come down and get some coffee, there'll be some. At the moment I'm thinking I'll go back to Manhattan tomorrow. There's something I have to do, so I can give you a ride. OK?'

'Couldn't we – I mean, wouldn't it be nice to stay here and chat for a little bit now.'

'Chat about what? My book?'

'Well, if you want. Or about anything, really.'

'No thanks, Georgina. I'm tired. Of course if you want to have sex with the great author, that's always a possibility.'

'Morgan!' Jesus! What was she supposed to say to that? Was he a Jekyll and Hyde character? Good Morgan – Bad Morgan? If so, she didn't understand what it was that brought Bad Morgan into being. 'Why do you find it necessary to insult me?'

'Because I'm tired of this shit. Come here.'

Georgie didn't move. Morgan grabbed her hand and yanked her up.

'Come here.' Putting his arms around her waist, he pulled her into him. He bent his head and kissed her with a fierceness which she found herself returning. Their kiss was so aggressive, she felt as if they were locked in battle. She waited for it to turn tender. It didn't.

Morgan stepped back, put his hands on her shoulders, turned her round so that she was facing away from him, drew her into his body and whispered in her ear. 'Look around you, Georgina. Tell me what you see.'

She was a little frightened, very bewildered, and incredibly aroused.

'I see a living room. I see two oars, I see two life preservers, I see a carved swordfish. Are we playing a game, Morgan?'

'What else do you see?' His hands were squeezing her shoulders.

'A lamp. A television set. A bookcase.'

Pushing her forward, frog-marching her from behind, Morgan let go of her when they were in front of the bookcase.

'Now what do you see?'

'Um . . . books.' She laughed feebly.

'What books?'

'Morgan . . .'

'What books?'

'All right. I don't understand the point of this game, but I'll play it if you're so dead set on it. Let's see – *The Sun Also Rises. The Great Gatsby. The Sound and The Fury. The Scarlet Letter.*' She looked at him. 'It looks like a bookcase full of books for a course on American literature. Do I have to name every single one?'

'Tell me what book *isn't* there.'

Georgie scanned the shelves.

'*Moby Dick?* I'm not an academic, Morgan. I don't know all of the great books written by American authors. Please, just tell me what's going on. I don't understand.'

Morgan put his hand in the air, signalling her to stop, left her side, went and stood in front of the fireplace. 'You know *my* book, don't you?'

'Duh,' Georgie wanted to say, but the look he was giving her stopped her. 'Yes, I know yours.'

'And it's not there, is it?'

Yet again, Georgie scanned the shelves. 'No. It isn't.'

'Why do you think it isn't?'

'Oh, God, I don't know. Morgan, is all this because I said you didn't write *War and Peace* before? Are you angry with me for that? I know we didn't start off on the right foot, but I thought that after sledding, after this evening . . . I thought you didn't mind any more that I came here to find you. I really do admire your work. I didn't mean to trash it. Are you worried that you haven't written the great American novel?'

Morgan, unaccountably, laughed.

'Is that it?' Georgie pressed.

'I haven't written the great American anything, Georgina.

227

I wrote a fantastic story about a spaceship when I was ten years old, but to my knowledge it has yet to win the Nobel Prize for literature.'

'But you wrote *Voodoo Women*.'

'Did I?' His eyes narrowed. 'What makes you think that?'

'You're Morgan Blaine.' Georgie found herself stepping back a pace. 'Aren't you?'

'Yes, I'm Morgan Blaine.'

'So . . .' Fear began to invade her, a terror that he really was unhinged, schizophrenic. She was alone in a house in the middle of nowhere with a schizophrenic. But Eliza was upstairs, she wasn't wholly alone. Did Eliza know how mentally unbalanced he was? Wouldn't Eliza have warned her? What had Eliza whispered in his ear?

'This is the deal, Georgina. I'm Morgan Blaine but there is also another Morgan Blaine. Another Morgan Blaine who is ruining my life.'

'Um. Does the other Morgan Blaine . . . does he . . . I mean when does he come out? At times of stress?'

I can help him, she thought, as concern mingled with fear. Maybe I can make him better.

Morgan stretched his mouth wide, put his hands out in front of him like claws.

'You mean at the full moon?' He tiptoed towards her, his claws still showing. 'You mean on nights like this when he feels the need to suck someone's blood?'

'Morgan!' Georgie retreated behind the sofa. 'This isn't funny. Stop it.'

'But I can't stop.' Rubbing his hands together, he made a horror-flick face. 'I'm thirsty. Fresh blood! Are you, by any chance, a virgin?'

Leaping in the air, Morgan landed on his back on the sofa and laughed. He was laughing so hard he reminded her of Jessica the night they shook up the champagne.

'This isn't funny.' She repeated. 'This isn't at all funny.'

'Yes it is,' he said between laughs. 'It's hysterical.' He wiped his eyes with his shirt before sitting up. 'It's the funniest thing that's happened since that stupid book was published and that idiotic man began to wreck my life. Well,' he shrugged, 'that's an exaggeration. He isn't wrecking my life, but he's making it damn annoying. Do you know how many people call me, assuming I'm *the* Morgan Blaine? Do you know how many people show up at my house in the city, doorstepping me, assuming I'm *the* Morgan Blaine? Do you have any idea what a pain in the ass it is? Of course, I should go ex-directory, I know. I haven't because I – because it's *my* name too, Georgina. Why should I have to change my life because some dipshit writer happens to share my name?'

'I—' Georgie reached out to steady herself but there wasn't anything to grab onto. 'You're not . . . ?'

'*The* Morgan Blaine? Nope, I'm not. I'm the other Morgan Blaine, the one in the oil business. I've taken a week off this week. My vacation.' He smiled. 'I travel a lot so I find it relaxing to come here and hibernate for a week in the winter. The summers here are full of summer people – know what I mean?'

'Why did you . . . why did you . . .' Georgie bit her lip. Tears were forming, she could feel them. Georgina Harvey didn't cry. 'Lie to me?'

'Why? Why lie to a fawning English groupie who admires a second-rate book so much she comes all the way to Connecticut and barges in on its author? I don't know.' He scratched his head. 'Why the hell not? You wanted to meet the great author, you met him. You wanted to discuss his silly book, I discussed it. I gave you what you wanted, Georgina. You met Morgan Blaine. Hell, bring me a copy of *Voodoo Women* and I'll even sign it for you. You can show it to all your friends in England. You can say you kissed the man who wrote those . . . those *godawful* sex scenes. How many points will you score for that back home?'

'Eliza.' Georgie was beginning to process what this information meant. 'Eliza was in on this too?'

'Eliza knows how fed up with this whole Morgan Blaine business I am. She wanted to have a little fun with it, so did I.'

'At my expense.'

'Well, sunshine, you asked for it, remember. Showing up here like that. What – did you think you'd have an orgasm just looking at me? Like in the book?'

Georgie turned her head away.

'I mean, if that isn't the most ridiculous scene ever to be written in the history of humanity, I don't know what is.'

She couldn't comment, she didn't want to look at him. Which was worse: the fact that he'd been secretly laughing at her all day, or the fact that she longed for him to kiss her again? She wanted to get into bed with him, talk about stupid song lyrics and have – what had he called it? Jungle sex. With hot chocolate afterwards. She wanted to go sledding again tomorrow morning; she wanted him to pin her to the snowy ground and whisper, 'Say uncle,' in her ear. And she knew perfectly well he wanted none of those things, not one. As far as he was concerned she was a fawning English groupie who had gone to unbelievable lengths to track down a second-rate author.

'I'm sorry to disappoint you, Georgina. After all the trouble you've been to.'

She wouldn't look in his direction or speak, she didn't trust herself to do either without crying.

'Well, I'm tired, it's been a hell of a day. I'm going to sleep. Goodnight, and please turn off the lights when you come upstairs.'

Doing an about-turn with military precision, he walked out

of the living room. At the threshold, he stopped, turned back, leaned against the door frame.

'You know, for a while there, I forgot why you'd come. I was going to apologize to you for making you unload the groceries and treating you so badly to begin with. But you never did forget why you came, did you? I wish I understood why you'd do something like that, Georgina. You don't strike me as the type of person who's a celebrity hound. But I guess headhunters are in the business of collecting scalps. Still, I thought, for a while . . .' He shook his head. 'Never mind. See you in the morning.'

He left the room. She could hear every stair thud as he climbed them.

What an incredible mess she'd made. And there was no way she could think of to clean it up. This was like the recurring nightmare she had of sitting in an exam room, naked, opening the test paper and not knowing one answer to any of the questions. She stood, motionless for a few minutes, then turned off the light, put her head down, trudged up the stairs and into the guest bedroom, undressed, put on the pyjamas, went into the ensuite bathroom, found a toothbrush and toothpaste, used them, and climbed into bed – all as if she were on autopilot. Closing her eyes, she tried to imagine herself back at home.

None of this has happened, she said to herself. Tomorrow I'll get back to the hotel and book the return flight. We can leave tomorrow night and life will go on and none of this will matter. I'll erase it from my mind.

I've met Morgan Blaine. He – the man who can draw me into a snowball fight, the man who can make me think a carved swordfish is a thing of beauty, is the wrong Morgan Blaine. Wrong for whom, though?

Ah, but Georgina, remember, you can never be sure, when the arrow wings its way into your heart that it has pierced the heart of the person you have fallen for. This person clearly thinks you're a deeply silly woman. Cupid's arrow hasn't gone anywhere near *his* heart.

It happens in business too, she reminded herself. You can find the perfect man for the job only to have him turn it down. Most of the time, if you offer a big enough salary and huge perks, you can convince him, but sometimes, once in a while, he'll turn you down however much you tempt him. He doesn't want the job, simple as that, and nothing will induce him to take it.

Could I try to sell myself to the wrong Morgan Blaine? she wondered, as she rolled over on her side. How would I do that? Buy different, non-weird clothes? Take a crash course on the oil industry? What difference would any of that make? I'd still be the woman who took a taxi from Manhattan to find the right Morgan Blaine. The wrong Morgan Blaine would never forget that.

And what if I told him about Project X? What would he think then? I can only imagine.

I hate romance. Love sucks. I can't function properly when I'm powerless, when things are out of my control.

Georgina Harvey rolled over on to her other side. Then back again. She put her arm over her eyes, then took it away and put the other arm over. She sat up, and lay back down.

I'll go into his room. I'll seduce him. We'll have sex in the country. I will refuse to leave until he falls in love with me.

She got up, out of bed and walked to the door. She stood with her hand on the doorknob. This is crazy, she said to herself, but opened the door nevertheless and stepped out into the corridor. Which was Morgan's room, which Eliza's? Tiptoeing down the hall, she stopped at the next door on the right and cracked it open as noiselessly as possible. Tiptoeing again, she approached the bed. She couldn't make out who was lying there, it was too dark to see properly. Dropping down on all fours, Georgie crawled to the side of the bed. Her eyes were getting more accustomed to the dark, but the body in the bed was obscured by the sheets on top of it. When she was up close to it, she paused, held her breath and gently lifted the sheet by a corner. The revealed head was turned on its side, away from her, but it was a male head, it was Morgan's head.

'Morgan,' she whispered. The head didn't move. 'Morgan,' she said. The head stayed still. 'Morgan.' She nudged his shoulder. 'Morgan.' She shook his shoulder. 'Wake up.' No movement, no change in his breathing pattern. He was sleeping the sleep of the dead. Georgie climbed into bed beside him. He was too big for her to push, so she lay, half-in, half-out of the bed, her arm draped over his waist. 'Morgan.' No response. 'Morgan!' She was almost shouting in his ear. How could she seduce a dead log? Go to the bathroom, get a glass of water and throw it in his face? 'Morgan!' Running her hands over his naked body, Georgie stopped herself short of grabbing his penis. There was seduction and there was rape. She began to lick his ear. He didn't move. She reached for his right hand and sucked his index finger, the finger which had had the splinter. Morgan Blaine's body shifted. He pulled his hand out of her mouth, he turned over on his front and his right leg shot out underneath the covers as his right arm pushed her away. Away, out of the bed. Away, onto the floor with a thud.

Georgina Harvey had been kicked out of bed.

Picking herself up, she leaned over his prone form. He was still sleeping soundly. At least he hadn't consciously kicked her out of bed, she hoped. Unless he was faking sleep as well as Meg Ryan had faked an orgasm in *When Harry Met Sally*, he had pushed her out of bed in a reflex response.

After a moment of indecision, Georgie left his room. She went back to her own bed and lay down on her stomach. After another minute she rolled over onto her back.

The earlier that snow plough comes the better, she thought. This is going to be a long night's journey into day.

Sadie had a roommate. Jessica was stretched out on the bed beside hers, tossing to and fro as if she were dreaming she was on a cruise in stormy weather. She was wide awake, though – every time Sadie was on the verge of sleep, Jessica would ask her a question or tell her another detail of her evening with Morgan Hancock. Desperate to get some rest, but unable to kick the even more desperate Jessica out of her room, Sadie would say, 'Mmm hmmm,' or answer her in the shortest possible way.

'You think I was right to leave, don't you, Sadie?'

'Mmmhmmm.'

'And Georgie has found Morgan Blaine?'

'She said she had.'

Silence would then ensue, followed by more tossing, followed by: 'Do you know what microbiotic organisms are?'

'No. I'm afraid not.'

Jessica had arrived in Sadie's room, poured out her story in a torrent of words, asked if she could stay and sleep there, as she couldn't face being alone, and then collapsed on the spare bed fully dressed.

'Don't you want to get changed?' Sadie had asked before she turned out the light.

'I can't move,' Jessica had replied. 'I'm exhausted. I'm shell-shocked. I'm probably suffering from post-dramatic stress syndrome.'

That comment, Sadie thought, wasn't just a Freudian slip, it was full evening dress. Sadie wasn't sure whether she felt sorrier for Jessica or for Morgan Hancock. The mistaken identity was a disaster for both of them. If she didn't have her rendezvous with the Gentleman in the morning, she knew she would have paid a lot more attention to Jessica's plight, but she did have the rendezvous and she couldn't stop herself from selfishly wanting sleep before it.

Toss. Turn.

'Do you think I should show up at Morgan Blaine's address tomorrow morning?'

'Maybe you should sleep on it. Decide what to do when you've had some rest.'

'Whoa!' Andrew had said on the phone. '*Two* Morgan Blaines. How cool is that? I think *I* should start up a headhunting company, one that recruits men who are named Morgan Blaine. We could have Prime Minister Morgan Blaine, President Morgan Blaine, every important person in the world will be named Morgan Blaine.'

Sadie had laughed, but that was before Jessica had come back with her sad tale. There weren't two Morgan Blaines. And, apparently, the name Morgan Blaine was the key to happiness. Jessica had forgotten all about falling in love at first sight. She'd passed off her feeling of 'rightness' in his flat as an after-effect of her fainting fit. A rose by any other name might smell as sweet, but Morgan Blaine by the name of Morgan Hancock smelled like a decaying microbiotic organism.

Life at the moment was definitely out of control. If anyone had told her she'd be sharing a hotel room with Jessica, in New York City, waiting for Georgie to come back after a date in a blizzard with a man who had written a book called *Voodoo Women*, and looking forward to her own breakfast date with a nameless man whom she had met on a bus, Sadie would have suggested they spend some quality time in a mental hospital.

Little did Lisa know, when she put that piece of paper on Sadie's desk, that she had laid a trail of explosive powder. Where would it end? Whose heart would get blown up and whose would survive?

'He has such a lovely smile,' Jessica murmured. 'Alfred Hitchcock is coming to my birthday party.'

Jessica, it appeared, would not stop talking, even in her sleep.

By the time she heard the sound of the snow plough crunching its way down the road, Georgie had regained control over her emotions. She had decided she was no longer in love, or even in lust, with the wrong Morgan Blaine. She'd been snowblinded and jetlagged and vulnerable, that was all. She'd imagined she was attracted to him, she had hated that kiss, she had no feelings whatsoever for this person in the oil business with a huge chip on his shoulder and a sleep pattern so deep it was impossible to disturb. Yes, he shared her non-comprehension about the phrase 'huckleberry friend' but that meant about as much as sharing a liking for scrambled eggs. She had momentarily lost perspective because of an afternoon of fun in the snow. She'd been, somehow, hypnotized into believing Morgan Blaine was the man of her dreams. George Clooney? He didn't look anything like him.

As soon as she got back into Manhattan, she would make the arrangements to leave. They'd go back home and continue with their lives. One way or another they'd get through and put this particular bit of horrible past behind them.

The wrong Morgan Blaine might have crept into her heart yesterday, but between the hours of four thirty and five a.m., she'd dated him, married him, had children with him and divorced him. How easy it was to imagine him as a hopeless husband, permanently angry and scornful. By four forty-five, she could hear him calling out, 'Get the goddamn lunch ready, you bitch'; by four fifty, she was trying unsuccessfully to wake him in the middle of a three-alarm fire, by five they were sitting across from each other in a lawyer's office. Thus the wrong Morgan Blaine had been vanquished from the heart he'd invaded.

Like the snow, Georgie thought, as she stood at the window

watching the plough's shovel clear it from the driveway. He's gone like the snow, piled into a mound on the side of the road.

I really, really don't like snow, whether it's here or up in the Arctic Circle.

As she turned away from the window and began to put her tartan suit back on, she could smell coffee.

That's that, she thought. I'll have a cup of coffee, we'll get on the road, I'll get back to the hotel and that will be that. He doesn't love me. He thinks I'm a fawning groupie and a celebrity scalp hunter. I don't love him. I think he's arrrogant and egotistical. End of story.

Her tights were halfway up her legs when she found herself wondering about something she knew she shouldn't be wondering about: had Jess found the *right* Morgan Blaine, had Jess already won?

Or was there still hope?

Chapter Twenty One

What do you wear for an eight thirty a.m. date in a coffee shop? Sadie had agonized over that question, finally deciding on jeans and a black turtleneck jumper. She had to tiptoe around the room as she was getting dressed so as not to wake Jessica. The night before she'd debated whether to tell Jessica about her breakfast date, but hadn't in the end because Jessica was so obsessed with finding Morgan Blaine she might try and stop Sadie from leaving. 'How can you go out in my time of crisis?' she could imagine Jessica moaning. 'I need you.' At some point in the last forty-eight hours she'd become Jessica Tanner's new best friend, but Sadie doubted that the friendship went deep enough to cover resentment. Human nature being what it was, Jessica would hardly like the idea of Sadie finding a mystery man when she had so spectacularly failed to find her own.

'Be back in an hour' she wrote on a notepad, then added, 'Just getting some coffee'. Careful, careful, she said to herself as she got her coat and went to the door. Pulling it open, she stepped outside, eased the door back into place with the nerves of a first-time burglar and ran to the lift. The door pinged open within seconds. She was free.

The snow had turned to slush in a dirty, drizzling rain,

the sidewalks were crammed with people going to work, pedestrians swearing when a car sprayed slush onto them or when their umbrellas clashed, but Sadie was paying more attention to the time than to her surroundings. Every few seconds she checked her watch, unsure whether she should arrive dead on time or be a few minutes late. She didn't want to walk into the coffee shop before he did, knowing she'd spend however long it took for him to get there worrying that he wouldn't get there at all. On the other hand, she didn't want to be so late he might, if he had arrived on time, leave. Eight thirty-five, she decided. That would be the perfect time. To get there then meant waiting for five whole minutes a block away, under the awning of a delicatessen. Her hair was wet, she hadn't dared spend too much time putting on make-up in case Jessica woke up, and she knew she wasn't looking her best, but she was too wired to care. At eight thirty-three exactly she sloshed her way to the coffee shop, at eight thirty-five, she walked into it. The same waitress was there, most of the stools were occupied, but none by the Gentleman. The tables at the back were full of people, none of whom was the Gentleman.

Of course, she thought. Of course he's not here. He's not coming. I knew he wouldn't. Why would he?

There was an empty stool at the end of the counter. She sat down on it and closed her eyes. One cup of coffee and she'd go back. She'd help Jessica find Morgan Blaine, or she'd help Georgie find Morgan Blaine, she'd help *anyone* find Morgan Blaine, she'd scour the city for Morgan fucking Blaine as long as it meant she'd be too busy to think about what a stupid, ridiculous fool she'd been.

Sadie checked her watch. Eight forty. The waitress behind the counter, who had told her not to worry about getting picked up by a stranger, was working like a maniac, filling cups of coffee and delivering plates of eggs. Desperate for a diversion, Sadie took the guide to New York out of her handbag and started to turn the pages. Her eyes travelled up and down, her brain not taking in a word of what was written. After she'd turned over the last page, she checked her watch. Eight forty-five. The waitress was now filling the cup for a middle-aged woman on Sadie's left.

'Could I have a cup of coffee as well, please?'

'In a second, hon.' She had orange hair, not far at all from the disastrous colour Sadie's hair had been dyed, but without the chocolate stripes, and red lipstick, sagging shoulders and a dirty, wrinkled brown uniform. Sadie hadn't noticed, the day before, how down-at-heel this woman was, but the day before she'd been too happy to see anything properly.

She swivelled the stool and looked at every table again. No Gentleman. He might have come in, checked the tables but not the counter, and left. As if. He might have come in, checked the tables and the counter but missed seeing her. Yeah, right. He might have had an accident. He might be stuck in traffic. Dream on, Sade.

A cup of coffee was plonked down in front of her. She looked at her watch. Eight fifty. She picked up the guide book. She leafed through the pages. She had a sip of coffee. Eight fifty five. She swivelled and looked at the tables, swivelled back and leafed through pages again. Nine a.m. The woman beside her lit up a cigarette. Sadie almost asked to bum one. Smoking would give her something to do. It would also, doubtless, get her right back in an addiction she'd broken five years ago.

So he wasn't coming. So what? It wasn't the end of the world. She'd get over it. There was no reason to feel as disappointed as she did. As she finished her coffee, she ran through the scenes of the morning before, slowly, trying to remember every single detail. Put it in a package, she told herself, wrap it up, put a bow on it and bring it back out whenever you're feeling ... feeling what? Depressed? Will it cheer you up or depress you even more? You know damn well it will depress you even more. Why did he bother to make a date if he wasn't going to show up? Why did Piers bother to live with her if he didn't love her?

Stuff the self-pity, Sadie. It's bad for the soul.

'Excuse me?' She called to the waitress, who scuttled over. 'Can I have my bill, please?'

'Sure, hon. That'll be – Jeez, Maurice, I forgot, didn't I?'

'Sorry?'

'You're the one from yesterday and I forgot. Where's my head? Be back in a sec. Wait here.'

Sadie watched as the waitress went to the far end of the counter, knelt down, retrieved something and came rushing back.

'The guy – the guy came in early – seven thirty or so. He said he couldn't meet up with you, some business thing, and to give you this.' Thrusting a white envelope at Sadie, she frowned. 'It was so damn busy in here. I'm really sorry.'

'It's OK.' *Everything* was OK. The Gentleman had come. And he'd left a note. The bulkiness of the envelope surprised Sadie, more than a sheet of paper was obviously in it, there was an object of some kind. The waitress hovered over her. Sadie didn't have the heart to tell her to go away.

'A watch? What's he doing giving you a watch?'

Sadie looked at the watch she'd removed from the envelope. It was an old Timex with a frayed brown leather strap. What the hell *was* he doing giving her a watch? She took the piece of paper out, put it on the counter and read:

To the mystery girl on the bus
  Sorry I couldn't make it this morning, someone truly mean and cruel scheduled an important breakfast meeting at the last minute. This watch is my deposit. It's old but it's trustworthy.

I'll redeem it when we meet again. This afternoon, at three? Coffee is on me.

   If, by any bad luck or worse mischief, you can't make . . .

'What's that? Worse what?' The waitress moved in closer, the almost nuclear power of her bad breath forcing Sadie back.

People who have been in accidents say that everything slows down, that things happen in slow motion. The car starts to spin out of control, seconds feel like minutes as it heads towards the tree, the impact comes as a final act in a long play. That's what people say, Sadie thought afterwards. But it isn't always true. In her case, it had all happened so quickly she had no time to take it in: the waitress's rank breath; her own immediate response to back away; the waitress's elbow coming forward; the coffee cup making a clanking noise as it fell over on its side; the brown liquid spilling. How long had it taken? Three seconds? It felt like a nanosecond. Her brain couldn't work fast enough to register the consequences, not at first.

'Fuck a duck!' the waitress cried. She grabbed a napkin from a counter-top dispenser and began to blot the piece of paper with it.

Looking down, Sadie saw a mess of illegible ink where the rest of the letter had been, a coffee-stained obliteration of words.

'Worse mischief.' Sadie said, looking down at the ruined letter. Had he written his name at the end? What had he signed it? Yours truly? Sincerely? Lots of love? Or love? Would lots of love be better than love? Technically, yes. Socially, no. Lots of people said lots of love to lots of people. Lots of love was like 'all my best', it wasn't a true declaration.

She could ask him this afternoon, if she really wanted to, what he'd signed it. That was the reason this accident was not a tragedy. She'd been able to read the most important bit, the arrangement for later. And the coffee hadn't spilt on his watch, either. All in all, as accidents went, it was a minor one.

'I'm so sorry, hon.' The waitress looked as if she were about to cry.

'Don't be. Honestly. No harm done.' *But please, please don't breathe near me any more.*

'Coffee's on me, OK?'

'Thank you.' All she wanted was to get out now. Sadie would gladly accept the free cup of coffee and leave. She picked up the still-damp piece of paper, put the watch in her bag and smiled.

'I'll see you at three.'

'Oh, damn, I'm off then. But tomorrow, hon? Will you two do an old lady a favour and come in tomorrow morning? This is so romantic and all. And happening right here in this dump. It's so exciting. He's given you his *watch*. I mean, a bracelet would be better. A necklace would be better than that. The first present my husband gave me? A subscription to *TV Guide*. And, believe me, it's been downhill since then on the gift parade. Anyway, I promise I won't spill anything if you come tomorrow. I'm not a klutz, not in a trillion years have I ever been a klutz.'

'I know, and thanks. I hope we do come tomorrow,' was the only thing Sadie could think of to say. The waitress was blushing so much she looked as though she were about to have a rendezvous with a mystery man herself. 'See you. Take care.'

'You too, hon.'

Returning to the slush-filled streets of Manhattan, Sadie walked through the rain with a smile on her face. She had his watch. His deposit. She had a date for later. It was disappointing that he hadn't been able to be there, but he'd made a huge effort to make up for that. *And* his non-appearance meant she could have a few more hours of anticipation. *This may be the best part*, she said to herself. *Enjoy it. When you actually meet him, he may be nothing like you hope.*

But I already love his watch, she thought, digging it out

of her bag and squeezing it tightly in her hand. I absolutely adore his watch.

'Bye, Georgina,' Eliza hugged her. 'And here's my number,' she pushed a card at her, 'in case you ever come out this way again. I'm sorry about yesterday. It was a joke, but I guess it's not so funny for you.'

'Oh, no, it *was* funny.' Georgie managed to smile. 'I deserved it after behaving so foolishly. I'm not normally quite so stupid. Anyway, it was lovely to meet you and I'll definitely call if I'm in the area again.' Morgan, Eliza and Georgie were all standing on the bottom porch step. Georgie turned to Morgan. 'You did say John Grisham lived in the woods, didn't you? Maybe he's somewhere very near here. Next time, I'll track *him* down. I might have better luck.'

Eliza, Georgie was grateful to hear, laughed. Morgan Blaine yawned.

'Do you want a ride, or are you going to walk, Lize?'

'I'll walk, thanks.'

'OK. See you soon' He stepped over, gave her a kiss on the cheek, a quick hug and headed for the car.

Georgie followed him.

'Have fun you two!' Eliza called, waving.

We have a snowball's chance in hell of that, Georgie thought, getting into the passenger seat. This ride is going to be worse than the taxi ride here. I never thought I'd be nostalgic for Mr ET, but I am now.

Morgan started up the car, they both put on their seatbelts and began the journey back. A couple of times, as they went down the driveway, the car skidded slightly, but Morgan controlled it.

'It's strange, isn't it?' he said as they came out onto the main road. 'You have to turn into a skid, which goes against all your natural reactions.'

'Mmm.'

Georgie wasn't going to get into a conversation, what was the point? He'd been perfectly polite as they drank their coffee in the kitchen, but nothing more. As soon as Eliza had joined them, he'd perked up a bit, but Georgie had felt like the odd man out as they discussed various members of their family. Morgan Blaine wasn't giving an inch in her direction. She was sure, now, that he hadn't been awake when he'd kicked her out of bed; he wasn't aware that she'd been in his room. If he'd known, he would have had to make a comment, he wouldn't have been able to resist. The wrong Morgan Blaine was not the type to be gracious. He was arrogant and egotistical.

Remember that Georgie, she said to herself. Concentrate on those two adjectives.

As they passed through a small, picturesque town, she saw a white courthouse. She imagined him in the quaint courtroom, in a wooden witness box, testifying against her. He wanted custody of their children. He was inventing stories about her to get it.

'I have an English friend,' he stated, as he changed into third gear. 'An older man, a barrister. He told me a story which I'd guess is apocryphal, but he swears it's true. He was here, in Texas, and was taking a plane to Hawaii. When he finds his seat on the plane, he's beside a woman who says, "Howdy, how're ya doin'?" My friend says, "Excuse me, madam, but I have no interest whatsoever in anything you may choose to tell me and I have absolutely nothing to say to you. The American habit of talking at random to no point is not one I happen to share. Kindly remain silent and allow me to read my book in peace until we reach Hawaii." The woman shuts up, about ten minutes later the plane pulls out of the gate and the pilot comes on the intercom. He announces the weather en route and all that stuff and then wishes them a turbulent-free trip to Alaska. My friend, of course, is on the wrong plane. The woman laughs. She laughs all the way to Alaska.'

'That's a good story,' Georgie said. 'Maybe you should try writing it.'

'Maybe I should.' Morgan Blaine shrugged. 'Maybe *the* Morgan Blaine and I could co-author a book. *Fans Who Have Stalked Us* – does that sound like a good title?'

'Brilliant.'

'Listen, Georgina, this stalking the famous business, it's a mistake whichever way you look at it. I happen to think *the* Morgan Blaine is a middle-of-the-road writer, but that doesn't mean he doesn't deserve his privacy as much as I do. Because he's written a successful book doesn't mean he should be stalked by some obsessive.'

Georgie flinched at the word.

'What right do you have to intrude on him? None. And the other way around, well, I've seen the pain it can cause. I had a female friend at college, she was a sweet, insecure, troubled nineteen-year-old. She read a good book, a *great* book which affected her so much, she wrote to the author. You know, a ten-page letter full of angst and soul-spilling. This author, a famous author, was momentarily out of the limelight. He hadn't written a book in a while and I suppose he was flattered by this fan letter. She'd put a return address, and he wrote back to her. They get this correspondence going and sure enough, he says he would like to meet her.

'*She* thinks he's going to explain life and literature to her. *He* wants to get laid. They meet, he gets her drunk, he has sex with her. Strangely enough, he doesn't let her in on the secrets of life and literature while he's screwing her. What would you call it? Book rape? Anyway, she wakes up with a hangover from hell the next morning and a feeling of shame so deep, it sends her already troubled psyche into overdrive. She ends up quitting college.

'Maybe she's gotten over it, maybe it was a, what do they call it? Learning experience. But at the time . . . Well, anyway, I understand kids wanting to meet baseball stars, I get that. I understand teenagers who have crushes on pop stars. But – what are you – thirty-one, thirty-two years old? You run a business. You're clearly a capable adult and you're chasing after a guy who writes about machete-wielding heros and voodoo women? Christ.' He shook his head. 'It's pathetic.'

Georgie stared out of the windscreen. Her body was shrinking in on her. Her heart was pounding. He'd chastised her. Like a parent would a badly behaved two-year-old. He was right. That was the problem. She knew he was right. He was worse than any headmistress or school counsellor. Morgan Blaine had made her feel like a complete idiot. And she had to spend at least another hour in the car with him.

My stepsister is chasing him too, she wanted to say. There's someone else in this world as stupid and pathetic as I am. That wouldn't help, not really. Nothing would help. She'd feel like a buffoon for the rest of her life. There was no rescue in sight. Harvey and Tanner could make trillions of pounds and she'd still remember this moment in this car and the feeling of humiliation that seared her.

Georgie's brain galloped desperately, searching for an escape route from shame.

1.   The car could crash now, they'd both die, and Morgan Blaine wouldn't be around to taunt her, even from a distance. But then she wouldn't be around either.
2.   The car could crash and only Morgan would die. That was a possibility. Why was he driving so carefully?
3.   She could kill Camilla Parker Bowles, marry Prince Charles and be Queen of England. Morgan Blaine would have to think differently of her then.
4.   What if she became the top headhunter in the oil

industry? She could be the person responsible for finding him the perfect job he'd always wanted.

5.   She could introduce him to Jess, he'd fall in love with Jess and be forever grateful.

No.

Think rationally, Georgie. What could possibly redeem this situation? Make the wrong Morgan Blaine see that he's wrong, not in general but about this specific instance.

If the right Morgan Blaine won the Nobel Prize for literature, at least he couldn't be seen as a middle-of-the-road author. But what are the odds of that? Low. If the right Morgan Blaine was a wonderful man, someone funny, intelligent, handsome . . . if he and Jess *did* get together, or if he became *my* best friend, maybe even more . . . if, one way or another, I could prove that finding him was a good, a brilliant plan, then making such a fool of myself would be justified. I could bring him to meet the wrong Morgan Blaine. I could say: see, finding Morgan Blaine *was* worthwhile. I am, after all, a very good headhunter. My instincts were right.

I *have* to find him, she said to herself as the car swung on to the highway. It's more important now than ever.

And if he's a wanker? He won't be. He can't be. He is a wonderful, fabulous, perfect man. Nothing like this . . . this arrogant and egotistical man beside me.

'So,' Morgan turned to her, 'now that I've given you my lecture, are you going to give up this crazy chase? Or are you going to go on with it?'

'I don't see that it's any of your business, either way.'

'Ah.' He laughed. 'Women in the bayou know their business. And that business is magic. You know, Georgina, I think you deserve a Christmas present. I think I'll buy you your very own magic wand. Or should I get some little dolls for you to stick pins in? Should I get one which looks like me? Would that make you happy?'

'Delirious.'

'Done.'

Georgie shifted, turned her body away from his and stared out of the passenger window.

'Do you want to be left in peace? Do you want me to kindly leave you in silence?'

'I want to sleep. I'm tired. I didn't sleep well last night.'

'That's funny,' Morgan Blaine said. 'I don't think I've ever slept so soundly.'

Georgie remained mute. The *right* Morgan Blaine will be wonderful, she kept repeating to herself. The *right* Morgan Blaine will be perfect.

'Sweet dreams then, Queen of the Snow. I'll wake you up when we get to Alaska.'

Jessica was sitting cross-legged on the bed, a Manhattan phone directory in front of her. There was Blaine, Morgan, on 308 East 81st Street, telephone number 228-3109. She'd been staring at it for five minutes. Picking up the phone beside her, she'd begin to dial the number, then stop half-way through and hang up. She'd done this approximately twenty-five times. This time her hand reached out for the phone, but was drawn, as if in the middle of a Ouija board, back to the directory. It hovered over the pages, landed and started flipping. Continuing to flip, with a will of its own, it finally ceased moving when it reached the first 'H' page. At that point, her finger took over automatically, tracing the names alphabetically until it found 'Hancock'. And then her eyes, of their own accord, searched for the name Morgan.

Hancock, Morgan: 212 West 102nd Street: 868-7026. Her other hand picked up the telephone. Her fingers dialled the number. Before the first ring, she hung up. The next time she raised the phone, she dialled a longer number.

'Hello?'

'Mum, it's me.'

'Hello, darling.'

'I'm in New York. I'm wearing the same clothes I've been wearing for twenty-four hours. I slept in them.'

'Jessica, are you drunk?'

'No.'

'Have you been to a party?'

'No.' Jessica sighed.

'Are you doing Christmas shopping over there?'

'No.'

'Well, you should. I hear they have very good bargains on designer clothes there at this time of year.'

'Mum? You wouldn't want anything to do with a man who wrote about microbiotic organisms for a living, would you?'

'Jessica,' Joanna laughed, 'you *are* drunk. Take a bath, get some sleep and go shopping.'

'Have you read a book called *Voodoo Women*?'

'Yes, yes I have. It was brilliant. I adored it. Why?'

'No reason.' Jessica sighed again.

'Ring me again when you're sober, darling. I've got to go. Oh, but tell me, any prospects there? Any lovely American men fighting over you?'

The invisible Ouija board moved Jessica's hand away from her ear and made it replace the telephone on the receiver. The next call she made was to Georgie's room. No reply.

Everything was Georgie's fault. Jessica could feel rage begin to take hold of her. Georgie was the one who had made them go to St Anne's. Yes, St Anne's had turned out to be fine, but that wasn't the point. It had been Georgie's idea. And it had been Georgie's idea to bring her into the headhunting business, and Georgie's idea to start this project, and Georgie's idea to come and find Morgan Blaine.

She is a control freak. And I allow her to be, but no more. Cheating, leaving me in the hotel while she went off to find Morgan on her own, that's done it. No more.

Jessica stared at the telephone for a long, long time. She then picked it up again and dialled 96.

'Room service. How can we help you?'

'My mother is desperate for me to find a man. I almost had sex with a scientist last night. I have these feelings for him but I know it would never work between us and besides I know he doesn't have them for me because I walked out on him. My stepsister and I are hunting a famous author. It looks like she found him first by blatantly cheating. I want to kill her. Please could I have an orange juice, a cup of coffee, two fried eggs and a new life.'

Chapter Twenty Two

Sadie was beginning to believe that life as she had known it would never be the same again. There was Georgina Harvey, looking like a sleep-deprived prisoner of war, lying on her – Sadie's – bed, dressed in a wrinkled tartan suit, an expression of haunted desperation in her eyes while Jessica, on the other bed, still in her Armani trousers and white blouse, resembled a cross between a thirteen-year-old girl after an all-night pyjama party and a soap-opera actress who'd spent too many years playing the same part. These were her employers. These were women she'd envied. If only Andrew could see them now, she thought. The Pod People with every ounce of sap removed.

A breakfast tray with half-eaten fried eggs lay on the floor. Sadie, sitting in the only chair in the room, wished she'd had something other than coffee; she needed some sustenance to deal with this pair of whacked-out women. When she'd arrived back from the coffee shop, she'd found Jessica staring into space in a zombie trance. Before she'd had a chance to ask her what was the matter, she'd heard a knock on the door.

'Sadie?' Georgie had called out. 'Sadie, it's me. Are you there?'

'Don't let her in,' Jessica, breaking out of her trance, whispered.

'I have to,' Sadie had replied, opening the door. When Georgie walked into the room, Jessica turned her face to the wall and kept it there.

'Jess?' Georgie took a step toward her stepsister. 'Jess? Jess?' Shooting a look at Sadie, Georgie asked, 'Is she non-speaks with the world or just with me?'

'You, I think.'

'Oh.' She kicked off her heels, went and lay down on Sadie's bed. 'I understand, Jess. You're right. And I apologize. I *am* sorry about yesterday. Cheating like that. I don't know what got into me. The point is, I paid for it.'

Jessica didn't move or speak.

'Listen. I found the wrong Morgan Blaine. There are two of them and I found the wrong one. I took a taxi ride from hell to some godforsaken place in some other state and it cost me a fortune and I was snowed in. The wrong Morgan Blaine is an arrogant, egotistical prat. I've suffered for my wrongs, I've done penance. It was a horrible trip.' Georgie lay back and flung her arms to the side. 'So I made a complete fool of myself. I deserved it, I know. But you can speak to me now.' Turning on her side, toward Jessica, Georgie sighed. 'While I was dealing for hours with a psychotic taxi driver who believes ET is real, you probably found Morgan Blaine. So what's he like, Jess? Please tell me he's fabulous.'

'I didn't find him either,' Jessica addressed this statement to the wall.

Sadie waited for Jessica to tell *her* story. Jessica didn't.

'But you went to Columbia, didn't you?'

'Yes, but I didn't find him. He must have had a day off.' This time Jessica's eyes were on the foot of the bed.

Uh oh, Sadie thought. What's happening here? Why isn't she telling Georgie about finding *her* wrong Morgan?

'All right. We both failed. My failure happened to be more humiliating – and, yes, yes, I know, that was how it should have been. But we could start again and go to Columbia now. We *have* to find him, Jess. At this point, the whole trip will be a total waste of time if we don't find him. I mean, just for the sake of finding him, you know? We can't leave now.'

You're right, you're right, we can't leave now! Sadie wanted to shout. I've got a date in a few hours. We can't possibly leave now.

'I'm not going back to Columbia. I don't want to go anywhere near Columbia.' Finally, Jessica had deigned to looked at Georgie.

'Why not?'

'I just don't. Don't push me. And you're not going anywhere without me. Not again.'

'Are you saying we should give up on trying to find him?' Georgie asked.

'I'm saying I wish I'd never been involved in any of this in the first place. You dragged me into it, the way you drag me into everything. I'm *glad* you had a horrid time yesterday, Georgie. I want you to know that.'

'I do know that.'

'Fine. You owe me an apology.'

'I *have* apologized.'

'Not enough.'

'Sorry. Sorry, sorry, sorry. Is that enough?'

'Not when you say it that way, no.'

Sadie was seeing her date with the Gentleman teetering on the edge of the abyss. Georgie and Jessica's relationship was unravelling by the second. In the taxi in from the airport, she had wanted an explosion to clear the air between them, but not now. This was the worst possible timing. If they continued in this vein, they'd be on the way to the airport in minutes. And Sadie would be with them.

Leaning over the side of the bed and grabbing her bag, Georgie extracted a packet of cigarettes from it, shook one out and lit it up. The idea of telling her this was a non-smoking room was one Sadie immediately discarded.

'Well –' Georgie exhaled a cloud of smoke – 'I can't apologize any more than I have and you can't accept my apology. What happens now? Should we pack our bags? The way you feel about it, it looks like finding Morgan Blaine is out of the question.'

'Finding Morgan Blaine is crucial!'

Both women turned and stared at Sadie when she blurted this out.

'Sadie?' Georgie raised her eyebrows. 'Why is it crucial to you?'

'Because . . . because if you don't find him, you'll always wonder what he's like. You'll think: if only we'd spent that extra day and found him. You've spent all this time and energy trying to find him, you should finish the job. Together. It would be—' Think, Sadie told herself, what pushes Georgie's buttons? What pushes Jessica's? 'It would be two things at once: a job well done, a successful enterprise *and* a . . . a symbolic one. The two of you working together as a team, which you are, you know. My brother and I are a team, even though we argue sometimes, and that's so important in life and finding Morgan Blaine is a whole kind of . . . kind of . . .' She was faltering. '*Fate* thing, too. Family, fate, business . . .' Enough, she thought, seeing their eyes register bewilderment. You're overdoing it. 'Anyway, if for no other reason, you should find him for curiosity's sake.' Don't, she prayed, ask me again why it's crucial to *me*.

Neither Georgie nor Jessica spoke. They were looking at her with such incredulity, Sadie had to drop her gaze. It landed on the Manhattan telephone directory.

'*Voodoo Women* was published by Vencourt Press. I remember I noticed when I read it on the plane. Look – hang on.' Sadie picked up the directory. Please, please, she thought as she thumbed through it. Please let Vencourt Press be in Manhattan. 'V – Vencourt. Vencourt Press.' Her hands were shaking. 'Here it is. 50 East 56th Street. Morgan Blaine must have an editor. Someone there anyway who will know where he is and I'm sure—' Her voice was, she knew, becoming manically high-pitched. She forced herself to tone it down. 'I'm sure you can convince them to tell you where he is and then you can find him and everything will be fine. You don't have to go to Columbia, Jessica. And I'm sure Georgie is truly sorry. It sounds as if she had a horrible time, wherever she was. Anyway, all I'm saying is that it's crucial you stay here and finish what you set out to do.'

'Sadie?' Georgie narrowed her eyes for a second, a second during which Sadie held her breath. 'Sadie, you're a genius. His publishers. Of course that's the logical place to go. I can't believe we didn't think of it before. How stupid could we have been? What do you think, Jess, should we go there? To Vencourt Press?'

'I wish we'd done that in the first place. I wish I'd never gone to Columbia.'

'Why? What happened at Columbia?'

'Nothing. Never mind. But Sadie's right. We might as well finish this.' Jessica rose from the bed, pushed her hand through her hair. 'But I want to get this straight right now. We'll go to find Morgan Blaine together. I'm going to my room, I'm changing and we're going together. Understood?' She was standing tall, her chin high. 'Is that clear?'

'Absolutely.' Georgina Harvey, Sadie was amazed to hear, sounded frightened.

'And whatever happens, afterwards, you and I are going to sit down and I'm going to talk. Things are going to be different between us from now on. Is that understood?'

'Jess, don't look at me that way – you look like you want to murder me. All right, whatever you say.'

'Right. I'll be in the lobby in an hour and a half.' With that pronouncement, Jessica Tanner left the room.

'Jesus Christ.' Georgie stared at the door, took another drag of her cigarette. 'What the hell happened at Columbia?'

At first Jessica didn't notice the light flashing on her telephone. She was too intent on getting out of her clothes and searching for clean ones which would be suitable for the occasion. Standing naked, flicking through the hangers in her closet, she congratulated herself on having, at last, stood up to Georgie. In a way, she reflected, that had only been possible because Georgie *had* cheated and couldn't pretend she wasn't in the wrong. That driven competitive instinct of hers had finally taken a step too far, and Sadie had been a witness. Jessica was justified in her anger, a fact which gave her the courage she needed to speak out.

She may be more intelligent than I am, but she screwed up this time, Jessica thought, smiling as she pictured Georgie stuck in a taxi for hours. There is justice in this world.

She found a Donna Karan grey wool dress which she knew emphasized the colour of her eyes, held it up against her to check herself in the mirror. Georgie would choose another fashion disaster. Excellent.

Jesssica found shoes, stockings, a scarf and laid the carefully co-ordinated outfit on the bed. She'd brought the BabyBliss hair iron, she'd brought the transformer to make it work in an American plug, her make-up was waiting for her in the bathroom, all she had to do was shower, wash her hair, dry it and get herself assembled. The embarrassing events of the previous day lay behind her. She had to forget Morgan Hancock, how badly she'd behaved by running out on him like that. He'd never forgive her, why should he? She could still see the disdain in his eyes when he'd told her Morgan Blaine was in the telephone book.

Meeting the right Morgan Blaine was the only thing she could think of which might help put that all behind her. Otherwise she'd spend the entire plane trip home and God knows how long after that replaying the mistake she'd made by running out of that apartment. This way at least she'd know exactly how much she'd sacrificed by succumbing to what she now understood clearly was her jealousy of Georgie, pure and simple.

As she went to the bathroom to turn on the shower, she passed the phone and saw the message light blinking at her. With a sudden feeling of dread, she picked it up and pushed the button.

'Jessica. It's Morgan.' A pause. 'The wrong Morgan.' Another pause. 'I just wanted to say I know I was harsh on you. You have every right to find Morgan Blaine – I guess he's the man of your dreams. That's no crazier than you being the woman of mine on the basis of one day and part of an evening together. You know, scientists say attraction is based on smell but what do we know, right? I fell for you when I heard you trying so hard to get that order for coffee right. Where's the science in that?' A cough. 'But that's over now. I understand I was temporarily insane, probably because, as John said, I don't get out enough. Anyway, I hope it works out for you. I'm going back home to Boston. I need a little break, I think. So good luck, Jessica.' Pause. In that particular pause Jessica saw Morgan Hancock's sideways smile. 'You blush in your sleep, did you know that? Take care of yourself. And try not to faint again – you never know where or with whom you may wake up. Oh, and thanks for unlodging that apple slice.' Pause. Click.

She didn't hang up. She stood, naked and shivering, with the phone at her ear.

Morgan. Morgan *had* forgiven her.

Jessica ran to the closet, grabbed the phone directory from the top shelf, looked up Morgan Hancock's number, ran back and dialled it. Answer, you have to answer. After twenty rings she pushed the button, waited for the tone, and dialled reception.

'Excuse me? Could you give me the number I need for directory enquiries – sorry – for information for a number in Boston, please? Thank you.' She wrote down the number. 'Thank you very much.' She hung up and dialled again.

'Could you find the number for a Morgan Hancock, please? Yes, Boston. Surname, Hancock, first name, Morgan. Surname *means* last name. No, I don't know the address. I don't even know if he's listed. His parents live in Boston. No, I don't know where they live. No, I don't know his father's first name. Why do you have to keep asking me all these stupid questions? Just please –' Jessica breathed deeply – 'please see if there's a Morgan Hancock. Maybe that's his father's name too . . . Can't you spend one minute looking? Would one minute kill you? Isn't this your job? For God's sake, it's an emergency!' Jessica sat down. She was, she knew, perilously close to fainting. 'No? You're sure? I can not believe how completely and totally incompetent you are.' She slammed the phone down, hurled herself onto the bed and put a pillow over her head.

He'd said he'd been temporarily insane. In her excitement, she'd mentally deleted that part of his message. Insane? What was so insane about falling for her? He'd also said it was over now.

That phone call had been a goodbye, not a 'when can I see you again?' Morgan Hancock had kissed and flown.

A picture invaded her consciousness. She could see him on the plane to Boston. There was a red-haired slut-vamp in the seat beside him, smiling. He smiled back at her. 'I see you're reading a science book,' the slut-vamp was saying. 'I adore science. I *love* microbiotic organisms.' He was choking on a piece of apple. The slut-vamp was trying to suck it out of his throat with a disgusting, hoover-like kiss. He was being unfaithful to her already. He'd forgotten all about her and was happily snogging someone else. He could choke to death on the apple as far as she was concerned.

Emerging from underneath the pillow, red-faced and breathless, Jessica spent a minute beating her fists against the mattress before standing up, walking slowly into the bathroom and turning on the shower.

I am about to find Morgan Blaine, I am in complete control of myself, I have a new sense of direction and purpose in my life, Morgan Hancock is a silly scientist who snogs sluts on aeroplanes, I don't love him, I never did, I was temporarily insane, too, she told herself as she stepped in.

A half a second later she was screaming bloody murder.

Jessica Tanner's new sense of direction and purpose in life hadn't included turning on the hot as well as the cold tap.

In the hotel lobby, Georgina Harvey sat in an uncomfortable straight-backed chair, tapping her foot up and down, waiting for Jessica. People were checking in, checking out, bellboys were loading, unloading suitcases, and Georgie was filling in time by working out how profitable a business the hotel one was. She calculated how many employees would be necessary, including bar and restaurant staff, placed that on a mental spreadsheet, factored in the rate for the rooms, the number of rooms, guessing at taxes and the effect of varying economic conditions on occupancy. How many cleaning staff per floor? 'Reasonably attractive.' How many rooms were single as opposed to double occupancy? 'It's pathetic.' Did any of the staff get overtime? 'Here we are, Georgina. Here's your hotel. You can go freshen up and renew your quest for the Holy Morgan.' Advertising. How much of an advertising budget did the Carlyle have? 'Well, this is goodbye, so goodbye. I'd wish you good luck, but you'd know my heart wasn't in it.

So what should I say? How about: good voodoo, and may the black magic be with you?'

Get out of my brain, she wanted to shout. Stop barging in on my thoughts. You're gone, I'll never see you again. Bugger off and leave my head alone. 'Say Uncle.' No, I won't. Screw you, the wrong Morgan Blaine. I'm going to find the right one.

Georgie saw Jessica get out of the lift and look around the lobby. She gave her a little wave and then watched as she approached. Jessica was gliding across the floor in a grey dress and matching grey cashmere coat, her heels barely making a noise. A vision of beauty as usual, Georgie thought, but there's something sad in her face. What is it? Sadie hadn't answered the question of what had happened at Columbia; either she was being loyal to Jessica or she didn't know. But something had occured to change her stepsister, Georgie was positive. All that 'we have to talk' business – where had that come from? And now why the downcast look in her eyes?

'Are we ready?' Jessica stood in front of her with her arms folded.

'Yes. Jess, when you said that things have to be different between us, what did you mean?'

'We'll talk about that later. Now is not the time or place.'

'Do you want to find some champagne and shake it up before we go?'

Rolling her eyes and sighing, Jessica said, 'Not that again. Let's get on with this, all right?'

It hurt. Georgie was surprised by how much Jess's reply hurt. As she rose from the chair, a terrible possibility occurred to her. Jess didn't need her any more. The little girl who had hidden underneath the bed had gone. The woman who could be coaxed out of a sad mood by champagne had disappeared. Jessica set off towards the street without even looking back to see if Georgie was following. There's something wrong with this picture, she said to herself, then realized what that wrong thing was. For the first time in their joint lives, Jessica was leading the way.

By the time Georgie caught up with her, Jessica had hailed a taxi. As Georgie climbed in, she took a quick look around to establish this wasn't the ET man, but there were no ET dolls and no other paraphernalia to signal any mental aberrations, only a 'No Smoking' sign. Jessica gave the address of Vencourt Press and sat back. Georgie looked over at her, and decided, when she saw how rigid Jessica's face was, not to make any further enquiries about Columbia.

'When we get there, I'll ask for his editor at reception,' Jessica stated.

You'll ask at reception. *You're* in charge now. All right. You'll never forgive me for yesterday. I'm beginning to understand that now.

'The receptionist at the building might not know. There might be lots of different companies in the same building.'

'We'll deal with that when we get there.' Jessica shrugged. 'Do you happen to know how far away Boston is from here?'

'Boston?' Why Boston? 'It's about five hours or so by car, one hour by plane. There's a shuttle service from New York to Boston. Planes leave on the hour, or half hour, I can't remember which.'

'Right.' Jessica nodded again, turned to look out her side of the window.

'Is there something you need to do in Boston?'

'Can't I ask a simple question without being cross-examined?'

'Jess – please. What's going on? Why are you being so secretive and defensive?'

'Because you're so controlling.'

'Ah.' Sliding as far away from Jessica as possible, Georgie turned and stared out the window on her side of the taxi. So that was it then. Jessica thought she was controlling.

I rescued her, for God's sake. How does that make me

controlling? She's angry with me because I *did* rescue her. Fine. If that's the way she wants it, casting me as the ugly controlling stepsister, she can have it.

They sat in silence, looking out of their respective windows for the rest of the trip. When the taxi pulled to the side of 56th Street, Georgie automatically reached into her bag to pay.

'I'll do it,' Jessica barked, handing a ten-dollar bill to the driver. 'I *am* capable of paying for a taxi ride.'

'I'm sure.' Georgie couldn't help herself, she slammed the door when she got out. 'This is *so* much fun,' she muttered. Yet again, Jessica was ahead of her, marching into the office building with the purposeful stride of a general about to review his troops.

'Excuse me,' Jessica was saying to the man behind the reception desk when Georgie caught up. 'How can I find Vencourt Press?'

'It's on the tenth floor. Who are you seeing there?'

'My brother.' Jessica smiled. She actually batted her eyelashes. 'Has anyone ever told you you look like Tom Cruise?'

'You gotta be kidding!'

Yes, you have to be kidding, Georgie thought. If he resembled any star, it was Benny Hill, but she could see how immensely flattered he was. Jess was turning on the charm, she was flooding him with it. The poor bugger didn't stand a chance.

'Honestly, I'm not kidding. You have his eyes and the same facial structure – it's amazing. What's your name?'

'Hal.'

'Well, Hal, my sister and I have flown from London to surprise our brother on his birthday. You don't mind if we go up without being announced, do you? It would spoil everything.'

'I don't see any problem with that. You know, I get off on English accents. Will you just say a few more words?'

Hal was a second away from drooling. Jessica reached out and took hold of his forearm.

'Hal, I'm Jessica, and this is Georgina.' She motioned to Georgie without looking at her. 'It's a pleasure to meet you.'

'You too. Do you know that Hugh Grant guy?'

'No, Hal, I prefer Cary.' Squeezing his arm before letting go of it, Jessica winked, waved and walked toward the bank of lifts.

'That poor man will go home tonight and tell his wife he looks like Tom Cruise,' Georgie said when they'd got into the lift. 'And she'll laugh out loud. You've probably ruined a marriage.'

Jessica didn't reply. A few seconds later the bell pinged, the door opened and they stepped off to find themselves in front of another reception desk. A middle-aged female sat behind it.

What's she going to do this time? Georgie wondered.

'Hello, we've come to see Morgan Blaine's editor.'

'Larimer Richards? Do you have an appointment with him?'

'I'm sorry,' Jessica took a step closer to the desk, 'I don't mean to be personal, but that scarf you're wearing is stunning. Can I ask you where you got it? I've been looking for something like that for ages.'

'This old thing?' The woman put her hand to her throat. 'I've had it forever.'

'Those colours are brilliant. Is it Gucci?'

'No.' She blushed. 'I wish. It's from a thrift shop, actually.'

'God, what a find! You must have an eye for fashion.'

'Well,' the receptionist smiled, 'I like to think I do.'

'You *do*, believe me, I work in the fashion industry, I know.'

'Thank you.' She was beaming now. 'Thank you very much.'

'We don't have an appointment with Larimer – oh, I'm sorry, what's your name?'

'Linda.'

'We're old friends of his, Linda, and we're only in New York for a day and we wanted to surprise him. You don't mind if we go in, do you?'

'I'm sure that will be fine. I just love your accent.'

'Thank you.'

'I *adored Notting Hill*.'

'So did I – So *do* I. I live in Notting Hill and that film has sent house prices sky high – it's a real bonus.'

'Gosh, I never thought of that.'

'Well, we'll just go and surprise Larimer now.'

'I'm sure he'll be thrilled to see you.'

'I hope so.'

How is it possible? Georgie asked herself, as they walked through the door of the reception area and into the main office. How can she *not* have found a man or the right job yet? Jess has talents I'd never known about. She's bloody brilliant. But I'm not about to tell her that now.

The office was open-plan with self-contained cubicles around the perimeter. Jessica stopped at a desk in the middle of the room, asked a young woman where Larimer Richards was and was directed to one of the cubicles in the corner. The door was closed, but that wasn't about to stop her. She simply rapped on it, turned the handle and stepped inside with Georgie close behind her.

Taking in the room with a quick look round, Georgie saw bookshelves, a fairly large oak desk, two chairs in front of it, a sofa against the side wall and framed cartoons hanging on the walls – so many that it looked like a gallery. The chairs were occupied; Georgie could see the backs of two male heads. Neither turned in their direction, but the man who had been behind the desk stood up and approached her and Jessica, his hand outstretched.

'My name is Larimer Richards.' Jessica and Georgie automatically shook hands with him, introducing themselves. 'I have a feeling I know why you're here. Why don't you sit down?' He gestured to the sofa. 'Make yourself comfortable. I don't usually have this many people in my office, but I think we can all squeeze in.'

The sofa was small, the size of a love seat. Their knees bumped into each other's when they sat down. As she crossed one leg over the other to give herself more room, Georgie caught sight of the man in the chair on their side of the room. He had turned and was facing them. He had glasses and was staring at Jessica with a strange half smile.

'Hello, Jessica,' he said.

'Oh, my God. What are you doing here?' Jess's body jolted, as if she'd been shot. 'You're supposed to be in Boston.'

Boston. This man was the Boston connection. But who the hell was this man?

'I decided to take a little detour.'

'Hello, Georgina.'

This came from the man in the other chair. He hadn't moved, he wasn't looking at her, but she knew his voice. She closed her eyes, opened them, putting her head to the side to see past Mr Boston with the glasses. He was still there, sitting with his legs straight out, crossed at the ankles. He was still there and he was still the wrong Morgan Blaine. Georgie put her head in her hands. Oh fuck, she thought. 'Fuck, fuck, fuck.'

Chapter Twenty Three

'Swearing doesn't become you, Georgina'

She'd said it out loud? Oh, no. But what was the wrong Morgan Blaine doing here? Instinctively, Georgie looked to Larimer Richards for help.

'Could you explain what's going on here, please?' she asked him. Back behind his desk, his elbow on the table, his chin resting in his palm, Larimer Richards looked as if he were having the time of his life. Georgie wanted to strangle him, knife the wrong Morgan Blaine, punch whoever this man with glasses was, run out of the room and never come to America again. This was clearly not a country she should be in. The place was full of deranged taxi drivers, maniac oil men and crazy editors.

'Well, let's see. Where shall I start?' He had the nerve to smile. He was, she had to admit a nice-looking man, probably in his mid thirties, dressed in a blue suit, white shirt and blue and red polka dot tie. There was an easiness to him, a kind of languid humour in his face, which made her think of summer. If he hadn't had that grin, if *she* hadn't been the object of his humour, Georgie thought she might have liked him.

'Around five minutes ago, these two gentlemen came to see me. They both want to meet my author, Morgan Blaine. One wants to meet him, as far as I can make out, because his name is also Morgan Blaine and he's tired of being confused with him, and the other –' he nodded toward the man with glasses – 'wants to meet him just because he wants to meet him. At the same time, they informed me that there are two Englishwomen desperate to meet Morgan Blaine as well. I, of course, was finding all this confusing, to say the least. Morgan Blaine has many fans, but none, as yet, has shown up in my office, or, come to think of it, travelled from England to find him. So, I admit, I was intrigued. When you two then came in here, I became even more intrigued. But as to what exactly is going on, well, all I can say is the obvious – you tell me. Please.'

Jessica had shrunk back against the sofa; all the bravado seemed to have drained out of her at the sight of the man in glasses. Who *was* the man in glasses? Georgie wondered again. Whoever he was, now was not the time to find out. Right now she had to make Larimer Richards understand. If he accepted that trying to find Morgan Blaine was not such a terrible thing to do, she could feel better – justified, even. And she was, she thought, in with a chance. Larimer Richards hadn't lectured her or actually complained about them coming to his office. He'd said he was intrigued, not horrified. He'd been smiling and gracious, not disapproving. There was a distinct possibility Larimer Richards would, with the right reaction, absolve her of any feeling of being 'pathetic'.

'We wanted to meet Morgan Blaine because we both love *Voodoo Women*. It's really as simple as that. Yes, we came a long way, but we felt like it. It was a spur of the moment trip.' She homed in on Larimer Richards' quite attractive eyes. 'What we think, Jessica and I, is that Morgan Blaine wouldn't think of our coming to see him as an invasion of privacy but as admirers coming to pay homage. Don't authors like having admirers, Mr Richards?'

'For the most part, they do, yes. Although there are exceptions. J. D. Salinger being an obvious one.'

'Excuse me, but don't writers deserve privacy? Do they actually like being followed to their country houses?' The wrong Morgan Blaine addressed this to Larimer Richards. 'Georgina took a taxi to my house in Connecticut. Doesn't that qualify as an invasion of privacy? And you –' swivelling in his chair, he stared at Jessica – 'were you planning to follow me to Connecticut next time I go?'

Jessica slouched down and hid her face in her coat, as if she were a convicted criminal hiding from television cameras outside a courthouse.

'Don't talk to Jessica like that.' Mr Boston, as Georgie now thought of him, suddenly spoke up. '*She* didn't do anything to you, it's not her fault. She's a romantic, that's all. A . . .' he pressed his fingers against his forehead, 'a hopeless romantic who faints. She loved the book, she wants to meet the author, she fell in love with him on paper, she wants to fall in love with him in the flesh. She came to find him, she found me instead. Don't pick on her.'

'Jesus, Morgan, you sound like you're in love with her.' Morgan Blaine sighed.

'No, I am not in love with her.' When he said this, Morgan Hancock visibly stiffened.

'Morgan?' Looking from one to the other man, Georgie began to think this entire trip was one long, surrealistic, truly fucked-up dream. 'Your name is Morgan too?'

'Yup.' Morgan Blaine stood up then sat down again. 'Morgan Hancock. And if you're wondering what he's doing here, if you're thinking there is some kind of Men Named Morgan Convention going on in the city, let me explain. Morgan met Jessica yesterday and Jessica thought he was Morgan Blaine – the author Morgan Blaine. When she found out he wasn't, she – big surprise – took off to find the real Morgan. Anyway, he's going to Boston today but he wanted to say goodbye to her and he couldn't get her at the hotel and he called me because he, along with everyone else in this goddamned world, thought my number was the writer Morgan Blaine's number, and when he explained himself on the phone, I told him I was coming here to try to find this guy and he asked if he could come along and I said, well why not? Join the "let's hunt down Morgan Blaine" party. OK, Georgina. Are you filled in now?'

'No.' She felt a seed of triumph sprout in her heart. 'No, it's not OK. Why do *you* want to find Morgan Blaine?'

'I'm sick to death of him. I want to tell him to change his name, to stop being *me!*'

'That is not only irrational, it is—' she stopped in order to emphasize the next bit, and to make sure she used the same tone he had used in the car. 'Pathetic.'

'Um, folks,' Larimer Richards' chin was still resting on his hand, 'can I suggest a solution to your problems? It really doesn't matter why any of you want to see Morgan Blaine, whether you want to pay homage to him or make him change his name or whatever, I'm sure he'd be more than glad to meet you all. What time is it?' He looked at his wrist, looked up again.

'It's ten to one,' Morgan Hancock replied.

'OK. Excuse me for a second here.' Larimer Richards stood up. 'I'm going to go make the arrangements to see him. I hope you don't mind, but I'm going to go with you. Somehow, I don't think I could miss this, you know? I'll be right back.'

After Larimer Richards left the office, silence reigned. The room was a veritable kingdom of silence. Jessica sat, her legs tightly crossed, her eyes closed. Georgie sat, her legs side by side, her eyes boring into the back of Morgan Blaine's skull, Morgan Blaine sat, his ankles crossed, staring out of the window and Morgan Hancock, having risen, paced around the room studying the cartoons on the walls.

'He's nice.' Jessica, when she opened her eyes, dropped this statement into the middle of the room. 'Larimer Richards is a nice man.'

'I like his cartoons,' Morgan Hancock added. 'Especially that one.' He pointed to one over the sofa. 'Adam and Eve in the garden of Eden, sitting under a tree, Adam is saying: "I think there's a book in this." They're all about publishing, but that's the best.'

Larimer Richards re-entered the room, rubbing his hands.

'OK, all set. It's all arranged. I've ordered a car because a taxi won't take all five of us. Are you folks all ready to meet the genius?'

'You bet.' The wrong Morgan Blaine jumped up out of his seat. 'Can't wait.'

'I can't either.' Larimer Richards smiled and ushered them out of his office.

The car ride was taken up by conversation between Larimer Richards and Morgan Hancock, both of them talking about science books: why some became bestsellers while most attracted only the specialist market.

'I'm afraid my books appeal only to other scientists,' Morgan Hancock stated, shrugging. He and Larimer Richards were in the jump seats, Jessica, Morgan Blaine and Georgie facing them. 'Jessica will tell you, they're not compulsive page turners, to say the least.'

'Your book was very good,' Jessica said quickly. 'I didn't understand it, that's all.'

'You read his book?' Georgie turned to her. 'When?'

'She didn't read it, I read it to her.' Morgan Hancock said. 'You know, that's more or less why I decided to come with Morgan to find the other Morgan; I want to meet a man who can read his book out loud and have people swooning over the words instead of yawning. *Microbiotic Organisms in Flux* could be marketed as a sleeping pill. I'm thinking maybe some of the author Morgan Blaine's talent for making sentences sing will rub off on me.'

'That's why you came?' Jessica leaned forward.

'That's why I came.' Morgan Hancock leaned back.

'Ah.' Larimer Richards laughed. 'You'll see, Morgan Blaine can definitely make sentences sing. He has a real way with words.'

'And with the ladies, I assume,' the wrong Morgan grunted.

'Some ladies, absolutely.' Larimer laughed again. 'Anyway, I'm interested in *Microbiotic Organisms in Flux*, I'm interested in science in general, so, Morgan H., what did you think of . . .'

Georgie tuned out as the conversation swung back to scientific books and Stephen Hawking. She wondered what had happened between Jessica and Morgan Hancock, how Jess had come to be read to by this man. It was a question of mistaken identity, Jessica had found the wrong Morgan when she went to Columbia. But why hadn't she talked about it? And why was she looking so depressed, when they were on the verge of meeting the right Morgan Blaine? The car had travelled downtown on Fifth Avenue, they'd been going for quite a while now and had passed through Chinatown. Did Morgan Blaine live in Brooklyn? Wherever he lived, she anticipated that when they met him, the wrong Morgan would be rude and abrasive, giving her the perfect opportunity to be civil and charming.

After the initial shock, seeing him again had been, in a way she couldn't explain, not entirely surprising. Her whole motive for finding the author Morgan Blaine had changed; now she wanted to meet him not to fall in love or beat Jessica in a game, but to prove something to *her* Morgan. His being here at the meeting made sense in its own weird way. Larimer's statement that Morgan Blaine would be pleased to see them was the first step to Georgie's rehabilitation.

Morgan Blaine in the flesh would be, *had* to be the crowning glory.

'So, here we are,' Larimer said as they pulled over to the side of the street. 'The food's great here.'

'This is where we're meeting him?' Georgie looked at the restaurant. 'Charlie's Clam House?'

'It's his local. He's here most of the day – when he's not writing, that is.'

They all climbed out of the car. Looking through the plate-glass window, Georgie saw a run-down establishment with a bar on one side and tables and booths on the other. When they went in, she looked around her and found men who were fat in the way only Americans, it seemed, could be, men with thighs that could be the foundations for houses, bellies that even women pregnant with quintuplets would be ashamed of – men sitting with paper bibs over their necks sucking at lobster claws, butter dribbling down their wobbling chins.

The Four Seasons, it wasn't.

'Hey!' Larimer called out, raising his hand.

A man in the last booth at the back stood up, his hand raised in reply.

Georgina Harvey finally got her longed-for sight of Morgan Blaine.

Chapter Twenty Four

Morgan Blaine.
Height: approximately 5′4″.
Weight: approximately three hundred pounds.
Age: approximately 55.
Marriage status: presumably single.
Ability to swim: doubtful, given aforementioned weight.
Driving licence: most probably, and most probably used in order to take others for long drives from which they never return.
Dress sense: don't even go there.
Education: the street?

Jessica Tanner, this CV flashing in her mind, giggled. It started as a small giggle, then turned into the kind of laughter young children fall prey to in church, the sort you can't stop because you know you should stop. It was rude, offensive, terrible. But she couldn't control it. She was shaking Morgan Blaine's beefy, ring-covered hand and trying to apologize and laughing too hard to get the words out. He was giving her a hard look to begin with, a Tony Soprano in a bad mood look, but the more she laughed, the more his look softened, until those small, sweaty eyes of his looked human.

'Hey, lady, too bad I didn't hear it, it must have been one hell of a funny joke.'

'I'm sorry,' she finally managed to get enough breath to say. 'I was just – I was just remembering something very funny.'

I was just remembering, she thought, how Georgie and I fought over you, the way we stared at that photograph in the book, how much *money* the plane trip cost. Not to mention the hotel. Oh, my God, she looked over her shoulder at her stepsister, Georgie, how much did this cost you? With that thought, the laughter started again and Jessica, ducking her head, slid into the booth, taking the seat at the far end. She'd been the first to be introduced to him, so she watched as the wrong Morgan Blaine, Morgan Hancock and then Georgie each shook his hand.

'Nice to meet you guys,' he said, his belly shaking along with his chins each time his hand pumped. 'Larry says you're fans.'

'We've been looking forward to meeting you, Mr Blaine,' Morgan Hancock said. Jessica was watching him closely. Shy scientist though he might be, he was handling this introduction with style. The sight of a mammoth, three-hundred-pound man with hooded eyes hadn't fazed him at all. Nor did his face display any sign of triumph. Morgan Hancock was genuinely interested in meeting the real Morgan Blaine, Jessica could tell. He, she realized, might be the only one of the four Morgan Blaine seekers who *was* genuine.

'Hey, my real name is Angelo, OK? Angelo Brown. This guy –' he reached across the booth and put his hand on Larimer's shoulder – 'Larry here is the one who came up with the name Blaine because I don't like Angelo Brown, never have. It's a dipshit name. So I didn't get to be a Hollywood star, so what? I could change it when I wrote the book. That's one of the bonuses of being an author, yeah?'

They were now all squeezed into the booth beside each other: Jessica, Morgan Blaine and Larimer Richards facing

Georgie and Angelo Brown. Angelo's bulk made it impossible to fit a third person on his side of the booth, so Morgan Hancock found a chair and sat at the end.

'You?' Morgan Blaine turned to Larimer. 'You gave him my name?'

'I had two friends at college. One was named George Morgan and the other George Blaine. When I was trying to think of a good pseudonym, I put them together and it sounded right. Sorry,' he grimaced, 'I had no idea there was a Morgan Blaine around who'd object.'

Georgie hadn't spoken, except to introduce herself to Angelo. Jessica could read her mood from her posture, her shoulders hunched, her hands clasped in front of her. She wasn't angry, her right eye wasn't swanning around in its socket, she was depressed. Jessica had seen her like this only once, when she had failed a physics test. The only reason she'd failed was because she'd been ill with bronchitis for weeks before and hadn't been able to study properly, but she took the news as if she'd been told she was due to be executed in the next twenty-four hours. That's what she looked like now, as if she were walking to the electric chair.

Why aren't I feeling the same way? she asked herself. I was as keen as she was on Morgan Blaine being a handsome, charismatic man, I wanted to fall in love with him too – at least at the beginning. Why am I sitting here, still trying not to laugh? Another picture floated into her brain. This time, instead of seeing Morgan Hancock on the plane, Jessica saw her mother, sitting in a chair. She was introducing Angelo Brown to Joanna, saying, 'And here he is, my husband, mother. I found him in New York. Isn't he perfect? Can you put the announcement in *The Times*, please?' To stop herself from laughing again, she covered her mouth with her hand. It's not Angelo I'm laughing at, she thought. That's the good part of all this. I'm not laughing at him, I'm laughing at my mother, and at Georgie, and at myself.

'So, Larimer,' Morgan Blaine ran his hand through his short-cropped hair, 'maybe we can do a deal. Give Morgan Blaine a middle name, perhaps?'

'Can't do that. Why don't you just go ex-directory?'

'You guys are confusing me.' Angelo put his hand flat on the table. 'All this name stuff. Another Morgan *and* another Morgan Blaine. It's too screwy. Anyone want a drink? Some food? I'm starving.'

'We can't stay for lunch, just for a few minutes,' Larimer said.

'The fuck you can't,' Angelo shot back. 'You're staying for lunch. My fans are here to meet me, I want to meet my fans, eat with my fans. Got it?'

'Got it,' Larimer answered quickly. 'OK. We're here for lunch, then. So why don't you order for us, Angelo? You know what's good here. We can trust you.'

'Sure. Six usuals,' he yelled over at the waiter. 'And two bottles of the usual. Oh, and some Perrier water with ice.' He turned back to Larimer. 'I know it's a yuppie drink, but I love that stuff. Plus, they got great ice here. Anyway, what's the deal? You guys want me to talk about my writing? You want an autograph? What?'

Georgie had turned her eyes up to the ceiling as if hoping for a helicopter to arrive and whisk her away from her nightmare, Morgan Blaine cleared his throat but didn't speak. Angelo Brown was looking at each of them, waiting for a reply.

'I guess we'd like to know how all of this happened,' Morgan Hancock said. 'How did you and Larimer hook up, for example. We'd like to know that. How did *Voodoo Women* come to be written?'

'Yeah, well, what happened is this. Larry was hitchhiking one summer, maybe ten years ago? I gave him a ride from Georgia all the way to Manhattan 'cuz that's where I was going anyway. We got to talking – it would've been a hell of a boring ride if we hadn't, you know? So after that we kept in touch, we'd have lunch or dinner, we'd chew the fat together. One day, he says: "Angelo, you've got a book in you." And I'm thinking: "No shit, Sherlock!" I like, know stuff, and ever since I was a kid I know I can write certain stuff – not like most of the guys I know. I have this writing thing going for me, don't know where it came from, but hey, why ask how, right? Just do it. Just say "yes", to put a reverse spin on that Nancy Reagan drug thing. So I did it, with a little help from my friends.' He smiled at Larimer.

Angelo had a large dent in the middle of his forehead. Jessica found herself staring at it, then looking away. Was it a birthmark of some kind? Or had someone taken a hammer to his head?

'What did you do before?' Morgan Blaine asked him.

'Packaging.'

'Packaging? Packaging what?'

'Just packaging, right?'

'Right.' Morgan Blaine nodded. 'Right.'

'So much of your writing is poetic,' Jessica stated. She was surprised to realize she was actually very interested in how this man had produced *Voodoo Women*. 'Do you read poetry or does it come naturally?'

'Yeah, I read poetry. My favourite poem? I need some silence here, OK?' Everyone at the table nodded. '"Stopping by Woods on a Snowy Evening", by Robert Frost. It's deep. There's a guy in the woods on a horse and he stops for a while, but he has to keep going, you know. It's snowing and all he wants to do is rest, like we all want to rest, but we can't, can we? We have to keep trudging through that fucking snow, yadda, yadda, yadda.' Angelo knocked the dent in his head with his fist. Jessica winced. 'Where's that fucking wine? The thing I like best? There's this part where the horse thinks. So he's making animals like humans. Which they are. What else you wanna ask me? I'm getting off on this. Fans. I get letters and shit but real live fans. Fans from a whole other country, that's something else.'

Six plates of spaghetti vongole with white sauce, two botttles of red wine and a bottle of Perrier, plus a bucket of ice were suddenly plonked down in front of them by three waiters. Angelo commands attention effortlessly, Jessica thought, remembering how she'd had the same thought about Stephen. That date, the whole Project X thing seemed like centuries ago, but all of that had led them here to this restaurant, to this table, where this mountain of a man was tucking a napkin into his brown and black checked nylon shirt.

'You gotta love clams,' Angelo said as he picked up his fork. 'Those hard shells, those soft bellies. Like me.' He looked down at his huge paunch and patted it. 'But no one would eat this belly of mine, even with butter, huh? Even with sauce. Unless we're talking serious cannibals.'

Jessica's eyes met Morgan Hancock's. After a few seconds when he looked away, she felt bereft, as if he had abandoned her on the dance floor in the middle of a perfect love song. The moment she'd seen him in Larimer's office, she'd felt a surge of hope, followed closely by despair as he explained his presence there. He hadn't come to the office to find her, he'd come to find Morgan Blaine. He'd even stated publicly that he didn't love her. She knew she shouldn't have had any hope in the first place; she'd walked out on him, after all, making it perfectly clear that he wasn't the object of her desire. But the minute she'd seen him some of the feeling of comfort she'd had in his flat had crept back into her heart. That sense of belonging and ease had, she now realized, made her stronger. It was what had given her the ability to schmooze her way past both receptionists and into Larimer's office. When she'd seen him again, it had immediately swamped her. All she wanted to do was kidnap him and take him back to his apartment, to feed *him* Valium and keep him a prisoner forever.

Given that was impossible, the only thing she could do was bide her time. As long as they were still in the restaurant and she was in his vicinity, she was in with a chance. She could wait and find a way to get him on his own after lunch. Then she could apologize and throw herself at his feet. 'I don't care what you do or what you look like or how much money you don't earn, I love you madly,' she would say. Well, no, maybe not those exact words. But definitely the 'I love you madly' part.

Jessica looked across at Georgie, crammed into the booth, dwarfed beside Angelo Brown. This isn't about you and me any more, she thought. This isn't about our relationship or my jealousy of you. It's not about my mother and her expectations, either. Whether or not I can convince Morgan to give me a second chance, the point is he has somehow, magically given *me* something. This is the land of independence and, finally, I'm beginning to find mine.

'The sex scenes were incredible too,' she said, but she was looking at Morgan Hancock as she said it. 'Just incredible.'

'Well, you wanna know my secret for that?' Angelo grinned. 'I write it like I do it and every time I do it I do it like it's the last time in my life I'm ever going to do it. 'Cuz a guy like me, I don't get what you'd call flooded with offers for fun times in the sack, you know. Babes aren't exactly turning down the sheets and leaping into bed for me. When I do get to where I want to be with a girl, I think, "Hey! this might be the last time ever." So I put a lot of concentration into it, you know? What can I say? It works.'

No one, clearly, knew what to respond to this; they all focused on their plates of food.

'So come on, you came all the way from England, ladies. Shoot. Ask me some more questions.'

'Yes, Georgina,' Morgan Blaine leaned forward, 'go on. Ask

him questions. He's dying to talk about his work. That's what you came here for, isn't it?'

'How . . .' Georgie was staring at her plate, twirling the spaghetti on her fork. It dropped off. 'How did you choose the setting? The bayou?'

'I spent a lot of time down there.' Angelo picked up a bottle and poured wine into everyone's glasses. 'Beautiful place. Beautiful people. And Rick? He was based on this guy I knew. You wouldn't believe this guy's magnetism. Now getting that down on paper, that was a challenge. The violent part, the machete scene? Pure inspiration. I was sitting in my truck in a traffic jam in the Holland Tunnel, and there were these teenagers in the car ahead blasting some shit music, and I thought to myself: if only I had a machete. A gun's too nice, too neat for these slobs. I wanna hack them up into tiny pieces. You know that feeling?'

'Uh huh.' Morgan Blaine nodded. 'I certainly do.'

'Right. And writers, they're supposed to write what they know about. I know all about witchy women, let me tell you. I married two of them. Then my cousin, she had this voodoo doll – she used to stick pins in it, pretending it was her low-rent boyfriend who cheated on her five times a day. That's where I came up with voodoo. Witchy women, voodoo dolls, put them together and you get,' he snapped his fingers, '*Voodoo Women*. It's symbolic, the title, you know? Women are magic. Men spend all their time trying to get to the magic of women, but us guys will never get it, not really. But the big thing is, women don't know they have it, not normally, which is why they have to sit around sticking pins in dolls of low-down cheating boyfriends. And the fact that it all takes place in that one month, in April? I figured the action taking place all in one day thing has been done already. James Joyce, right? He got there first. So having it all in April, that was from a poem I heard.'

'A poem?' Jessica asked. 'Which poem?'

'That T. S. Eliot guy. That one where he says April is the coolest month.'

'Ah.' Larimer Richards smiled. 'The coolest month. You never told me that, Angelo.'

'Hey, I figured you'd pick it up on your own, being so literary and everything. You people don't like the food here? You want me to get you something else?'

'No, no,' Morgan Hancock said. 'We're all interested in what you're saying, that's all. The food is great.'

'Yeah.' Angelo stuffed a wad of spaghetti in his mouth, chewed, swallowed, took a half of glass of wine in one sip. 'So, that's the thing. The whole male–female dynamic like. What do women want? They want to be listened to, they want to be made love to, they want to be given presents, they want to be protected. And you know, they'd get all that if only they knew the power they have over us boneheads. But because they don't know, they let us have the power, they kind of like give it away, you know. Which is flat-out stupid. Eva, she doesn't give it away. She knows her business, the magic business. Which is why she finds Rick and why – after a few plot twists, 'cuz you got to have some twists – Rick proves to her he can give her all these things. The clearing they met in? That's symbolic too. There are all these woods – woods, right? Get that reference? Anyway, there are all these woods that separate men from women, all these overhanging branches of misunderstanding you have to hack your way through, but then, if you get beyond those, you find the clearing.'

'Hang on.' Georgie actually, Jessica saw, grabbed Angelo's wrist. 'Are you saying we get to the clearing if we – if females – understand our magic?'

'You got it, doll.'

'And that magic consists of?'

'You can't define magic. You can only feel the power of it.'

'Oh.' Georgie hung her head, picked up her fork and tried once again to twirl her spaghetti. Once again, it flopped back down on the plate. 'I see, I think.'

'So what do men want?' Morgan Blaine asked.

'Women!' Angelo shouted out. 'Babes! Broads! Men get the women, the magic rubs off on them. My next book, *Lightning at Dawn*? It's about these men who are lost, who are working their asses off without knowing even that the whole point of working your ass off is to get the girl. My hero doesn't understand shit until he gets struck by lightning on a fucking golf course. *Then* he begins to get into his groove.'

'Um, what about gay people? Where do they fit in?' Morgan Hancock asked.

'Beats me!' Angelo laughed. 'That's for someone else to write about. I can't figure it out. Like I said before, you can only write what you know about.'

'But you just said you've been married twice.' Morgan Blaine finished his glass of wine and wiped his mouth. 'What happened? Did the magic fade?'

'It didn't fade so much as explode all over the place. Those babes were too much for me and my bank balance – what can I say?' Angelo grinned.

'Not a lot, I guess.' Morgan Blaine grinned back.

'OK.' He held up his hand. 'Enough talk. None of you is eating. Time to shut up and eat.'

They all obeyed him instantly, scooping up forkful after forkful of spaghetti as if a terrible punishment was waiting if they didn't clean their plates of every last mouthful, fearful of saying a word until they'd finished the job. Jessica was amazed that she managed to devour it all. She was even more surprised that she got through two glasses of red wine easily; normally she never drank at lunch.

'Good. Good eating. You need to fatten up, doll,' Angelo

addressed Jessica. 'And you,' he transferred his attention to Georgie, 'you need to lighten up.'

Georgie looked down at her plate like a child who has been told off for having bad table manners.

'I don't understand why you said you taught at Columbia.' Morgan Hancock's face twisted in evident puzzlement before it suddenly registered a flutter of fear. 'Oh.' He turned to Larimer. 'Oh. Does it have to do with Angelo's previous career in, um, packaging?'

'Let's just say Angelo wanted a different occupation as well as a different name. He chose the Columbia job. I advised him this wasn't a good move and we could get in trouble, but he insisted. Strangely enough, Columbia has never contacted us about that. But if there were any problems, I'm sure Angelo could make them see sense. Anyway, they'll probably be asking him to teach a course there any day now.' Laughing that easy laugh of his, Larimer clapped Angelo on the back. 'We have to go now. I'll get the bill.' He signalled for the waiter. 'Vencourt can pay for this. How's it going on *Lightning at Dawn*, Angelo? Do you have the last half to show me?'

'Not yet. Soon. I promise, boss.'

'I'll hold you to that.' Larimer paid the bill, stood up. 'Listen, I'm unbelievably late for a meeting so if you want a ride with me, we'll have to run now.'

The others stood up and said their goodbyes and thank yous to Angelo.

'Hey, it's been my pleasure.' Angelo beamed. 'Larry, you should do this more often – bringing my fans here. This place could turn into one of those thingamajiggies? What's it called? A saloon. Yeah. A literary saloon.' He struggled to get up from the booth, gave up and sat back down. 'Time for my dessert. More food to fatten my belly for those serious cannibals, right fans?'

'Right.' Everyone said in unison. Georgie had to duck under

the table to get out on the other side. After she'd managed this, he motioned for her to lean over to him, then whispered something in her ear which made her blush.

When they were back in their original positions in the car, Jessica asked Georgie what Angelo had whispered to her.

'Nothing,' she replied. 'Nothing.'

This time, Morgan Blaine, Morgan Hancock and Larimer had a three-way conversation, the two Morgans peppering Larimer with questions about Angelo, Larimer answering them. Jessica leant back against the seat, half-listening. The other half of her brain was reflecting on lunch, not only her new-found feeling of independence, but also the surprising affection she felt for Angelo Brown. He got words wrong, he had said 'saloon' when he should have said 'salon', he'd misquoted Eliot, he, she felt she could safely assume, hadn't been to university either, but he'd written a book – a bestseller. Academic excellence, a highly polished intellect, weren't always neccessary for success.

If he can make something out of his life, I can too, she thought. And I'd like to do it with Morgan Hancock beside me, because he would understand and support me. He'd listen to me, he'd make love to me, he'd give me presents, he'd protect me. And Angelo was right – that's what I want from a man. All I have to do is understand my magic to get it.

Crossing her legs and flicking her hair back, she smiled at Morgan Hancock, thinking: magic, magic, feel my magic. There was no response. Morgan Hancock was listening to Larimer Richards talking about his ride from Georgia to New York with Angelo. Jessica sighed, re-crossed her legs, conjured up a sexy, dreamy look in her eyes and beamed it at him, willing him to look at her. His eyes didn't move from Morgan Blaine who was asking about *Lightning at Dawn*. As Jessica was preparing to swing her legs yet again, she felt Georgie elbow her in the ribs.

'Stop kicking me, Jess,' she said sharply.

'You know,' Morgan Hancock was talking to Larimer, 'I'm so glad I came along on this trip. This is the most fun I've had for a long time.'

More fun than you had with me in bed? Jessica felt suddenly car sick.

'Totally ace.' Morgan Blaine nodded. 'Us boys are having a blast. How about you girls? Are you having fun?'

'I liked him.' Georgie replied. 'He's not arrogant. He doesn't lecture people. You *were* wrong, Morgan, it *was* a good idea to meet him.'

'But you wouldn't have—' Morgan didn't finish the sentence.

'I wouldn't have followed him to Connecticut if I knew what he looked like? No. All right? That's what you want to know, isn't it? How shallow and superficial I am? I admit it. I'm shallow and superficial. I'm controlling. I'm not . . . I'm not . . .'

There were tears, real live tears pouring out of Georgie's eyes. As soon as Jessica saw them, all she could think of was how to stop them.

'You're not superficial, Georgie.' Jess was close to shouting. 'And you—' She faced Morgan Blaine. He was the one responsible for Georgie's tears. *She* could criticize her stepsister, yes, she could call her controlling, but this man, this stranger, had no right to make Georgie miserable. 'You don't understand anything. We came to find Morgan Blaine because we spent months going out with abominable men, because we set up a project for ourselves – we were going to headhunt a man for ourselves, use our files to find someone decent and available. All we found were these . . . these hopeless, awful men. Each candidate we interviewed was worse than the one before. And then we saw a piece of paper with Morgan Blaine's name and it was as if Fate was guiding us here. He was in our files –

God knows why or how, but there he was, in our files, and of course we wanted him to be attractive. I mean, wouldn't you? Don't tell me men don't care about looks. Don't tell me men don't care even *more* about looks than women.'

'You were *headhunting* yourselves a man?' Morgan Blaine's jaw hadn't actually dropped, but his mouth was wide open.

'That was Project X?' Morgan Hancock's eyes weren't actually hanging out of their sockets, but they were bulging. 'You were using a filing system to find a man? You were *interviewing candidates?*'

'Whoa.' Morgan Blaine was shaking his head. 'Those poor suckers.'

'My God.' Morgan Hancock put his hand to his forehead.

'Have you two ever thought about writing a book?' Larimer Richards asked.

The car was stopped at a traffic light. Georgie reached out, pulled the handle and fled. Jessica took one second to decide whether she was going to stay and try to make Morgan Hancock understand or follow Georgie.

It wasn't hard to catch up to her stepsister, not this time.

Chapter Twenty Five

Sadie was twirling on the same stool she'd been on in the morning. Back and forth, she twisted, looking at the Gentleman's watch in front of her on the counter each time she came to the centre. Three fifteen. She'd arrived on the dot of three. There was a young boy instead of the old waitress behind the counter, one who looked vaguely Greek but who swore like an American. After ordering a coffee, she pulled the note from the Gentleman out of her pocket and read it. And re-read it. Ten minutes of going over the same lines and wondering what the obliterated last part of it said, and she was beginning to believe she was the victim of an elaborate and cruel trick. That thought started her twirling; she couldn't bear to sit still any more.

Being stood up once, especially with a note and a watch as an apology, was one thing; twice, well, it might begin to make you paranoid. Not that she wasn't in a paranoid state already. It was as if a primer of fear and anxiety had been laid, all set for the painting of rampant insecurity. On the phone to the office, while Jessica and Georgie were at Vencourt Press, Sadie had handled various business problems caused by Georgie's absence. Working was a good way to pass the time until three, and Sadie was glad to have it as a distraction. She'd

288

hung up afterwards, ordered a hamburger from room service and switched on the television. While she was watching the news, the phone rang – Lisa was on the other end, desperate for news of the hunt for Morgan Blaine. Sadie told her only that Jessica and Georgie had gone to his publishers; she knew filling Lisa in on all the events of the past day would have been equivalent to broadcasting them nationwide.

'God, I hope when they find him, he's like I said he was.' Lisa sighed. 'I hope, actually, they never come back. One way or the other if they do, I'm screwed, I just know it.'

'I won't tell them, Lisa. You don't have to worry. Are you still at the office?'

'God no, it's seven thirty. I'm at home. I'm calling because Piers rang for you at work earlier – when he found out you were away, he asked for me. He says he needs to talk to you. He gave me his home number, said he'd be there all night. Do you want it, or not? I say don't do it. Don't give the bastard the satisfaction.'

Piers? Piers? Was he ringing to set up that coffee date he'd suggested – what was it – three months ago? Or . . . Sadie stared at the television screen. A woman with big blonde hair and a manufactured face was eyeballing the camera with as much gravity as a frozen expression could allow.

'Sade? Do you want his number?'

'Yes. I can decide later whether I'll ring him or not, but yes, I might as well have the number.' As soon as she said this, she knew that she was going to dial the number Lisa gave her.

'OK – here it is.' Lisa reeled off the digits. 'But do not, and I mean this, Sade, do not give him an inch. If he wants you back, he's going to have to fight for you and fight hard, yes? Do you understand the importance of this? You can't give in straight off or he won't respect you.'

'I'll be cool,' she said. 'I promise.'

'Good girl. Ring me back as soon as you've talked to him, OK? I need to know what's going on.'

'OK.'

Sadie said her goodbye and hung up, thinking: this, in a way, is perfect timing. I have my three o'clock rendezvous, I have back-up, my mystery man to sustain me whatever happens when I talk to Piers. If I have to talk to him again, this is the best time to do it. But why *am* I talking to him again? Why not leave it as it is? Because I can't. That's why. I just can't. She clicked off the television and picked up the phone, dialling in a hurry because she didn't want to consider the wisdom of what she was doing. Piers answered on the second ring.

'It's Sadie,' she said. 'I got a message from Lisa that you wanted me to call.'

'Sade, yeah, hi. You're in New York?'

'Mmmhmm. There was a big snowstorm here yesterday.'

'Yeah. Great. Must have been fun. Anyway, the reason I called, was to ask you a favour.'

Come back to me? Was that the favour he wanted to ask? I miss you, I love you, come back to me?

'Ask,' she said, then held her breath.

'Well, you know I was promoted? That was great and I was pleased, but the new job isn't exactly what I thought it would be, it doesn't give me real scope or authority, not as much as I want. I think I should talk to a good headhunter, and what better headhunting agency for someone like me than Harvey and Tanner? I thought you could set me up an appointemnt with Georgie – go right to the top, not muck around with anyone lower down the ranks. I'll take you out to dinner afterwards – how does that sound?'

Sadie threw the receiver at the pillow, then sat staring at it. 'God damn you, God damn you,' she muttered, shaking her head. 'God damn you for being so stupid, you stupid woman.'

Even though I wasn't sure what I'd say if he did ask me back, I wanted him to ask.

'Piers?' she'd picked up the phone. 'Sorry, I'm in the middle of a meeting. I'll have to get back to you.'

'Oh, right. Do you know when you'll be able—'

'Have to go. Bye.'

Never. That's when I'll get back to you. Never.

Did it matter, this hideous phone call? Did she care that Piers had only rung to use her? At three o'clock, the Gentleman would walk in to the coffee shop, sit down beside her and smile. And those eyes of his would wipe every trace of Piers Tate from her heart.

This was a difficult feat for the Gentleman to accomplish, however, when he wasn't there.

Sadie stopped twirling. It was three thirty-five. She'd told herself she'd leave at three thirty but she had let another five minutes go by. If she didn't leave now, she probably never would. At the rate she was going, she'd end up applying for a job in this place.

Why do people keep saying things they don't actually mean? Sadie wondered. Why did he say he was going to meet me if he wasn't?

Picking up the Gentleman's watch, she hesitated for a few seconds. Should she leave it with the boy behind the counter, along with a note of her own, complete with the name of her hotel? And her English address and phone number?

No way. He gave it to her. She'd keep it. There was no point in leaving a phone number or an address. He wouldn't use either. He'd said something he didn't mean and she had been gullible enough to take him seriously. After putting a dollar bill down on the counter, Sadie left. The waitress won't get to see us together tomorrow morning, she thought, as she began the walk back to the hotel. She'll be disappointed. I hope she asks him what happened when he comes in next time and pours a pot of boiling coffee over his head.

'Well,' Georgie was leaning on a plate-glass Gap window, wiping tears from her eyes with her sleeve, 'I presume they're not following us, are they? They haven't jumped out of the car and come to sweep us away.' She snorted. 'We're not just fans who came to find an author, we're scheming women who headhunt men.'

'I shouldn't have told them.' Jessica had her arm around Georgie's shoulders. 'I'm sorry. I don't know why I did, I couldn't stand seeing you cry and I thought – I don't know what I thought.'

'It doesn't matter.'

'Yes, it does. I ruined things.'

'There was nothing to ruin, Jess. Morgan, my Morgan, already thought badly of me. That was only the icing on the indigestible cake, that's all.'

Georgie had known it the minute she saw Morgan Blaine aka Angelo Brown in Charlie's Clam House, she'd understood, with a profound sadness, that she was still in love with the wrong Morgan Blaine, not because she was disappointed Angelo weighed three hundred pounds, but because she was actually relieved. She realized that she didn't want some charming, handsome author sitting in that booth. If Angelo had been God's gift to women, she would have loathed him. At first this reaction didn't make any sense, but as she sat through lunch she began to understand why she'd had it: if Angelo had been a hunk, she would have felt defensive on her Morgan's behalf. What right did some good-looking, smug, rich author have to be parading around with the same name as the man she loved? This might be – it was – a wholly irrational thought process, but, she reflected, that's what love does. It makes you crazy.

She knew she should have felt pleased that Morgan liked Angelo and had admitted finding him was a good idea, but that fact didn't change the basic problem. Morgan would never believe her if she told him how she felt. He'd always think she'd been staring unhappily into her plate of clams because Angelo was not a dream date. How could he accept her version of events? She wouldn't, if she were him. Had their situations been reversed, she'd be sure the man chasing a female author across an ocean wasn't in it only for a literary kick. He'd want to find a sex goddess as well as a page-turner. Which would make him superficial and shallow.

And if she'd then been told that the man had used his company to cull dates from? That he'd approached finding true love as a business deal? Even as work-oriented as Georgie was, she knew she'd find this information off-putting, to say the least.

'Are you in love with him, Georgie?'

'I'm afraid so. How about you?'

'Ditto.'

'Well, we've certainly made a mess of things. Maybe we should go back to Charlie's Clam House and ask Angelo to fix it for us. I'm sure he has ways of bringing people round.'

'I wish. You know, it was the way my Morgan said "interview candidates" that killed me. He said it as if we'd committed some unpardonable sin. We didn't, did we? I mean it really wasn't that different from a dating agency. Why did they look *so* shocked?'

'We would have looked just as shocked if they had told us the same thing.'

'Maybe I'm not really in love with him, maybe I just imagined I was.'

'I tried that one, too, Jess. It didn't work. Come on,' Georgie stepped away from the window, 'let's go home.'

'You could go after your Morgan. You could—'

'Chase him, stalk him again? I don't think so.' Georgie smiled. 'I think he's had enough of that. You were right when you said I'm controlling, but even I know when I've lost control over a situation. But you could go after your Morgan.'

'After he said he didn't love me? After he looked at me the way he did in the car? I don't think so either.'

'Then let's go back to the hotel, drink our way through the minibars in our rooms and get on the evening flight back. The sooner we leave this place the better.'

Jessica shook her head, and kept shaking it.

'I'm so stupid,' she said.

'Join the crew, sis.' Georgie hugged her. 'I'm really, really sorry for getting us into all this in the first place.'

'Promise you'll never do it again?'

'Word of honour. From now on, when it comes to anything romantic, I'm saying uncle.'

'Uncle?' Jessica stepped back. 'Uncle who?'

Sadie spent a long time staring out of her window at the office building opposite before taking the watch out of her bag, unfastening her own, slipping it off, then putting his on her wrist. This will remind me, she thought, not of my disappointment, but of a nice experience which wasn't all that I wanted it to be, but which, for a short time, was exciting and lovely. The Gentleman may have let me down, but I can remember that scene on the bus and the teenagers on their date and smile. At least I can try to. I can try very hard. I'm tired of looking backwards and wondering what I've done wrong. It's time – she looked at the watch – to let go of the past.

'Sadie? Are you there?' It was Georgie's voice, accompanied by a knock on her door. She shook her thoughts off with the same physical movement she used to shake off water after a swim in cold water.

'Hi,' she opened the door, 'how was it? Did you find him?'

Georgie and Jessica came in together, with indecipherable but matching expressions on their faces. Had they found him or were they still in the midst of tracking him down? She couldn't tell.

'Yes, we found him.' Georgie went to the chair, sat down on it. 'We'll tell you all about it on the flight back. Could you call BA and book us on the flight tonight? Upgrade yourself to business class while you're at it. You've been a star through all this, Sadie. I truly appreciate all you've done for us on this – how should I call it? Madcap – that's it – madcap trip, plus, of course, the entirely insane Project X.' Georgie pulled out her cigarettes and lit one. 'I need this. When I get back to London, I'm never going to smoke again. But I need this now. Oh, and by the way, it's time you moved up in the company. Do you want to be a researcher, Sadie?'

'Yes.' She stood, stunned, trying to take all this in. 'I do.'

'Good. As soon as we get back, I'll arrange it. You know I believe in promoting from within, and after this . . .' she waved a lit match in the air. 'After all this, I suspect you could use a change. Jessica and I are going to get drunk. We'd like to know if you would like to join us. Until we land at Heathrow, you are – officially – not employed by Harvey and Tanner. This afternoon and evening are off the record, so to speak. Can you handle that? A girls' night out with us?'

Sadie looked over at Jessica, who nodded and smiled.

'I think so,' she replied.

'I think you can, too. Let's get that minibar open.' She stood, walked over to the minibar, knelt down and opened it, extracting a small bottle of champagne. 'This will be good for starters, right Jess?'

'Shake it up.' Jessica swung her body around so she was lying on her stomach, her face at the end of the bed, cupped in her hands, her elbows supporting her, her ankles crossed up behind her. 'Go for it.'

Someone has sprinkled fairy dust, Sadie thought. They like each other again. How long will it last, though? When we get back, will they regret this girls' night out, will Georgie rescind the promotion, will – she mentally stepped on her train of thought and stared down at her watch. Let it go, Sade, she told herself. Stop rewinding the tape, stop fastforwarding it too. Live in the present and let it go.

Chapter Twenty Six

April in Paris. Georgie sat at a café table on the Champs Elysées, a cup of coffee and a postcard of the Eiffel Tower in front of her. At the top of the postcard she drew a shaky outline of France, put an 'x' in the middle, wrote the word 'Paris' beside it. Beneath the map, she drew an arrow pointing up to the 'x' and penned the words, 'This is a foreign city. There are many oil deposits here. The picture on the front is a giant oil derrick, commonly mistaken for a tourist attraction.' Then she addressed it to Morgan Blaine, 308 East 81st Street, NYC, NY, USA, placed stamps on it and put it in her bag to post when she got back to her hotel.

She'd sent him similar postcards from Venice, Amsterdam and Rome when she'd gone on business trips. Of course, she'd had no response, she didn't expect any. Morgan Blaine had gone back to his usual life, which didn't include her. But if the postcards made him smile, she'd be in his thoughts, anyway. He couldn't escape her totally, not quite yet.

Postal stalking – was that a crime? Georgie smiled, thinking of the defence she'd mount. 'I was just showing him Europe, Your Honour. He's an American, he needs to have a broader picture of the world, especially as his president doesn't have a clue.'

Or, 'A man named Angelo Brown, when I was saying good-bye to him in a restaurant, whispered "Kick your sweetheart Morgan Blaine's ass some, babe, he's been staring at you on the sly all through lunch. But remember, a guy like him? He'll fight you every step of the way." You see, someone else knows we should be together, Your Honour. Angelo picked up on the vibes between us. Sending postcards is my little way of kicking ass. That's all.'

Georgie wasn't sure what the next stage in this campaign would be; whether she'd write him a letter, or ring him, or what. At times she considered doing what she'd done before and flying to New York, but she knew she should bide her time. He had to understand this was no whim. The feelings she had for him hadn't diminished over the past four months, they'd increased. If he took that on board, he might consider taking her on board as well.

Cupid, when he'd drawn back his bow, had aimed with consummate skill. Yes, she could carry on her business perfectly well, and yes, she could function on a day-to-day basis, but now she had stopped thinking of a relationship as part of her success story. She no longer cared whether she and Morgan Blaine lived happily ever after, even whether happy ever after was possible or not, she only wanted to get the chance to try. If it doesn't work, it doesn't work, she said to herself. I'm willing to take that gamble.

Picking up her mobile, Georgie punched in a number.

'Jess? It's me. How's it going?'

'Fine.'

'The course is good?'

'Excellent. How's Paris?'

'Beautiful. Sunny. Full of tourists. I'll be back tomorrow night.'

'See you then.'

'Right.'

It was funny, even Jessica's voice had changed in the last few months. It was lighter, yet at the same time more confident. Jess was getting her act together, in a way Georgie almost envied. Not only had she found out what she wanted to do, but she was clearly going to be very good at it. Which would make her successful in two occupations: one, this landscape gardening she had taken up, with a commitment Georgie had never known her to have for anything before; and two, her revised role at Harvey and Tanner. By day, Jessica studied gardening, with a passion, by night she was the perfect public-relations woman. At parties, at the opera, at any social event, Jessica would promote H&T with all those public-school types who still had clout in the world of the City.

Georgie had seen her at work a couple of times at some of those gatherings doing what she'd done so effectively the morning they'd stormed into Vencourt Press. Complimenting people, schmoozing her way through the room, she worked it with grace and aplomb, toeing the flirtation line without crossing it. Jess was a natural PR person and Georgie wondered why she hadn't thought of using her talent this way before.

Because she hadn't wanted Jess to have any talents, that was the shaming answer. She'd been so jealous of Jess's natural beauty, she hadn't wanted her to have any other strings to her bow.

I kept thinking I wanted her to get a life of her own, but part of me was very comfortable with the idea that she never would, that she'd be entirely dependent on me – a fact which made up for all those stares and attention she got from men.

New York had changed everything. The night after they arrived back in London, even though they were suicidally hungover and tired, they'd stayed up and broken through a barrier as they talked, both finally coming out with all the incidents which had caused resentment to smoulder for years.

It would have made great TV, Georgie thought. Stepsisters coming to terms with the past. The new understanding they had as a consequence of that night didn't mean life was entirely frictionless; they still responded according to old patterns occasionally, but that had to be natural. It would take some time to get used to a new, more equal relationship.

Georgie looked around her at the throng of people walking by, many of them couples arm-in-arm, all of them looking happy in the sunshine of spring. She pictured Morgan, with those strong, long legs of his striding down the Champs Elysées, a harpoon in his hand.

Ah, she thought, come over here, Morgan. I'll show you Paris in the spring, I'll show you Rome in the summer, I'll show you Venice in the autumn. And in the winter, you can show me Connecticut again. Only this time you won't kick me out of bed.

Now that's worth waiting for.

Jessica used the same florist each week; they knew her there now and were used to the bizarre element of her order. Along with a bunch of flowers, she insisted they send one apple. The first time she'd made this request, the person on the other end of the line had baulked, but she'd held her ground and finally, the florist had caved in and agreed.

'Same address?' the woman, who Jessica now knew was named Deidre, asked.

'Same address. Tulips, this time, and an apple.'

'Done.'

'Thank you.'

When she hung up the phone, Jessica envisioned Morgan, in his apartment, the tulips in a vase on his desk, the apple – where would he put the apple? On his bedside table, she hoped. She never sent a card and he never responded, but that non-response, she thought, was a good sign. At least he wasn't stopping her from sending them. If he wanted to badly enough, she was sure, he could have found her address and written a 'Don't even think about it' letter. The flowers, each week a different sort – and the apple would remind him of her. That was enough for now.

Jessica looked at the book on landscape gardening in front of her. She was amazed by how easily she understood this subject and how close it was to her heart. Gardens were like bodies waiting to be dressed in the right clothes. Each season demanded a different approach, a new line, and all the elements had to blend and match, like shoes and handbags and accessories should match a dress. Sometimes it was right to use bright colours next to each other, so bright they came very close to clashing, sometimes a more subtle blending was called for. And gardens, like bodies, came in different shapes and sizes. She loved this kind of designing, knowing instinctively, too, when a garden should be a jeans and sweatshirt sort of look and when it should be evening wear.

I didn't do well at school because I wasn't interested in the subjects, she thought. I hated the City because I didn't understand the language. This – flowers, nature, – is a sort of poetry, and I get every single line of it.

Those photographs on Morgan's wall were what had led her to her new passion. They kept reappearing in her dreams after she'd come back from New York, the pictures rearranging themselves into kaleidoscopic patterns of flowers, each one set in a different type of landscape. Her subconscious was fashioning gardens every night, ideas which stayed with her after she'd woken up.

After two weeks in her old position at Harvey and Tanner, she'd walked into Georgie's office and announced her resignation. 'I've decided I want to study landscape gardening. But I'll help out by promoting H&T at parties and all those poncy functions I still get invited to. I'll spread the word at Ascot and Henley and so on – in return for a favour.'

'What favour?' Georgie had asked. The relief Jessica felt when she didn't hear Georgie's laughter or a comment such as 'landscape gardening sucks' gave her the courage to carry on.

'If I do a good job promoting, you can help me set up a landscape-gardening business when I've learned enough about it to do it properly. I'll need financing and you can help me. If that's all right with you.'

'It's fine, Jess,' Georgie replied. 'Excellent, in fact.'

So much in life depended on having a sense of direction, Jessica thought. It had taken her years of floundering before she found a plan, but once she did find it, her entire psyche had shifted. She could ask for what she wanted with authority; a big slice of fear had been cut out of her – how, she wasn't quite sure. Sometimes she thought it was all down to that one afternoon and evening with Morgan, at others, she felt Angelo, in a weird way, had contributed. Certainly the long night of talk with Georgie, when they had traded their jealousies and insecurities as if they'd been bartering at a sibling rivalry market place, had made an impact. Whatever the cause or causes, Jessica wasn't hiding in that mountain-top café any more.

There's only one thing missing in my life, she said to herself as she turned a page. But I'm working on it. I'm planting the seeds.

Andrew was hustling his girlfriend out of the flat, Sadie knew. He was doing it deftly, but Sadie could hear Theresa saying goodbye, followed by the silence of a stolen kiss before the door opened and closed.

I have to get out of here and let him lead his life in private, she thought as she made herself a cup of tea in the kitchen. He'd never ask me to leave, but it's time. The week before,

Lisa had mentioned she needed someone to share her flat, as her roommate was moving out to live with her boyfriend, so that was a possibility.

Sadie could imagine Lisa's place, stocked full of health pills and moisturizers, shelves of neatly lined up eye pencils, lip pencils, brushes. It might be a little daunting at first, but she could get used to it. Lisa had been so grateful that Sadie had never revealed her part in the hunt for Morgan Blaine she was sure to offer her the room. And they did get along well – as long as Lisa didn't give her advice on where or how to fix her hair.

'Hey, can I have a cup while you're at it?' Andrew asked. He was looking dishevelled, with a self-conscious smile on his face.

'Sure. I hope you didn't make Theresa leave on my account.'

'No, no, she's going to the gym. Can you believe it? On a Saturday morning?'

'A lot of people do.'

'No one who has ever dated me.' Andrew sat down at the kitchen table. 'Any girl I've ever been with has picked up my lethargy by osmosis.'

'Maybe she wants to look like Demi Moore.'

'Demi's history, Sade. I've moved on to Penelope Cruz.'

'You should have moved on from Demi years ago, she's been history for a long time.'

'Poor Demi.' Andrew sighed. 'How fleeting is fame. Where have all the flowers gone? she must ask herself.'

'To Holland?'

'To Holland.' Andrew laughed. 'So, what are you up to tonight?'

'Nothing. TV. The usual.'

'Sade—'

'Don't. Andrew. It's OK, really. My social life will pick up soon, don't worry.'

'I do worry.'

'Because you feel guilty that you have someone and I don't. I promise you, you shouldn't. I'm fine. Work's great, I'm doing well. I'm happy.' Andrew narrowed his eyes as he took the cup of tea she handed him. 'Really. I am.'

'OK. I believe you.'

'You know, I never asked. What did happen to Theresa's boyfriend? Did she leave him before you rang her, or did she leave him for you, or did he leave her? What?'

'Well,' Andrew hung his arm over the back of his chair, 'he had a headache one day and he took some aspirin, but they didn't work. So he went to his GP, who, after lots of tests, referred him to a hospital that specializes in tropical diseases. No one could work out exactly what was wrong with him—'

'How awful.'

'I know, I know. Anyway, no one could work it out, and he became more and more frustrated. His headaches were getting worse and worse. He thought he was going insane. Actually, he *was* going insane. One day, after a whole bunch of other tests, he went crazy and attacked the doctor.'

'Oh, no.'

'Oh, yes. He tried to strangle the doctor, but the nurses dragged him off.'

'This is terrible.'

'I know. So he was tried for assault and convicted. But on the way to gaol the prison van crashed into a scooter and went off the road and he escaped. He jumped into the Thames and swam for his life but a rogue flying squirrel attacked him on the riverbank. Sadly, he died.'

'Of a flying squirrel bite.' Sadie winged the piece of toast she was eating at Andrew's head. 'I can't believe it. I can't believe how long it took for me to catch on to that one. You bastard.'

Picking up the piece of toast from the floor, Andrew threw it back at her.

'You are *seriously* slow, Sade. The City is rotting your brain. Right,' he stood up, 'I'm going to get changed. I think if Theresa is going to go to the gym, I should go for a run, to try and get into shape. I'm not fat, but I'm not fit either.'

'You're going for a run? You, Andrew Hawkes, running? Are you pulling my leg again?'

'No, this is for real.' He paused at the threshold, smiled, threw his hands in the air. 'What can I say? Young love.'

'Young love,' Sadie murmured as he walked out of the kitchen. 'It's a killer.'

She hadn't obsessed about the Gentleman, but she hadn't forgotten him, either. How could she when she still wore his watch? Her adventures in New York, however, were stored in a part of her memory bank she didn't try to access often. They were, in effect, a no-go area.

The trip back on the plane, after she and Georgie and Jess had drunk all the alcoholic contents of the minibar in her room, then moved on and done the same in their two rooms, had been wild. Jessica and Georgie had discussed every aspect of their meetings with the two Morgans, then the trip to Vencourt Press, the lunch with Angelo Brown, and the car ride when they'd told about Project X. In the cab to JFK, they'd wailed about how they'd lost the loves of their lives. As they waited to board, they'd laughed at the various absurd situations they'd found themselves in, and on the plane, they'd repeated most of what they'd said in the hotel, wailed some more, laughed some more, taking time out occasionally to quiz her about her own life.

Despite being as drunk as she could remember being since her early university days, Sadie remembered every word of what turned out to be a ten-hour marathon of talking. By the time they landed, she felt she knew them better than she knew any of her friends, that the intimacy of their conversation had been intense. How life at the office would be after this girls' night out, she couldn't fathom. Georgie had said at the beginning it was a night 'off the record', yet how could they *not* treat her differently? She pictured being invited to their house for dinner or out to parties with them, and wasn't sure whether she should go or not. Lisa, she knew, would be gobsmacked by this new state of affairs.

It will be awkward, Sadie thought. But I'll manage it somehow.

As it turned out, she didn't have to manage a thing. As soon as she walked into Harvey and Tanner, life pre New York was back in place, with one exception – Georgie had kept her promise to promote her. In every other aspect, both Georgie and Jessica behaved as if that trip hadn't happened. Hurt, at first, and uncomprehending, Sadie had attempted to get back to those hours spent flying the Atlantic, but Georgie and Jessica, though polite and friendly, weren't reciprocating.

Had they forgotten everything? she wondered. Possibly. They'd drunk the business-class section pretty dry as well. Sadie could recall it, only, she thought, because talking to them like that had been such a strange sensation it overrode the effects of alcohol.

Searching for any other explanation for their behaviour, she remembered meeting a ghostwriter at a barbecue an acquaintance of Piers had given. 'The worst part about ghostwriting,' the woman, who was about ten years older than Sadie, had said, 'is that you develop a relationship with your subject, you learn so much about him or her, you spend so much time with them, you begin to think you're their new best friend. When the project's over, they always say they'll ring, they'll keep in touch, blah blah blah. And they never, ever do. They've paid you, you've done your job, that's it. End of story, end of being part of this famous person's life. It's a shock, and what's funny is every single time it happens, it's still a shock.'

Sadie had, in a way, been paid to be Jessica's and Georgie's confidante. When the plane touched down, her job as confidante was finished. In some sense, that did make her life easier. But occasionally she'd wonder what had happened in their respective lives. Now that she was no longer their PA, she had no idea who was phoning in or who had lunch with them. How about Morgan Blaine and Morgan Hancock? she asked herself. What's happened to them?

What's happened to the Gentleman?

'So here I go, pounding the pavement.' Andrew had a pair of shorts on that came down to his knees, and a T-shirt with the words: 'I Used to be Snow White, but I Drifted' on it. He was lacing up a pair of old trainers.

'Socks might be a good idea.'

'Oh,' he looked up and nodded, 'good point. Socks. And, for protection, some anti-flying-squirrel-bite vaccine. You did put that in the medicine cabinet, didn't you?'

Sadie was happy Andrew had found Theresa again. She liked Theresa. And Theresa's re-appearance in his life had spurred him on to apply for a better job. He'd get one, she knew. He was moving forward very quickly, whereas she, in every area of life except work, was stalled. She'd been out with a few men, but on each date she found herself looking at the Gentleman's watch more often than she should have, and not always for the purpose of telling the time.

Moving out would kickstart her, she hoped. But what was life with Lisa going to be like? Sadie tried to imagine Lisa catching the groceries, it was a doomed effort.

'We don't have a medicine cabinet, Andrew.'

'Shit. Tell you what, I'll pick one up on my run. A little sprint down the North Circular and full speed into IKEA, where I'll also pick up one of those oven-hood extractor things – I think life is pretty meaningless without one of those – and a medicine cabinet. Anything else you want while I'm there?'

'Brad Pitt.'

'He'll be in with the garden umbrellas, right? I'll bump Jennifer Aniston into the warehouse. He's yours, Sade. It's done.'

Chapter Twenty Seven

Jessica had a routine, her days were mapped out and ordered. At nine every morning, she'd get a cup of coffee at the café in Battersea Square, sit and read a paper for half an hour, walk back home, study, go into town at noon, pick up a sandwich from Prêt à Manger, attend her course, come back to Battersea, go to the gym, head for home and either get ready for a night out or scan the listings for something good on television to watch for a night in. At times, when she was socializing, she would be asked out for dinner by a man, but she always refused politely. She was a one-man woman; the fact that the one man in question was thousands of miles away and hadn't shown any interest in her for months was beginning to get to her, though. How long do I keep sending the flowers and the apple? she asked herself more and more often. Morgan Hancock had had six months of weekly flowers; if he was never going to acknowledge her, should she give up?

On this first Monday morning in June, the sun had, after weeks of hiding, deigned to show itself; she put on a sleeveless sun dress and sandals and, while brushing her hair, had stared at herself in the mirror. Monday was the day she rang the florist; was this the Monday she should pack it in and leave him be? Louisa and he probably laughed about her; Jessica could hear Louisa saying, 'Maybe we *should* have had her committed, Morgan, she's obviously nuts. These flowers are ridiculous. And what's with the apple?'

What *was* with the apple? She wanted to remind him of that moment when he'd hugged her in the hall. They'd had a life and death experience together, didn't that count for anything? Obviously not. He said she'd saved him, but she knew she hadn't. All she'd done was thwack him on the back.

Jessica threw the brush on the table, turned from the mirror, the decision made. Enough flowers. Certain plants didn't grow in certain climates. She'd attempted to grow love in a hothouse of her own making but it was refusing to blossom. Georgie hadn't even contacted Morgan Blaine; she'd never lower herself by keeping in touch when he had turned his back on her. Why should she, Jessica, be any different? The time had come to forget his sideways smile, the way he'd take his glasses off and then replace them straight away, how safe she'd felt in his arms when he'd carried her. And his kiss.

She would throw away all those scientific books she'd bought and had hidden from Georgie, ones she would open and attempt to read for about twenty seconds before giving up. They could go in the rubbish, she could be free.

Walking to the Café de Paris with her newfound determination, Jessica felt a wave of relief. I don't have to wait any more, she thought. I won't care that there's nothing from him in the post or that there are no messages from him on the answering machine. I'm over it. Thank God.

She sat down at one of the outside tables, ordered a cappuccino, reached for her sunglasses and opened her paper. Ascot was on, she'd have to find a hat for her trip there. So many things to do, so much to look forward to. Life was full of possibilities; she'd been holding herself back from them. She was an independent woman now. Morgan Hancock could laugh away with Louisa or some new girlfriend he'd found.

Did she care? No. Not at all. She might even try to find out what had happened to Daniel Canter. Were his parents still in the country? She could ring them up, ask them – no, no, Jessica, she said to herself. You're not going to chase a man ever again. You don't need a man. Sex is a waste of time. Romance is stupid.

'Could I have a *café con lait*, please? Or is it *café avec latte* or—'

Thousands of tons of rocket fuel ignited, thrusting her heart off its launchpad. She turned toward the voice and went into orbit, reaching outer space in one split second.

'Hello, Jessica. Jessica— Oh, shit!' Morgan Hancock was at her side. 'Breathe deeply, put your head down. I know about fainting now. You have to keep your head down.' His hand was on the back of her neck, pressing it downwards. Her sunglasses fell to the floor. 'Water!' he called out to the waiter. 'We need some water here. Quick.'

Jessica pulled herself back from the brink of unconsciousness just as Morgan Hancock was flicking water on her face with his fingertips.

'I'm all right, I'm all right.' She put her hand in the air. 'Enough.' Her head came up for air. 'I'm OK.'

'Are you sure?'

'I'm sure.' She smiled, wiping the water drops from her face. 'How did you find me?'

'It was pretty easy.' Pulling up a chair beside hers, he sat down. 'When I got to your house this morning, I waited outside and followed you here.'

'Why didn't you just ring the bell?'

'I wasn't sure you'd be alone. Anyway, I figured it was my turn to stalk you.'

'Morgan . . .' Jessica breathed in his clean air; even after a plane trip, he smelled fresh. He had on khaki trousers, a dark-blue cotton shirt. His nose was sunburned, freckles had

311

appeared on his boyish cheeks. 'You are *so* gorgeous,' she said. 'You look about ten years old.'

'Do you want to know why I came here, Jessica? I had to. My apartment is unlivable in, all those flowers, I couldn't bring myself to throw any of them out, so there are tons of dead flowers everywhere. I was beginning to feel like I lived in a mortuary. Plus, with all those apples, I'm thinking I have to go into the cider business. It has to stop.'

'I'm sorry.' Jessica drew back in her chair. 'I was only—'

'I know. Trying to make me understand that Morgan Blaine doesn't matter any more, whether he's Morgan Blaine or Angelo or whomever. And you know, at first I was shocked by the nature of that project of yours, how cold and calculating and cynical it seemed. I couldn't get over it. Then I thought, why? Why is it bad? People have a hard time finding romance, any way of trying to make it easier makes sense. Besides, I kept seeing you in my bed. It was really hard to sleep with you there when you weren't actually there if you see what I mean. So what with no sleep and the dead flowers and John raving on about you every time I saw him, I thought: time to book a flight. The professor in flux better get moving before you give up on him.'

Morgan took off his glasses, focused on Jessica and took her hand in his.

'Morgan—'

'Shh,' he said, putting two fingers up to her mouth. 'We're in the clearing, Jessica. Look at me.'

She did. As she looked into his eyes, she felt herself start to tingle, then shake. Something very strange was happening inside her. A warmth was building like waves which her body was surfing on. Each wave brought her closer to some undefined shore, making her clench each time it broke. Am I fainting again, she wondered, before she heard herself moan. What's happening to me? Closing her eyes, she saw a surfboard flying, she felt an explosion as it beached. She shook with the impact of it.

'Oh my God.' She covered her face with her hands. 'Oh my God. I don't believe it.' She shook her head. 'You have no idea. You don't know. Oh, my God.'

'Jessica – are you all right?'

She had gone from the beach to the Alps, and was standing at the top of a mountain, her skis on. All it would take was the courage to slide one foot forward and she'd be on her way. Down a black run. If she fell . . . if she fell, well, so what if she fell? Jessica took her hands away from her face.

'Marry me,' she said. 'You have to marry me, Morgan. If you don't, I swear I'll kill you.'

This was wonderful and then again it wasn't, Georgie thought, as she looked at Morgan and Jessica sitting beside each other on the sofa. Their hands were on each other's knees, approximately every twenty seconds they'd kiss. All right, the kisses weren't very long, but they were long enough to make Georgie feel queasy. She was fourteen, fifteen years old again; Jessica had pulled and she hadn't. God, did life ever *really* change? Not only had Jess pulled, she'd got bloody engaged, in the space of what? One cappuccino, apparently.

Stop this. Feel happy for her, she told herself. So Jess hadn't informed her she'd been sending Morgan flowers, so what? She hadn't informed Jess about her postcards, either, and she certainly wasn't going to now. Morgan Blaine wasn't about to fly over and get engaged to her at the Café de Paris, which was the only outcome which would make all of this fine.

Pull yourself together. Step on this rivalry. Be a good sister and a good friend. Don't think about how much you'd like to get a cold jug of water and pour it over them. But Jesus, couldn't they unlock their mouths for a minute?

'Um . . .' Georgie coughed. Jessica broke away from the kiss and smiled.

'Sorry, I know public displays of affection aren't very nice for the people watching.' She squeezed Morgan's knee. 'I just can't help it.'

'No problem.' Georgie waved her hand in the air. She wanted a cigarette, desperately, but she didn't have any. 'I was thinking. You should have a party, an engagement party to celebrate. You'll be here for a while a least, won't you, Morgan? You're not taking Jess away instantly?'

'No, no. Of course not. I have to meet her parents, I'd like to meet her friends. No, if it's all right, I'll stay for a couple of weeks while we get all this organized.'

He wasn't good-looking, but he was *nice*-looking, Georgie thought. Not a patch on Morgan Blaine, that was for sure. Morgan Blaine. Where the hell was Morgan Blaine when she needed him? Kicking some other poor woman out of bed?

'Well, have fun with Joanna.' Georgie allowed herself a smirk. 'That should be entertaining.'

'My mother will be fine. Morgan went to boarding school. That will do the trick for her.'

Yes? And how much money does he make writing about microbiotic organisms? You think Joanna won't die a death when she hears what he does for a living? Georgie knew Jess was thinking what she was; she could see a slight nervous twitch pass over her face.

'Anyway, forget Joanna. Forget parents. Let's have a party. How about on Saturday? I'm sure we could organize it by then. We could have it here, get the same caterers I use at Harvey and Tanner. Come on, Jess, it would be . . .' Georgie hesitated.

'Fun.' Jess laughed. 'You said that about Project X, I know. But this will be different. *Everything* is different now.'

Yes. Love changes everything. Who sang that silly song? Who wrote it? Oh, no, they're kissing again.

'Listen, I'm going to go upstairs to make some phone calls and get this party in motion. You two should go out to dinner at the Italian, it's a very romantic restaurant, Morgan, you'll love it.'

Please, please go out and leave me alone for awhile. I have to digest this. I need to get over it. Not only is Jess getting married, she's moving to New York. Which leaves me . . . alone.

'Sounds great.' Morgan Hancock took off his glasses and immediately put them on again. That habit in itself would drive me bonkers, Georgie thought. But he does have a lovely smile.

I should have, the minute I came in and they told me about this, taken the champagne out of the fridge, shaken it up and let it explode all over the room. That would have been the right thing to do. Jess would have loved it.

So why didn't I?

'Well, I'm off to make those calls.' Georgie got up and started to climb the stairs.

Why didn't I?

Because if I had, I would have, for the second time in my life, burst out crying.

Chapter Twenty Eight

The party was in full swing when Sadie arrived, the ground floor of Jessica and Georgie's house was teeming with people. It was a perfect summer's evening, everyone was wearing the clothes they probably only got to put on once or twice a year, hot-weather wear which rarely saw the light in England. She was surprised to have been invited, even more amazed that Georgie had asked her to bring Andrew along as well.

'If things get really boring, you and your brother can throw some eggs around,' Georgie had said when she'd come into Sadie's office. 'I remember you telling us about that on the plane. Actually, that's about all I do remember of the plane trip.'

Andrew, when Sadie informed him of the invitation, said, 'Wow! A chance to meet the Pod People! I couldn't possibly miss out on that.'

So they'd come in together, and while Sadie tried to spot Georgie and/or Jessica among the throng, Andrew tried to spot where to get a drink.

'Ah,' he nudged Sadie in the ribs, 'there's a garden out the back, see? And a long table with a man behind it. He looks suspiciously like a bartender. Let's head in that direction.'

Sadie followed him, still scanning the living room for her

employers. She thought she could see Jessica at the far end of the room, but wasn't sure; some man moved in front of the woman who might be Jessica before she could tell for certain. The room was as packed as Heathrow at Christmas time, people jostling for position, spilling drinks in an effort to stay upright as others moved past them. Grateful that there'd be some air in the garden, even more relieved that Andrew was there with her, Sadie kept close behind him as they wended their way through the living room and out into the garden, which was marginally less crowded.

'Apparently, he's a scientist,' she overheard a woman saying as she went by. 'Must be a nuclear scientist.'

'Whew,' Andrew exclaimed when they finally reached the bar. 'They make you work for a drink here, don't they? Any sign of the Pod People?'

'Not yet.'

'Good. We're safe. Two white wines, please,' he said to the bartender. 'Well, do we do the mingling thing or find a corner of the garden and talk among ourselves? Over there, under that tree, there's a place for us to stand. People will then doubtless be drawn to us like magnets.' He handed Sadie her wine. '*They'll* have to mingle with *us*. That's the better option.'

The garden was decorated with fairy lights, and, as Sadie stared at her fellow guests, she felt a hollowness in her stomach. All these people who knew each other, who were conversing easily with each other and she and Andrew under a tree, hiding, in effect. She hadn't wanted to mingle, either, but she wished she could be the type of person who found mingling with strangers easy. Instead, on the occasions she tried, she was too aware that people looked over her shoulder for someone more interesting or made a pitiful excuse to move on. She'd have to learn not to be so defensive, but this was not the night she'd be able to start her first lesson.

The news of Jessica's engagement to Morgan Hancock had both pleased and saddened her. She was glad Jessica had found happiness, but Morgan Hancock reminded her of New York and New York reminded her of the Gentleman. She tried not to ask the same question again, but she couldn't. Why hadn't he shown up at the coffee shop?

Andrew, after she'd related the story to him, said what she expected he'd say, 'He probably died on the way there, or was run over and is paralysed like in that old movie. In either case, it's better not to know, right? Forget him, Sade. He has to be better than the World's Most Obnoxious Man, but not showing up like that makes him a serious contender for the title.'

'You guys have found the perfect place here. Mind if I join you?' The man who had approached them and asked this was tall, with an American accent.

'Be our guests. See,' Andrew nudged Sadie, 'I was right. People are flocking to us already. I'm Andrew Hawkes,' he held out his hand, 'and this is my sister, Sadie.'

'Hello.' The American switched a bottle of beer from his left to his right hand and shook hands with Andrew, then with Sadie. 'I'm a friend of Morgan's. I just got here and I can't find Morgan or his fiancée, or her sister who is apparently hosting this bash. I came in with a friend but he seems to have disappeared on me. So I thought I'd chill out here for awhile.'

'Have you known Morgan for a long time?' Sadie asked.

'Seems like centuries. How about you two? What's your connection?'

'I work at Harvey and Tanner.'

'Ah.' He nodded. 'And you? Do you work there too?' He turned to Andrew.

'No, I'm a hanger-on.'

'Listen, it's important to hang on. Do you think there's any chance those waitresses floating around with platters of food will come in our direction?'

'Not a chance in the world.'

'You're right.' The American smiled at Andrew. 'I guess we'll have to rely on liquid sustenance.'

'What did you say your name is?' Sadie asked.

'I didn't. I didn't want to confuse you. It happens to be Morgan as well. Funnily enough, the world is full of Morgans.'

'Morgan Blaine?' Sadie almost dropped her glass.

'Yeah, but not *the* Morgan Blaine. Let's get that clear now. I didn't write *Voodoo Women*.'

'I know you didn't.' She stared up at him. 'I don't believe you're here.'

'Whoa. Is this the man who kicked the chief Pod Person out of—'

Sadie elbowed Andrew sharply.

'I was in New York with Georgie and Jessica when they met you,' she said quickly, before Andrew could finish his wildly indiscreet sentence.

'Don't tell me you were looking for Morgan Blaine too,' Morgan grimaced, 'I can't take it.'

'No, no. I was there to help with work. I mean, I was there with them, but I wasn't . . . I wasn't . . . I was more of a hanger-on.'

'Hanging-on runs in the family? Don't worry –' Morgan waved his hand in the air – 'you don't have to explain yourself. It must have been one hell of a trip, though, if you were sitting on the sidelines.'

'It was.' Sadie nodded. She liked this man a lot. He had a handsome weatherbeaten face and wry eyes.

'So, Sadie, tell me, what's it like to work for Georgina? Does she beat you if you don't deliver the goods? Are we talking Scrooge before he had the visit from the ghosts or after?'

Choosing her words very carefully, Sadie began to answer his question.

Georgina Harvey, on her way to the bar in the garden, saw a man standing under the tree at the far end, talking to Sadie and another man. Something about his posture, particularly his shoulders, stopped her in her tracks. He looked like . . . he looked like . . . no, it wasn't possible, she was imagining it. Wasn't she? Circling around the back of the bar table, she caught sight of his profile.

Morgan Bloody Blaine was standing in her garden, talking to Sadie Hawkes.

How? When? Why?

Georgie grabbed a glass of champagne from the bar, but kept her distance. What the hell was he doing here? Had he come to see her, or had he come to celebrate Jess's engagement? Or both? Or neither?

Morgan Blaine reached out and put his hand on Sadie's shoulder. He was laughing, Georgie could see. About what?

Georgie swigged her glass of champagne, took a step forward, stepped back. How was she supposed to handle this? If he *had* come to see her, wouldn't he be searching the house for her instead of standing happily underneath a tree talking to Sadie? No, he'd come just for the party, which meant the only way to handle this was to be unbelievably cool.

Walking as steadily as she could, repeating 'act authorized' with every step, Georgie approached the threesome under the tree.

'Hello, there,' she said when she reached them. 'Hello, Sadie, hello Morgan. And you, whoever you are,' she turned to the third person, 'it's nice to meet you. I'm Georgina Harvey.'

'I'm Andrew Hawkes, Sadie's brother,' the man said, holding out his hand to shake hers. 'Thank you for inviting me to this party.'

'Oh, my pleasure. Absolutely. My pleasure. So nice of you to come.' She couldn't bring herself to look at Morgan. If she looked at him, she would lose all her cool immediately. So she stared at Andrew Hawkes as if he was the only person there. 'I hope you didn't have to come far.'

What was this? She was speaking as if she were the queen. But she couldn't stop herself.

'Shepherd's Bush. It was easy, actually.' Andrew looked as discomfited as she felt.

'Hello, Georgina.' Morgan Blaine spoke. His voice had that teasing tone she had prayed it wouldn't. What was he going to do? Lecture her about sending him postcards?

'So, Andrew. Sadie told me you throw eggs. That must be . . . it must be satisfying. I've been thinking I should try it myself.'

'I don't throw them except when we're putting away the groceries.' Andrew shifted from foot to foot. 'But I suppose it would be a satisfying thing to do in general.' He was blinking wildly. Probably, Georgie thought, because my stare is so intense he has to shield himself from it, but there's nothing I can do about that. There's no way I can even begin to look at Morgan Blaine.

'Georgina, much as I would like to continue this scintillating conversation on the joys of egg-throwing, I think you and I should go somewhere and have a talk.'

Why was the thought of being alone with Morgan Blaine suddenly so terrifying when that's all she had wanted for months? Make me disappear, she thought, her body sagging. Someone please wave a magic wand and make me disappear. I want to faint like Jessica and be unconscious for the next twelve months. At least. When I wake up maybe I'll be rid of this attack of paralysing shyness.

'Well, it's been just great meeting you both,' Andrew said. 'Come on, Sade, back to the bar!'

'No. No.' Georgie reached out and grabbed Sadie's elbow. 'Don't leave. Stay and talk some more.'

'We'll be back,' Sadie said.

'Let them go.' Morgan waved them away. 'They need a drink. And we need to talk.'

Georgie watched Andrew and Sadie walk off together. They'd abandoned her, but to what fate?

'My God, Georgina,' Morgan laughed, 'you're blushing.'

What kind of fool am I? Georgie thought, as her eyes travelled in every direction except the spot where Morgan Blaine was standing.

Now, that's a song I could have written the lyrics of with no problem whatsoever.

Andrew had gone to steal a plate of food from one of the waitresses and Sadie had spent the time he was away from her having desultory conversations with people she didn't know. After the, 'What do you do and what are you doing here?' beginnings, they'd taper off into, 'Isn't it a lovely evening?' and finally end with, 'I've just seen an old friend, I should go and catch up.' Glancing towards the tree, she saw that Morgan and Georgie were no longer there. Georgie had seemed petrified in his presence. How was it that she could be so effective in the City and such an emotional wreck in the face of one American man?

Men, Sadie said to herself. They're not worth all this misery and angst. Love pits women against each other, it ruins parties, it is bad for the heart. Men should all go away somewhere and not come back until women have learned to live without them.

How long should she stay at this party? Darkness was descending, people, she could sense, were beginning to think of moving on to dinner. In half an hour or so, it would be time, she thought, to make a move. She wished Andrew would come

322

back. Where were Morgan Blaine and Georgie? And what was happening between them? Would there, against all the odds, be a happy ending for the planners of Project X? Maybe she should hire them to find a man for her after all.

'Excuse me,' a voice spoke behind her. 'Do you happen to have the time?'

Sadie looked at her watch.

'It's eight fifteen,' she said, realizing by the 'fif' of 'fifteen' that she recognized the voice.

'If you were going to walk off with my watch like that, you could have told me.' The Gentleman was by her side. He took hold of her wrist. 'Would you mind very much if I took back my deposit now?'

She felt him unbuckle the strap and lift the watch from her wrist. She watched him put it back on his own.

'I told you, I'm always late. Not having a watch has made me even later than always.'

'What?' Sadie's eyes were fixated on his wrist. 'Why? I mean, what are you doing here? I don't understand.'

'Well, *I* don't understand either. You disappeared from my life and you took my watch with you. And now I find you in this garden. Excuse me, but what are *you* doing here?'

'I work at Harvey and Tanner.' She'd shifted her gaze from his wrist to his eyes. Green. They were even more green than she'd remembered.

'You – you work with Georgina and Jessica? You know, I missed that meeting of ours because of them. By the time I got to the coffee place, you'd gone. And when I went there the next morning, hoping to find you, the waitress told me all about spilling coffee over my note – which might have explained why you didn't call me. My number was at the end of the note. Every morning I hoped you'd show up there. You never did.'

'You missed our meeting because of Georgie and Jessica? I still don't understand.'

'Larimer Richards.' He held out his hand. 'Editor of *Voodoo Women* among other books. I got held up that day because we were having lunch with Morgan Blaine the author. Anyway, Morgan Hancock invited me and the other Morgan Blaine – are you confused yet? – to this party and we couldn't resist coming.'

'Oh my God.' Sadie started to laugh as she shook his hand. 'This can't be happening.'

'Believe me.' Larimer Richards slowly took his watch off and slowly fastened it back onto Sadie's wrist. 'It is.'

Morgan Blaine had taken hold of Georgie's hand and led her away from under the tree in the garden, through the crowded living room, and up the stairs.

'Which is your room?' he'd asked at the top and she'd pointed it out. He then pulled her into it, kicked the door shut, sat down on the chair and motioned for her to sit on the bed.

'Interview time,' he said.

'Excuse me?' Georgie sat down. Clearly he was going to lecture her again, she didn't know what the topic would be this time, but she didn't think she could take it.

'I'm interviewing you, Georgina. You're a candidate and I'm interviewing you.'

'A candidate for what?'

'Take a guess.'

'Morgan – please. I promise I've suffered enough for my mistakes.'

'Now, Ms Harvey.' He leaned forward. 'I know from my files that you have a good grip on geography and have travelled extensively. That's a plus point. Your taste in literature is a little suspect, so that's a minus.'

Georgie dragged her hands down her face and shook her head.

'Please just leave me alone. You don't have to torture me.'

'You do have a strong understanding of the absurdity of bad lyrics in songs,' he nodded, 'which is crucial. And you are willing to put yourself out on a limb, that's for sure.' He templed his fingers. 'As for "The Seven Habits of Highly Effective People", I'd say you possess at least five of them. What you need to do is to work on the win-win mentality. You're stuck in the win-lose dynamic which will hamper you in your dealings. However, you are absolutely ace when it comes to snowball fights. And that, as you may know, is requirement number one.'

Georgina Harvey studied Morgan Blaine's face. Carefully. What she saw made a smile sneak across her own.

'What are the other requirements for this position?' she asked.

'Persistence in the face of male obstinacy.'

'I have that. Definitely.'

'Indeed you do. Let's see – the ability to fall asleep in a car when someone else is driving.'

'I'm good at that.'

'Indeed you are. And – now, this is more demanding – you must have technical expertise.'

'What sort of technical expertise?'

'The quick and painless removal of splinters with a household needle.'

'Ah,' she said.

'Ah.' He nodded.

'Anything else?'

'Not that I can think of now, although you understand, this is only the first interview. But it's your turn now. Do you have any questions you'd like to ask me?'

'Only one, Mr Blaine.'

'Which is?'

'Can you swim?'

'I am, Ms Harvey,' Morgan Blaine said solemnly, 'a veritable fish.'

POCKET

B O O K S

IT'S MY PARTY
Cindy Blake

Isabel has secrets. Her biggest secret is a burning passion for her business partner, David. Together they run PARTY TIME, organising fashionable parties and until now they've been doing very nicely . . . until, that is, Stryker McCabe sets up a rival business and starts to steal their biggest clients. David is furious. Isabel is livid. They need to stop Stryker from poaching their business, but how?

Isabel's other secret is that she plays poker every Saturday night in a casino. When she spots Stryker at the table, she hatches a scheme to get even with him. After all, she may be a loser in love, but she's always a winner in poker.

Now, with Stryker falling for Isabel's charms and David's marriage heading for the rocks it begins to look as if anything could happen. And anything does . . .

PRICE £5.99
ISBN 0 671 02264 4

POCKET
B O O K S

I SAW YOU FIRST
Cindy Blake

'Remember how you felt when you first fell in love? I bet you felt more powerful than Arnie Schwarzenegger. So don't say "Hasta la vista, baby", say "Hi there, darling, I'm back. The me you first knew. And I'm raring to go!!"'

Bestselling self-help guru Lisa Thomas is in London to promote her latest book on how to rediscover the first flush of love. And she's determined to do this via an infomercial – a corny TV ad that worked in the States, but she hasn't bargained for a cynical British audience . . .

In a hilarious, irresistible romantic comedy all hell is about to break loose as Lisa wreaks havoc amongst her new British friends – Toby, the actor chosen to appear in the ad, his down-trodden girlfriend Christina, Declan, the man in charge of marketing Lisa's book in the UK, and his super-efficient girlfriend Alison . . .

£5.99
ISBN 0 671 01600 8

POCKET
B O O K S

This book and other **Cindy Blake** titles are available from your book shop or can be ordered direct from the publisher.

0 671 02265 2	**The Last Available Man**	£6.99
0 671 02264 4	**It's My Party**	£5.99
0 671 01600 8	**I Saw You First**	£5.99
0 671 02883 9	**Second Wives**	£5.99
0 671 85418 6	**Foreign Correspondents**	£5.99

Please send cheque or postal order for the value of the book, free postage and packing within the UK; OVERSEAS including Republic of Ireland £1 per book.

OR: Please debit this amount from my

VISA/ACCESS/MASTERCARD_____

CARD NO:_____

EXPIRY DATE_____

AMOUNT £ _____

NAME _____

ADDRESS_____

_____

SIGNATURE_____

www.simonsays.co.uk

Send orders to: SIMON & SCHUSTER CASH SALES
PO Box 29, Douglas, Isle of Man, IM99 1BQ
Tel: 01624 836000, Fax: 01624 670923
www.bookpost.co.uk

Please allow 14 days for delivery. Prices and availability subject to change without notice